HELL'S PARADISE

HELL'S PARADISE

Brian Freemantle

This title first published in Great Britain 2001 by
SEVERN HOUSE PUBLISHERS LTD of
9–15 High Street, Sutton, Surrey SM1 1DF.
Originally published in 1977 in Great Britain under
the title *H.M.S. Bounty* and pseudonym of *John Maxwell.*
This title first published in the USA 2001 by
SEVERN HOUSE PUBLISHERS INC of
595 Madison Avenue, New York, N.Y. 10022.

British Library Cataloguing in Publication Data

Freemantle, Brian, 1936-
    Hell's paradise
    1.   Christian, Fletcher, 1764-1793.
    2.   Bounty, Mutiny, 1789
    3.   Historical fiction
    I.   Title
    823.9'14 [F]

ISBN 0-7278-5633-2

Printed and bound in Great Britain by
MPG Books Ltd., Bodmin, Cornwall.

For Peter and Romayne,
with much love

'The law, sir! Damn the law: my will is the law
and woe unto the man that dares to disobey it!'

Captain William Bligh

Fletcher Christian

' ... he was a gentleman: a brave man: and every officer and seaman on board the ship would have gone through fire and water to have served him ... '

Edward Christian,
in an appendix to the published text
of the *Bounty* Court Martial, October 1792

William Bligh

'... a man with integrity unimpeached, a mind capable of providing its own resources in difficulties, without leaning on others for advice, firm in discipline, civil in deportment and not subject to whimper and whine when severity of discipline is wanted to meet emergencies ... '

Sir Joseph Banks,
Bligh's patron, March 15, 1805

Acknowledgments

Pitcairn Island is one of the remotest inhabited spots in the world, a volcanic chip of land one mile across and two miles long, lying almost midway between Panama and New Zealand. The nearest commercial airstrip is 1,300 miles away in Tahiti. Shipping companies ask for bookings to be made with either Panama or New Zealand as the listed destination, so unsure are they that weather conditions will permit passengers to disembark.

I never imagined, therefore, that there would be any possibility of my reaching the island to research this book, much less that I would have the opportunity to live among people only fifth-generation descendants of Fletcher Christian and his mutineers.

That I did was due to the Royal Fleet Auxiliary and their vessel, the *Sir Geraint*. For making the trip initially possible, I thank Major 'Tony' Dixon and Lt-Col. Peter Hicks, at the Ministry of Defence.

To the master of the *Sir Geraint*, Captain James Bailey, and his officers I will remain forever grateful for their friendship and hospitality during the two-month South Pacific voyage.

I shall always remember with gratitude and affection the welcome given to me by Pitcairn chief magistrate Ivan Christian and his wife Dobrey, with whom I lived. And appreciate the willing help I received from the islanders to the sometimes intrusive enquiries I made.

Pitcairn, of course, represents only a part of the study made for this book. The staff of the London Library responded to every request with an enthusiasm and cheerfulness that is a feature of any dealing with that institution. So, to them, a final 'thank you'.

Introduction

This is a work of fiction, not history.

Fully aware of the irritation it may cause some historians of the period, I have made appear simultaneous events in the lives of Captain William Bligh and the man who led the mutiny against him on the *Bounty*, Lieutenant Fletcher Christian, which did, in fact, occur some years apart.

I have done this — consciously — for several reasons. For the fictional book it is intended to be, it makes for ease of narrative. I hope, too, that it enables me to highlight the conflicting characters of the two men.

And then it makes it possible to suggest the hidden secret that caused Fletcher Christian to rebel against the man who had been his friend, casting him and seventeen other crewmen adrift to what he could only have believed would be their certain death. For nowhere in the mass of surviving documents, records, first person accounts or on the island of Pitcairn itself is there a satisfactory answer to the question: why?

Bligh was not a tyrant, imposing the lash at the slightest infringement of regulations. He was an irascible nagger, certainly. He demanded a high standard aboard his ships and when it wasn't achieved, the lash came from his tongue, not the cat-o'-nine-tails. Compared with other recorded punishments by contemporary captains, by eighteenth-century standards Bligh was soft-handed with his crew.

When, on the outward voyage of the *Bounty*, the crew deck became soaked by the storms of Cape Horn, he turned his own quarters over to his men so they could sleep dry. They didn't like it, but he made them eat a carefully considered diet, rightly recognising ahead of his time that scurvy came from a vitamin deficiency. He reached Tahiti after a ten-month voyage with only one suspected case of the illness, an unparalleled record for the time.

So why?

Would an educated man like Christian, whose brothers were barristers and whose family was steeped in law, have considered mass murder because he had fallen in love with a native girl in Tahiti? Or because Bligh had harangued him to the point of tears in front of the whole crew for stealing a coconut? These are the explanations offered by Bligh, in the existing log of his amazing, 3,600-mile survival voyage and then in a book he wrote of the incident.

The transcript exists of the court martial of ten mutineers arrested in Tahiti and arraigned at Portsmouth on September 12, 1792. The dialogue and evidence I have created for the participants is based on recorded fact, moving, I hope, towards my conclusion. That recorded fact comes very little from the court hearing, however. Not once were any of the witnesses or prisoners asked to suggest a cause for the insurrection.

Bounty midshipman Edward Young followed Christian to Pitcairn, fomented a civil war on the island between the natives and the mutineers and then, in an act of dying contrition after all but one of the mutineers were dead, wrote a detailed account of events leading up to the mutiny and of their subsequent existence on one of the loneliest islands in the world.

Today that account is, according to the islanders I have met and interviewed, still hidden somewhere on Pitcairn, secreted upon the orders of the last surviving mutineer, Jack Adams. Before he died, however, Adams made the record available to one of the British sea captains who had located their island sanctuary and the man copied sections from it. In his journal, Young confessed to his part as agent provocateur in the mutiny and wrote at length of their early, savage years on Pitcairn.

Missing from the document, however, was any acceptable explanation for why Fletcher Christian went before dawn on that April morning in 1789 to rouse Captain Bligh at cutlass point with the words: 'I am in hell.'

One man knew. Fletcher Christian told him.

A few minutes before sailing for the last time from Tahiti to form what is today Britain's smallest colony, Christian took aside midshipman Peter Heywood. Before they pulled too far away, Edward Young, standing nearby, heard Christian begin to talk of 'the reason for my foolishness'. The Portsmouth court martial exonerated Heywood from any complicity in the crime, accepting his story that he was carried away against his will. Heywood rose to the rank of captain and swore an affidavit that in 1808, walking along Fore Street, Plymouth, he saw a figure he recognised. He called out Christian's name and the man turned, showing himself to be the mutiny leader. The man fled and although he gave chase, Heywood lost him.

Heywood was quite willing to provide these and other details for a book written about the *Bounty* uprising by a relative, Lady Belcher. About only one thing did he refuse to talk – that secret conversation with Christian on the greyish-black Tahitian sand.

Could Christian have escaped from Pitcairn?

There are several accounts that other vessels came upon the mutineers before the officially accepted discovery in February 1808, when the Boston-registered whaler *Topaz*, under the command of Captain Mayhew Folger, anchored in surf-lashed Bounty Bay.

And in the *Dictionary of National Biography*, Sir John Laughton writes: 'It is in a high degree probable that, whether in Captain Folger's ship in 1808 or in some more venturesome way, Christian escaped from the island and returned to England.'

John Adams told several conflicting stories about Christian, finally asserting that he had perished in the civil war that broke out when one of the mutineers demanded from a Tahitian native the woman who had accompanied him to Pitcairn from Tahiti.

Adams and Edward Young's journal both recorded how Christian was ostracised on the island.

On September 17, 1814, a British sailor, Captain Pipon, interviewed Adams and then wrote of Fletcher Christian:

It appears that this unfortunate, ill-fated young man was never happy after the rash and inconsiderate step he had taken but always sullen and morose, a circumstance which will not surprise anyone; this moroseness, however, led him to many acts of cruelty and inhumanity which soon was the cause of his incurring the hatred and detestation of his companions here; one cannot avoid expressing

15

astonishment when you consider that the very crime he was then guilty of towards his companions who assisted him in the mutiny was the very same they so loudly accused their captain of.

Bligh's mission in the *Bounty* had been to transplant the breadfruit plant from Tahiti to the West Indies, to provide cheap food for the slaves on Britain's sugar plantations there.

He returned to England after that 48-day, 3,618-mile voyage to be lionised in eighteenth-century London. He was presented a hero to George III, became a friend of the King's son, the Duke of Clarence, was cleared of any blame in losing his ship and promoted full captain.

Within three years – after completely succeeding with the breadfruit transplantation during a second expedition – his reputation was publicly smeared by the powerful families of Fletcher Christian and Peter Heywood.

Throughout a lifetime of spectacular dispute, Bligh was involved in the North Sea Fleet mutiny in the Nore in 1797; in 1805 he was reprimanded at a court martial for tyranny, unofficer-like conduct and ungentlemanly behaviour on the complaint of one of his lieutenants; and in 1808 he was overthrown as Governor-General of New South Wales, Australia, in an illegal rebellion.

In 1817 he died, aged sixty-five. His tomb is in St Mary's churchyard, Lambeth, London.

Christian died, according to legend, in Cumberland, where he was born.

On the wall of Cockermouth Grammar School was recorded the fact that he was once a pupil, together with the poet William Wordsworth.

Other than that, there is no monument to him.

Neither is there on Pitcairn.

BOOK ONE

' ... I would rather die ten thousand deaths than bear this treatment any longer ... I always do my duty as an officer and as a man ought, yet I receive this scandalous usage ... I am in hell ... '

Fletcher Christian, April 28, 1789,
at the moment of mutiny

Like an occasional fly on the chest of a sleeping man, the *Bounty* rose and fell softly in the Pacific swell. It should have been cool, so early in the morning, but there was no wind for the sails that sagged empty from the masthead and the heat draped over the tiny, almost stationary vessel like a thick blanket.

And few people slept comfortably.

Only Captain William Bligh appeared undisturbed. He even wore a nightcap and nightshirt, but the door of his cabin was ajar, to catch any breeze. He stirred from time to time, mumbling in some private dream, but did not awaken. The difficult part of the voyage was over now: he was returning home, in triumph. He was a contented man.

It was too hot in his bunk for the ship's master, James Fryer. Seeking some relief, he had arranged bed-covering into a mattress and was lodged precariously on top of his sea chest, dozing fitfully and half aware of the ship's sounds around him. The two loaded pistols he always kept at hand were on the far side of the cabin, locked in a small cupboard. They were at sea now, miles from the nearest island and safe from any surprise attack, so the precautions weren't necessary any more.

Charles Norman, the carpenter's mate, had abandoned sleep altogether. He stood at the rear of the vessel, gazing down at the bubbled whiteness the huge, scavenging shark created, arcing and scything around the *Bounty*. Charles Norman liked fish, much better than human beings. He'd told people that, several times. But they hadn't taken much notice, because Charles Norman was thought to be mad.

He would have warned Fletcher Christian, had he known what the second-in-command was planning. But the carpenter's mate was the last person to whom any confidence could be entrusted.

It was only a few minutes before the end of midshipman George Stewart's watch. It would stink down below, among the sweating, unwashed men, he knew. He stayed aloft, breathing deeply, like a swimmer about to make the plunge. The volcano on Tofoa, twenty miles away, was a spectacular sight, belching towards a full-scale eruption but already with great gouts of fire and lava shooting from it, like a roman candle.

The island was too far away for Fletcher, thought George Stewart, worriedly. And too dangerous, now, with the prospect of its being destroyed by the volcano.

Christian was insane, Stewart decided. With good reason, perhaps. But definitely insane. The man would have to be dissuaded, for his own safety. Stewart began making his way towards the hatchway, pausing to look towards the stern. What was Norman staring at so intently? he wondered. He shrugged, uninterested. Norman was soft in the head. Nothing he was doing could be important.

Like Norman, William Muspratt had decided to get up on deck. For'ard, near the galley, he inhaled the fresher air. A hatchet lay near the breakfast logs and on impulse he decided to split some for the cook. It would be a guaranteed way to get extra rations. Almost immediately came the protest from Michael Byrn, the ship's sightless fiddler.

'Hell's teeth, shut up and let's get some sleep. It's not four yet.'

'Shut up yourself, you blind bugger,' shouted back Muspratt. He stopped though: it was too hot to chop wood. And who needed extra rations anyway, in weather like this?

In his bunk below, the sleepless Christian heard the footsteps approaching and drew back, instinctively, as the canvas screen was pulled aside from his starboard berth. From childhood, Christian had been bothered by excessive perspiration, so bad he stained things the moment he touched them. He was soaked now, his shoulder-length hair coiled in wet ringlets, his face smeared and greasy. And it wasn't the heat, decided George Stewart, staring at the man who was to take the watch at 4 a.m. The acting midshipman was shocked by the appearance of Christian, with whom he had become friends during the sixteen months they had been at sea. Christian *was* as mad as Norman, on deck above, thought Stewart again. Maybe even madder.

'For God's sake, Mr Christian. What is it?'

'You know, well enough.'

Stewart sighed. Bligh was a bastard, an unmitigated, bullying bastard, to have reduced a man to this state. Perhaps another officer wouldn't have been so badly affected, but Christian was a sensitive, highly strung man and Bligh should have recognised the effect of his behaviour. They'd known each other long enough, after all.

'You'll not escape,' insisted Stewart.

'I've got to. Somehow.'

There would be a lot of men who knew of Christian's plan to desert the ship, reflected Stewart. The ship's carpenter, William Purcell, was certainly aware, because he'd provided the planks with which the second-in-command had lashed together a make-shift raft, utilising the masts of the ship's launch. He'd given Christian some nails, too, to trade with the natives if he reached an island. The cook, Tom Hall, had supplied a roasted hog. So he knew. And any intelligent man, having seen the petulance with which Bligh had treated Christian during the two weeks since they had sailed from Tahiti and witnessed how, the previous night, after that blazing, childish row, Christian had gone from friend to friend, bestowing his personal belongings as gifts and finally throwing letters and papers overboard, must have guessed the man was in a desperate, almost demented, state of mind.

'There'll be sharks near the boat,' warned Stewart, unaware of Norman's interest in the stern of the vessel.

Christian gestured, uncaring.

'It could be a year before we finally get back to England,' reminded Christian. 'Do you think I can stand the man for that long?'

'If you reach an island, you'll be slaughtered,' predicted Stewart. 'This isn't Tahiti any more. The natives are hostile, cannibals maybe. If you get ashore, you'll be killed.'

'Maybe I'll find a friendly island.'

Stewart sighed, exasperated. Enough of Christian's friends knew, thought Stewart again. Should he round them up, to over-power the man for his own good? But that wouldn't work. Bligh would have to be informed. Yet Bligh couldn't be told the truth because the reason for their action would put Christian in irons for the rest of the voyage, then get him hanged at Spithead for desertion. So the captain would construe it as an attack upon the second-in-command and accuse them of mutiny. And *they* would be hanged at Portsmouth.

But the word lodged like a burr in Stewart's mind. They were thousands of miles from England, in an area where few Europeans had explored before. And God knows they had reason enough to take command of the ship. You only hanged for mutiny if you were caught.

'You're not alone in your feelings for the captain, Mr Christian,' said Stewart, suddenly.

Christian shifted in his cramped bunk. He smelled, he realised. Damn the sweat. Yes, he thought, he hated Bligh now. He felt suffocated by the man. He was always conscious of him. Of those staring, pale eyes that followed every movement, eager for mistakes, either real or imagined, any cause for yet another irrational outburst.

'But I'm the victim of his madness,' complained Christian.

'You're badly treated, right enough,' sympathised Stewart, detecting the self-pity. He paused.

'Yet there's hardly a man better liked than you aboard this ship.'

Once the praise would have pleased him, Christian accepted. Always he had enjoyed being liked and respected. Doubtless the reason he'd welcomed Bligh's friendship, all those years ago.

Now Stewart's assertion brought him no pleasure. Bligh had drained him of all the feelings he had once had.

'It's no good, Mr Stewart. I'm trapped with the man and can stand it no longer. Even to die would be a better fate than staying aboard the *Bounty* a moment longer.'

Christian shuddered, unexpectedly, reminded of Stewart's warning about sharks. Sometimes the men had amused themselves by throwing bones and rotting meat into the water, watching those huge mouths with their saw-edged teeth crush and tear at the bait. He closed his eyes, imagining a leg or an arm being ripped away from his body as he spread-eagled on his raft, trying to paddle towards the uncertain safety of an island he couldn't see.

Stewart frowned at the shaking of his friend. Christian was chilled, he decided. Men's minds often went when they were fevered.

If Christian were caught trying to slip over the side, Bligh would make the man's life hell on earth, Stewart knew. Or even more of a hell than he was making it at present. He'd clap him in irons, of course. And keep him, like a pet bear or dog, paraded every day to be goaded and taunted. Before the voyage was over, Christian would undoubtedly be insane.

'It's near four,' cautioned Stewart. 'Little more than an hour before sun-up. You'll never leave the ship without being seen, sir. We're making so little way they'd get the cutter launched and you inboard before you'd been in the water thirty minutes.'

'Unless a shark gets me,' qualified Christian.

Stewart frowned, caught by the remark. Was Christian discarding the ridiculous idea of a raft? he wondered.

'There are people on board who would follow you, if you chose another course,' prompted Stewart, guardedly.

Only inches separated the faces of the two men, hunched in the fetid berth. Christian stared at the Scotsman, waiting. Stewart gazed back, saying nothing more.

'It's time I went on watch,' said Christian, at last.

'Desert and you'll die,' said Stewart, desperately.

'I know.'

'Then talk to your friends.'

'And I still might die.'

'It'll be a better chance.'

'Out of my way, Mr Stewart.'

2

The faint easterly made it cooler on deck, but sweat still dripped from Christian, soaking his shirt. He looked towards the shapes of several men lining the rail, watching the eruption of Tofoa, and remembered Stewart's warning.

The man was right, he knew. Even if the sharks didn't get him, the raft he had put together the night before and which lay concealed now beneath the cutter would probably break up before he reached any island.

And the natives *would* kill him, if he landed without the visible protection of the *Bounty*. Even with the ship and its guns in evidence, the natives often weren't scared. Only three days earlier, he'd been lucky to get the men away alive when the watering party he had commanded on Anamoka had been attacked.

Of course, Bligh had blamed him for what had happened, undermining his authority by ranting in front of the crew of which he was supposed to be second-in-command, saying it was his fault the natives had stolen the worthless axe and demanding to know why he hadn't ordered his men to use the guns with which they'd been issued, to prevent it. Christian sighed. Bligh *was* going mad, he thought, remembering the diatribe in minute detail. It had been one of the most positive indications yet of the man's closeness to insanity, castigating him for not using the muskets less than three hours after giving specific orders that although they had been issued, the weapons were not to be fired. The self-pity bubbled up again. How could he be expected to work a ship under a man whose mind butterflied from order to order in constant contradiction?

He put aside the question, thinking of the natives again. They fought with stones, he knew, battering their victims until they were pulped to death. It would take a long time to die, guessed Christian. And hurt a great deal.

He stood, quite alone on the deck, his eyes pressed closed. Oh dear Lord, he thought, what am I to do?

He had to get away, he knew.

He heard the rest of the watch approaching and opened his eyes, embarrassed. It was still dark enough to conceal what he had been doing, Christian realised, gratefully. He didn't want gossip that he had begun his watch standing on deck, praying.

'Sir?' asked Thomas Ellison, seeking an order. Christian smiled down at the tiny, baby-faced youngster, still only seventeen. Like the rest of them, the boy had had himself tattooed in Tahiti, Christian knew. His right arm was still flushed and puffy around the inscription of his name and the date upon which it had been done, October 25, 1788. His parents would probably beat him for it, when he got home to England.

'The helm,' ordered Christian, briskly. He looked over Ellison's shoulder, to John Mills. The gunner's mate was a raw-boned, taciturn man who'd sailed the world. At 5 ft 10 ins he dwarfed the youth.

'At the conn, to guide him,' ordered Christian. Mills would keep the boy out of trouble, he knew. Not that anything was likely to arise on this stifling night that could cause any trouble. Stewart had been right; the ship was scarcely making headway.

Matthew Quintal and Isaac Martin came towards him, expectantly. They were tattooed, too, Christian knew. Quintal had his ass covered in pictures, copying the idea when he knew that Christian had had it done. It had taken them both a week before they could sit down again.

'Coil the loose lines,' instructed Christian, brusquely. 'Prepare to swab down.'

Both Quintal and Martin had suffered from Bligh, Christian remembered. He tried to recall the number of floggings that had been inflicted on both men, but gave up. He snorted, halted by a sudden thought. Had he not been an officer and therefore above such punishment, how many lashes would Bligh have chosen for him?

He went slowly along the creaking ship to the quarter-deck, to relieve William Peckover. The gunner didn't like him, suspected Christian. Once it had worried him.

'Hot night, Mr Christian,' greeted Peckover. He was a large, shambling man, always ready at grog time. But a good seaman.

Christian nodded.

'How's it below?'

'Bad,' said Christian.

'Then maybe I'll stay on deck.'

Christian didn't reply.

Peckover nodded towards the stern.

'Norman has found a new friend,' he said, amused.

'What?'

'A shark,' said Peckover. 'Very big. Norman is talking to it, idiot that he is.'

The gunner moved away, humming softly to himself.

A following shark would be on him the moment he hit the water, Christian knew. No matter how quickly he followed the raft, it would take at least five minutes to swim to it and sprawl aboard. So he'd have no chance. Which meant that the carefully made raft was useless. And that he remained trapped.

Still the professional seaman, Christian looked around for the rest of his watch, then shrugged. John Hallett and Thomas Hayward would both be still asleep, he guessed, careless as always of their duties. He would let them stay. There was little they could do and he liked neither of them. The last thing he wanted was forced conversation with two youngsters whose prattling irritated him. If Bligh discovered he'd done nothing to rouse them, there'd be trouble, Christian knew. It didn't matter. Very little seemed to matter, any more.

Christian was surprised to see Edward Young coming towards him. Young was his friend, almost as close as Stewart. Too hot to sleep, Christian guessed. It would get worse, after sunrise.

Young was a direct, rough seaman who drank too much. He was quite ugly, thought Christian, his nose broken from some forgotten brawl and nearly all his teeth rotting blackly in his mouth. The Tahitian girls hadn't liked him, Christian remembered. Before they'd agree to his making love to them, they'd made him eat pineapple and drink coconut milk, to sweeten his breath.

'What's it to be then, sir?' opened Young, with his customary directness.

Christian moved his shoulders, uncertainly. It wasn't just

Bligh any more, he thought, feeling the emotion rise in his throat. Everyone kept on to him, prodding and demanding. He tried to control the irritation. Edward Young was his friend, the man to whom the previous night he'd given some of the belongings he most treasured. The man's concern was genuine, he knew, not the prying of someone trying to confirm a half-heard rumour.

'Mr Stewart thinks we should seize you, to prevent your killing yourself. He thinks you're mad,' added Young.

'And what account would you give the captain?'

'That's the only thing preventing us.'

'I'll get away, somehow,' said Christian, lamely. The knowledge that there was no escape was settling insidiously in his mind.

'You've got friends aboard,' said Young.

He was speaking very quietly, Christian realised, his head only inches away. The Tahitian women had been justified: his breath smelt very badly.

' ... friends who would follow any lead you might make ... ' added the other midshipman, pointedly.

The same prompting as George Stewart, reflected Christian. Why did they need him to lead?

'There'll never be another opportunity like this,' said Young, urgently. 'Look at your watch ... '

Christian stared around him at the men under his command, then answered his own question. The officers wanted him to lead because they knew he commanded the respect and leadership of the men on the lower deck. He wished Young would stand away a little.

'What do you mean, Mr Young?'

The midshipman shifted, annoyed at Christian's refusal to acknowledge the facts.

'Every man of them with reason to hate Bligh, almost as much as yourself,' insisted Young, hurriedly. 'Sound them out ... they'll be behind you, just like we will ... '

'You can be hanged for inciting a mutiny, sir, just the same as mounting one,' warned Christian.

'Nothing will go wrong, once it starts,' argued Young. 'Every man who might oppose you is below now, asleep.'

Christian shook his head, unwilling to make the commitment.

'What's the alternative?' demanded Young. 'It'll take months to get home, months when you'll be the whipping boy for that madman Bligh. He'll turn you mad, Mr Christian. Mad, like he is.'

'He's already come close to it,' mused Christian, softly.

'We could put them in the cutter,' enlarged Young. 'And give them provisions. That way they'd get to an island ... '

And be killed there, thought Christian. A mutineer. And a murderer. The Christian family was a proud and honoured one; only he had chosen a career at sea. The others were barristers and would, he knew, become judges. Was he to besmirch a family whose very vocation was the upholding of English law by committing the most serious crime in the statute book?

'It's ridiculous,' he rejected. 'I'll hear no more of this, Mr Young.'

'He's turned against you,' insisted Young. 'Think on what he was threatening during the row yesterday – that he'd have you and others of us jumping overboard in the Endeavour Straits, rather than remain aboard with him. That wasn't just an idle expression. He meant it, Mr Christian. He means to pick and nag until he breaks you.'

It was true, thought Christian. Bligh wouldn't stop. He'd keep on, through every hour of every day. And it could be so long before they reached Portsmouth again. So very long.

A gush of red spurted through the distant volcano cone, brightening the already lightening sky and the sound of the eruption, like far-away thunder, rumbled over the ship. At the stern, Charles Norman leaned over the rail, muttering to the shark. In his cabin below, the ship's master twisted, trying to find a more comfortable position on top of his chest, and in the cabin opposite, Bligh muttered a jumble of words, one of which sounded like 'honour', before settling back to sleep.

'There won't be another chance,' repeated Young, turning back along the deck. 'Think on it, Mr Christian. By morning, it will be too late. And if the raft is discovered and traced to you, as it must surely be, then you're lost anyway.'

Young walked away with short, thrusting strides and Christian remained at the rail, looking down into the ship. He closed his eyes again, scurrying thoughts filling his mind like dry leaves in autumn.

A spontaneous uprising *could* succeed, he knew. Everyone to whom he had confided his determination to abandon the ship had conceded some personal reason for hating Bligh. At the moment they were like driftwood swirling unconnected in a whirlpool. Only a catalyst was needed to bind them together. And he could provide that element of cohesion, Christian knew. To become an outcast, a man denied the possibility of ever returning to his own country. They were thousands of miles from England, certainly. But one day, somehow, the news would arrive there. And his family would be humiliated. He balanced the argument in his mind. A family probably humiliated in several years' time, compared to the daily, unremitting humiliation for month upon month. And perhaps not even ending with their arrival at Portsmouth. When he came to get another ship, Bligh would damn him in every report and character assessment, Christian knew, haunting him with his vindictiveness for the rest of his life. Thousands of miles away, he thought again. Years before anyone really knew: if ever. Lost at sea would be the official belief. Sadness in the family, certainly. But not disgrace. Pride even: lost at sea, with his ship.

They'd hang him if they *did* find out. At Spithead, before the jeering fleet. As an example to others. Wouldn't hurt, though, not like being ripped apart by a shark. Or pounded to death by savages. Just a quick, sharp jerk. And that would be it.

Christian began walking from the quarter-deck, a lightness numbing his body: he felt as if his limbs were moving without his control and that he couldn't have stopped if he had wanted to. And a part of him wanted to stop. Immediately.

At the mizzen he paused, halted by a thought. If it went wrong, he couldn't let Bligh arrest him. The torture, until they got home for trial, would be unbearable. Mr Young would be right. He would end up certifiably insane. With his seaman's knife, Christian cut away a length of line attached to one of the heavy sounding leads with which they established the depth of the water in harbour or in shallows, hefting it in his hands to test its weight. It would do, he thought, pleased with the idea. He looped it around his neck, tightly securing the cord. If too many men opposed him to follow Bligh and it became clear the uprising was to fail, he'd throw himself overboard and the weight of the lead would pull him down. He'd drag the water into his lungs. He had the will-power to do it. It wouldn't take long to drown: or become unconscious, even. He'd be able to achieve it before the sharks struck.

He pulled his sweat-damp shirt over the weight, feeling it heavy against his chest.

He'd have to hurry, thought Christian, the decision made. Soon it would be daylight. He would have to guarantee support before then.

'Dear Lord,' he said, softly, moving on again. 'Please help me.'

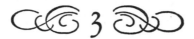

3

Quintal looked up as Christian approached, straightening from the rope he was looping. Since their matching tattoos in Tahiti, Quintal had regarded Christian differently from most superior officers, even though he accorded the man the respect due to his rank.

'It'll be a hot day, Mr Christian,' he said, looking hard at the officer. Christian was drenched in perspiration already, he saw.

'Are you all right, sir?' he asked, looking at Christian intently. The man's face was set and he seemed to be looking at something far away.

'Well enough,' replied Christian. It would have to be a careful approach, in the beginning. If Young and Stewart were wrong, Christian wanted ground upon which to retreat.

'It's going to be a long voyage home,' opened Christian. 'Maybe longer than a year.'

'Aye, sir,' said Quintal.

He was a short, stocky man, not afraid to fight, Christian knew. And he made no secret of his dislike of Bligh. But was it sufficient for him to become a mutineer?

'I'm worried about the captain,' embarked Christian, cautiously. His stomach dipped, as it did sometimes when the ship slipped too quickly into a storm trough. The moment of commitment, he thought.

Quintal let the rope-end fall, studying the second-in-command intently. This wasn't a casual conversation.

'Worried?'

'His rages are almost constant now,' said Christian. 'It'll be a hell trip.'

And you to be the chief sufferer, thought Quintal.

'It will be that,' agreed the seaman, guardedly. His back was still marked by the flogging that Bligh had ordered. And there would be more, he knew. Bligh had him singled out, for no reason at all. The man would find cause for further punishment.

'There's none who are happy with him,' asserted Christian, growing bolder.

That was true enough, accepted Quintal. But Christian shouldn't have said it. He should have been frightened by this conversation, Quintal thought. Instead, he found himself excited. Mr Christian had picked him out, he decided.

'Ours has been a fair relationship,' prompted Christian.

'Aye, sir,' agreed Quintal.

'Do you trust me?'

'Of course.'

'Completely?'

Quintal nodded.

'Aye, sir, completely.'

'Do the men trust me?'

Quintal nodded again, feeling the first twitch of apprehension.

'What about the other officers?' demanded Quintal. People were hanged for mutiny, he thought. And that's what they were discussing, he was sure.

'With me,' assured Christian. 'Those that count.'

It was like dancing to the music of the blind fiddler, Byrn, thought Quintal, going around in circles with little point and arriving back where you started.

'What are you proposing, Mr Christian?' he demanded, directly.

Christian hesitated, suddenly scared.

'I'm going to seize the ship,' he blurted. 'Seize the ship and cast Bligh adrift.'

Quintal stared at the wild-eyed man in the half darkness, silenced by the confirmation.

'But there'll be no murder,' qualified Christian, imagining Quintal's reaction to be that of reluctance. 'No violence at all. And they'll have provisions. Are you with me?'

Still Quintal did not reply and Christian shifted, nervously. If Quintal rejected him, he was lost. The conversation would be around the ship within hours. Bligh would hear of it, without doubt. And demand an explanation. He'd have the ship searched, too, and find the raft. Christian felt the weight around his neck. Was it sufficiently heavy to bear him down? he wondered. Please God, make it so.

'I'll follow you, Mr Christian,' undertook Quintal, breaking the silence. He smiled at the relief on Christian's face. 'And I know the others will, too.'

Christian reached out, clasping the seaman's shoulder. It was too friendly a gesture between an officer and a lower deck man, he recognised. But he discarded the hesitation.

'We'll not fail,' he promised.

Quintal nodded, his growing excitement erasing any doubt.

'Muskets,' he said, immediately. 'We'll need muskets.'

For a moment, Christian paused. Then he said: 'Thank God Mr Fryer is such a lazy bugger.'

For several months Joseph Coleman, the armourer, had been entrusted with the keys to the arms chests, given the chore without Bligh's knowledge because the master was irritated at being awakened by seamen wanting muskets to shoot fish or birds first at sea and then in Tahiti.

'I'm doubtful that Coleman will join us,' cautioned Quintal.

'I'll not invite him,' said Christian. He gestured and moved off towards the armourer's berth. Quintal followed, so closely their bodies touched going down the companion-way.

Christian stopped by the sleeping man. Another point of commitment, he thought. Abruptly he reached out, grabbing the armourer's shoulder.

'A shark, Mr Coleman,' he said, softly. 'The keys, if you please. I'll have some meat for you.'

Coleman reacted automatically, burrowing the keys from beneath his hammock pillow and handing them over without even looking at Christian.

Behind Quintal sniggered his nervousness and Christian turned quickly, pushing him away before the noise could arouse the now sleeping man.

'Sorry,' apologised Quintal. 'It just appeared so easy.'

'It won't be easy,' warned Christian.

Back on deck, they stood together, gazing down at the keys.

'We can do it,' said Quintal, almost in disbelief. 'We've got the means to do it.'

'But not sufficient men,' rejected Christian.

'Isaac's been flogged,' reminded Quintal, nodding to the other seaman on the opposite side of the deck.

Isaac Martin was an American, a crop-haired, sallow man, almost 6 ft tall. Like almost everyone else, he had been tattooed in Tahiti. He was very proud of the star on his chest and often worked stripped to the waist. When he did, it was still possible to see the marks of Bligh's beating.

Christian and Quintal approached the man together and this time Christian was more positive, seeking instant support.

Martin frowned at the second-in-command, moving uncomfortably from foot to foot.

'Who's following you, Mr Christian,' he demanded, carefully.

'Most of the people below,' guaranteed Quintal, gesturing expansively to the orlop deck.

Martin shook his head in disbelief.

'Where are they?' he insisted.

'They'll follow,' assured Quintal.

'I've no more reason to love Bligh than anyone else,' said the American. 'But I'll not involve myself in a scheme that won't work.'

'So you're not with us?' asked Christian, immediately apprehensive.

'Let's see your following,' said Martin.

It was Quintal who moved, turning without any command and running barefoot down the hatchway to the lowest deck in the ship. He knew the hammocks of every man and went unerringly to those of his friends of whose support he was convinced.

Charley Churchill, the master-at-arms, twice flogged and put into irons for desertion in Tahiti, listened without question to Quintal's whispers and nodded, just once, swinging out of his berth.

Burly William Mickoy, scarred in two places from knife fights, was perhaps Quintal's closest friend on board.

'Too long overdue,' he accepted. 'Have we guns?'

'Aye,' said Quintal, holding up the keys like a talisman.

'Then we can't fail.'

Alexander Smith immediately committed himself. So did Matthew Thompson, at forty one of the oldest seamen aboard and the first man to label Bligh a tyrant. Jack Williams, the slow-talking, slow-moving Guernseyman, thought about Quintal's approach for several minutes.

'You've my support,' he agreed, at last.

Separately, to avoid arousing the suspicions of the other crewmen who stirred and twisted in their hammocks, the mutineers slowly mounted the ladders, fighting against the excitement that made them want to hurry, trying to appear men bothered by the heat going aloft for some relief.

Only Quintal and Thompson remained below, moving towards the arms locker. The keys in Quintal's hand jingled with the man's nervousness.

'Damn,' said Quintal, softly. He stopped in the alley and Thompson stumbled into him. Sprawled over the arms store, asleep but completely securing it, lay fifteen-year-old John Hallett, the midshipman missing from Christian's watch.

'We must have weapons,' muttered Thompson, his conviction immediately faltering.

Quintal nodded. Mickoy had demanded the same, he recalled. Support for the overthrow would blow away like sea mist in a rising wind if they couldn't get to the muskets.

'The other store,' suggested Quintal.

Both men, worried now, hurried on deck, making for the knot of men grouped nervously around Fletcher Christian. It could be only minutes before the activity aroused suspicion, Christian knew.

'We can't get to the arms chest,' reported Quintal, speaking softly to avoid alarming the uncertain men. 'Hallett is asleep on it.'

Christian groaned.

'And Thomas Hayward is sleeping on the second one,' he responded. He had checked the arms cache while Quintal was rousing the others below, hoping desperately there'd be no bar to the first chest.

'Without guns, we're lost,' said Quintal, unnecessarily.

And for having gone this far, I will swing at a rope's end, thought Christian. It would be day soon, he realised, staring over the rail towards the lightening horizon: in daylight, they'd be seized in minutes.

He turned incisively to the men around him, pushing away his fear.

'Thompson, Quintal, come with me,' he ordered. 'The rest of you spread around the deck: don't hold together.'

Hallett was on his back when they got to the wind-drafted arsenal, his chest lifting in breathy snores.

Christian motioned Quintal and Thompson further into the companion-way, where they were half hidden, then kicked out at the foot of the young midshipman.

'Up, Mr Hallett. Up,' he said, head close to the boy. He wanted no one but Hallett roused. 'You're an hour late on the watch; you could be on report for this, sir.'

The boy jerked awake, bewildered. He pulled up, mouthing for words.

'Up, sir! About your duties.'

Hallett, mind still fogged with sleep, stumbled into a half crouch, moving instinctively towards the hatchway, oblivious to both Thompson and Quintal.

Quintal moved swiftly, the key already in his hand.

Now the positive commitment to crime, realised Christian, as Quintal swung the lid up off the chest. Fletcher Christian, proud son of an even prouder family, second-in-command of a ship engaged upon an expedition that had the interest of King George III himself, assured before he was fifty of an admiral's flag, had become a mutineer. For the briefest moment, his resolve wavered. A mutineer, he thought again. And made so because of a man who slept not fifty feet away and had driven him to the point of despair.

The other two men were standing back, waiting for his lead, Christian saw. He gazed down at the weapons neatly arranged before him. If it still went wrong, he would need to fight people off, until he could get to the rail to cast himself over. Abruptly he moved, reaching into the chest. He clipped a bayonet on to a musket, then looped his arm through the canvas webbing. Into his belt he thrust a pistol and then took up a box of shot. He paused, then snatched at a cutlass. He'd prick Bligh with it, he decided. He'd make the bugger cringe.

'Stand guard on the chest,' Christian ordered Thompson. 'Only those supporting us are to have guns; if any try to rush you, put a ball over their heads. But *over* their heads, remember. I'll have no one dead.'

'There's the other chest,' warned Quintal. 'If they seize that, they could stand us off.'

'Aye,' said Christian. 'But we're armed now. We can shift Hayward.'

Christian emerged cautiously from the hatchway. Until this moment the tiny gathering of men could only have aroused passing curiosity. But now he was festooned with weapons, like a make-believe pirate at those country fairs he'd once enjoyed in Cumberland. No one who saw him would have any doubt what he was about.

Keeping in the shadow of the booms, he moved with Quintal towards the second chest, nodding to those mutineers he passed to go to where Thompson stood and arm themselves.

'He's gone,' he said, needlessly, when he got to the chest. He gazed around, suddenly alert. If Hayward had discovered what was happening and gone to awaken Bligh, the uprising would collapse now.

'There,' pointed Quintal.

Christian looked towards the poop. The second midshipman was engrossed with the soft-minded Norman, gazing down at the great fish swimming sentinel behind them.

There was movement from the left and Christian turned to see Mickoy approaching. The seaman gestured over his shoulder.

'Tom has thrown in his lot with us,' he reported.

Thomas Birkitt, fair and solid-bodied, his face holed with pockmarks, nodded and smiled nervously. There was still the rest of his watch, remembered Christian. Ellison would be with him. And Mills, when he saw the growing size of the mutineers. And the doubtful Isaac Martin had seized a musket, he saw.

For'ard came the sound of chopping as Muspratt started again on the breakfast kindling.

'See if he'll commit himself,' ordered Christian, to Quintal.

From the direction of the poop Hayward, bored with Norman's shark, moved forward, then stopped at the sight of the mutineers.

'What in the name of God ... ?' he demanded, his voice trailing away in disbelief.

'Quiet, sir!' silenced Christian. He'd shouted, he realised; an over-reaction to the first challenge. He'd have to control it. Nervousness was contagious.

'Have you given mind to what you're doing, Mr Christian?' pressed Hayward, immediately aware of what was happening.

'I ordered you quiet.'

39

'It's a hanging crime, sir.'

'Too much has passed to be vexed about that,' said Christian, emptily.

He detected movement in the shadows near Hayward and swung the musket towards it. Hallett, blinking rapidly from the combination of fear and the effect of sleep, moved into the light. He looked first to Christian, then to Hayward for guidance. When none came, he moved closer to Hayward, seeking protection from the older unarmed midshipman.

Christian jerked his head at Martin, then indicated the two young officers.

'Guard them,' he instructed. 'They're to stay where they are.'

'What now?' asked the attentive Quintal, at Christian's side.

'Bligh,' responded Christian, shortly. 'We go to get Captain Bligh.'

4

William Bligh stirred in his tiny cabin and turned on his back, comfortably lulled between sleep and full consciousness, immediately thinking, as he had constantly since their departure from Tahiti two weeks earlier, of the honours that would be accorded him when he got back to England. It would be marvellous, he knew. To be famous. And respected. He'd have to be promoted, of course. Not just to full captain, which should have happened anyway before the *Bounty* had left England and for the failure to do which the Admiralty would be properly criticised when he returned. But even higher. He'd probably make history, he thought, twisting on to his back and shrugging his nightshirt around him. The youngest admiral in the King's navy. Betsy would be so proud. And the children, when they understood what it meant. Admiral William Bligh! It had the proper sound about it: an important sound.

The recognition for what he had achieved would be immediate, of course. The Royal Society, which had organised the expedition and especially selected him to command it, had promised a gold medal if he were successful. And he had been, he knew. Beyond even their expectations.

Not ten feet away, in the main cabin which had been completely converted into a greenhouse, with lead-lined floor to capture and recycle water and lamps for artificial heat, were over a thousand breadfruit plants, carefully potted and held secure in their special racks.

The climate of Tahiti matched almost perfectly that of the West Indies, where he would anchor within months. The botanist they carried with them was convinced the breadfruit would transplant without the slightest difficulty. So he would earn the gratitude of all England, Bligh knew. Every landowner and person of importance in the country had a fortune invested in the sugar plantations of the West Indies. He'd seen the wealth for himself, after Betsy's uncle, Duncan Campbell, had given him the merchant ship *Britannia* to command when the Admiralty had stood him down after the American war.

Unimaginable riches, he reflected, sleepily. And dependent entirely upon slaves. It had been only natural for the British establishment to become worried after American independence because the colonies had supplied the food for the chained and shackled workers. Now, because of what he'd done, there was no longer any need for concern. He was providing an alternative. More, even. The cultivation on the spot of the breadfruit, with its year-round crop, would provide even cheaper food than that which they had had to import. So their profit would be even greater from now on.

Oh yes, decided Bligh, the people who mattered in England would have every reason to be grateful to him. Very grateful indeed. King George would probably present him with the Royal Society medal, he thought happily. The sovereign's patronage of the gardens at Kew, established by his mother, showed the royal interest in botany. So there was reason beyond the good he had done for his country. Yes, the King would definitely honour him. And that would secure his place in society, opening to him every door in London.

It was right that he should finally get some recognition, he thought. The anger roused him further and he opened his eyes, staring through the gloom at the bulkhead inches away. What had happened after James Cook's last voyage had been a travesty of justice, he reflected, in familiar bitterness. He was as good a hydrographer and cartographer as that damned Grimsby coaster captain: at least half the charts and drawings produced after the *Resolution*'s Pacific journey had been his and he'd been given no credit. There was hardly a mention that he'd been Captain Cook's sailing master, even. He'd put that right, though, once he'd become famous; he'd publish his own account of the *Resolution*'s hunt for the north-west passage and Cook's death in Hawaii. And take care, very cleverly and without appearing to correct any previous accounts, to show who deserved credit as the better navigator.

He had no need to arise for another hour, he thought, lazily. Perhaps even longer. He closed his eyes, seeking sleep again. Life, he thought, was very good.

Around him the ship creaked and winced and far away he could hear the scuffle of the watch on deck. They'd turned out to be a bad crew. It might have been different, he supposed, had he been able to sail with the usual company of marines to guarantee internal control. But the space needed for the plants, which meant everyone, even himself, was uncomfortable and cramped, had made that impossible.

No captain could have taken greater care of his people, he told himself. He had imposed a special diet on the outward journey to keep them free from scurvy and even given over his own cabin when the gales soaked their quarters. Yet they had repaid him by insolence, carelessness and ingratitude.

Even Mr Christian. Perhaps Mr Christian worst of all. Bligh opened his eyes again in the darkness, annoyance bunching in his throat. Why? he wondered, recognising the recurring question. Why had Fletcher Christian, whom he had made a friend not just on this voyage but on the *Britannia* as well, turned upon him?

It had been Tahiti, Bligh determined. There was no place on earth more like Sodom and Gomorrah. Where else did women crowd, three or four to a man, groping and pulling at him, demanding a European child? And men, too, cockaded and perfumed, but still men, flaunting themselves in opposition to the laughing girls, lifting their skirts in open invitation to any aberration.

In almost every festival performed for his benefit, until he'd insisted it should stop, there had been disgusting scenes of blatant sex, with men and women distending their sexual parts in obscene gestures. He shuddered at the recollection.

The men had been satiated and spoiled by the island and its easy life. Even Mr Christian.

It was only natural, he supposed, that the man should miss Tahiti. Mr Christian had been shore commander of the breadfruit plantation for nearly six months and had known the relaxations better than most men aboard. He'd even, finally, made a wife of one of the native girls, a chief's daughter. Actually given her a European name, Isabella. And a child, yet to be born.

Yes, very natural to miss it, during these early weeks. But the man would get over it, Bligh convinced himself.

The episode on Anamoka had upset Mr Christian. And that stupid argument the previous night over the theft of the coconuts. He'd been correct, of course, Bligh knew; he always was. For six months they had known little discipline, so it was important to remind them they were at sea again, sailing under the King's Regulations. Even something as insignificant as a missing coconut, especially one belonging to the captain, had to be challenged and the culprit seen to be punished. It had just been unfortunate that Mr Christian had taken it and had had to be publicly rebuked.

Perhaps, thought Bligh, I should try to curb my impatience. Certainly with Mr Christian. Yes, definitely with Mr Christian. To bully and drive was the only way to get the crew ship-shape. But Mr Christian was different. It was stupid not to have realised it before, decided Bligh, in rare self-criticism. He closed his eyes again, turning towards the starboard bulkhead.

Damn Tahiti, he thought, before drifting back to sleep.

5

There were five of them, in single line, hugging the weapons against them to prevent any sound, feeling their way soft-footed down the companion-way into the after cockpit.

Fletcher Christian led, stomach churned with doubt, his ever-wet hands slipping greasily along the stock of the musket. Bligh's cabin was small, he remembered: two men in it were a crowd. So a cutlass would be easier than the cumbersome, long-barrelled gun lengthened even further by the fixed bayonet. He shifted the sword to his right hand, in readiness. He'd never seen Bligh frightened, he realised. Angry, certainly. Irrational, to the point of insanity, many times. Every emotion, in fact. But never fear. But he'd witness it now, Christian promised himself. He'd make the man grovel, he determined, remembering his thoughts over the arms chest. Christian shook his head, like a man trying to dislodge an irritating insect, annoyed by the persistent doubt. The accusation kept repeating itself, like a litany, in his mind. Fletcher Christian, mutineer: Fletcher Christian, murderer. Not my fault, he tried to contradict. Not my fault at all. Mutineer, he thought again. Murderer.

Quintal followed Christian, still excited. He had to fight against the strange desire to laugh, tongue clamped between his teeth, biting himself to force away the nervousness. Churchill and Smith were bunched together next in line, needing physical contact for reassurance, and Birkitt, at the rear, kept glancing behind him, as if fearing a surprise attack.

They huddled together outside Bligh's cabin, staring through the crack which the man had left for ventilation. It was almost light now and they could make out the figure of the sleeping captain. He was on his back, one arm hanging loosely over the side of the cot. It was a neat, fussily kept room, every article of uniform folded and neatly stowed in its appointed place in its locker.

Christian felt the eyes of the other men upon him, expectantly. He tightened his grip upon the cutlass and shrugged the rifle further back upon his shoulder, tensing at the noise it made. The men were strained forward, like hunting dogs awaiting a command.

He moved his head, identifying Quintal, then indicated the closed door of Fryer's cabin immediately opposite that of the captain. If Fryer had his pistols to hand, he could be a danger, Christian knew. Quintal nodded in understanding, then twisted at the same time as the apprehensive Birkitt at the sound behind them. Jonathan Sumner appeared, pistol held before him in his right hand. The new mutineer smiled, hopefully. Damn the man, thought Christian. He'd given the strictest orders that no one else was to come below decks. If they started milling around so soon, it would be impossible to isolate the mutineers from those who might remain loyal to Bligh. It would only need one loose shot and there would be carnage.

He'd punish the seaman later, he decided. He paused, stopped by the thought. How would he punish him? The captain of a ship punished by the right of his appointment, as the holder of the King's commission. By what right did a mutineer punish? None, he realised. His only authority would be that which those who followed him would permit. And any order they disliked could be ignored. They were all just common mutineers, levelled by their complicity in crime. He was no longer an officer, Christian realised. He'd abandoned the right. Just a common mutineer now, like the rest.

He prodded Quintal, then indicated Sumner. If the damned man wanted involvement, then he could have it. Let him be the second man to face Fryer and the uncertainty of his pistols.

The tight-packed group were shuffling, the feeling among them mounting. Within minutes, thought Christian, his support would start to erode. He breathed deeply, preparing himself, then pushed against the cabin door with the point of the sword. It was wrong, he thought, immediately. Too slow and unsure. He should have burst in, frightening his victim with the noise. As if trying to recover from a mistake, Christian slapped at the captain's arm with the flat of his sword, but misjudged that gesture, too. It hardly snicked the sleeve of the nightshirt, echoing instead against the edge of the berth. The other men were jamming in behind him, urging him on, so that he was scarcely a foot from where Bligh lay.

Christian swivelled the butt of the musket, bringing it up against Bligh's legs, hitting him awake.

'Awake, sir!' he shouted. It sounded banal. Here I am, discarding my honour and perhaps my life and I rouse the man like a mother chiding her son for being late for school, he thought.

'Up,' he shouted again, unable to find better words.

Bligh blinked awake. And did nothing. The man, whose nearly every communication with his crew was conducted at a roar and who became enraged at the slightest infringement of regulations or authority, was numbed in his bewilderment.

'I've taken control of the ship,' announced Christian, formally. 'You're no longer in command, sir.'

Nothing he said seemed to be right. Weren't men supposed to use momentous words on occasions like this?

Bligh still appeared unable to comprehend what was happening, Christian saw. The man's mouth was moving, fish-like, as he groped for understanding.

Finally Bligh moved, wedging himself up on his elbow. Christian remembered the promise he had made himself. He brought the cutlass up, awkwardly, jabbing the point at the side of the captain's throat.

Even now, Bligh's reaction was wrong, decided the mutineer, prepared for a screaming, disjointed harangue and hearing instead quietly uttered words.

'Mad,' said Bligh, simply, straining away, his voice rusted with sleep and disbelief. 'You're completely mad.'

'Aye, sir,' agreed Christian. 'And I know well enough who made me so.'

Bligh tried to shake his head, but it drove the sword-point into his throat and he stopped, head held unnaturally to one side. From the moment of awakening, he had not taken his eyes from those of Fletcher Christian. The unwavering, brittle-blue gaze had always unsettled him. Christian looked away, disconcerted, to where the sword pricked the man's smooth neck.

Bligh wasn't scared, realised the mutineer, sadly. The confounded man would rob him even of that satisfaction, like he had robbed him of everything else.

'Murder!'

Bligh seemed conscious for the first time of the enormity of what was happening. He screamed the word, suddenly, jerking back further in his bed, so that the cutlass point was temporarily away from his throat. Everyone jumped and was immediately embarrassed by their reaction.

'Murder! To arms!'

Christian pinned him again, driving his head up, the doubts he'd had washed away by the momentum of the events.

'Aye, sir,' he said. 'There may well be murder. And I'd be justified in doing it, well justified.'

Bligh stared back, balefully. He still wasn't frightened, Christian knew. Damn the man: damn him in hell. He pushed back against those crowding into him.

'Give me room, I say,' he demanded. 'Don't crowd upon me so.'

Bligh appeared to be listening, expecting to hear the sound of his rescuers.

'There's no man on this vessel who will help you,' predicted Christian.

'You,' said Bligh, softly. 'You, Mr Christian. Of all people.'

'Tie him up,' demanded Churchill, from behind. 'He's a shifty bugger. Let's not leave him loose.'

The captain's screams had echoed throughout the ship and there was noise everywhere now. Churchill moved away, making more room in the tiny quarters.

'Hand down some rope,' he yelled up the companion-way, unable to see who was above. 'Something to secure the captain.'

There was the sound of shuffling, but no reply.

'A line,' shouted Churchill. 'Give me a line.'

It was Mills, one of the first to follow Christian, who responded. He went to the mizzen and cut off a section of the cord matching that which Christian still wore around his neck, weighted by the suicide lead. He threw it down and Churchill bustled past Christian, grabbing at Bligh's hands. Christian moved back, glad to be away from the unremitting stare. Churchill pulled the tiny, fat-bellied man out of his cot, then turned him, to face down over it. The balding master-at-arms screwed the cord tight into the captain's wrists, as determined as Christian for him to cry out in pain. Bligh winced, but said nothing. The end of his night-shirt was caught up as he was tied, so that his thighs and buttocks were exposed to the grinning men. It would have taken the smallest tug to cover the man, but no one moved, enjoying his humiliation.

In the cabin opposite, the startled Fryer was staring at the wavering pistol held by Sumner. It had been a frightening awakening, the sound of Bligh's screams coming at the very moment his door opened, splitting back upon its hinges. He crouched up, still unsure, trying to see into Bligh's quarters. Men were milling about in the captain's cabin, colliding and getting in each other's way. There was no order among them, he saw.

Quintal stood between him and the cupboard in which the pistols were kept, Fryer realised, coming back to his own sur-roundings. He'd be blown apart before he could get his legs off the sea-chest. It was the time for talking, not fighting. Perhaps that would come later. There was much to learn first.

'What's afoot?' he demanded.

'Mr Christian has seized the ship,' reported Quintal, eagerly. 'The captain has been overthrown.'

'What's to become of him?'

'Cast adrift,' said Sumner. 'With the pig's rations he's expected us to eat.'

'In what?' asked Fryer, thinking clearly now. He wasn't frightened, he realised, in sudden self-admiration. Fryer was a sharp-featured, querulous man whose annoyance throughout the voyage at Bligh's over-bearing, nagging attitude to his officers and men had finally led to his refusal to sit at the captain's meal-table. But the man's overthrow was wrong. Without Bligh in command, he thought, it would be difficult to get the *Bounty* to a place of safety. Certainly Fletcher Christian would have difficulty in doing it: Fryer didn't share Bligh's confidence in the younger man's seamanship.

'The cutter, sir,' said Sumner.

'Then he'll die,' said Fryer, immediately. 'The bottom has rotted out and well you know it. You might as easy throw him overboard to the sharks and be done with it.'

'It's a matter for Mr Christian,' avoided Quintal, hurriedly. He kept looking over his shoulder, more interested in what was happening in Bligh's cabin.

'You'll hang, you know,' warned Fryer. They weren't completely committed, he guessed. If he worked cleverly, he could sabotage the uprising. He decided to experiment.

'Go to the captain's cabin, if you so desire,' he allowed.

'Thank you, sir,' said Quintal, instinctively, moving back. He snapped around at Fryer, knowing he'd been tricked.

'Take care, Mr Fryer,' he warned, uneasily.

Quintal was definitely unsure, decided the master. If Quintal were, then they would all be uncertain.

'What's happening?' demanded Sumner, snatching glances behind and trying to keep the pistol upon Fryer at the same time. The seaman was nipping at the inside of his lips and moving from foot to foot, uncomfortably, like a child wanting a chamber pot.

Quintal glanced resentfully at Fryer. 'I'll go and see,' he said.

Fryer stared after Quintal, observing Bligh for the first time. The captain's nightcap hung lopsided like a mongrel's ear and his nightshirt was caught up. He looked ridiculous, thought Fryer.

'On deck,' said Churchill, in the opposite cabin. 'Let's get the bugger topside, where everyone can see he's done for.'

It might bind the mutineers to him, to see that Bligh was a captive, thought Christian. Or be the signal for a counter-attack by those loyal to the man.

He was conscious of Quintal crowding into the cabin and turned, alarmed.

'Mr Fryer? Who guards the master?' he demanded, looking into the facing cabin.

'Securely held,' reported Quintal, carelessly. 'Sumner can watch him. I wanted to see what was happening here.'

They were rabble, thought Christian, worriedly, disorganised rabble following whatever whim took them.

'Get aloft,' he ordered, trying to convey his anger. 'Gather the support.'

Later, he thought, he'd discipline the man. He and Sumner both. One command had to be replaced by another.

'Let's stop this, Mr Christian,' said Bligh, sensing the disorder. 'Before it goes any further.'

Christian laughed at him, without humour.

'That time has long since passed, sir.'

'Do you really know what you're about?'

'Freeing myself of you.'

Bligh frowned: 'There won't be a port you can put into ... no civilised land where you can berth, not even for a day ... '

'The world is too big,' refuted Christian.

He turned, at the movement by his elbow.

'Almost the whole ship is with us,' exaggerated Quintal, returning. 'And those not in open support show no sign of backing the captain.'

The man had been too quick, reluctant to quit the centre of the action, thought Christian. So the assurance was worthless. He cocked his head, listening to the noise above him. Men were running everywhere, without purpose or direction.

'Who's under guard?' demanded Christian.

'Mr Fryer,' listed Quintal. 'The gunner, Mr Peckover, has rejected us. So has Purcell, the carpenter. And William Elphinstone, the other mate, won't commit himself.'

'Take heed,' ordered Christian. 'There are too many weapons about. Ensure those that hold them are truly with us.'

Quintal nodded, then indicated Bligh.

'How many men are to go overboard with him?'

'I don't know yet,' said Christian. What right had Quintal, a lower deck seaman, to question him? And in so disrespectful a manner?

'The cutter's no good,' cautioned Quintal. 'She'd go under within the hour.'

'Mr Christian!'

The mutineer turned back to Bligh.

'There's still much for us to say,' suggested the captain.

'We've done our talking,' rejected Christian. It was remarkable how calm Bligh was, he thought. Just one outburst: he had pictured the man screaming in constant rage. Nothing was unfolding as he had expected.

'An hour will make no difference with what you're about,' pleaded Bligh.

Christian smiled, pleased at the tone in the man's voice. Perhaps he was scared after all, he thought, hopefully. He always had been a devious man. Perhaps he was just better able to conceal his fear than most people.

'There's little for us to say to each other,' prolonged Christian, enjoying the feeling of superiority.

Several minutes elapsed before Bligh spoke again.

'Please,' he said, at last.

It was a word he had never heard Bligh use before, realised Christian, in sudden surprise. It would be good to savour the man's humility.

The mutineer turned to Quintal.

'The captain and I will talk privately,' he said. 'I want everyone else up on deck, in control there.'

'What do you want to speak alone for?' demanded Quintal and Christian jerked back at the impudence, remembering his earlier doubts about authority.

'Because I choose to do so,' he replied.

'That's how it will always be, Mr Christian,' judged Bligh, as he watched the doubtful men back away from the cabin. 'They'll do as they like now.'

Every eye had been upon him, Christian knew. Now up on deck every mind would be questioning, wondering at his resolve. He felt the sounding lead thump against his chest as he slammed the door. It might still be necessary, he thought.

6

'Untie me, Mr Christian.'

'No.'

'At least release my shirt, sir, so I can cover myself.'

'No.'

He couldn't touch the man, Christian realised. Was it revulsion? he wondered. Or fear?

Bligh was half turned, offering as best he could his bound wrists. His legs were varicosed, Christian saw, the veins knotted and roped over his calves. Unclothed, he was an ugly little man.

'Please, Mr Christian.'

'I said no, sir.'

Bligh straightened, looking at the younger officer sadly.

'You'll not succeed in this enterprise.'

'I will,' insisted Christian, desperately.

'The people will rise up to free me. Be sure of it.'

'Where are they then?' demanded Christian. 'There's no one on this ship now who doesn't know what's happening. You've no support, sir. No support at all. You never have had.'

'There's no more serious crime,' tried Bligh.

He wouldn't get his wish, Christian realised, unhappily. Bligh wouldn't beg. Damn him.

'I know that well enough, sir,' said the mutineer.

'I've been a fair captain, Mr Christian.'

The second-in-command spat, unable to put into words his amazement and disgust at the assertion.

'Fair!' he echoed. 'You're a tyrant, sir, a bullying, insecure swine who takes a strange delight in driving men until they can stand no more.'

'Is that what they think?'

'It's what they *know*. There's hardly a man who hasn't been driven to the point of going overboard because of your treatment.'

'And is that what you think?' demanded Bligh.

'You know well enough what I think,' said Christian.

Bligh was twisting his hands behind him and Christian brought the sword up, threateningly.

'Only the shirt,' said Bligh, coolly. 'I'm only trying to dislodge the shirt.'

'Leave it,' ordered Christian, unsure. 'I'll not suffer you to move about.'

'You're very frightened, aren't you, Mr Christian?' jabbed Bligh.

'Oh no,' refuted Christian, shaking his head to enforce the hollow denial. 'Not fear, Captain Bligh. I'll own to only one feeling towards you, I despise you, sir. Despise you.'

'It wasn't always so,' said Bligh.

No, thought Christian, sadly. How anxious he'd been to work under Bligh, he remembered, after the stories that had spread of the man's expertise as a navigator, cajoling and begging anyone he thought might help him to become a member of the man's crew. Christian had used every influence he could muster among his powerful, well-connected cousins and uncles to pressure Bligh, particularly when he'd discovered the Christians were acquainted with the family of Bligh's wife. Even Bligh's rejection that his officer list for the *Britannia* was full hadn't deterred him, he recalled.

'Wages are no object,' he had written back. 'I only wish to learn my profession and if you would permit me to mess with the gentlemen, I will readily enter your ship as a foremaster, until there is a vacancy among the officers. We midshipmen are gentlemen, we never pull at a rope: but I should even be glad to go on one voyage in that situation, for there may be occasions when officers may be called upon to do the duties of a common man ... '

Bligh still had the letter, Christian knew, carefully preserved in the document case somewhere in the cabin. How many times, wondered Christian, as they had sat at that cramped dinner table had he heard how that letter had appealed to the man.

' ... officers may be called upon to do the duties of a common man ... ' The phrase recurred in Christian's mind. Or the duties of a common mutineer ...

'No, sir, not always so,' he conceded.

'Let's turn back,' urged Bligh, anxiously. 'It's not too late, not yet.'

Christian shook his head.

'I'll muster the entire crew,' promised Bligh. 'Assure them the whole matter was a mistake, an error between us that we've resolved ... '

'Stop, sir!' rejected Christian. 'The whole ship's in arms ... they'll be at the rum, before long. Do you imagine any one of them would willingly put themselves back under your command, after what's passed in the last few hours? They'd rather kill you outright. Or themselves.'

'You have my word I'll victimise no one.'

'Your word!' accused Christian, contemptuously. 'Your word, sir, is the most valueless thing about this vessel.'

'How so?' demanded Bligh, nostrils flaring in the familiar prelude to an irrational tirade.

Rarely, thought Christian again, suddenly alert, had he known a man less able to control his temper. Yet apart from that moment-ary slip, now subdued, the two of them could have been discussing an everyday problem of the voyage, rather than an event that was going to alter both their lives from that day on.

Bligh's behaviour, with his promises, was a ploy, accepted Christian warily, a super-human exercise of will by a man on the lip of insanity to secure his release. Once Bligh were set free, he would go berserk. Maniacs were often very cunning, thought Christian.

He brought the cutlass up again, jabbing it towards the other man. Was it to frighten Bligh? Christian wondered. Or to reassure himself?

'You are not a simpleton, Captain Bligh,' lectured Christian. 'One of the worst captains ever to sail under the English flag, perhaps. And a thief and a cheat, to boot. But not a fool. So don't appear surprised at the worth your men set upon your promises.'

Bligh's face was tight, Christian saw. He was trying hard to control the outburst, the feeling shaking at his body.

'Take care, sir,' grated Bligh, through clamped lips. 'Were my hands not tied, then upon my honour ... '

'I know well enough what you'd do,' broke off Christian. 'There's been hardly a day when we haven't suffered the ways of your demented mind.'

He might not be able to inculcate fear into the other man, realised Christian. But he could reduce him to an impotent anger and for Bligh to be unable to vent that annoyance in some punishment or beating would probably hurt him as much. It was very important to make Bligh suffer, decided Christian.

'There could be another course open to us, rather than setting you adrift,' he began, gently.

Bligh stared at him, head cocked to one side.

'We could return you to England in irons, for a court martial. King's Regulations permit a trial for tyranny on the accusation of a junior officer,' said Christian.

Why was he playing with the man? wondered Christian. He had no intention of taking him prisoner.

'And pray, sir, how would you work the ship for a voyage of 12,000 miles, with every other officer under guard?' challenged Bligh. 'I haven't forgotten what Quintal said. Your only support is the scum of the lower deck.'

He *was* a clever man, admitted Christian. He wouldn't be deflected, he decided. He'd ridicule Bligh, one way or another.

'A court martial would be a good way to discover what happened to the ship's rations,' he continued. 'And of learning how much money was *really* spent in victualling.'

Bligh's face was puce and a vein throbbed in his forehead. He'd touched the nerve, Christian knew. As a merchant captain, commanding the *Britannia* for Duncan Campbell, Bligh had earned £500 a year. Coming back into the King's service, yet not promoted to full post captain, had meant his salary had dropped to £70 a year.

There wasn't a man aboard who didn't know how Bligh had made up that deficiency. Or who hadn't suffered because of the man's determination to line his own pocket.

'I made not a penny piece at the expense of the crew,' hissed Bligh.

'Balderdash, sir,' said Christian. 'What you supplied as beef on the outward voyage and no doubt listed full charge for was donkey, without a doubt. No one could nor would eat it. The whole lot went overboard.'

Bligh straightened, listening intently to the disclosure. He was sure the men had taken it.

'And there was no reason, apart from not wanting to resupply, for cutting down the bread ration either,' insisted Christian. 'Replacing the loss with extra rum would, I'd wager, be seen by a court martial for the device it was, a sop to avert any protest from the men.'

'It was necessary to preserve our supplies,' seized Bligh, defensively. 'We *were* beaten back from Cape Horn. The voyage took months longer than expected.'

'There was bread enough, even with the rerouting. It was obvious we would refit in Capetown, if we failed to round the Horn. So there was never any danger to supplies,' countered Christian.'

It was his own private trial, decided Christian, enjoying himself. Bligh was an arrogant bugger, always convinced he could succeed in everything. It was good to show him nobody had been deceived by his cheating.

'And John Williams would be a good witness at any enquiry into your honesty,' said Christian.

'Do you think the Admiralty would take the word of an illiterate, common seaman against a commissioned captain?' sneered Bligh.

It was working, thought Christian, triumphantly. Bligh was confused and uncertain. That he remembered immediately the incident involving Williams indicated his guilt.

'Supported by the word of the cooper, who would swear that the cheese barrel had already been broached when he examined it, I imagine they'd accept the word of Williams that upon your specific instructions he took the cheeses to your lodgings at Portsmouth, for the use of you and your family.'

'Lies,' declared Bligh, desperately.

'As you insisted during the outward voyage,' recalled Christian. 'Not a man believed you then and neither do they now.'

Bligh shifted and Christian saw his hands were whitening, so tight had Churchill secured them. He must be in great pain, thought the mutineer.

'Satisfied?' demanded Bligh, suddenly.

Christian did not reply.

'You're like a child,' accused the captain. 'Bottled up with imagined grievances, breaking toys in its bed chamber.'

'My grievances aren't imagined,' said Christian.

For several moments they stared at each other, eyes held. Neither wished to be the first to look away.

'This is all the fault of Tahiti,' said Bligh, suddenly.

Christian frowned.

'Tahiti infected you,' insisted Bligh. 'Spoiled everyone.'

'Rot, sir.'

'Everyone,' repeated Bligh. He was staring down now, talking almost to himself. 'Infected with sex and debauchery, like a disease.'

'And you the only one to stay aloof and free from taint,' mocked Christian.

Bligh laughed, an attempt at a contemptuous sound.

'That's the difference, perhaps, Mr Christian. I'm not an animal ... I didn't have to rut and fornicate ... '

There was a vicarious thrill in being a torturer, thought Christian.

'Because you *couldn't*,' said the mutineer. 'You were the captain, a man who always had to have respect. You couldn't touch it because it would have been public knowledge, on board and ashore. And you feared they'd laugh at you, didn't you? You couldn't risk being laughed at, could you, sir!'

Bligh stared back, meeting the challenge.

'Have you forgotten Mrs Bligh, who offered you her friendship, Mr Christian? And my babies, whom you held upon your knee?'

'No,' replied Christian, immediately. 'Convince me that you hadn't forgotten them either, sir.'

Bligh looked away, silenced. His face was pinched with the pain the ties were causing upon his wrists, Christian saw. He heard the scrape of feet outside the door and half turned, apprehensively. The door opened, without a knock, and Quintal appeared.

'What's about?' he demanded.

'Is all quiet on deck?' asked Christian, ignoring the question.

'Right enough. But the men are growing restless. They don't know what's happening.'

'They'll know, soon enough,' promised Christian.

'We've looked at the cutter. It's useless,' said Quintal.

'The launch then. Give them the launch,' ordered Christian. 'Start unshipping it.'

'What will that leave us with?' said the seaman.

'The *Bounty*. We'll need no more,' said the mutineer.

'That doesn't rest well with me,' argued Quintal. He remained standing in the doorway.

'I don't give a damn what you like,' yelled Christian. 'Go aloft and do as I say.'

Still Quintal hesitated and Christian swept the butt of the musket against the door edge, slamming it in the man's face.

'You've no authority, Mr Christian,' said Bligh, again. 'They were already a scurvy lot. You knew that, right enough. You'll not be able to lead them.'

'Quiet, sir!' ordered Christian.

'Don't do it,' tried Bligh, sensing the other man's lack of conviction.

'It's done,' insisted Christian. 'Done and nothing can alter it.'

The nose flared again and into Bligh's eyes came the glazed, staring look that always showed at moments when his control was almost gone. But his voice remained level, little more than a whisper, the words spaced and evenly spoken.

'I'll see you destroyed for this, Mr Christian. I shall survive and do everything in my power to bring you down. I'll not rest until you're twisting at the rope's end and the name Fletcher Christian is damned throughout the length and breadth of England. You're a lost man, Mr Christian. A lost man.'

'I was a lost man the very moment I stepped aboard a ship commanded by you,' said the mutineer. 'One of us will be destroyed by this day. And if there is a God, sir, then that person will be you.'

He jerked open the door he had so recently closed, gesturing towards it with the cutlass.

'On deck,' he commanded.

Bligh didn't move.

'My shirt,' he pleaded. 'Please let me cover myself.'

He would not touch the ropes, decided Christian. Or the man.

'Let them see what sort of man there is beneath that starched and proper uniform,' rejected Christian, perversely.

'Damn you,' said Bligh, his temper gone now and the words coming in a roar. 'Damn you in every hell.'

He shook his head, like a dog throwing off water, and the nightcap fell to the floor. Without it, he looked slightly less stupid, thought Christian. But only slightly. He was still a ludicrous sight.

Bligh groped with difficulty along the still darkened alleyway, ignoring the call that came from Fryer's cabin as they passed before it. At the foot of the companion-way, Bligh stopped, gazing up at the quilt of faces looking down expectantly. They *would* laugh at him, he knew, when they saw him. He turned back to the following man.

'Mark my oath, Mr Christian,' he warned, his voice even again. 'Mark it and mark this day. There will never be a moment, for the rest of your life, when you will be able to forget what passed between us.'

He had never thought it possible for so much hatred to exist between two people, thought Christian, staring back at the man. He jabbed out at Bligh's exposed buttocks with the point of the sword, snickering when the man skipped aside to avoid being pricked.

'Get aloft,' said the mutineer. 'I want them to laugh at you.'

7

Christian's arrival on deck, driving Bligh before him, was like that of an orchestra conductor mounting the rostrum, bringing gradual silence from the players he was about to lead. The hush fell over everyone. They were shadowed and grey in the peculiar twilight preceding the immediate dawn and everyone stopped moving, apprehensively.

There was no laughter at the captain's appearance, Christian realised, disappointed.

'There's the bugger!'

It was a bravado shout, like a small boy trying to create an echo in a dark tunnel to prove he wasn't afraid of anything hiding there. It came from Churchill, who appeared immediately embarrassed by what he had done, snatching around, grinning, eager for smiles of response.

Ellison smirked and nodded. So did Birkitt. But the sight of Bligh, humiliated and bound, appeared to unsettle the men rather than bind them to him, as Christian had anticipated.

Passing doubt, Christian reassured himself, prodding the captain forward. They'd rally round, soon enough. They'd all be with him in the end. He knew they would.

'Here. Bring him here,' said Quintal, by the mizzen mast.

Christian hesitated at the command. The stern area was obviously the most secure place to parade the captain and ensure that he couldn't escape. But who the hell did Quintal imagine he was, giving orders? Didn't he realise who the new commander was?

'Aye,' encouraged Ellison, sensing the uncertainty among those grouped on deck. 'Bring him here. I'll stand guard over him. One move and I'll skewer the dog.'

Bligh's head was held forward, but he was looking intently around, identifying everyone who spoke. Creating mental lists, decided Christian.

The mizzen *was* the only place, accepted Christian, moving the captain on. Churchill came alongside, pistol cocked and ready, and Smith and Birkitt positioned themselves behind Bligh, so that the captain stood in a circle of men, with the mast forming a barrier to one side. It would take a concerted attack to free the man, Christian realised, gratefully.

'Just the slightest cause,' Birkitt said, pushing Bligh more to sustain his own courage than to instil fear into the captain. 'And I'll blow your damned brains out.'

'Hasn't got any,' insisted Churchill and they all sniggered.

Children, worried Christian. Frightened, nervous children, even in the way they were speaking. Bligh would recognise it, he knew. And attempt to capitalise upon it.

He was too encumbered, realised the mutineer. At the moment the crew were bemused by Bligh's appearance, but it would not take long for them to sneer at the weapons with which he had armed himself. He handed his cutlass to Alexander Smith, who was standing nearby, then unclipped the bayonet from the musket. Just that would be sufficient, he thought. He detected Bligh straining against his bonds and reached out, managing to grab the trailing cord without physically touching him.

Now he's my dog, thought Christian, happy at the reversal of roles. My dog, at the end of my leash, and he'll have to perform the tricks that I command. He jerked the rope, to remind Bligh who was the master. Just as childish as Churchill, he recriminated almost immediately, loosening his hand on the rope. Careful. Mustn't become hysterical. He was in charge now, in positive command. Couldn't relax, not for a moment.

Heightening the theatricality of what was happening, dawn broke, the sun pulling up on the horizon and washing over the ship, like the lights coming up immediately after the curtains had been raised on a stage. Better able to see the state to which the captain had been reduced, a murmur flickered through the assembled crew, but Christian was unable to discern immediately whether it was sympathy for the man or approval for what had happened to him.

'Here he is,' announced Christian, loudly. He was still being the bully, he knew. And enjoying it. 'Here's the man who's cheated and lashed and kept us short of our victuals.'

The murmuring was increasing. It was approval, recognised Christian. The men were with him. The majority anyway. And that's all he needed, the majority. And weapons.

'I'll forget nothing of this, sir,' said Bligh, speaking very softly and only to Christian. 'Not one moment of it.'

He was trembling again, fighting against the temper. Bligh was like that volcano, far away to starboard, thought Christian. Always about to erupt.

'Look at him,' he commanded, like a fairground barker. His voice almost cracked and he gulped, quickly. 'No more tyranny, lads ... no more lash, for no reason at all. We've deposed him. He's ours now, to do with as we like ... '

Ellison started forward, his mouth moving.

'Pig,' he shouted and spat into Bligh's face. The captain jerked back but couldn't wipe it and the spittle ran slowly down his cheek.

Ellison looked away, down to the deck for acceptance, but only one or two people nodded and smiled approval.

'Let's not slack,' shouted Christian. 'I want that launch swung outboard.'

Activity would prevent them thinking, decided the mutineer. And if they didn't think, they couldn't have doubts. He wished Ellison hadn't spat upon Bligh. It had created sympathy, he knew. And he didn't want that emotion building up for the man.

Christian gazed about him, trying to estimate his support. He was sure of Churchill, Smith, Quintal and Birkitt. Ellison and Muspratt were armed and loyal. Both Edward Young and George Stewart would be with him, he was sure. They'd practically incited the uprising anyway. They couldn't abandon him now. The eager Sumner was down in the well, with James Morrison the mate, unloading the yams and fruit from inside the launch, making it ready for those to be cast adrift. Thompson was still guarding the arms chest, preventing a counter-attack. Another supporter. Enough, decided Christian. He was going to succeed. He'd have been happier with more, but perhaps the support would grow as the idea of overthrowing Bligh settled fully in their minds.

Quintal hurried up, grinning at the new intimacy he imagined existed between himself and Christian.

63

'Mr Fryer wants to come on deck,' he reported. 'Says it's important to talk to you. Shall I tell him to go to hell?'

Damn the man, thought Christian. He'd have to be very careful of Quintal, he decided. Power was going to the man's head like a pint of the best rum. If there were a second mutiny against his command, Christian thought, Quintal would lead it.

'No,' he said, sharply. 'You'll do nothing of the sort. Bring him here.'

Quintal frowned and stood there, arrogantly.

'That might be a doubtful course,' he said.

'That's a decision for me,' insisted Christian. 'Go and get him.'

Would the master throw in his lot with them, wondered Christian, as Quintal made his reluctant way below. Fryer hated Bligh, like they all did. For weeks communication between them had been restricted to the barest minimum necessary for the running of the ship.

Christian's hopes at the man's intentions wavered when he saw Fryer's face. There was no support in that look, he knew. The master gazed without sympathy at Bligh, then at Christian. He appeared to be waiting for the mutineer to order away from their hearing the common seamen who clustered around, guarding the captain. And he would have liked to have dismissed them, realised Christian. He felt uncomfortable with them, knowing the barrier of authority between officer and men had been irretrievably breached. He couldn't tell them to leave, he accepted. They might defy him and it was too early for his tenuous command to collapse.

'These men can hear anything that passes between us,' he told Fryer. His voice was weak, he knew, like a man reciting the lines of a speech that somebody else had written.

Still Fryer hesitated, unsure. Then he shrugged.

'This is a sorry business, Mr Christian,' he said. Then, adamantly, he continued: 'And it's got to stop. And stop now. Damned quick.'

Christian had never thought of Fryer as a brave man. Rather, he was a moaner, constantly complaining about the conditions and Bligh's behaviour, but doing nothing practical about it apart from cutting himself away from the man. Yet he was speaking now in direct challenge to a group of armed men who, for all he knew, were as prepared to commit murder as they were to

64

mutiny. Was it real courage? wondered Christian. Or surface bravery?

'It will,' assured Christian. 'When he's been set adrift.'

Fryer shook his head, in refusal.

'Let's talk about this privately, Mr Christian. Just the three of us ... '

He paused, looking to Bligh for confirmation.

' ... I'm sure if it's abandoned now, the captain is prepared to put it out of mind ... '

Instead of replying, Bligh threw back his head, control ebbing, and bawled out, 'Get Mr Christian! Attack, for God's sake, attack!'

Once again every movement in the ship ceased and Bligh misconstrued it as response.

' ... Seize him, quickly,' he urged, dribbling in his desperation and jiggling from foot to foot at the end of his securing rope. 'You, Isaac Martin. Come on, man, don't bugger about. And you, Jonathan Millward. You've a musket, man. For God's sake, use it. Shoot him down, like the dog he is.'

No one moved.

Christian swung the bayonet first towards Bligh, who stood, blinking in surprise that nothing had happened, and then in the direction of Fryer, who gazed back at him quizzically, not believing his determination to use it. Why was it, wondered Christian, that no one laughed? The whole thing was unfolding like a farce.

'Would he?' said Christian, to Fryer. 'Can you see him forgiving and forgetting that he's been brought bare assed up on deck, to be laughed at by those he's terrorised for so long?'

Fryer misunderstood the reply as lessening conviction on the part of the other man and moved to reduce it further.

'We've become well enough acquainted on this voyage, Mr Christian. So harken to me. No matter how badly you feel you've been treated ... '

Again he stopped, looking at Bligh.

' ... and God knows, of everyone you've been bullied and harried more than most. And earned all our regard for the way you've taken that treatment ... but no matter how bad it was, it doesn't merit the course you're taking ... '

Christian snapped forward, suddenly losing his temper.

'How in God's name, sir, do you know what is justified and what isn't?' he demanded. He felt his eyes flood and blinked against it. Bligh had reduced him publicly to tears not twenty hours before, with the accusation that he was a thief over those coconuts. It wouldn't happen again.

'Nobody can know my treatment at the hands of this man,' he said. He jerked the rope he still held, so that Bligh was forced forward. Jump, little dog, thought Christian. Jump when I tell you to jump.

'Every day,' continued Christian, the self-pity surfacing again, 'without respite he has nagged and bullied and sworn. He's tried to break me, Mr Fryer. He's tried to take away my will and my mind, so that I would leap automatically to any command ... '

Christian was completely distraught, realised Fryer. More than distraught, even. Demented perhaps. And he was armed and followed by at least a dozen men with guns who would, initially anyway, obey any order he gave them. The man would have to be handled very gently. From Bligh he intercepted a look of apology for the outburst. And so he should be sorry, thought Fryer. The man had thrown away an opportunity, judged the master. Alone in a cabin, he was sure, he could have weakened Christian's resolve. Perhaps even overpowered him: he looked almost on the point of collapse. But Bligh, predictably, had been too stupid to realise it. It was typical of the man. He was a fool.

'Take him to England under guard then,' urged Fryer. 'Bring him before a court martial.'

Christian shook his head, indicating the crewmen who had block and tackle fixed to the launch now, ready to swing it over the side.

'How long do you imagine their determination would last, Mr Fryer?' he asked, rhetorically. 'Especially as we got closer to England and the prospect of justice from an Admiralty forced to choose between its captain or crew. No, sir, I'll not keep him aboard, to foment my overthrow. He's to go overboard.'

'He might as well,' said Fryer, interpreting the word literally. 'Casting him adrift will just prolong his death. He'll surely die. You know he will.'

'So be it,' dismissed Christian. He suddenly felt very tired. He had been without sleep for nearly forty-eight hours, he realised. He squinted against the rising sun and felt an overpowering need to close his eyes completely. How good it would be to be able to walk away from it, he thought. Just go below and crawl into his hammock and know that when he awoke Bligh would be gone. For ever. He wished the man dead, he accepted, considering Fryer's warning. He wanted him dead yet hadn't the courage to kill him outright. Which was cowardice.

He squeezed his eyes tightly, trying to drive away the fatigue, then opened them wide. On the far side of the quarter-deck, standing apart from everyone, was Jonathan Smith, Bligh's servant. At that moment Smith looked towards him and Christian held the gaze, gesturing him forward. Smith approached apprehensively, eyes moving between the mutineer and the captain. He waited for the man to look directly at him, to guess his attitude. There was dislike in the expression, Christian saw. Dislike and contempt.

'Rum,' ordered Christian. 'Break out the grog, for everyone ... '

He hesitated, looking back to Bligh.

' ... and bring him some clothes,' he added, suddenly disgusted with himself for what he had done in bringing Bligh on deck unclothed. It had been stupid. Stupid and juvenile, the sort of thing Bligh might have done to humiliate somebody whom he hated. The men would despise him for it, not admire him, Christian decided.

Smith waited, not moving immediately. Abruptly, so quickly that Christian had no time to bring up his bayonet to prevent it, Smith reached out and snatched at the caught-up nightshirt. It came down to Bligh's ankles, concealing his behind.

'It'll do until I return,' said Smith, to Christian.

He wanted to prove I've no longer any authority over him and that providing he's brave enough he can do what he likes, judged Christian. Was that how it was to be from now on, he wondered, everyone determined to prove themselves, even lowly servants like Jonathan Smith?

Bligh's head was still lowered and he was muttering, as if his reasoning had gone. It was names, realised Christian. The man was reciting names to himself, attempting to mark them in his mind, determined, if he survived, to provide the authorities with a full list of the mutineers.

The man had set himself a difficult task, thought Christian. Even he was still unsure who supported him and who didn't.

Smith returned very quickly with the captain's uniform. There was still some inherent respect for Bligh, realised Christian, as he watched Smith struggle to help the tethered man into his breeches and shirt. Perhaps it was more for the title than for the man, he thought, watching the way Churchill and Sumner and Millward stood back, actually half looking away as Bligh's night-shirt came off. But it was still respect. Every minute that the man stayed aboard increased the risk of a counter-mutiny.

Christian took his rum neat, waving the glass for a second tot. Smith provided it, then, not bothering to conceal his hostility, moved from man to man, careless with the ration. Only the youngster Hallett insisted on water to dilute it and Christian was suddenly aware of a new alertness about Bligh. He was hoping they'd get drunk, realised Christian. He was very cunning.

'Smith will go with the captain,' Christian said, briskly, to Fryer. 'And the two midshipmen, Hallett and Hayward.'

The master nodded, not looking to Christian but to Bligh.

'It would be better if I stayed aboard, would it not, captain?' he said.

Bligh looked up, head cocked to one side. He looked like a parrot, thought Christian, about to recite its words. A very alert parrot, whose beak it would be wiser to avoid.

'Aye, Mr Fryer,' he accepted, readily. 'Stay aboard.'

Too quick, realised Christian, instantly. No words had passed between the two men, he knew. But there had been times when he had been looking at neither and they must have been able to determine some action by looks and half-nods.

'Oh no, Mr Fryer,' said Christian.

'Sir?' questioned the master.

'We *were* acquainted on this trip,' agreed Christian. 'But I view that friendship with reserve, sir. It would be an ideal time, wouldn't it, to mount a counter-attack, at the very moment we're all engaged in setting the captain adrift? You'll not stay aboard to organise that, Mr Fryer. You'll go with the captain.'

'The boat's ready.'

Christian looked down at Sumner's shout.

Through the crush on deck, Christian saw the ubiquitous Quintal thrusting forward, head moving from side to side. The damned man was even giving orders, already seeing himself the second-in-command to Christian's captaincy.

Quintal arrived at the mizzen, nodding his head in half deference. Yes, decided Christian, that was very definitely the role the man saw for himself. Where were Young and Stewart? Those were the men he wanted as his junior officers, not an upstart from the lower deck.

'What is it?' he demanded, allowing the annoyance to show in his voice.

'Alone,' said Quintal, conspiratorially. 'I'd like to talk to you alone.'

Christian hesitated, looking back to where Fryer and Bligh stood. They were closer now, he realised. Near enough for a whispered conversation.

'Keep close watch,' Christian instructed Churchill. He waited. 'An eye on *both* of them,' he added, indicating Fryer.

He walked a few feet away and turned to face Quintal, trying to show by the expression on his face his disapproval for the way Quintal was behaving.

'What?' he asked.

'Not as good as we thought,' said Quintal, confirming Christian's thoughts at the man's self-promotion. 'We haven't the support.'

Christian frowned.

'I reckon there'll be almost twenty people who'll want to go with Bligh,' added the seaman.

Christian swallowed, silenced by the number. Although he hadn't admitted it to himself, Christian had expected his overthrow of Bligh to be accepted almost unanimously. And even from those who did not wholeheartedly approve, he had anticipated tacit acceptance of the new command. He'd never expected almost half the crew to choose abandonment in an open boat 12,000 miles from England, making it quite clear that but for Christian's possession of the weapons, he would already have been deposed. Twenty people in an open boat, reflected Christian. Fryer's words intruded into his mind again. To cast Bligh adrift would be murder, the man had said. And he was right. There was little chance of his surviving: the war canoes would be upon them the moment they came in sight of land. He'd always known his decision would mean Bligh's death, Christian accepted, with belated honesty. Bligh's death and those of the three or four most closely allied to him. But twenty people would be mass

69

murder ... mass murder of people with whom he had drunk and laughed and whored and whom he had regarded if not as friends then certainly as shipmates.

'Even the launch will be overcrowded,' said Quintal, adding to Christian's self-recrimination.

'They'll not be dissuaded?' tried Christian.

'For what?' dismissed Quintal. 'To band together to attack whenever they felt like it. We might be able to watch over one or two who disagree. But there's not enough of us to guard twenty people. We've scarcely enough to work the ship as it is.'

Christian nodded. The man was right, he knew. Such a number of dissidents couldn't be kept aboard. Where the hell were Young and Stewart? He needed advice and counsel. He halted at the thought. Captains of ships made their own decisions, he told himself. And that's what he was now. The captain. The man in supreme command. He didn't like it, Christian realised. He didn't like it at all.

'Then they'll have to go.'

'It's a lot of people,' said Quintal. The man knew what would happen to them and was reluctant to be a party to such slaughter, Christian guessed. How many of those following him so fervently would back away from killing their friends when the time came to force them into the launch? If Bligh realised his opportunity, accepted Christian, he could re-seize the ship.

He looked beyond Quintal to where Smith stood, close to Bligh.

'Rum,' he shouted, to the servant. Perhaps drunk it would be easier for them. Was the nervousness discernible in his voice? Please God, don't make it so, he thought.

'Rum,' he repeated, his voice stronger now. 'More rum for everybody. And get that launch into the water.'

Bligh was smiling, Christian saw. The confounded man was smirking across the gap that separated them. Had he guessed? Christian asked himself. Had Bligh realised he could win, even now? Or was it just his madness, that tendency to grimace for no reason that was one of his more irritating habits?

8

The boat launched badly, hitting the water stern first and the prow slapping down moments later like the handclap of a teacher calling her pupils to attention. Christian, who was standing amidships, jumped at the sound, fearful that the launch, like the cutter, had rotted and broken up. If that had happened, there would be no way of getting rid of Bligh and his supporters, other than by throwing them overboard. And Bligh's following appeared to be growing, Christian saw. William Cole, the bosun, was for'ard, in deep conversation with Purcell but avoiding any looks towards Christian. Instead, both men kept glancing towards the spot where Bligh and Fryer stood. They were awaiting a signal, decided Christian, nervously. The rival factions were beginning to form into two separate groups.

It wouldn't do much good, but Hayward and Hallett would automatically swing behind any official effort to recapture the ship, Christian guessed. All they needed was one central figure around whom to gather, like the dissidents had followed him, thought Christian. And once a counter-revolt began, it would soon gather strength.

'The boat?' he shouted to Sumner, near the rail. 'Is the boat all right?'

There was open fear in his voice, but Christian was careless of it, his only concern now to get Bligh and the men who might follow him away from the *Bounty*.

'Aye,' assured Sumner, detecting the tone and looking back curiously at his new leader. 'Safe enough. Shipped a little water, but none that can't be baled in a few moments.'

'Overboard, then,' commanded Christian, hurriedly. 'Get them overboard. Look lively, now.'

No one moved to follow the order, he saw, desperately. Each mutineer was staring around him, no one willing to be the first to herd the men to their deaths.

Cole and Purcell were coming towards him, Christian saw, apprehensively, their bravery growing as they detected the increasing disunity among the mutineers. It meant there would be four people abaft the mizzen who opposed him, calculated Christian.

'It's to a certain death you're sending us,' said Cole, contemptuously.

'Stay then,' retorted Christian.

'I'd rather die than be associated with a mutiny,' said Cole. He was a burly, sea-weathered man whom Christian had always admired. He would have been a sobering influence had he thrown in his lot with them, thought Christian.

'The launch is ship-shape enough,' Christian tried to reassure the man. 'And the sails and masts are good.'

He could vouch for that, thought Christian. The previous night he'd made his escape raft from them. It must be still down there somewhere, among the debris thrown out as the launch had been swung overboard. He hoped someone had realised it and stowed the masts back in the boat.

He looked towards the man alongside Cole. William Purcell had helped him in his desertion plans, he remembered, providing nails with which to trade with the natives and rope to lash his fragile craft together. The carpenter was a weak, vacillating man, Christian knew. Willing, eager in fact, to assist in a desertion and damning in his criticism of Bligh as he did so, yet the man lacked the courage to join in open opposition when the opportunity arose. A carping, always-complaining coward would be no loss, decided Christian. But his ability would. They'd need a carpenter.

He stared around, trying to locate Charles Norman. The carpenter's mate had abandoned the shark and was standing in the stern, frowning at what was going on around him, his lips moving in private conversation with himself.

Christian turned back to Sumner, who had positioned himself at the head of the ladder.

'Norman stays,' he instructed. 'We'll need him.'

Sumner, confused by the statement, looked to the simple-minded man, then back to Christian.

'Purcell's going with the captain,' enlarged Christian. 'The captain.' Even after overthrowing the man and attempting his ridicule, the term of respect came so naturally. The men he now led would never call him captain, Christian realised.

Down in the well he heard snatches of laughter. It was a nervous, almost hysterical outburst, recognised the mutineer, trying to locate it. Mickoy was drunk, Christian realised, watching the flushed, stumbling man as he moved around the deck, musket slung across his back, sniggering for no reason. The man could have been overpowered in a moment, Christian knew. So could Mills. The middle-aged gunner's mate was slumped against the thwarts, head lolled on his chest. There would be others, he accepted, desperately. It had been ridiculous to break open the rum.

'I'll need my tools,' demanded Purcell, with increasing determination, reminded of his professional ability in the exchange between Christian and Sumner.

'Aye,' agreed Christian, immediately.

'No,' protested Churchill.

The master-at-arms came around from behind Bligh, his face working with anger, and stood close to Christian.

'Damn it, man,' he said, clearly regarding Christian as an equal. 'With his tools and the luck to land on a friendly island, there's no knowing what sort of vessel they'll be able to build.'

'I've said he can have them,' said Christian.

'And I say he can't.'

Christian felt Bligh and Fryer shift behind him and swung the bayonet towards them. It would be a good moment to fight, Christian realised. They would only need to overpower him and the mutiny would collapse like an open mainsail in a gale. It would be madness to continue the argument with Churchill, he thought, revealing their weakness.

'Let's talk no more of it,' he tried to dismiss, but Churchill shook his head, sensing victory.

The appearance of Edward Young saved Christian, who turned upon the absent midshipman with the anger he felt for Churchill.

'In what hole have you been skulking?' he demanded, too loudly.

He heard laughter again, but controlled this time. He looked towards the mizzen and saw Bligh smiling at him, mockingly.

'Not long, Mr Christian,' he said, calmly. 'Not long before your enterprise collapses.'

'What's the matter?' asked Young, to his right.

Christian twisted, not knowing whom to address first. Oh God, he thought. Oh dear God. The captain, he decided. He had to reinforce his authority to the man who was the most direct challenge to him.

'Stay here,' he shouted at Young, knowing the man's awareness of discipline would make him obey the command more readily than the seamen had been doing for the past hour.

He stalked towards Bligh with the bayonet held before him but the captain didn't flinch away and it was Christian who had to lower the weapon to avoid driving it into the man's stomach. Christian stood there, reduced to foolishness by the action, and Bligh laughed again, a forced sound, but still wounding in its mockery.

Bligh was controlled again now, Christian realised. Fryer must have lectured him about the stupidity of irrational outbursts, which would only remind the mutineers of the sort of man of whom they were ridding themselves and strengthen their resolve. Instead, guessed the mutineer, they had decided upon near silence, letting the uprising destroy itself by its own disorganisation.

'Mind one thing, Captain Bligh,' said Christian, vehemently, emotion building up in his throat, so that his face reddened, as if he were choking. 'If events turn against me, then I'll not be denied my revenge. I'll not have this put aside without the satisfaction of your death.'

Bligh believed him, he thought. The sneer on the man's smooth face flickered uncertainly, and he swallowed several times. I succeeded, thought Christian, feeling the euphoria flood through him. For several seconds, at least, I succeeded in frightening the man. But it wouldn't last.

'Abandon this madness, sir,' intruded Fryer, still believing he could talk down the mutiny. 'It's doomed, as you must know ... '

Both Smith and Birkitt were unsure now, Christian realised, looking beyond the two captives. There hadn't been an exchange the two guards had missed during the last hour and both men had recognised the confusion.

'Into the boat,' yelled Christian, looking at Birkitt. 'Get Fryer into the boat as soon as it's pulled close to the ladder.'

Birkitt straightened at being addressed, but made no move towards the master. Not one order obeyed, thought Christian, exasperated. Each man was looking inside himself, acting as the mood took him. It was anarchy, complete anarchy.

'What's happening?' demanded Young, on the far side of the mizzen.

Christian hurried to him, needing support.

'The whole thing is collapsing, that's what's happening,' he said, his voice a whisper. 'You urged me to this, Mr Young. You and Mr Stewart, with your assurances that everyone was behind me, to a man ... '

' ... and ... '

' ... and almost half the crew are openly defying me and siding with Mr Bligh,' cut off Christian. His emotion broke and his fears poured out at the other man.

' ... I've had to stand here all alone, trying to hold the thing together, while you two hid away below ... '

There was a whine in his voice, he knew, the complaint of a child fearing he'd been left alone in an empty house.

'I was not hiding,' denied Young, without strength. He hurried on, knowing he had to say more. 'I was testing your support.'

'A lie, sir,' threw back Christian. 'I tested my support hours ago. It took Quintal not fifteen minutes to gauge it.'

Young shuffled before his friend.

'I'm with you, Mr Christian. You know that.'

'Then show yourself to be,' said Christian, anxiously. 'I need you behind me. And some order. Everyone is doing whatever enters their head. Unless we get some command recognised, we'll all be in irons before this day ends.'

Bligh had been right, hours ago, thought Christian. They were a bad crew, officers and lower deck alike.

Christian swivelled at a shout and saw Churchill gesturing over the rail. Purcell was staggering along the deck, weighted down by his toolbox, and the master-at-arms was yelling at Sumner to prevent its going into the launch. But Sumner appeared not to hear, turning instead towards the stem of the ship. Purcell, apparently oblivious to all around him, struggled on down the gangway with his box.

'I'm buggered if he'll have it,' said Churchill, moving away from the captain and the master he was supposed to be guarding.

'Stay at your post, sir,' yelled Christian, abandoning his determination not to argue with the man again in front of Bligh and Fryer.

Churchill paused, gazing back towards Christian.

'A pox on what you say,' he refused. He scrambled down into the launch, threatening Purcell with his pistol, groping into the toolchest with his free hand.

'Matthew,' called Churchill, without looking away from the carpenter. 'Here, Matt, take this.'

Quintal responded immediately, positioning himself halfway down the ladder and creating a middle link in the chain, with Sumner at the top, to pass back the tools that the master-at-arms was seizing at random and returning to the ship.

Other men were moving towards the launch and Christian tensed, his immediate fear that it was the first movement by crewmen loyal to Bligh. Then he saw they carried bundles of possessions and scraps of food and realised that, unbidden, they were following Purcell into the boat, removing from any mutineer the responsibility for personally ordering them into the small vessel. The botanist, David Nelson, was going, Christian saw. He'd lived with the man, in adjoining tents, throughout their stay in Tahiti and had come to like him. Taciturn, perhaps. And silently critical of the sexuality into which the crew had plunged with sudden abandon. But a fine man. Without his expertise, Christian knew, the breadfruit plants would not be in their greenhouse amidships. Nelson would suffer, having to abandon the plants he had tended with such care. He had seen almost as much honour in the expedition as Bligh had anticipated. Lawrence Leboque, the sail-maker, had decided to stay with the captain. And Robert Tinkler and Robert Lamb. Tinkler paused at the rail-edge, looking up at Christian. It was in the able seaman's bedroll that Christian had hidden the food he had intended taking with him when he deserted. Tinkler had found it and recognised the bag as belonging to Christian. He'd known its purpose, Christian remembered. Without judgment the man had returned the food hoard, absolving himself with just seven words: 'I want to know nothing of this.' And still he wanted to know nothing; poor Tinkler.

Christian felt a jump of regret at the sight of the gunner, William Peckover, scrambling down the ladder. There might not have been friendship between the two men, but Peckover was a solid, reliable man who could be depended upon in moments of emergency. 'Reliable' stayed in Christian's mind. All the stalwart men were going with Bligh, he thought. And all the hotheads were staying aboard the *Bounty*, becoming mutineers with the eagerness of children introduced into a new game of which they would soon tire. Thomas Ledward, the acting surgeon, was going into the launch with his medical supplies. And George Simpson, his assistant. So they were without a physician. Because of the promiscuity in Tahiti there had been many outbreaks of venereal infection, recalled the mutineer. He'd caught it himself and been cured by Ledward. Where would they get their treatment now? he wondered. It was said that, untreated, the disease sent a man mad. The two useless midshipmen, Hallett and Hayward, came stumbling from the hatchway, holding on to each other's clothing like abandoned children, both clutching a knotted shirt of belongings. Hayward was crying, Christian saw, his nose running to mix with his tears.

'I'm getting all the good men,' said Bligh, from behind. 'You're left with just the scum, Mr Christian.'

'No, Mr Bligh,' corrected Christian, heavily, looking back at him. 'I'm ridding myself of some scum, too.'

Bligh's mouth snapped shut. Christian saw Fryer seize the captain's arm in warning and Bligh stood there fighting an internal battle with his temper. So they still thought they could regain control by remaining calm, realised Christian.

Jonathan Smith, the newly courageous servant, came out of the entrance to the captain's quarters with logbooks and charts. but at the ladder-head Sumner stopped him, retrieving the maps.

'To be set adrift, without even a route to follow,' accused Fryer, seeing the incident.

'We could tow you towards Tofoa,' offered Christian, without thought.

'Holy Mother of God,' exploded Birkitt.

Christian looked up in surprise at the outburst. The second guard was storming away, leaving only Alexander Smith to watch over the captain and Fryer.

'Come back,' shouted Christian, desperately. 'Consider what you're doing, man.'

Birkitt ignored him, not even bothering to turn at the protest. Christian twisted again, looking for Young. He'd had a musket, he remembered. The other midshipman had vanished again. A coward, Christian thought; an abject bloody coward.

'Shoot,' ordered Christian, going back to Alexander Smith. 'If they so much as make a move, put a ball into them.'

Smith nodded, doubtfully. He wouldn't do it, Christian realised. With a little encouragement, the man would abandon his post, like Churchill and Birkitt before him. Birkitt was by the ladder now, gesturing to Quintal and Churchill, waving his arms back towards where Christian stood.

'The thieves fall out,' mocked Bligh.

'A matter of indifference to you, sir,' retorted Christian. 'Your fate's decided, whatever happens.'

'Sure, Mr Christian?' said Bligh. He almost appeared to be enjoying himself, thought Christian, worriedly. The man definitely saw events swinging back in his favour, even though the majority of his supporters were away from the *Bounty* now.

Bligh half turned, looking at Alexander Smith. The thick-set, sturdy man shifted uncomfortably under the examination.

'Smith,' identified Bligh, as if seeing the man for the first time. 'Alexander Smith! Tell me, Mr Smith, what are you going to do when this matter is reversed and that madman comes towards me with the bayonet? Are you going to stand there and let him run me through? Or are you going to put a ball into his head? Protecting the captain's life like that could absolve you from whatever has gone before ... earn you a commendation, even ... '

'Pay him no heed,' yelled Christian. 'It's a trick, nothing more.'

'Think on it, Alexander Smith,' encouraged Bligh, his usually strident voice soothing and soft. 'Think of your choice: protect the captain's life, to be honoured. Or stay a mutineer and be hanged. And you will be hanged, you know? You'll dance at the yardarm, unless you abandon it right now.'

Christian ran to the man he hated, prodding the bayonet into the sagging flesh of his belly.

'Enough,' he threatened Bligh. 'Or by God I'll get it over with now.'

He jabbed the weapon forward, pricking the skin, enjoying it when Bligh winced. Their faces were only inches apart. He could actually see his own features mirrored in the man's eyes, realised Christian. Bligh's breath smelt sickly sweet.

'One more word,' Christian repeated, 'and this knife will be through your belly.'

'No, it won't,' challenged Bligh.

The man wasn't sure whether he'd complete the threat, Christian knew. But he still had the courage to argue. He was a brave man, decided Christian, in reluctant admiration.

'You won't kill me, not in cold blood,' said Bligh, his voice strengthening. 'You might, by setting me adrift in a boat, with no chance of survival. But that would be different, wouldn't it ... you wouldn't have to see it happen ... '

'Kill him. Go on, kill him.'

The demand came from behind and Christian turned. Churchill and Birkitt had returned from the ladder-head and were staring at the confrontation.

'Kill him,' Churchill said again. The man had been given nearly fifty lashes when he was recaptured after his desertion in Tahiti, remembered Christian.

'I said there would be no killing,' replied Christian, uneasily. He sounded foolish, he knew; death threats one moment, backing away the next.

'Here's your new commander, lads,' Bligh shouted to them. 'Quivering with the vapours. Tuck him in sound at night, so he won't see shapes in the dark.'

It was a poor jibe, but effective, Christian knew. He had been robbed of any authority over those who followed him by his very action in leading the uprising. Now Bligh was undermining any respect they might have retained. Fryer's counsel was proving very dangerous; the taunts were more damaging than any blows would have been.

'I'm permitting only the barest necessities,' reported Churchill, belligerently, gesturing back to the boat. 'There'll be no tow to any damned island.'

First Quintal, now Churchill, thought Christian. If Bligh and his remaining supporters weren't away from the *Bounty* within the hour, the mutiny would be over.

'*I'll* decide what they're to have,' insisted Christian. He had to restore some command, he knew. He felt the lead against his chest as he walked over to the two mutineers; it still might be needed.

'They'll have food,' he ordered. 'And navigation equipment ... '

He hesitated, preparing the threat. 'And from you, sir, I'll have obedience,' he completed.

Christian stood directly in front of Churchill, the bayonet tight in his hand. He'd never killed anyone, he realised, suddenly. But he might have to kill Churchill, to bring the men back behind him. What would it be like? he wondered. Would the blade go in easily, without striking a bone? Would Churchill die immediately? Or linger, thrashing at his feet? Would the blood splash on him, still warm, staining his hands for a moment and his mind for ever?

Mutineers and loyalists alike were watching, further along the deck, Christian realised. The revolt could end at this moment. He detected movement to his right. To look would mean taking his eyes from Churchill's face. And if he did that, it would be taken as weakness. He stared ahead, unflinching, waiting to be attacked. The figure came into his vision and he saw it was Young, musket in hand. The midshipman positioned himself behind Christian, the backing implicit, and Christian felt the tension seep away. Confronted by two officers, Churchill capitulated, lowering his eyes and nodding respectfully.

'Aye, sir,' he accepted.

It was ironic, thought Christian, that the discipline to which the man was instinctively, if belatedly, reacting had been beaten into him by Bligh.

Christian turned to Young, gratefully.

'Stay here,' he ordered. 'Keep close to the captain ... '

Still the respectful 'captain', thought Christian, going to the upper rail and gazing down into the boat. There were about fifteen people already there, he saw, knee-deep in hastily grabbed bundles. Littering the bottom were hammocks, twine, rope, sheets of canvas and sails and a jumble of boxes. But no food, he realised. The launch was almost too low in the water. With food to come and the remaining men, there would be dangerously little freeboard.

'Victuals,' he shouted to Sumner. 'Get provisions in. No more belongings until the food is stored.'

It was Jonathan Smith who again rose to the responsibility, summoning Tinkler and Simpson from the launch to help him. Christian stared down, mentally checking the supplies as they were loaded aboard. One hundred and fifty pounds of bread went in first, he saw. Smith was a sensible man, going immediately for the basic food. Meat was the next thing the man collected. Sixteen pieces of pork was hardly enough, Christian thought, counting it as it was handed down. But to increase it might lead to opposition from Churchill or Quintal. And he might not win another confrontation. They had lines in the launch, he could see. And the sea was full of fish. Better to say nothing, he decided. And safer. Six quarts of rum and six bottles of wine were stowed at the stern of the launch, presumably where Bligh would sit, and then Smith handed four empty butts into the boat, in addition to the twenty-eight gallons of water. They'd be well able to catch whatever rain fell, Christian tried to reassure himself. Immediately came the contradiction. There would be eighteen men in that launch. What if it didn't rain? And there were no fish to catch? It was a torturer's death, he told himself. They were being cast adrift to starve or thirst to death.

Cole bustled up from the launch, heading immediately for the quarter-deck.

'I want a compass,' he said, imperiously, addressing Christian. It had the makings of another dangerous situation, realised Christian, startled by the man's arrogance. Cole's arrival put three unafraid men on the quarter-deck, with Hallett and Hayward still loitering nearby. And there were only Smith and Young, besides himself, to oppose them. He had to get rid of Cole immediately.

'Take it,' he agreed.

'No.'

The protest this time came from Quintal, as the bo'sun began opening the binnacle. The man who had first joined Christian had come back unseen from the launch, and was standing with his musket held loosely across his body, half threatening to level it. At least Quintal's arrival balanced the numbers with Bligh's men, thought Christian. And created another problem.

'What's he want a damned compass for?' demanded Quintal. 'There's land not five miles away.'

The man was drunk, Christian decided. A bayonet was hardly the weapon with which to challenge a drunken man with a musket at the ready. For the briefest moment he pressed his eyes closed again. How tired he was, he thought. Not just the fatigue that came from lack of sleep, but the lassitude and disgust arising from what he was doing. He'd made a mistake: a horrendous and terrifying mistake, ending one hell and immediately creating another for himself. He was damned, thought Christian. Damned forever. And all because of William Bligh.

Quintal had brought the musket up further, he saw. A musket ball would be a quicker way to die than being dragged down through the water by an uncertain weight, he thought, suddenly. How easy would it be, he wondered, to goad the man into using the gun? Quintal was a violent man. And very drunk. He'd used a knife, in lower-deck brawls, Christian knew. A man who would use a knife would use a gun. Quintal swayed, cockily, happy that Cole was standing before the compass box waiting permission to take the equipment out. Badly drunk, Christian thought again, seeing the movement. And so he might miss, wounding instead of killing him. Wounded, he would be captured by Bligh. No, it would have to be by drowning, if at all.

Christian walked over to the box, putting himself between Cole and Quintal, took the compass out and handed it to the bo'sun.

'I said he wasn't to have it,' shouted Quintal.

'Go back to the launch,' Christian said to Cole, ignoring the man behind him.

He turned back to Quintal, looking beyond him to Bligh and Fryer. Get rid of them, he thought, wearily. Just get rid of the immediate danger of Bligh and his men and perhaps he could get below, to rest.

Quintal was still pointing the gun but there was no determination in his attitude. There never had been, accepted the mutineer. It had been a challenge without substance.

He waved the man towards their captives.

'Into the boat,' he said, embracing Alexander Smith in the order. 'Get Mr Fryer and Mr Bligh into the boat.'

They moved at last from the mizzen, shuffling forward in a ragged half-circle.

Churchill had a bottle of rum open in his hand, Christian saw as they approached the ladder, and he was almost as drunk as Quintal. The master-at-arms was barring the final descent into the launch of Jonathan Smith, loaded with Bligh's chart cases, logs and personal papers. The captain's servant was a determined man, thought Christian, remembering his earlier attempt to take them aboard.

'No,' refused Christian, as they came up to the scene. The only way to avoid trouble with Churchill and Quintal now was to agree with whatever they said, he decided. 'You can only have the charts and the log tables that are already inboard. You'll have nothing more.'

'Afraid I might use them to dangerous purpose?' said Bligh, from his left. 'I'm a good enough navigator to survive, you know.'

'Let's kill the dog and be done with it,' belched Churchill, blinking to clear his rum-blurred vision.

'All right,' said Christian, moving away. 'Go ahead and kill him.'

Let him, decided Christian, positively. Let the drunken fool put a ball into Bligh and end the whole business. He didn't care any more. It didn't matter whether Bligh lived or died or he lived or died or anyone lived or died. He swayed, like the drunks clustered around him. So weak, he thought. He felt so weak and tired.

'No killing.'

It was Edward Young who spoke, from behind, the edge of command still in his voice.

'Out of the way, Mr Churchill,' the midshipman continued, thrusting his way into the group. 'Give them pathway to the launch.'

He seized the barrel of Churchill's musket and pushed it across the man's chest, forcing him back from the ladder opening. Churchill stumbled away, clutching his bottle and giggling.

Young shoved roughly at Jonathan Smith's shoulder, hurrying him towards the ladder.

'What about the captain's things?' tried the man, once more.

'They stay,' said Young, crisply. 'You next, Mr Fryer.'

The master paused at the deck edge, staring down into the wallowing launch.

'My God, she's low in the water,' he said, almost to himself.

'And will be lower,' said Young, still brisk. 'Come now, Mr Fryer, don't delay.'

'Let me stay,' pleaded Fryer, turning to Christian.

At last his courage has gone, thought Christian. He never thought it would get this far and now it has he's scared.

'No, Mr Fryer,' refused Christian. He jerked his head back towards the rear mast. 'You threw in your lot with the captain back there and did your damnedest to get me put down. You made your choice. Now you can stay with it.'

'Scum,' cried Fryer, in desperate defiance.

'Get aboard, sir,' said Christian, dismissively.

The man scrambled away and Bligh came forward, still unafraid.

'I never thought you'd actually do it, Mr Christian,' he said.

'Not the first time you've been wrong about me,' replied Christian, heavily.

'I meant what I said, back there in the cabin,' threatened Bligh. 'I'll damn your name and you with it in every part of the civilised world.'

In the cabin, it had seemed a serious threat, remembered Christian. Now it didn't matter at all. Nothing mattered any more. He was sickened by the whole affair.

He turned to Alexander Smith.

'In my locker,' he said. 'My sextant. Get it for me.'

He turned back to Bligh.

'I'm already damned, sir,' he said. 'There's little worse you can do.'

'Weapons,' demanded Purcell, from the launch. 'You must give us weapons. We can't go ashore on these unknown islands without muskets.'

The request was met with derision by Quintal and Churchill.

'A shooting match, is that the game?' mocked Quintal, waving the musket. 'Ship to ship, man to man?'

There was a real risk of one of the mutineers letting off a musket very soon, thought Christian. And no one aboard any longer to treat a wound, he added, looking down at the two physicians in the boat.

Alexander Smith hurried up, the instrument in his hand.

Christian held it as if testing its balance, then moved around Bligh, bringing the bayonet up to sever the rope. The man's hands were whitened almost bloodless and where the cord had

84

been were purple grooves. Bligh must have been in agony for hours, realised Christian. Yet he'd refused to give them the satisfaction of showing it.

He thrust the instrument towards Bligh.

'It's a good sextant,' he said. 'You know that, well enough.'

Bligh frowned, confused at the gesture. Quintal and Churchill were watching, a few yards away.

'No tow,' insisted Birkitt, reminded of the half promise that had driven him enraged from the mizzen and afraid Christian would offer more concessions. 'We can't allow a tow.'

'Try it and we'll use their boat for target practice,' reinforced Churchill.

They probably would, thought Christian.

'All right,' he accepted. 'No tow.'

And there would be no discipline against those who had ignored his commands, he knew.

Bligh's hands were too numb for him to hold the sextant. Instead he clutched it against his body. Still he lingered at the top of the ladder. The anger began to pump at the vein in his forehead and Christian knew there was to be a burst of temper.

'There'll not be a day when I don't think of you,' said Bligh. He tried to control the rising emotion and his voice jumped, unevenly, so that the watching men giggled, misinterpreting the tone as fear.

Only Christian didn't smile. There was nothing about Bligh he found amusing, he thought.

'I'll think of you, Mr Christian,' continued Bligh, sneering. 'I'll know the torment you've created for yourself. And I'll laugh at it.'

'Be gone, sir,' said Christian, contemptuously. He waved his hands before him, like a man trying to drive away a summer insect. 'Get into the boat before it's too late.'

'Too late for whom? You? Or me?'

Christian turned away, tired of the protracted scene. He'd stood on deck for almost four hours, he thought. The sun pressed down on him, burning through his shirt. His own odour, sour and stale, offended him.

Behind him he heard Quintal and Churchill driving the unsteady Bligh down the steps.

Morrison ran along the deck, cutlasses across his forearm. He slowed when he saw Christian.

'Only swords,' he apologised. 'They'll be no danger in the boat with swords. It'll be some protection, on the islands.'

'Aye,' nodded Christian, ready now to permit almost anything. 'Let them have swords.'

The drunken group of mutineers didn't see the weapons until they landed in the boat. Churchill turned angrily upon Morrison, standing at the rail from which he had thrown them. The master-at-arms lashed out with his hand to hit the mate. He missed, wildly, almost throwing himself off balance.

'Fight,' slurred Quintal, fumbling with the musket. 'They're going to fight.'

'Stop it,' said Christian, his voice strained. 'For God's sake, stop it.'

He looked to Alexander Smith. He wasn't as intoxicated as the others, he decided.

'Cast them adrift,' he ordered. 'Get that launch away from the *Bounty*.'

He had not intended to look at Bligh again. But it was impossible to remain staring inboard until the boat was out of sight, Christian accepted.

Bligh drew him like fire attracting a child who knew it would be burned if it reached out towards the flames but tried to grasp them anyway. The man was in the stern, already in command, the sextant and the compass on the seat beside him. He would try hard to survive, thought Christian. Very hard.

The castaways had heard Quintal's threat, he guessed, gazing down from the poop. Bligh had his men at the oars, putting distance between them and the *Bounty*. Purcell was rummaging in the bottom of the vessel, trying to raise a mast to tack against any wind, and Bligh's curses at the man's slowness echoed back to the ship.

When they were twenty yards away and out of immediate danger from the muskets, Bligh let his men rest their oars.

'Not a day,' he called, his bruised hands cupped to his mouth so that Christian would hear him. 'Not a day without torment. Remember that, Mr Christian.'

'Oh God,' said Christian, quietly. 'Oh dear God, what have I done?'

BOOK TWO

'... one of the hardest cases which can befall any man is
to be reduced to the necessity of defending his character by
his own assertions only ... '

Captain William Bligh, 1792, in
a written rebuttal to Edward
Christian's attack upon him

9

Although September and unseasonably cold, even for autumn, the main cabin of the *Duke* would become hot by the middle of the afternoon, decided the court martial President, Lord Hood.

And the enquiry would doubtless last more than a week. Confounded nuisance. Damned stupid to stick to tradition and have them aboard a warship at all, determined the sharp-faced, autocratic admiral. Much better facilities ashore, in Portsmouth barracks. Safer, too. Not that the men arraigned before them looked much danger. Hardly surprising really. After the ordeal they'd been through it was a miracle any had survived at all. Just ten out of the fourteen who had been seized in Tahiti by the search ship *Pandora* in March 1791. More would have survived the *Pandora* shipwreck, thought Hood, if they hadn't been incarcerated in cages on deck and left in chains until minutes before the vessel had been abandoned. The *Pandora*'s commander, Captain Edward Edwards, had been exonerated for losing his ship and those who had died. Too sweeping a verdict, decided Hood. Wouldn't have happened here, not in his court. Still, they had been suspected criminals. Couldn't have expected better.

He glared around the room, glad the open ports in the fantail behind would bring him air. The others further into the cabin, particularly on the witness bench, would suffer. Too bad.

Unfortunate business, the *Bounty*, determined the President, shifting his sword to make himself comfortable. Admiralty had handled it quite wrongly, in his view. Important not to be tainted by their mistakes, though. Have to examine the whole thing properly; get right to the root of the matter. Discipline was the thing to remember. Discipline and the King's Regulations. Couldn't have damned ruffians seizing ships; example had to be made, to see it didn't happen again. Pity they'd suffered so much already. And that Bligh wasn't to give evidence personally. Another mistake. The Admiralty would regret not waiting, decided Hood. It would not have amounted to more than a few weeks. According to reports they were getting from the fast packets, Bligh was already homeward bound. Only eighteen months since their arrest, after all. Few more weeks wouldn't have mattered. It would have enabled justice better to be done. That was the important thing. Still, not his decision. Have to accept orders, that's all.

Lord Hood looked at the men sitting before him, wondering who would be the spy for the Christian family. There would definitely be one, he knew. Ever since the mutiny and Bligh's well-publicised account of what had happened, the relatives of Fletcher Christian had worked unceasingly to sway public opinion. Hadn't done very well so far, despite the advantage that the man's brother, Edward Christian, was one of the best lawyers in the country: rumour had it he was to become a judge very shortly. Another story said he was here, in Portsmouth, for the enquiry.

The President concentrated upon those defending the accused men. That was where the informant would be, he guessed. Among the lawyers. Their sort always stuck together. Wouldn't allow any legal trickery, decided the admiral. Not that there was anything to worry about. He was going to conduct a very thorough and completely fair investigation, keeping strictly to naval law but bringing out all the facts. There would be nothing permitted which could give rise to criticism of a court of which Lord Hood was President. He coughed, indicating his readiness to start, and dutifully the blur of conversation subsided.

'Prisoners will stand,' ordered the clerk.

Lord Hood lounged back, studying the men as they rose, already aware of the identities of the accused from the Circumstantial Letter which set out the evidence to be produced and which had, by the same tradition that decreed the enquiry be held aboard ship, been circulated to the officers conducting the court martial. Some of the prisoners would have to be discharged, Hood knew. In a deposition before the court, Bligh had exonerated completely the blind fiddler, Michael Byrn, who was groping to his feet, head held respectfully to one side to locate from the sound which way he should face. Charles Norman had been kept on the *Bounty* because Christian had wanted the skills of a carpenter, not because the man had thrown in his lot with them, Hood remembered. And Thomas McIntosh had been carried away against his will. Bligh had been emphatic about that, as insistent as he had been that the armourer, Joseph Coleman, had taken no part in the affair. Evidence would have to be called, before their discharge, though. Justice very positively had to be seen to be done at the enquiry. He had always to keep in mind what would happen after the court martial, Hood knew. The affair had already dragged on for three years and become a *cause célèbre* in English society. It wouldn't end, he guessed, with whatever was to happen in an overcrowded enquiry room on a British man-o'-war.

He moved on, studying the rest of the prisoners awaiting the charge to be read to them. Why was it, wondered the admiral, lips twisting in disdain, that they'd all seen fit to have those disgusting pictures indelibly marked upon their bodies? Tattooing, it was called, he believed. Captain Cook had referred to the native practice, in the journal of his Pacific voyages. And Bligh, too, in the narrative of the disastrous journey on the *Bounty*. Shouldn't have let the men deface their bodies like that, determined the admiral. It was pagan. How could a man expect to maintain discipline in his ship if he let his crew descend to the level of unchristian savages? Point to bear in mind, decided Hood. He wondered if the thought had occurred to the rest of the court martial officers. Must remember to mention it during their deliberations.

The midshipman, Peter Heywood, appeared very frightened, thought Hood. To be expected, accepted the admiral. He was only a lad of seventeen, after all. Came from a good family, too. Well connected. Little secret that for months now there had been every pressure possible brought to bear to show the boy an innocent victim of events that had swept him along in their wake.

The bo'sun's mate, James Morrison, seemed better controlled. But then he was a grown man. And intelligent, too. The document he'd submitted, indicating he was going to conduct his own defence, showed an education far higher than most seamen. Better than some officers even, mused the President, glancing along the table at which the court sat. Some could hardly write their damned names.

Thomas Birkitt and Thomas Ellison had been very actively

involved in the insurrection, recalled Hood, coming back to the shackled men and feeling the edge of the Circumstantial Letter. They seemed to have accepted their fate already, he thought, watching as the men stood, heads contritely bowed, even before the evidence against them was presented.

Jonathan Millward was apprehensive, too, realised the President, coming towards the end of the line. Several times since the enquiry had opened, the man had turned to the last prisoner, William Muspratt, as if seeking encouragement, but the bearded Muspratt had ignored him, staring fixedly at some point at the stern of the ship, his lips moving in apparent repetition of the accusation being laid against them.

The clerk was coming to the end of the preliminaries, Hood realised, and arriving at the actual charge.

' ... against each and every one of you that upon April 28, 1789, you did mutinously run away with the said armed vessel, the *Bounty*, and by so doing deserted from His Majesty's service ... '

Where was Fletcher Christian? wondered Hood, as the court martial settled itself after the formal opening. The men before him now were meaningless, he decided, as unimportant as the pilot fish who unquestioningly follow the lead of a shark. Fletcher Christian was the key. And he had vanished.

But Bligh's absence was the most irritating. It was not for him to question the wisdom of the Lords Commissioners of the Admiralty. Or of the King himself, upon whose direct instructions the *Pandora* had been dispatched. But to rely upon Bligh's evidence from a deposition that could be introduced into the court but upon which there could be no cross-examination was a mistake, Hood felt. Particularly with the man so near England. He had little doubt the Christian family would use it to their advantage: their determination to harass Bligh appeared implacable. It was almost as if they were preparing the way for the mutineer's eventual reappearance. Surely they didn't think they could so discredit Bligh that Fletcher Christian could some time in the future return to England? No, dismissed Hood. Whatever their purpose, it could not be that. There could be no mitigating circumstances to prevent the man's immediate arrest and subsequent hanging. Edward Christian would know that, well enough. It could only be the determination of a proud family to salvage something of their reputation.

It was just possible, the President tried to rationalise, that there would be advantage in not having the major participants before the court. The witnesses might possibly speak more openly, without the restricting presence of either man. And frankness was damned important: from the brief details set out in the summary of evidence, Lord Hood couldn't understand why the mutiny had occurred in the first place.

He coughed again, clearing his throat this time.

'This is to be, in many ways, an unusual enquiry,' he opened. 'We are to hear evidence into an armed uprising, three years ago and thousands of miles from these shores, led by the second-in-command against his superior officer. It will be unusual in that neither the alleged leader of the mutiny, Fletcher Christian, nor the captain, William Bligh, will appear to give evidence. Fletcher Christian cannot appear because no one knows where he is ... '

The President paused, deciding to break away from his carefully rehearsed statement.

' ... but let me say every endeavour will be made at this hearing to discover his whereabouts.'

He stared up, looking at the lawyers again. Let that get back to the Christian family, he thought, defiantly.

'Captain Bligh will not give evidence personally,' picked up Lord Hood. 'Because he had already embarked upon the second voyage to Tahiti and from there to the West Indies before the apprehension of the accused and it was not thought proper by the Lords Commissioners of the Admiralty to delay this trial until Captain Bligh's uncertain return ... '

They *should* have delayed, determined Hood again. It could not be a proper trial without him. The Admiralty was a bumbling collection of fools.

' ... such a decision was reached,' he hurried on, alert to the bustle of note-taking that was occurring at the lawyers' bench ' ... in the sound belief that the full and detailed facts of the uprising have been carefully taken down and notarised by a lawyer, to be presented at such time as I and my fellow officers deem necessary.'

Hood sipped from the glass of diluted wine on the table before him. He had been right, he decided. Already the overcrowded room was getting too hot. Thank God he wasn't among those poor buggers way at the back of the cabin. He looked towards the witnesses, wedged on their narrow bench.

' ... for not only do we have the written evidence of Captain Bligh,' enlarged Lord Hood. 'We have, for this enquiry, the castaways most closely involved in the insurrection whose evidence we can hear first-hand. We shall hear from the master, James Fryer. From the bo'sun, William Cole. From the gunner, William Peckover. From the carpenter, William Purcell. And from the two midshipmen who were in the watch of Fletcher Christian and who were among the first to be aware of the uprising, Lieutenants Thomas Hayward and John Hallett.'

Another glance up at the lawyers. There! thought Hood, triumphantly. They might be without Bligh, but no fault could be found with a witnesses' list like that.

' ... and about the facts of the mutiny itself,' he continued. 'There appears little doubt ... '

He paused, looking first to the prisoners, then to the lawyers, waiting for a contradiction. No one challenged him.

' ... therefore the purpose of this enquiry, which I intend to be as far-reaching as possible, is to determine the circumstances that led up to those facts and the reasons for them ... '

Someone appeared to be smiling at the back, thought Hood, curiously. It was Fryer, he recognised, squinting in the semi-darkness of the cabin. What, he wondered, did the master find so amusing about what he said?

At the insistence of Bligh, Fryer and Purcell had been accused of near revolt before a Dutch enquiry at Timor after their incredible survival in the open launch, recalled Lord Hood. And both had been found culpable during the investigation. The evidence of Fryer would have to be examined with particular care, thought the President. And perhaps some pointed questions directed at the man. Odd, reflected Lord Hood, that there had been a second uprising, particularly in the middle of a 3,600-mile voyage which no one knew they were going to complete so miraculously and when, presumably, men should have been bound by the common need for survival rather than splintered by dissent. It really was damned inconvenient that Bligh wasn't going to be before him in person: inconsistencies like this were going to arise frequently before the end of the enquiry. Bligh must be a damned funny man.

'... because neither Fletcher Christian nor Captain Bligh are present, I intend conducting this court martial with complete impartiality and purposely to introduce evidence that would have come from one or other of them, had they been here. For that reason, although the facts are not in dispute, I am going to have the clerk read out the details in the Circumstantial Letter, according to naval regulations. That will conclude the hearing for today. We will begin tomorrow with the evidence of the master, James Fryer . . .'

That had made the bugger jump, thought Lord Hood, relaxing back into his chair but with his eyes still upon the master at the rear of the cabin. The man had started forward in his seat at the announcement and the smile had gone from his face. That would teach him to grin in a court of which Lord Hood was the presiding judge. What was going on in the *Duke* was damned serious, not an occasion for stupid giggling. There were a lot of questions he would put to Mr Fryer when the man took the witness stand.

God, thought Hood, it was confounded hot. It had been a wise decision to rise at noon.

Edward Christian sat, knees beneath his chin, in the window seat of his lodgings at Sally Port, the pot of porter forgotten on the table beside him. There was no breeze at all to move the curtains and the clouds were tumbling up over the Isle of Wight and gathering at Spithead. The day would end in thunder, he decided. It would be uncomfortable out there on the *Duke*, he thought, looking over the Narrows as the warship slowly veered to starboard as the tide turned. But he'd still have given a thousand guineas to be there, in person, so he could have actually questioned in the environment of a court men who had been with Fletcher and knew what he had had to endure from Bligh. He'd have got the truth, the lawyer knew. He always had, which was why he had risen so high in the legal profession. It hadn't been easy, though, after the slander that Bligh had spread to involve the whole family. It had hindered his career, Edward knew. At one time, aware of the opposition he was facing, he had actually considered abandoning the law altogether.

He smiled at the recollection. Now he was being selected for appointment as a judge. He'd have forgone even that, he thought, to have been out there, aboard that warship, stripping away the deceits and excuses with which everyone involved would by now have covered their part in the mutiny. In that they'd had guidance enough from Bligh.

Edward Christian sighed, turning towards his forgotten drink and sipping the beer, without interest.

But he couldn't attend. So therefore it was pointless to speculate about it. Far better to concentrate upon the daily reports from John Bunyan, the eager young lawyer who was defending the midshipman Heywood and who appeared flattered at the interest from the older man. Through Bunyan, Edward hoped, he would be able to introduce the sort of questions and accusations he would have made had he been there in person.

Edward Christian was a man very different from his seafaring brother. He was a short, precise and scholarly person, of abrupt incisive movements, hair receding to form a wide forehead above which he habitually lodged his spectacles. In a family remarkable for their sense of purpose, Edward Christian was probably the most determined. And for the past three years that resoluteness had been directed solely to the defence of a younger brother damned to ridicule by a man who had become a favourite of London society and even honoured by King George himself.

It had been a solitary and largely unsuccessful campaign, he acknowledged, staring back out of the window as the first full splashes of the thunderstorm slapped against the sill outside. Bunyan would get wet, he thought.

It had been in October 1789, two months after he had written it from the Dutch settlement at Timor, that Bligh's dispatch of the mutiny of the *Bounty* had first become public knowledge and the hero-worship had begun. That a man, with just a sextant, compass and book of longitudinal tables, could have safely navigated a vessel with just seven inches of freeboard for a distance of over 3,600 miles and saved the lives of seventeen other castaways had been a tale to enrapture London society. The adulation had increased with the official enquiry, during which the name of Fletcher Christian had been vilified, and then been confirmed with the publication of Bligh's book. It was said there was hardly a house in London without a copy and that the strutting, bouncing figure of Captain Bligh was a familiar sight, moving from salon to salon, autographing copies as he went, always with another untold anecdote of Christian's villainy.

He'd reverse it, Edward vowed. No matter if it took him the rest of his life, he'd destroy the esteem in which Bligh was held. And discover what had really happened to make his brother lead a mutiny.

And there was little legal doubt that his brother had been the ringleader, he reflected, sadly. Edward had reached that objective conclusion, regrettable though it was, long before learning the outline of the evidence that was to be presented to the court martial and about which he had read in the Circumstantial Letter that Bunyan had allowed him to study the previous night.

But there *had* to be mitigating circumstances, he knew. More than that, even. A proper, understandable explanation. Just had to be. As boys they had been inseparable in the Cumberland dales and valleys near Cockermouth. At Cockermouth grammar school it had been unthinkable they would not sit side by side and when Fletcher had determined upon a career in the navy, it had been Edward who had accompanied him to join his first ship at Liverpool. No man knew another better than he knew Fletcher. And that was why Edward had no doubt that there was something which would explain completely why Fletcher had involved himself in the overthrow of his captain. And he'd discover it, vowed the lawyer. He'd discover it and use it to make William Bligh a pariah in the very society in which he was at the moment so revered.

He turned at the knock on his door and saw, immediately it was opened by the inn servant, the polished, anxious face of Bunyan.

'Come in, sir! Come in,' invited Edward. The other man was soaked, he saw, water running from his hair in tiny streams.

'A towel, Mr Bunyan? And some refreshment? A little wine, perhaps?'

The younger lawyer nodded, head buried in the cloth that Edward had offered him.

'Well?' demanded Edward, urgently, when Bunyan had dried himself.

'Little enough to tell,' replied Bunyan, wishing he had a better report for the man recognised to be one of the leading barristers in London. 'It was a formal opening, nothing more.'

'No evidence?'

Bunyan shook his head.

'None,' he said. 'Lord Hood has said he'll call Fryer when the court resumes tomorrow.'

Edward nodded, slowly. Fryer would know more than anyone, he decided. He would have been the man most associated with both Bligh and his brother. In the restricted conditions of the *Bounty*, a plan of which he had studied and knew by heart, the ship's master would have been aware of everything that passed between the two men.

'He's important,' stressed Edward. 'Get all you can from him, particularly about what sort of man Bligh was. Don't forget there was an enquiry, immediately after they arrived in Timor, upon Bligh's complaint. There'll be no love for the man, I'll wager.'

Bunyan nodded, accepting the wine from the returning servant.

'How far do you think you'll be allowed to go with your questioning?'

'A goodly way,' guessed Bunyan. 'The President insisted he would make it as extensive an enquiry as possible ... said he wanted to be fair to your brother and Bligh ... '

That was interesting, decided Edward. Why should the President make such a point? Did it mean the Admiralty weren't happy with the account they had so far received from Bligh? God, it was infuriating that he couldn't attend the damned hearing.

'What about your client?' he asked, politely.

'I've a good chance, I think,' said Bunyan, smiling gratefully at the interest. 'He was little more than fifteen when it happened ... a child, almost. There appears to be some evidence of his having seized a weapon, but to what point nobody is clear.'

Edward nodded.

'Make much of the confusion,' he advised. 'The Circumstantial Letter indicates there was uproar.'

'Bligh's deposition says otherwise,' contradicted Bunyan. 'He insists it was a planned affair.'

'Then it must be attacked,' said Edward, urgently. 'For the sake of your client. And for my brother. A conspiracy would be the worst thing that could be proven.'

Bunyan moved his head in acceptance of the advice, sipping his wine, slowly.

'What about Hood?' demanded Edward.

Bunyan considered the question.

'An authoritarian, from all I've learned. Strict believer in discipline. But a fair man.'

'He'll allow some latitude in the questioning, then?'

'I trust so,' said Bunyan, fervently. 'I got that impression from his opening today.'

'Handle it gently,' counselled Edward. 'These court martial panels are laymen, who resent trained lawyers. At the first hint of being patronised, they'll be against you.'

'I know,' said Bunyan. 'I'll be very careful.'

I hope so, thought Edward. Bunyan was his only contact with the court and if the man antagonised Hood and the other officers, then the chance to intrude into the hearing would be lost.

'I've had a long conversation with the man Morrison, as well as my own client,' offered Bunyan. 'Morrison is a clever man, defending himself. Neither he nor Heywood believe your brother has perished.'

Edward started up at the statement.

'Where then? Where the hell is he?'

Bunyan gestured, helplessly.

'They've no clue. The *Pandora* spent another three months going from island to island after the Tahiti capture ... and found nothing. But they did discover charred spars, bearing the *Bounty*'s name, indicating a fire at sea.'

Edward waved the variance away, impatiently, wanting to believe Fletcher was still alive.

'If only he could be found,' said Edward, distantly. 'If only Fletcher could be produced, to refute before a court of law all that has been said against him.'

'He'd do so as a defendant,' reminded Bunyan.

'I know he would,' agreed Edward. 'But I'd be defending him. And by God, sir, I'd get to the truth of this affair.'

The older man was unsure of his ability to cross-examine the witnesses, realised Bunyan, unhappily.

'I'll do my best,' said Bunyan, allowing the edge of annoyance into his voice.

'I know you will, sir ... know you will,' assured Edward, effusively. 'I was just dreaming. If only Fletcher knew what was being done for him ... '

10

They didn't want him any more, accepted Fletcher Christian. Or need him, even. Perhaps they never had. He'd served a function, like a paper flag behind which people could walk on a parade. Now the event was over, so the flag could be put aside, an occasional reminder but not something to be concerned about.

Certainly not followed.

Only to Isabella was he important, he thought, smiling across the clearing in front of their house. She became aware of his attention and smiled back, contentedly. Their older son was clutching her arm, watching her breast-feed the child born only weeks earlier. Christian wondered if the woman knew how necessary she was to him. Without Isabella, he thought, he would have nothing.

He cosseted her too much, he accepted. She was a Tahitian, after all, a woman used to every sort of freedom. So his attitude would be unnatural. And he knew the other women gossiped that he stayed too much around the house and laughed that on an island the size of Pitcairn he always wanted to know where she was going and how long she would be away from the house.

And it *was* stupid, he knew.

But he couldn't help it. Didn't want to, even. Isabella and the other women thought of it as jealousy, he decided. So let them. Perhaps the mutineers did, too. His behaviour would be as odd to them as it was to the natives. He didn't give a damn what they thought, any of them. And it wasn't jealousy, not the normal sort, anyway. It was fear, he knew, a numbing, suddenly-awake-in-the-night sort of fear from which there was no release. He had nothing else but Isabella: nothing at all. He should have felt more for the children, of course, but the emotion wasn't there.

He loved them, he supposed, in the accepted way. He worried when the older boy got too near the rocks and had been anxious when the baby had developed a cough, so soon after being born. But that was concern more than love. And that's what he had for Isabella. Love. He supposed he'd loved her before they had sailed from Tahiti, all those years ago, on the homeward voyage to England, although he hadn't realised it then because it was an emotion he did not know how to recognise. Bligh had known it, he guessed. He'd called her a whore, Christian remembered, the very day they had sailed. He strained for the recollection.

' ... sad farewell to your whore, like all the others ... ' Something like that. Yes, Bligh had known.

But it had taken Christian several years to realise what it was he felt about her. And become frightened at that acceptance.

'I love you,' he said. How many times did he say that during the course of a single day? Too many, he thought. The words had become flattened by over-use.

Her reaction to the expression of affection always amused him. She nodded her head vigorously, as if agreeing it was right he should do so, then made the usual response.

'Me too.'

'You should say you love me,' he chided, gently. Her command of English was very good, far better than his Tahitian, but sometimes the words refused to form in the proper queue.

'I love you,' she said, accepting the correction and gazing down, shyly. It was odd, thought Christian, how a woman who knew no inhibition in physical love could still be embarrassed at the words.

'I love Thursday,' she added, kissing the older boy. 'And Charles, too. Is that right?'

'Yes,' he assured her. 'That's right; that's very right.'

Was that a rebuke? he wondered, an indication that she knew he did not feel about the boys as he should? No, he dismissed, immediately.

The older boy would be four years old soon, realised the mutineer. It had seemed fitting at the time to name him after the day and the month in which he had been born, Thursday October Christian. Now it seemed wrong. But then most of the things he had done seemed wrong, thinking about them in the lonely exile of Pitcairn.

Nothing had been right, he reflected, after that April morning so long ago. Nothing at all. Christian was surprised the recrimination was still so bitter. Immediately he found the answer. With no future, it was natural to live constantly in the past.

' ... *not a day without torment* ... '

Bligh's words were as clear now as they had been when the man had stood in the stern of the launch, mouthing his threats while the rabble who had followed the uprising had jeered and milled about him on the poop.

And the man had been right, accepted Christian. The anguish had been with him at the moment of mutiny and had hardly left him since. Had it not been for Isabella, Christian would have long ago carried out the idea that had come to him as he had walked to the mizzen and cut away the sounding lead. The cliffs upon which the women they had brought with them from Tahiti scrambled and clawed for birds' eggs were very high and the sea-washed rocks below savagely sharp. It would all be over very quickly. Just a little pain, that's all. And now physical pain seemed so unimportant, compared to the constant mental ache.

He'd known from the start how difficult it would be to get the men to accept his leadership, he remembered. Quintal, now the constant challenger, had shown his attitude within minutes of the mutiny, even before Bligh had been seized. So their rejection of his command should not have irritated as much as it did. But it wasn't really their refusal to obey, he admitted. Their lack of respect hurt far more. There were hardly any of them who didn't regret the situation in which the mutiny had placed them. And they blamed him for leading them into it, behaving always as if he had secured their support by trickery. Which was unfair, he decided. Bloody unfair. Only one man was to blame for what had happened that day aboard the *Bounty*.

William Bligh.

Had he survived? wondered Christian. Unlikely, he decided, realistically. The mutineer knew too well how hostile the natives could be, even confronted with the visible evidence of a heavily armed ship like the *Bounty*. And less than twenty-four hours after the launch had been set adrift, those torrential thunderstorms had lashed the whole area, so what chance had a small boat, with only seven inches of freeboard, stood in conditions like that?

No, he thought, Bligh was dead. Thank God. Yes, he decided, expanding the thought. Thank God. It was right that he should be dead. What if he hadn't perished? What if he had reached safety somewhere, as he had feared the man might in those early, fear-driven days? If Bligh had survived, he would have carried out his threat, Christian knew. There wouldn't be a civilised part of the world where a warrant did not exist for his immediate arrest. He closed his eyes, visualising how the launch had wallowed in water soon to be driven into waves over thirty feet high. No, he reassured himself. Bligh would be dead. Had to be.

And I might well be, reflected Christian, settling back to his reminiscence. His was a living death, made bearable only by Isabella.

It *had* been a good idea, he convinced himself, to have the men make uniforms from the spare sails immediately after the uprising. Natives were impressed by the manner of a man's dress: Bligh had taught him that. For their six months in Tahiti, the captain had sweated daily in his coat, vest and sword, knowing they automatically earned the respect of every islander he encountered. The arrival upon an unknown island of a ship in which the men all dressed the same would increase tenfold the natives' acceptance, he had argued. And so they had obeyed him, he remembered. Only just. But they'd accepted the order, not so much because he had given it but because that residue of discipline from Bligh's command was still there and because they had been too frightened then to oppose him, realising completely in those initial hours what they had done.

They'd complained. But without any real strength. Quintal had led the dissent, of course, with his bumptious arrogance.

'Worse than Bligh,' Christian had overheard him say, three days after the uprising, as the men had sat cross-legged on deck, stitching at the seams.

'Good teacher,' Mickoy had replied. And they'd both laughed, enjoying their joke. But even that had been gained from the reassurance of the past. They were as scared as everybody else, Christian had known, despite the bravado and the cursing. The rum-drinking had made that obvious. Christian had made no effort to stop it, knowing he could not succeed by open challenge. The men would have rejected him immediately, taking from him the thin platform of authority upon which he still stood. So every night they had washed away their apprehension until they were unconscious, the *Bounty* nosing almost unmanned through the Pacific swell.

Had he realised their feelings, like a true leader would have done, then perhaps they would have accepted him in the role he had then sought. But he had been too engrossed in his own remorse to consider theirs.

So all he had done was inflate to ridiculous proportions the need for uniforms, carping as Bligh had done in the past, knowing the Quintal comparison was inevitable, but careless of it.

Whether or not the uniforms were made had become an issue of major importance in his mind. If the outfits were completed, he had convinced himself, then everything was going to be all right: they would acknowledge his leadership, not put every order to the committee of dissidents that appeared to be forming. Without consultation, conscious of his role as their nominal leader, he had chosen Tubai as a refuge. Tahiti was obviously the first place any searchers would look if Bligh survived—he had left the *Bounty* sneering at their eagerness to get back to it. Tubai was only three hundred miles away, so conditions should have been almost identical, he had decided.

But they weren't.

No women had come giggling to meet them, offering themselves. No men had paddled out in canoes, anxious to trade.

Instead, there had been almost constant hostility, with the mutineers having to fight for every yard of land they wanted. Christian had decided upon a fort-like compound, with the ship's guns mounted at the four corners to repel any searchers. His efforts to create it had become ridiculous. As quickly as the sailors dug trenches and created earth and wattle walls, the Tubains tore them down. Every food and water expedition had become the target for guerilla attacks. The night after Christian had ordered the ship's guns fired, as a show of force, the natives had crept undetected into their compound, stolen muskets and lashed them together in the shape of a funeral pyre to mock them when they awoke.

Christian had tried to minimise the defeat.

'Tahiti, lads,' he had urged, as they had manhandled the guns back aboard. 'Think on it — the women we know! The friends we have there, who'll feed and shelter us without expecting anything in return!'

Predictably it had been Quintal who had focused their disgust. Christian had never been able positively to prove it, of course, because they would have laughed at him had he enquired. But he was sure it had been Quintal's idea to bundle together the uniforms upon which he had been so insistent and commit them overboard, in imitation burial.

Had that been the end of his control? he wondered. Perhaps not entirely. They still took sea orders from him, but even that gesture was without meaning. They obeyed because he was the only man left who could read all the charts and use every instrument. It was more a case of his working for them than they for him. He'd been let down by his friends, Christian decided. George Stewart, the damned man who'd first brought out the idea of an uprising, had lost stomach for it by the time they had reached Tahiti. Accepting without apparent concern the risk of arrest from any search boats that would come had Bligh survived, it had been Stewart who had led the break-up of the mutineers. Christian had intended to leave behind those who had been unwilling participants, like the midshipman Heywood and the carpenters Charles Norman and Thomas McIntosh and the blind violinist, Michael Byrn. But he hadn't expected so many others to risk a rope's end against the uncertainty of following him in the *Bounty*. Twenty-four men had remained on the ship when Bligh had been set adrift. And when he had sailed the second time from Tahiti, in the middle of that September night in 1789 to trap aboard some of the sleeping women who might have been unwilling to accompany them into exile, the number had dwindled to eight.

Nearly all of those who had stayed behind had been the most willing mutineers, he remembered. Ellison, who'd wanted to run Bligh through; Birkitt, whom he had feared might band together with Churchill and Quintal and overthrow him during the actual mutiny; Churchill himself, the man who'd done more shouting than anybody; Thompson, who'd guarded the arms chest and by so doing guaranteed the success of the uprising.

Christian sighed, enjoying the sun upon his face. How quickly they'd lost faith in him, he reflected. Just over four months and men he'd regarded as his most ardent supporters had decided the possibility of death was preferable to his leadership.

Would they still be in Tahiti, he wondered, undetected and surrounded by every sexual indulgence and luxury? How good their life would be if that were so, instead of being trapped like he was among a community of little more than twenty people, with hardly any of them prepared to engage in the most trivial conversation.

The remark of Quintal's had been accurate, he thought. He had become just like Bligh, despised and ostracised by everyone around him.

He would have sailed back to Tahiti if he had had a ship, Christian knew. And been glad, almost, if a British man-o'-war had been waiting in Matavai harbour to arrest him.

But he didn't have the *Bounty*. It had disappeared in flames, before they had even had a chance properly to strip it and certainly before any destruction had been decided, either by him or by discussion with the other hard-core mutineers. It had been Edward Young, he remembered, stiff-legged from the rum he had consumed, goaded by Quintal, both of them groping drunkenly from the hold with torches in their hands, giggling at what they'd done. Young had almost died in the blaze, recalled Christian. Pity he hadn't. It had been Young, following so closely upon Stewart, who had fomented the idea of a mutiny. Twice, thought Christian, he had been trapped by the man.

And now the mutineers appeared more willing to take notice of Young than they did of him.

Perhaps, thought Christian, he should suggest they build another escape craft, like the one they had constructed when the women had become so discontented with life on Pitcairn. It had only been done to placate them, with no care to trim or design and the vessel had capsized immediately they had launched it, convincing the women that return to Tahiti was impossible. But they *could* get back, Christian knew. Providing enough attention was paid this time to the balance of the vessel. And that they planned their departure for the best weather, to avoid the squalls and storms.

Being on Pitcairn was like being locked in a cupboard, Christian thought. On Tahiti he would be able to breathe again, as if the door had suddenly been thrown open.

And to return would have a practical advantage as well. There was a dangerously uneven balance of men and women on Pitcairn. Jealousy was building up, he knew. When it burst out, it would bring bloodshed.

There was no question, thought Christian, that he would kill rather than share Isabella with anyone. He might have stood back from the commitment to murder in the past, but about her he had no doubts; to keep Isabella entirely to himself there was nothing he would not do.

'Why do you look so angry?'

He smiled across at her question. Thursday had become bored, he saw, and was striding off fat-bottomed to join the other children.

How lovely she was, he decided, studying the woman, admiring the gleaming, polished hair that made a curtain down her back, her open face always poised for laughter, even here on Pitcairn.

It would have been wonderful to drive with her in the carriage to Brigham Church on a Sunday and then go back, for family dinner, to the farmhouse at Moorland Close, aware of the admiration that would come from his brothers for having captured such a beauty.

'I was thinking how much I loved you,' he said. It would be good to have other words, he thought, rather than those she must be bored at hearing.

'I laugh when I love. I am not angry,' she said, frowning.

She would never manage the confusing nuances of the language, thought Christian. He was beginning to prefer the simple directness of Tahitian himself.

'It was an angry thought,' he tried. 'I was imagining how it would be to lose you.'

There was never a moment, he thought, when that concern was far from his mind.

'Lose me?'

Again she frowned, head lodged to one side in misunderstanding.

'But how could you lose me? I am yours ... '

The worry deepened as the doubt occurred to her.

' ... unless you are not happy and don't want me ... '

He went to her, urgently, cupping her face between his hands and staring down into her wet-black eyes.

'Oh my darling,' he said. 'Don't ever think that. No matter what happens, there will never be a moment when I don't want you … '

He paused, recalling his earlier thoughts.

' … if you were to die. Or be taken from me in a way I couldn't prevent, then I would kill myself. I've lost everything. Except you.'

She smiled, still uncertain.

'Are you sure … I would understand … '

He brought his hands around, so that she could not speak.

'So sure,' he said. 'So very sure. I'll always be there, when you turn to look for me.'

'The constant lovers.'

Christian recognised the voice, without turning to face Quintal.

'The sort of tenderness that Sarah might appreciate,' retorted Christian. It was no secret that Quintal beat the girl who had happily followed him from Tahiti and to whom he had given an English name, as they all had to their women.

'She's happy enough,' blurred Quintal. He was drunk, Christian saw, as he was by mid-afternoon most days. William Mickoy had brought with him to Pitcairn the ability to make a still that he had learned as a distillery worker in Scotland and once the rum had been exhausted, they had both adapted to the native drink made from the root of the taro plant.

'What do you want?' demanded Christian, hostilely.

'Want? Why should I want anything?'

'Social visits aren't a practice on Pitcairn,' rejected Christian.

Quintal nodded, despite his drunkenness.

'Aye,' he said, sadly. 'That's right enough. I never thought that on a South Sea island, where it is always summer, with food waiting on the trees to be picked and a woman content with me, I should be so unhappy.'

The attitude of them all, thought Christian. Boredom was eating into them as destructively as the worms that had devoured the boat in which he had wanted to set Bligh adrift.

'He's a fine child,' tried Quintal, gesturing after Thursday.

The mutineer nodded, pleased with the admiration despite his dislike of the man.

'That's hardly surprising, though,' continued Quintal, smiling down at Isabella. 'With such a lovely mother.'

Christian frowned at the crude compliment. He wished her breasts had been covered. She sat quite unashamed, smiling up innocently at the man's remark.

'What are the others doing?' asked Christian, to regain the man's attention.

He knew by now he should have adjusted to the fact, but it always distressed him that so little happened to them on the island that there was virtually nothing to talk about. They were atrophying, he thought, like the fossils they sometimes found in the rocks on the seashore, among the relics of the Polynesians who had long ago abandoned the island.

'Tending their plots,' said Quintal, uninterested. 'Some of the women are egg-collecting, up on the cliffs.'

'I think we should be careful of that,' said Christian. 'Those rocks are dangerous.'

Quintal looked up sharply at the thought that Christian was attempting to issue an order, even now. There'd been enough of that immediately after the mutiny, when the damned man had behaved as if he were a reincarnation of Bligh. Quintal relaxed. Christian was staring into the ground, hardly aware of what he was saying. The time when Christian could issue orders had long passed and everyone accepted it.

'They're safe enough,' Quintal said. 'They're as sure-footed as goats.'

'I was thinking of Tahiti today,' said Christian, almost to himself.

'I often do,' confessed Quintal.

'Pity the *Bounty* was destroyed.'

'Would you go back?' demanded the sailor.

'If I could,' conceded Christian.

'It could mean arrest. And a hanging.'

Christian looked slowly up at the man who had been the first to follow him, holding his eyes. Quintal was bloated with alcohol, he saw, his nose purpled with aimless veins and his eyes wet and rheumy.

'Aye,' nodded Quintal, at last. 'It would be good to go back.'

11

Bligh stood easily at the conn, his body shifting automatically with the gentle movement of the ship, gazing through the evening haze towards the shoreline of Plymouth. The early lights glittered at him, far away, and he smiled, sighing.

It was always a satisfying moment, coming home. And he had so much to come home to, he reflected, handing the eyeglass to the officer of the watch and leaving the poop for the seclusion of his cabin.

He wanted to be alone, to savour the anticipation of the arrival in London. It would be wonderful, he knew, surpassing everything that had happened before. Deservedly so.

He had succeeded. Again. So it would happen once more. The adulation of a London society still enraptured by his survival from the *Bounty*. The admiration of a King who properly recognised him as the most brilliant navigator of the day. And now the additional gratitude of all those landowners whose fortunes he had guaranteed on this second expedition by successfully transplanting the breadfruit.

Nelson was more famous, he conceded. As much for the scandalous affair with the Hamilton woman as for his seafaring ability. But he was the only one. No one else could match his achievements, Bligh decided. Nor were likely to. So he had earned the fame. And the respect.

Betsy would be so proud, he knew, remembering her nervousness and the tears and the fainting spells at the excitement of being received at St James's Palace by King George and Queen Charlotte after the survival from the *Bounty*. But this time the children were older and would be better able to appreciate how important their father was to his country. And he *was* important, Bligh knew. His name would feature in the history books.

They'd berth at Plymouth at first light, he recalled. But it would be another week before he could get up the Channel to Portsmouth and then to Greenwich. So he'd send his wife a letter by horse courier, warning her of his impending arrival. She would be as surprised as Sir Joseph Banks, to whom another letter should go, so the Royal Society could inform the King of the details and prepare for the necessary reception.

According to everyone's calculations, he should still be a fortnight away. But that was because the estimates were made for ordinary sailors. And William Bligh was not an ordinary sailor. Which Britain now knew.

Normally an abstemious man, Bligh poured himself a glass of Madeira and stood, making a solitary toast.

'Success,' he mouthed, very softly, feeling slightly embarrassed. 'Sweet success.'

And it *would* be sweet, he knew. Sir Joseph had repeated the promise, just before he had departed for his second voyage to Tahiti, of a gold medal from the Society if he got the breadfruit to the West Indies. And the *only* person who could possibly make the presentation would be the King. So it would be the court again, with all its pomp and ceremony. He hoped Betsy wouldn't faint this time.

Would there be more? wondered the man, hopefully. He had guaranteed the fortune of already rich men by this voyage. A gold medal would be the public recognition of his efforts. But there should be another reward. How pleasant it would be, he thought, if the plantation owners could be made to realise he existed on the meagre salary of a ship's captain, without any outside income. And that to sustain the position in London to which the fame of his exploits was thrusting him cost a great deal of money. Perhaps, thought Bligh, he could find an acceptable way to broach the problem with Sir Joseph. The man knew everyone of influence in London. And could organise a privy purse within weeks if he were acquainted with the need. And there was a very definite need. Betsy never complained, but Bligh knew she found life very different in London from what she had known as the daughter of a rich land- and shipowner on the Isle of Man. There was as much cruelty as kindness in the society into which they were being admitted. Gossip and tittle-tattle was the communication of the women and Bligh was aware his wife would have enjoyed a larger wardrobe and a greater selection of jewellery in order to compete at the funetions to which she was daily invited.

Yes, he decided, taking a second Madeira, he'd tell Sir Joseph of his difficulties. It would be an easy subject to introduce. He would approach the man for advice, as if expecting nothing but counsel. Sir Joseph was a kind man: perhaps the best friend he had. He would take the nod and act swiftly, Bligh was sure. He paused, considered, then dismissed a new idea: he would not tell Betsy his plans in the letter he was to write. It might create too much hope and he hated disappointing her. In any case, in the holds were bolts of silk he had purchased to make several new dresses. So whatever happened, she would not be embarrassed this season.

What would have happened to the arrested mutineers? he wondered, suddenly, his mind moving on. He had heard from an incoming man-o'-war in Antigua that they had been seized at Tahiti. He'd always known they'd return there, to the sex. Had he not written as much, in the log supported unsteadily on his knee in the stern of the launch, not three hours after they had been set adrift?

The log would be available as evidence, together with the affidavit he had sworn before embarking on the current voyage. Would the court martial have begun? It hardly mattered. Because Fletcher Christian wouldn't be there. Only *his* punishment was important. Bligh had harried the officers on the warship, after hearing their news, demanding to know the names of those arrested, even reciting from memory the identities of the scum who had overturned him. They hadn't known the names, not all of them anyway. But they had been sure of one thing. Fletcher Christian, whose part in the infamy everybody in England knew because of the account Bligh had published, was not among them.

So what had happened to him? That was the only thing of interest, not the fate of those who had stupidly followed. Let him be dead, prayed Bligh, fervently. Let him have died as painfully as he had expected me to die. Bastard.

He said the word, aloud, his voice high, then jerked around, alert for any sound in the alley outside that would have indicated he could have been overheard.

Only the creaking of the slumbering ship came back to him and he relaxed.

'Bastard,' he said again, quieter this time.

He sat at his desk, pulling quill and paper towards him. He'd write first to Sir Joseph, he decided. And ask about the court martial, so that the man could be prepared for the questions upon his arrival at Greenwich. If it had not been already convened, then perhaps he could give evidence in person, thought Bligh.

It was important that he should, if possible. And find out what had happened to the man he hated.

12

It was going well, decided James Fryer, feeling the apprehension seep from him. Very well indeed. He had been nervous, imagining the angular-faced President would turn his evidence into an inquisition, but for the past two hours Lord Hood and the rest of the court martial officers had sat in attentive silence, only occasionally making notes.

Now the *Bounty* master waited, his account finished, alert for the questions.

Lord Hood straightened in his chair, leaning forward on the long table that had been positioned across the main cabin. Thank God the thunderstorms had cleared the air, he thought. It was much more comfortable today. He'd sit during the afternoon, he decided.

The President had made few notes, relying on his memory for the points he wanted clarified.

'So until the moment when Quintal and Sumner burst into your cabin, at the same time as you heard the captain's shouts, you had no indication whatsoever that the crew were in a mutinous state?' he queried.

'No, sir. None whatsoever.'

'Yet Fletcher Christian, who led it, was a fellow officer ... and Stewart and Young both midshipmen ... you'd have been in daily contact?'

'Yes, sir.'

'No, sir,' rejected Hood, sharply. Fryer jumped, startled.

'I cannot accept,' challenged the admiral, 'that there had been no hint of this matter before.'

'I knew nothing of it,' insisted Fryer, eyes fixed just above Lord Hood's head.

'Was the *Bounty* a happy ship?'

The question came from Captain Sir Andrew Snape Hammond, who sat on Hood's right. As they had risen the previous day, Hood had decreed other members of the court could put questions directly, instead of going through the President. The stupid formality added hours to any enquiry, the admiral had insisted.

Fryer shifted, uncomfortably. It *was* going to be an inquisition, he thought.

'Well, was it?' pressed Hood, curious at the master's hesitation.

'I have known happier vessels,' tried Fryer.

'Sir,' warned Lord Hood, softly. 'We are enquiring here into one of the worst cases of mutiny so far to be examined by a naval court ... a case in which, if the evidence we have so far heard is true, a captain and seventeen of his men were cast adrift to what should have been their certain death ... '

He paused, staring at Fryer until the man met his gaze.

'I will not accept, Mr Fryer, the sort of answer you have just given. I will repeat the question. Was the *Bounty* a happy ship?'

'No, sir,' said Fryer, shortly.

'Why not?' demanded Snape Hammond. He was a crumpled, mottled-faced man who sat slumped in his chair in an attitude of inattention which was invariably misconstrued as boredom.

'There were several reasons,' said Fryer.

'Then let's have them,' said Lord Hood, briskly. The man's reluctance to answer was annoying the President. There was more to the mutiny than they had so far learned from the evidence, he decided.

' ... it had been a long voyage,' suggested Fryer. 'We had had a bad time trying to get around the Horn, fighting gales for most of a month before turning back ... '

'Conditions encountered by His Majesty's vessels every week of the year,' rejected Snape Hammond, positively. 'And such conditions were long past, anyway ... '

Fryer swallowed. Lord Hood ruled his life by discipline, the *Bounty*'s master knew. To indicate criticism of Bligh's treatment of the crew would meet with no sympathy.

'There were times,' groped Fryer, uncertainly, 'when the men complained about their food. When they felt they were being badly treated ... '

Was the man a fool? wondered Hood. There wasn't a ship in

the King's navy upon which men weren't disgruntled with their victuals.

'This enquiry would be greatly speeded, Mr Fryer, if you were able to respond directly to what we ask,' threatened the President, tightly. 'Why, sir, was the *Bounty* an unhappy ship?'

'It was often difficult,' responded Fryer, 'to adjust to the ways of the captain.'

It was a bad reply and when he saw their reaction, the nervousness lumped in his stomach. The court martial officers sat unmoving, every eye upon him. Each man was a captain, a demander of unquestioned obedience from the rabble, often snatched from the streets of Portsmouth or Greenwich or Liverpool and pressed into service under the King's Regulations. To imply that a captain's conduct was wrong, as he just had, would need a lot of justification.

'We want to know more of that, sir,' said Captain Sir Roger Curtis, from the centre of the officers' bench.

'Captain Bligh had strong ideas about the diet of the men,' Fryer tried to recover. 'He insisted they eat and drink certain things.'

Hood sighed, irritably. The man was trying to twist away, he decided.

'To what purpose?' he demanded.

'To keep away the scurvy.'

'And did it?' asked Snape Hammond.

Fryer nodded. 'There was some illness, just before we arrived in Tahiti. The ship's surgeon said it was scurvy, but Captain Bligh disagreed.

Hood frowned. 'Had Captain Bligh any medical qualifications?'

'Not that I know of, sir.'

'One outbreak of something that might have been scurvy, on an outward voyage of ten months,' elaborated Snape Hammond. 'That would indicate the captain's victualling was right and proper?'

'Aye, sir,' agreed Fryer, hopefully.

Among the prisoners, Morrison was scribbling hurried reminders for his cross-examination.

'Why, then, the discontent?' pressed Hood.

'The men didn't like it, sir.'

'Seamen don't like many things, Mr Fryer. That's not sufficient to make an unhappy ship,' insisted the President.

'No, sir,' accepted Fryer, dutifully.

'Then perhaps you'd explain properly what you meant by saying it was difficult to adjust to the captain's way,' said Snape Hammond.

He had no choice, decided Fryer. But it would hurt him, he knew. There were twelve officers on the court martial panel, with influence throughout every fleet. He would be condemned within weeks as the man who had described the *Bounty*'s commander as a poor captain. That Bligh deserved that criticism, instead of the hero-worship he'd received, was immaterial. Fryer's only concern was that his own career would not be harmed by what was said at the enquiry.

'Captain Bligh,' he began slowly, still seeking a safe course, 'was a very violent man ... of unpredictable temper ... '

They didn't understand, thought Fryer, seeing the expression of doubt and suspicion settling on their faces. It was difficult for anyone to understand what Bligh had really been like, he accepted.

'You mean he occasionally shouted and cursed?' smiled Snape Hammond, attempting sarcasm and looking among his fellow officers for smirks of appreciation.

'No, sir,' said Fryer, positively. 'I mean he *always* shouted and cursed ... without a moment's pause ... '

'Mr Fryer,' reminded Snape Hammond, annoyed his joke had soured. 'We are talking of the King's navy, not a finishing school for English gentlewomen. Are you seriously asking this court to accept that men were driven to the point of mutiny and murder because their captain shouted and swore at them?'

It did sound ridiculous, realised Fryer. No one would ever know unless they had sailed with the damned man. He hoped they wouldn't probe into the open boat business, thought Fryer. They must know of the enquiry in Timor.

'I mean, sir,' replied the master, 'that the captain's criticism of everything and everyone was like water pouring constantly upon a stone, until it destroyed the strongest resistance. No one was ever right, except Captain Bligh.'

Hood sighed, better pleased. They were getting there, he thought. It was a laborious process, but gradually the evidence was coming out. The President decided upon an experiment.

The prisoner Morrison, who had decided to defend himself, had actually remained on the *Bounty* and might know more than most. Not only that, he would not have the apparent reluctance of Fryer to speak about it. And the lawyer Bunyan, entrusted with saving young Heywood, was sitting flushed at his table, as if bursting with questions to ask. He would allow the defence to interrogate Fryer, Hood decided. The court could always re-examine upon fresh evidence obtained.

He muttered briefly to the officers alongside him, then nodded to Bunyan. The young lawyer started up immediately, grating the chair over the decking in his eagerness. Fryer faced him warily, conscious the man would be better briefed than the court martial officers had been.

'Mr Fryer,' lured Bunyan, gently. 'Will you tell the court if, at any time, you saw my client, midshipman Peter Heywood, actively participating in the uprising upon the *Bounty*?'

'No, sir,' replied Fryer, relieved at the first question, 'I did not.'

'Did you at any time see him under arms?'

'No, sir.'

'Do you recall seeing him at all?'

Fryer considered the question.

'No,' he admitted, at last. 'I do not remember seeing him.'

'Why would that be, do you suppose?'

Fryer shrugged. This was an easier examination, he decided, relaxing again. The man's only concern was to prove the innocence of his client and about that Fryer had little doubt. He had never understood why Heywood had been arraigned.

'I would imagine because he was detained below.'

'Against his will?' pressed the lawyer.

'That would be my assumption.'

'That was possible, was it?' asked Bunyan.

'Sir?' said Fryer.

'It was possible for the mutineers to detain those unwilling to participate in the insurrection?'

Fryer smiled at the stupidity of the question.

'Of course, sir,' he said. 'They were armed, after all.'

'Yes, Mr Fryer,' seized Bunyan. 'They were armed. And how could that have been, when according to regulations the keys to the arms chests should have been in your possession?'

Fryer felt the attention of the officers to his left and bit at the inside of his cheek. He'd been trapped, he thought, annoyed.

'The keys were not in my possession, sir,' he admitted.

'Oh, Mr Fryer?' said Bunyan, apparently surprised. 'Why not?'

'I had entrusted them to the armourer, Mr Coleman.'

'Why?'

'The habit had arisen, early in the voyage, for the men to shoot at birds and fish. It got so bad I couldn't get a fair night's sleep ... so I gave Coleman the keys, so he could deal with the constant demands.'

What sort of man had Bligh been, wondered Hood, slumped back in his chair and happy at his decision to turn the questioning over to the defence, who could rant constantly about discipline until his men mutinied and yet be careless of how weapons were controlled on a ship unguarded by marines?

'Is it usual for seamen to shoot fish and birds?' probed Bunyan.

Fryer was cautious now, considering every question before replying.

'Not uncommon,' he said.

'To the point where it becomes impossible for the custodian of the keys to sleep properly?'

The lawyer was very clever, decided Fryer. And very determined. Yet he seemed to have taken his questioning beyond that necessary to protect his client, Peter Heywood. Fryer wondered why. The same thought was occurring to Hood. So Bunyan was the unannounced representative of the Christian family, guessed the admiral. It meant the young man had been instructed by one of the best legal brains in the country. And that, coupled with the financial resources of the Heywood family, there had been unlimited money available to prepare for the examination.

'Perhaps there was more of it on this voyage than others upon which I've sailed,' conceded Fryer.

Bunyan was nodding, as if the answers were conforming to those he expected.

'Why would that be, do you suppose, Mr Fryer?'

The master shifted uncomfortably. There appeared no way, he thought resentfully, that he could avoid harming his career prospects.

'There was an abundance of birds and sharks,' he tried. 'And the men had time in which to hunt them.'

'What did they do with them?' demanded Bunyan, suddenly harsh.

'What?' floundered Fryer.

'The birds and fish the men killed. What did they do with them?'

'Ate them,' confessed Fryer, simply.

Bunyan was smiling happily, he saw.

'To a question from Sir Andrew Snape Hammond,' reminded Bunyan, 'not one hour ago, you agreed that Captain Bligh's victualling was satisfactory. Now you tell the court that the crew's pursuit of additional food was such it prevented you getting a good night's sleep.'

'A seaman can always find room for more food,' attempted Fryer, hopefully. No one smiled, as he had thought they might.

Bunyan spread his hands towards the court, as if the master's answer had confirmed a point he wanted to make.

'You told my Lord Hood that until the men entered your cabin at gunpoint, you had no hint of mutiny?' embarked Bunyan, at a new tangent.

'That's right, sir.'

'Not a whisper?'

'I knew it was a discontented ship, no more.'

'Hadn't there been any discussion upon it?'

'Sir?'

'Isn't it the practice for the senior officers, the captain and the master and the senior people, to eat together? And during these meals, aren't the problems of the vessel discussed?'

Fryer nodded, reluctantly. 'It is usually the practice to mess together,' he conceded.

'Usually?' picked up Bunyan.

'I did not eat with Captain Bligh,' blurted Fryer, in sudden admission.

Bunyan was definitely a Christian man, determined the President, head shifting back and forth at the exchange between the two men. It had been an excellent idea to conduct the enquiry this way.

'Why, sir?' encouraged Bunyan, softly.

Fryer did not reply immediately. He stood, head bowed, trying to arrange the words in his mind so that the answer would not bring a fresh onslaught.

'The captain and I disagreed,' he said at last, inadequately.

'About what?' demanded Bunyan.

About what? mused Fryer. One didn't disagree about one particular thing with Captain Bligh. You disagreed with everything: his arrogance and his conceit and his parsimony and his greed and his bullying. Particularly his unremitting bullying.

'There had been numerous disagreements between us,' said Fryer. 'As I tried to explain earlier, it was often difficult to understand the captain. He would issue instructions one day and when one attempted to obey them in slightly different but still applicable circumstances the following day, it would be judged wrong.'

'Are you saying he was unstable?' jabbed Bunyan, hopefully.

'I am saying he was unpredictable,' refused Fryer.

Hood waited, expecting the cross-examination to continue about Bligh's stability, but abruptly Bunyan switched direction again.

'So Captain Bligh ate all alone?' he suggested.

'No,' contradicted the master.

'Ah,' said Bunyan, apparently correcting himself. 'Of course, I had overlooked the ship's surgeon.'

'Before his death, Mr Huggan, like me, had refused to sup with the captain,' said Fryer, miserably.

'Mr Huggan, too,' pursued Bunyan. 'Now why would that be?'

'Mr Huggan drank a great deal,' explained Fryer. 'The captain objected.'

'Is that all?' demanded Bunyan.

There seemed few secrets about the ship that the man didn't already know, decided Fryer, staring at Bunyan.

'Mr Huggan objected to the captain's conviction that he knew better on matters concerning the health of the crew,' said Fryer.

'So who was the rare man able to share the captain's table without the apparent distaste of every other officer?' pressed Bunyan.

'Mr Christian,' replied Fryer, softly.

The admission stirred through the court and several officers appeared to note it on pads before them.

'Mr Christian!' echoed Bunyan. 'Mr Christian, whom we are told led the mutiny, was the only man able to tolerate Captain Bligh?'

Fryer's head was almost sunken upon his chest now and sometimes it was difficult to hear the man's replies to Bunyan's persistence.

'The two men had been friends for a long time,' said Fryer.

'How do you know?'

'It was very clear on the early stages of the voyage, when we sailed from Portsmouth for our first stop at Tenerife.'

'Do you know Captain Bligh's opinion of Mr Christian?'

Fryer nodded. 'There were indications enough,' he said.

'What were they?'

'He thought Mr Christian a fine seaman', said Fryer. 'He promoted him second-in-command after Tenerife and showed him great attention.'

'What do you mean by "great attention"?' asked Bunyan. 'Do you mean in matters of seamanship?'

'Yes,' agreed Fryer, doubtfully.

'And?' prompted Bunyan.

'In matters of personal friendship.'

'Give the court an illustration of what you mean, Mr Fryer,' insisted the lawyer.

Fryer hesitated. Then he said: 'It was no secret that the captain gave Mr Christian the key to his personal liquor cabinet, so that he could help himself whenever he saw fit. Mr Christian boasted of the favour sometimes.'

'This was on the outward voyage?' qualified Bunyan.

'Yes, sir.'

'During which time you and the late Mr Huggan became so irritated by Captain Bligh's behaviour that you refused to sit at his table?'

'Yes, sir.'

'Why didn't Mr Christian share your irritation, do you suppose?' asked Bunyan, ingenuously.

'He was normally spared the captain's temper,' replied Fryer, as if suddenly annoyed.

Once again the lawyer surprised Hood by abandoning what appeared to be productive questioning.

'The captain was a strict disciplinarian?' asked Bunyan.

'Yes,' agreed Fryer.

'And remained so in Tahiti, while the plants were being cultivated for transplanting?'

'Yes,' said Fryer, doubtful again.

'Perhaps you'd like to qualify that answer,' invited Bunyan, sensing the man's attitude.

'As I've said, he was a difficult man to satisfy. He had men flogged for infraction of regulations, yet permitted them to keep aboard any women they liked.'

That was not unusual, thought Hood. A common way of keeping seamen from deserting was to dispatch marines to fetch whores aboard.

'For how long?'

'Months, in some cases,' enlarged Fryer.

Hood frowned. That was a stupid relaxation, decided the President. And there had been that disgusting tattooing, he remembered.

'So the men were happy?'

'Happy, yes, sir,' agreed Fryer. 'But they were often confused by the captain.'

'And Mr Christian was still Captain Bligh's only friend?' demanded the lawyer.

Fryer hesitated and Bunyan waited, not hurrying the man.

'It was different in Tahiti,' he said at last.

'What does that mean, Mr Fryer?'

'They saw much less of each other. Mr Christian was appointed shore commander. He spent nearly the whole time living under canvas on the plantation established by the botanist, Mr Nelson.'

Bunyan nodded, as if the explanation had satisfied a number of doubts in his mind.

'But they were still friends?' he insisted.

Again Fryer hesitated and this time the lawyer pressed him.

'But they were still friends?' he repeated.

'Less so,' said Fryer.

'Why was that?' demanded Bunyan.

'I don't know,' admitted Fryer. 'In Tahiti, something happened.'

'What?' intruded the President, frightened that Bunyan, whom he considered had missed questions before, might ignore this one.

'I don't know,' said Fryer again, unhelpfully. 'Mr Christian appeared to annoy Captain Bligh a great deal.'

'Which was unusual?'

'Yes.'

'And how did Captain Bligh manifest that annoyance?'

'He was very savage to Mr Christian.'

'And what was Mr Christian's reaction?'

'He just suffered it,' said Fryer.

'Knowing that you had fallen out with the captain, didn't Mr Christian discuss the matter with you?'

'No,' insisted the master. 'He did not.'

'So you do not know his feelings at this apparent change in the captain's behaviour towards him?'

'Oh yes,' said Fryer. 'That was easy to see.'

'And it was?'

'Deep hurt. And distress. Captain Bligh was constantly undermining Mr Christian's authority.'

'So it was a very different ship that left Tahiti than that which arrived?'

The master nodded agreement.

'Was the captain's attention to detail the same?' asked Bunyan. He had been speaking for almost three hours and his voice was creaking with hoarseness. He glanced down at his clerk and saw one notebook was already full. Edward Christian, waiting patiently at the inn, should be very grateful, he decided. He was establishing a picture of the *Bounty* far different from that which the enquiry had known when the hearing began that day.

'Perhaps worse,' conceded Fryer. 'Some sails which should have been checked had been ignored and were found to be rotten. And insufficient care had been taken to protect the ship's boats from worm; the bottom of the cutter was found to be almost eaten through. That's why the captain wasn't cast adrift in that boat, during the mutiny.'

'Whose responsibility would that have been?' came in the President again, sure of the answer.

He was lost, thought Fryer. After today's hearing, he'd be lucky to get a berth as a common seaman in a merchant fleet.

'I had given explicit instructions several times during our stay in Tahiti that they should be examined,' insisted Fryer, desperately.

'But not checked to your own satisfaction that the orders had been carried out?' defeated the President.

'No, sir,' admitted Fryer.

'So again you were at odds with the captain?' came back Bunyan.

'Not as much as I had expected,' admitted Fryer.

'Why was that?'

'Captain Bligh seemed to vent his annoyance more upon Mr Christian.'

'Really!' probed Bunyan. 'Yet the failure had not been his?'

'No,' agreed the master. 'But for the first few days after we sailed from Tahiti, Captain Bligh seemed only to criticise Mr Christian.'

'About what?'

'Everything,' generalised the witness. 'Finally it was a row about coconuts. Mr Christian was reduced to tears.'

'Coconuts!' echoed Bunyan, incredulously.

Fryer smiled, in nervous embarrassment.

'Everyone had traded just before we left Tahiti,' explained Fryer. 'The islanders have no knowledge of iron and regard a nail as a pauper regards a guinea. The ship was packed with every provision available, bought with a few nails. And every man had his own supply of coconuts, even Captain Bligh. A day or two before the mutiny, he decided one had been stolen. So he mustered the whole crew and demanded the culprit own up, otherwise the rum would be stopped and the rations reduced by half.'

'For a coconut!' pressed Bunyan. 'He made this threat because of the loss of one coconut?'

'Yes, sir,' said Fryer. 'Mr Christian admitted to it. He said he'd been thirsty and had taken one for its milk, intending to replace it.'

'What happened?'

'The captain went into a tremendous rage. He insisted that not one coconut but half his supply had been stolen and cut the officer's rum ration by half.'

'He imposed that penalty upon a man to whom he'd willingly provided the key for his own liquor cabinet on the outward voyage?' asked Bunyan, curiously.

'Yes,' agreed Fryer.

'And Mr Christian was deeply affected?'

'Mr Christian was a much pressured man,' expanded Fryer. 'Captain Bligh had told him he would only need him to help get the vessel through the dangers of Endeavour Straits and then he would make his life such hell that he would jump overboard to his death rather than face it.'

'So Mr Christian carefully planned the overthrow of Captain Bligh?'

'No, sir,' disagreed Fryer.

'What?' demanded the President.

'I mean it wasn't carefully planned, sir,' qualified Fryer. 'It has always been my thinking that it was a spontaneous thing. Captain Bligh felt otherwise.'

'How do you know that?' demanded Bunyan.

'He spoke about it often, after we were cast adrift.'

'I'm glad we've reached that point,' smiled Bunyan. 'Let's talk about the open boat voyage.'

Fryer clenched his hands behind his back.

'It was an incredible voyage,' tempted Bunyan.

'Yes, sir,' agreed Fryer, cautiously.

'Remind the court of it,' demanded the lawyer.

'We all thought, in the first few minutes, that we were lost,' remembered Fryer. 'The sea was to within inches of the gunwales ... there were eighteen of us in the boat and hardly room to sit down. We got the launch as ship-shape as possible and Captain Bligh said we were setting sail for Timor.'

'How far was that?' intruded Bunyan.

'1,200 leagues.'

'Over 3,600 miles?' clarified the layman.

Fryer nodded.

'We landed at Tofoa,' recalled Fryer. 'But the natives attacked, trying to stone us. In escaping, John Norton, the quarter-master, was killed. They tried chasing us in their canoes, but we threw clothes overboard. In stopping to pick them up, the natives lost the chance to overhaul us.'

'Whose idea was that subterfuge?' asked Hood, curiously.

'The captain's,' said Fryer. 'After that, we decided to keep at sea as much as possible. We made land on several islands to gather shellfish and on three occasions we were almost beaten under by storms ... '

'Was your food sufficient?' asked Bunyan.

'Captain Bligh firmly rationed it.'

'To what?'

'An ounce and a half of bread a day ... an ounce, raw, of any seabird we captured ... we even ate the innards ... and a gill of water ... '

'Scarcely enough to live?'

'Scarcely,' agreed Fryer. The man *did* know of the enquiry demanded by Bligh, the master knew.

'There was an unusual incident when you arrived at the Dutch settlement, was there not?'

'Sir?'

'Was there not, on the instigation of Captain Bligh, an official enquiry into the conduct of yourself and another man to be a witness at this enquiry, Mr Purcell?'

'Yes, sir,' agreed Fryer.

'Well?' insisted Bunyan.

Fryer hesitated. Damn Bligh, he thought. Damn Bligh and the *Bounty* and Fletcher Christian and the very day he'd become associated with any of them.

'Captain Bligh alleged we were near mutinous on the voyage ... ' said Fryer, at last.

'Were you afraid for your life, in that launch?' demanded Bunyan.

'Aye, sir. All the time,' agreed Fryer, definitely.

'Yet, afraid though you were, there was serious dissent between you and your captain?'

Fryer nodded. He felt very tired, he realised.

'Why?'

'We ... Mr Purcell and myself ... believed he was taking more than his fair share of the food.'

'Was he?' broke in Hood.

'It was never proven,' conceded Fryer. 'In Timor we publicly withdrew the charge and the captain said he would forget the matter.'

The President sensed the changing mood among the officers around him. This was a very different account than that which they had expected to hear, he thought.

'Would you serve again with Captain Bligh?' demanded Bunyan, suddenly.

'A naval officer serves upon whichever ship he is appointed,' replied Fryer, formally. After today, he thought, he'd be lucky to serve with anybody, anywhere.

'Would you serve again with Captain Bligh?' insisted Bunyan, doggedly. 'Or would you ask the Lords Commissioners of the Admiralty to reconsider their decision?'

'I would ask the Lords of the Admiralty to reconsider their decision,' conceded Fryer.

Bunyan sat down, abruptly, content at what he'd done. He stared at Fryer. Poor bugger, he thought. A shifty, unpleasant man, perhaps, but he'd been mauled in that questioning.

The prisoner Morrison strained for the President's attention and Hood nodded, curtly. It took Morrison only minutes to establish that he had provided the castaways with weapons and in full view of the launch been threatened by Churchill because of his action. Hood frowned when the man resumed his seat. He had expected more questioning on the lines opened by the lawyer. Perhaps, thought the President, the prisoner was content with what Bunyan had brought out.

Hood shifted, cramped in his chair. It had been a long sitting, he thought.

'We'll adjourn,' he announced, without reference to the other officers.

'An odd affair,' offered Sir Andrew Snape Hammond, as they filed out of the cabin.

Hood nodded.

'Can't see, from the evidence, that there's any doubt about the guilt of most of them,' said the President.

'Oh, not at all,' agreed the officer. 'The mutiny is clear enough. But Bligh seems to have brought much of the troubles upon his own head.'

'He does that,' agreed Hood. 'An odd man ... a very odd man.'

Edward Christian had been reading the notes of Bunyan's clerk for over an hour, hunched close to the candle and never once looking up from the thick sheaf of paper on the table before him. From the occasional grunt the younger lawyer guessed that Fletcher Christian's brother was very satisfied.

At last the older man pushed the transcript away and smiled across at his colleague. Before speaking he went to the decanter and poured them both wine.

'Magnificent, Mr Bunyan,' he congratulated. 'I could not have succeeded better myself.'

And he couldn't, Edward accepted. The man had exceeded his every hope.

'I detected a very different attitude in the court, too,' said Bunyan, warmed by the praise.

Edward went back to the desk and began carefully arranging the papers into their original orderly pile.

'I shall publish this, in manuscript form,' decided Edward, suddenly. 'This and whatever else you succeed in establishing, during the hearing.'

Bunyan frowned, unbalanced by the announcement.

'To what end?' he asked.

Edward hesitated at the question, then smiled. Of course, he realised, the other man wouldn't know the depth of his determination.

'To tell the world about Captain Bligh,' he elaborated. 'And wipe away the disgrace from my brother's name.'

He lifted his glass, gazing down at the other man.

'I give you a toast, Mr Bunyan. "To the destruction of Captain William Bligh." '

13

No one came to the cave, high in the cliffs on the lower reaches of which he could just see the women collecting their eggs. Christian had found it within weeks of arriving on Pitcairn and withdrawn more and more to it, his own solitary retreat, as his relationship with the other mutineers had worsened.

At first it had been his look-out point, the spot to which he clambered almost daily, musket and shot in hand for the last redoubt, expecting to see a sail on the horizon that would mean Bligh had survived. As the years had passed, that fear had reduced to the vaguest, rarely considered apprehension, but the hideaway had retained its importance, the place to which he could go, away from Isabella even. To examine his past, as a rich man might study a favourite painting.

Far below lay the concealed village they had built upon Pitcairn, each plot carefully designated and marked in its irregular circle, like the huge Sunday pies he could remember his mother baking when he was a boy in Cumberland. So many years ago, he thought, nostalgically. And so far away.

It was a neat village, congratulated Christian, gazing down. He'd planned it, he remembered, going through the pretence of a committee, but cleverly manipulating the discussion to achieve the layout he wanted, every dwelling well concealed from the sea behind thick banyan trees. Each house had been finely thatched in pandanus palm in the Tahitian manner that the women had taught them, and the breadfruit and the sweet potatoes and the yams laid out in their tiny plantations, as David Nelson and William Brown had created their gardens in Tahiti all those years ago.

If he looked very hard, squinting against the sun, he could isolate in the houses the spars and beams they had salvaged from the *Bounty* before Young and Quintal had fired her. So stupid, he reflected, in constant regret.

Jack Williams was in his garden, he could see. A good worker, Jack. But growing increasingly discontented since his wife, Pashotu, had fallen to her death egg-collecting on the cliffs upon which he sat. There were only three women to be shared among the six native men they had brought with them from Tahiti and they were already becoming disgruntled at the segregated society that had arisen on the island. Christian suspected Williams intended taking one of their women as a new wife. And that would trigger the threatened bloodshed, he thought. He was surprised the others didn't seem to realise the danger, casually leaving their muskets and cutlasses unguarded in every house.

His one-time friend, Edward Young, appeared, child on hip, and almost immediately Alexander Smith, who had years ago confessed to sailing on the *Bounty* under an assumed name and had now reverted to his proper identity, Jack Adams, joined him from the house next door. As Young's friendship with Christian had soured to a mutual dislike, Young's comradeship with Adams had grown and now the two men were almost inseparable. It was a useful association, accepted Christian, realistically. Apart from the bruised pride of rejection, he didn't seek to be the community leader. It was a role that came far more naturally to the two men gossiping far below. They had both accepted completely that they would end their days on the tiny, high-rocked island and were content with it. Not for years had he heard either of them recriminate about what had happened on the *Bounty*: tomorrow's crop of yams was far more important than yesterday's mistakes.

As high as he was, Christian heard the singing and isolated first Quintal and then his friend Mickoy, slowly picking their way from the spot on the outskirts of the village where Mickoy distilled his taro liquor.

The trouble-makers, identified Christian. If Williams hadn't appeared so determined to take one of the native women, Christian would have guessed Quintal and Mickoy the likeliest cause of dissent with the Tahitians. Both men treated the natives like slaves, driving them to tend their gardens and plots and beating them at the slightest indication of defiance.

He saw Young and Adams turn but even from that distance there did not appear to be any conversation: both men despised the seamen as much as he did, Christian knew. Irritated at being ignored, Quintal and Mickoy performed a charade of greeting, bowing and shouting, and finally Young and Adams responded, choosing the easy way out. It was becoming the demeanour on their island, Christian thought. The easy way out, to avoid a confrontation that might destroy the uneasy calm of which they were all aware but did not want to recognise.

' ... *not a day without torment* ... '

The daily thought ... the daily memory. Bligh haunted him, realised Christian, the spectre always at his shoulder, cackling and gloating. He hoped that whatever death the man had suffered had been a painful one. How much better it would have been, reflected Christian, suddenly, if Bligh had survived to undergo the agonies in which he lived, like a man with an illness slowly eating away at his flesh. But Bligh wouldn't be in torment, had he survived. Victims of mutinies were heroes. Bligh had always thought himself a hero, remembered Christian. One of his favourite dinner-table conversations was of encountering Nelson and realising how similar he was in stature to the admiral revered throughout England.

For a while, until he had realised Christian had identified it and was laughing at the stupidity, Bligh had even aped the man's mannerisms, stumping the quarter-deck with the impatient tread regarded as one of the great admiral's affectations.

Bligh had had many acts, Christian recalled. He had been a man of pretence, adopting manners and attitudes to suit the mood of a moment, like a chameleon colouring itself to its surroundings.

Not even Elizabeth really knew her husband, he reflected, closing his eyes to picture the full-nosed, gentle woman, conscious of her plumpness and always slightly in awe at the bustle of London, compared to the calm of her Isle of Man home. To her, Bligh had been a man destined for greatness, someone in whom there was no fault.

She had indicated as much, he remembered, on the last occasion he had been at Bligh's house in Lambeth. Bligh had just selected him for the *Bounty* and on that occasion the act had been that of the magnanimous benefactor, patronisingly accepting the gratitude of a young man benefiting from his influence and largesse.

'Mr Bligh is so good,' the woman had confided eagerly. 'Such a good husband. And father to the girls. And bound for such great things ... '

The head had come forward, a habit of the woman when excited.

' ... the King knows of him, would you believe ... '

Poor woman, thought Christian.

Far below the stumbling seamen continued their promenade of the village. The native men stood aloof, contempt visible in their attitude, but the women giggled as they passed, nervously amused.

They were approaching his house, Christian realised suddenly. He saw Isabella appear with the baby after its feed and carefully place him in the crib that Christian had made, then straighten at the men's approach. Thursday bustled importantly around from the back of the house and stood, plump arm around his mother's legs.

She was very beautiful, thought Christian, gazing down. Taller than most Tahitian women and with an aristocratic, commanding bearing that came from her birth as a chief's daughter. It was too far away to see, but Christian did not think she was laughing, as the other women had done.

Too far away. The fear was like a hand, feeling at his stomach. He'd sat so long in the damned cave, awash in self-pity, that he'd exposed Isabella to risk.

' ... *always be there, when you turn to look for me* ... '

The promise echoed in his mind. She was looking for him now, he knew. So where was he?

He thrust away through the opening, crabbing along the narrow ledge that girdled the cliff in the first of the haphazard criss-cross of paths, like the sandal thongs around the legs of the ancient Greeks.

The ledge was narrow here, in places only half as wide as a man's foot, which was why his cave was so secure behind its screen of banyan trees. Christian shuffled along it carelessly, whimpering in the frustration of having to move so slowly, stones and displaced rock cascading into the sea heaving hundreds of feet below.

Normally he descended with his face against the rock, arms and legs spread for hand- and footholds. Now he traversed facing outwards, only his heels on the ledge and the musket clutched desperately in his right hand like a balancing pole, so that he could watch constantly the scene being enacted in miniature below.

They were bowing and genuflecting again, but this time he detected an anger in their movements that had been missing when they had confronted Young and Adams.

And he knew why, thought Christian, embarking on another path that would take him at the commencement of its descent even further away from the woman. The drink had removed the cover from a feeling that even they, the scum, normally managed to conceal. Only Isabella had remained utterly faithful since their arrival on Pitcairn. The other women had continued as on Tahiti, sleeping as the mood or inclination took them with different mutineers and even, occasionally, with the Tahitian men who had accompanied them into exile. In the later years the relationships had become more monogamous, but even now none of the mutineers could ever be sure that his partner wouldn't lift her skirts or open her mouth for another of the men if she felt like doing so. Isabella had been approached, of course. Christian knew that. In the early days, there had even been a strange pride that Isabella, unquestionably the most beautiful woman on the island, had been so attractive to the other men, the feeling heightened by his confidence that she would always reject them.

His heel skidded off the rock and he groped to his left, feeling the skin scrape off his ankle and then even further, into his calf. He drove the musket down on the ledge, and hung there, his body bent and supported on one side by his right foot and at the other by his left arm, propped against the gun. There was hardly any sensation at all in his left leg, hanging limply in space. He could feel the warmth of the blood, though, sticky as it pooled in his shoe. He would unbalance completely, he realised, if he brought his right arm over to put himself into a crawling position. And there was insufficient room to crawl on the ledge, anyway. The muscles began to cramp in his back and his arm started to shake with the strain of supporting the weight of his body. He moved his hand backwards, along the rock face, fingers flickering for a crack or an outcrop he was unable to look back to locate.

Below he could see the charade continuing. Quintal, the more daring of the two, had actually gone into the garden, gesturing the reluctant Mickoy to follow him. The older boy had instinctively sensed danger and had started to cry, Christian saw, and Isabella had lifted him into her arms, nudging her face reassuringly into his head. She wouldn't be afraid, he knew. Not Isabella. She'd never known the feeling, in her youth on Tahiti. And here, on Pitcairn, she'd always been so sure of Christian's protection.

He felt something. It wasn't a wide crack; little more than a fissure splitting downwards through the rock. Gently, frightened of losing it, he traced his forefinger along, hoping it would widen. But it didn't. Desperately, feeling them split and chip, he drove his nails into the tiny crevice, struggling his body up. He pressed against the gun butt, levering from the other side. If the rock broke away under his fingers, he'd go over, he realised. He'd be dead before he hit the water, he knew; all the air would be driven from his lungs by the fall. And as he fell, Isabella would be defiled. Debris began slipping over the edge, disturbed by the swivelling action of the one foot he still had anchored. The feeling was returning to the other leg now, the pain snatching up almost to his groin: it would swell very quickly, he guessed. Damn the sweat, he thought. It was running into his eyes so that he could hardly see and making slippery the hand that gripped the musket. He tried lifting his left foot, very slightly, moving his heel for it to catch on the ledge. At the first attempt he missed, and again grated it against the rock, stripping off more skin, but got a foothold when he tried again. The whole leg burned with the pain now and he could hardly put any pressure upon it. He manoeuvred fully upright, feeling his legs and arms tremble with the strain imposed upon them.

It was still going on down below. Mickoy was in the garden now, hands outstretched. But he wasn't reaching for Isabella, Christian realised. The movement was towards Quintal, an effort to restrain him. And Quintal appeared less sure of himself now. Isabella was facing him quite fearlessly, the contempt obvious in her stance, Thursday wedged astride her hip.

Christian moved on, pain spurting through him as he used his left leg, his body feeling hollowed out by the ordeal on the ledge. Flies, attracted by the sweat, swarmed around him, settling on his neck and face and refusing to move despite the constant dog-like shaking to disturb them. He wanted to stop, until his breathing became easier. And to wipe the perspiration from his face, so that the insects would go away, if only for a few seconds. But his ankle would swell even quicker, if he ceased using it. And the men were still down with Isabella. As the cliff bottomed out, spreading into the jungle, he lost the elevation that had made it possible for him to look down upon his house. And it became worse, not knowing. Quintal had only been feet away when he'd last been able to see them. He could be upon her now, knocking the child to one side, scrabbling at her skirts, arm across her throat to prevent her crying out for help.

The path was widening, becoming the thoroughfare used by the women to collect their eggs. Christian stumbled forward in a clumsy, hopping gait, twice sprawling face down when his injured leg collapsed beneath him. It would have been easier had he reversed the musket, using it as a crutch. But that would have blocked the barrel and Christian wanted a weapon, primed and ready, when he confronted the men in his garden. Breath was grunting from him in choked, bitten-back sounds but the flies were gone now, finally driven off by the increased movement. The huge banyan trees began to thin, their roots spread out like the legs of a man on stilts, and then he reached the clearing.

He paused, momentarily, able to see his house again. The relief went from him in a groan, the sound of a man from whom a great pain is suddenly lifted. Quintal and Mickoy were still in the garden. And Isabella was still facing them, challengingly.

'Isabella.'

His exhaustion strained the first shout to a croak and he snatched breath into his lungs and yelled again, with enough sound to reach them this time. Mickoy turned, frightened despite his drunkenness, and faltered back to the garden perimeter, where he stopped, uncertainly. Quintal, nervous too but less willing to appear so before a woman he was trying to impress, turned towards the village but remained where he was.

Christian hobbled on, musket across his body. The grunts were sobs now, prompted by relief and stoked by anger. Careful, he thought. Mustn't cry. Mustn't break down, like he had during the last argument with Bligh, immediately before the mutiny. Filth like Quintal and Mickoy would see it as weakness; maybe even try to take Isabella away by force. And he wouldn't cry in front of her, either. She wanted a strong man, a protector.

At the entrance he swept the gun sideways, clumsily, catching Mickoy with the butt. It struck the man's hip, hardly bruising him, but the force was sufficient to unbalance him and he staggered sideways, more surprised than hurt.

Quintal tensed, warily, as Christian brought the musket up. He pointed it at the man's belly: it would take a long time for him to die if he put the ball there, he thought. And he wanted Quintal to suffer.

'Careful, now,' said Quintal, edging back.

He wasn't really drunk, realised Christian. Not as drunk as Mickoy, anyway. The man had merely pretended to be, giving himself an excuse for what he had attempted to do.

'Get away from my house,' said Christian, his breath still uneven, so the words switchbacked from him, lessening the intensity of the threat. 'Get away from my house ... for ever. Or in God's name, Matthew Quintal, I'll kill you.'

Thursday detected the danger again and began to cry. The sound awakened the baby and it began to whimper, too.

Quintal smirked, still uncertain but slightly more confident.

'What's wrong?' he attempted, humping his shoulders. 'Man calls by to pass the time of day ... gets met by a cocked musket ... '

'I saw you, Quintal,' took away Christian. 'From up there, on the cliff ... I saw you.'

'Saw what?' challenged the other man.

'Isabella is mine ... only mine ... ' said Christian. He was better controlled now, his breath recovered. 'I don't want scum like you anywhere near her ... or my children ... '

Christian heard Mickoy but didn't turn to see the man limping back to the entrance. He'd placed himself badly, decided the mutineer. It was impossible to watch both men at the same time. But Isabella could see Mickoy, to warn him, he realised. And he was the lesser danger of the two, anyway.

' ... I should kill you,' said Christian. 'And mark me well, Quintal, I will, by God I will, if I know you've been within fifteen yards of my house ever again. Or even looked at Isabella ... lusting after her ... '

'Would you, Mr Christian?' demanded Quintal, cockily.

The man wasn't frightened any more, decided Christian.

'Would you kill me, like a real man should? Or is it another empty threat, the sort we've come to recognise? You're not a brave man, are you, Mr Christian? You shout a bit and look good, but you rarely finish anything off, do you? If you'd had any courage, real courage, you'd have killed Bligh. But you couldn't, could you?'

Christian hit him. He hopped forward, awkwardly, reversing the musket and sweeping it up, aiming for the man's groin. But Quintal began to move when he saw Christian coming, doubling his body, so that instead of the stock landing where Christian had intended, it struck the man's shoulder, knocking him sideways. The blow unblocked the impotent anger and Christian struck out again, bringing the weapon down two-handed against the side of Quintal's head, wincing with satisfaction as the skin split, and then again, twice more, against the man's shoulders as he fell away.

'Wouldn't I?' he screamed, his voice out of control. 'Wouldn't I, Quintal?'

He jabbed again with the butt at each question, experiencing an almost sensual feeling at the sight of the man curled up at his feet, head shielded by his arms and legs drawn up to protect his crotch.

He could see Mickoy now. The man was still standing outside the garden, his mind too fogged to do anything but stare.

Christian looked back to Quintal. He wanted to kick him. But if he did, he'd fall over. He almost laughed at the thought, only just managing to stop it. Hysteria again, he recognised. He held the musket correctly now, jabbing Quintal with the barrel. The man had unwound, very slightly, and was squinting up, his face contorted in hate.

Quintal had been humiliated in front of Isabella, realised Christian, happily. And he'd appeared the protector he had always promised the woman he would be. And others were watching, he realised. Both Young and Adams had come to the square and he could detect movement in Isaac Martin's hut, where the native women usually gathered in the afternoon.

'Out,' commanded Christian, savouring the attention. 'Get out. On your hands and knees, like the pig you are.'

He was goading Quintal with the gun, driving it past the protecting arms to the man's ribs, rasping the breath from him.

Quintal rolled into a crawling position and scrabbled forward, the blood from his head dripping before him.

Christian stood, unable to follow, but with the gun held ready. Quintal wouldn't doubt him after that, he decided. No one would doubt him after today.

No heart to finish anything. So that's what they thought, did they? Well, they'd see. They'd see just how far he'd go if anyone came near Isabella again.

'Just once more,' he shouted. Mickoy was helping Quintal up now, both staggering in the dirt.

'So much as look at her or come near this house and I'll put a ball into you,' Christian yelled. There was no need to go on shouting, he thought. He'd proved himself.

Quintal turned, looking at him. The man's face was smeared with blood and the side of his head was ballooning up, the bruise already marked out purple against the whiteness of his neck. He made as if to speak, but then appeared to change his mind. He just shook his head, stopping almost immediately because of the pain, then moved off slowly through the tiny settlement.

That night Christian made love violently to Isabella, driving into her so that she gasped with each thrust and she clung to him, more frightened than excited. He climaxed before her, shuddering with each spasm, and she feigned the sensation as well, feeling his need. Immediately he rolled away on to his back and she frowned, curiously. He was normally a considerate lover, always waiting for her. Tonight he'd been like an animal. The ugly man would have been like that, she knew, the drunken one who had come to the house that afternoon.

'Kept you safe,' he said, suddenly.

'Yes.'

'Said I'd keep you safe. And I did.'

'Yes,' she said again. Why was he talking like this? she wondered.

'No one will bother you again, you see.'

Unable to reply, she reached out, feeling for his hand. He was shaking, she detected.

'You were very brave,' she said, sensing he wanted praise. It was stupid, she felt, to have created such hatred in a community as unusual as theirs. Quintal had never been a threat to her, she had decided.

'I love you,' he said.

'Me too,' she replied, as always.

Why, she wondered, staring towards him through the darkness, was he crying?

'Oh damn,' said Christian, softly.

14

At least the children would not be disappointed, resolved Elizabeth Bligh, bustling around her sewing room. An outing to the Vauxhall Gardens wouldn't be as exciting as being able to see, from the discretion of the upstairs landing, all the important people arriving at the house, but they would still be able to wear the dresses she had made for the occasion. Parade them off, even. And she'd buy them some sweetmeats, she decided: they wouldn't have had that treat had the soirée been held. She must remember to make a joke about that. That was the best way to treat it, as a joke.

It was Harriet and Mary for whom she felt most upset. And not just because the eldest girls had been denied the opportunity to attend, for an hour at least. Both were sensitive girls. And old enough to realise that there was something peculiar about the unusual number of refusals that had been returned to their mother's invitation.

And it *was* peculiar, determined the woman. Five acceptances. And twenty refusals, all pleading prior engagements.

She'd been very careful about that, remembered Elizabeth, making discreet enquiries among her new, exciting friends several weeks before the planned date. Certainly her understanding had been that Saturday was completely free.

She lifted the remodelled dress, holding it in front of her. She'd done it very well, she reassured herself. No one would know she had transferred the bodice from another gown, cleverly weaving a snippet from the hem of the skirt into the revers facing.

And if there were so many other functions being held, she thought, returning to her musing, why hadn't she been invited to one of them? Not a year before it had been a weekly problem to decide which affair to attend. And before Mr Bligh had embarked upon the second expedition to the island where that awful mutiny had occurred, they were being invited to as many as three parties a day, sometimes every single day of the week. Such an exciting time, she thought, wistfully.

She strained behind, buttoning the dress, then pirouetted before the glass. Perfect, she decided, happy her figure was still firm after six children. Mr Bligh was still very proud of her, she knew. Darling Mr Bligh.

Elizabeth looked away quickly at the noise, embarrassed at being discovered admiring herself by Mary. The girl stood in the doorway, smiling.

'You look lovely, mama.'

'And so do you,' replied the woman, honestly.

The pale blue brought out perfectly her daughter's dark colouring and white skin, so much like her father's.

'The twins want to say goodnight,' reported the girl.

The two youngest girls, Frances and Jane, came in solemn-faced, miserable at missing an outing. Elizabeth allowed them to stay while they put on their bonnets and arranged the folds of their parasols, then kissed them off to bed with the housekeeper, Mrs Bolton.

The coach arrived on time and Elizabeth sat next to the girl named after her, with Harriet and Mary facing them.

'Will there be boys there?' pressed the young Elizabeth, eagerly.

'Hush!' rebuked her mother. 'I'll not have talk like that.'

It was hard bringing up the children with Mr Bligh constantly away, thought the woman as the carriage crossed the bridge and turned along the Vauxhall road. They definitely missed their father's control. She was very lucky, she decided, that Harriet and Mary were such sensible girls.

The vehicle was slowed by the crush of people going to the entertainments and the youngest girl gazed out, fascinated.

'The trial has begun in Portsmouth of those dreadful men,' said Mary, softly, so that little Elizabeth would not hear.

The woman frowned.

'Mrs Bolton told me,' added the girl.

The housekeeper was a busy-body, decided Elizabeth Bligh.

If she weren't so necessary in the running of the household, she would have dismissed her long ago.

'I know,' said the woman.

'Mrs Bolton says there is little other discussion in high circles ... daily accounts are being received, all the way from Portsmouth,' enlarged Harriet.

'Mrs Bolton is a gossip,' said Elizabeth Bligh, sternly. She would have to talk to the woman, she resolved. It was quite wrong to tittle-tattle to the children about matters like this.

How much she wished Mr Bligh were home. He'd know what to do about the pamphlets. Not that they'd cause any harm to his reputation. That was already established, she thought, confidently. But it was distressing that such shameful things were being allowed to circulate.

It was a pleasant evening, despite being so late in the year. Elizabeth walked slightly ahead of her children, happily aware of the occasional glance of recognition. It thrilled her to be the wife of such a famous, respected man. Only to herself would she admit the conceit. And that's what it was, she recognised. She actually felt superior to most of the women to whose houses she was invited, even the titled, aristocratic ladies. Because the majority had inherited their distinctions, King George being far too wily to allow the custom of patronage to pass from his hands into those of Mr Pitt or Mr Fox. Mr Bligh had earned his honour. And was often envied because of it, she knew. That's why the accounts from Portsmouth were being read so avidly. It was only to be expected, she supposed, that someone of Mr Bligh's achievements should attract such jealousy. It was still disturbing, though.

Elizabeth was just off the main concourse, buying the girls the sweetmeats she had promised, when she saw them.

Lady Harpindene, with her constant friend, Mrs Wittingdon, were promenading towards her, exaggerating the use of their parasols and smiling from side to side, conscious of the attention they were receiving as the leaders of that season's society. Elizabeth suspected that neither were as friendly with the Prince of Wales as they tried to convince everyone they were.

The country, remembered Elizabeth. Both had written in their letters of apology that they were going with the Prince to his beloved Brighton, and that the visit would occupy most of the week. A long-arranged engagement, both had insisted.

Determinedly, Elizabeth moved away from the stall, directly into the women's path. They stopped, momentarily disconcerted. As always, Mrs Wittingdon, a pale, blonde-haired woman of quick, nervous gestures, who constantly deferred to her titled cousin, looked to Lady Harpindene for guidance.

The baronet's wife recovered quickly. She was an overweight, painted woman who enjoyed the notoriety of cuckolding her husband with youngsters hardly out of their teens.

She smiled, reaching forward.

'Mrs Bligh!' she gushed. 'Upon my life, an unexpected delight!'

Behind her, Elizabeth heard the rustle as the girls bobbed their curtsies and felt the flush of pride.

'Indeed, Lady Harpindene, a surprise,' greeted Elizabeth, pointedly. She nodded to the woman's companion. 'Mrs Wittingdon,' she greeted.

'Mrs Bligh,' responded the merchant's wife. If Mr Bligh were successful on the second expedition, it was families like the Wittingdons who would double their fortunes, reflected Elizabeth, enjoying the woman's consternation.

'Your soirée,' said Lady Harpindene, holding her hands in the manner of someone reminded of an overlooked event. 'Why, whatever happened to your soirée?'

'Cancelled, madam,' reported Elizabeth. 'It appeared to conflict with so many other things.'

'Such a shame!' contributed Mrs Wittingdon, looking to her companion for reaction. Lady Harpindene dabbed her nose with a silk handkerchief, momentarily hiding her face.

'Yes,' agreed Elizabeth, tightly. 'Such a shame. As unfortunate, perhaps, as your country outing ... Brighton, wasn't it, with the Prince?'

Lady Harpindene frowned, forgetting the excuse.

'The country,' she echoed, recovering. 'Yes, such a nuisance. Postponed, don't you know. The Prince is becoming more involved with the King in the affairs of state ... so little time for himself.'

It was common knowledge, thought Elizabeth, that the Prince and the King were engaged in one of their periodic disputes over the Prince's debts and that their only communication was through intermediaries and ministers.

The women stood stiffly upright, each seeking an escape.

'Such a pretty dress,' congratulated Lady Harpindene. 'I always say, don't I, Polly, that Mrs Bligh has such lovely dresses?'

'Lovely,' parroted the companion.

Elizabeth was glad of the almost complete darkness. Neither would be able to detect her blush, she knew.

'But isn't it one ... ?' continued the woman, trailing the sentence as if embarrassed by it. 'No, of course not ... silly of me.'

'What, Lady Harpindene?' said Elizabeth. She wouldn't be harassed by the other woman, she determined.

'... *so* silly,' giggled Lady Harpindene. 'Had the oddest feeling I'd seen the garment before ... but I can't have done, can I?'

'No,' said Elizabeth, immediately. 'Such an easy mistake to make, with fashion changing so quickly.'

Lady Harpindene swirled her parasol, like an animal trainer about to give a command, and Mrs Wittingdon twitched, preparing herself for reaction.

'We must move on, Mrs Bligh,' apologised Lady Harpindene. 'Unsafe to be on the streets of London after a certain time, don't you think?'

'Yes,' agreed Elizabeth, standing aside. Behind, the girls dipped their farewells.

'We must meet, very soon,' threw away Lady Harpindene, moving on to the main thoroughfare.

'Very soon,' echoed Mrs Wittingdon.

Bligh's letter from Plymouth was waiting for her when she returned to Lambeth.

'Mama,' said Mary, worriedly.

'What?'

'You're crying. Why are you crying?'

'Happiness,' said Elizabeth, after the briefest pause. 'Your father is coming home. He's done all he was dispatched to do ... such a wonderful man, your father.'

'Mama,' said Mary, much later. 'Are those ladies we met this afternoon very important?'

'Why?'

'I didn't think I liked them very much.'

'No,' said the woman. 'They're not important ... not important at all ... '

She hadn't made the jokes she'd intended, realised Elizabeth. It was becoming increasingly difficult to laugh, she thought. Thank God Mr Bligh was coming back.

15

'A raft!'

The interjection came from the President, almost at the end of William Purcell's evidence. The *Bounty*'s carpenter shifted, uneasily. He had seen Fryer attacked and had taken the stand frightened, knowing the same thing could happen to him; twice he had carefully avoided mentioning the help he had given to Fletcher Christian the night before the mutiny, even though he knew the disclosure was inevitable.

'Yes, sir,' he replied. 'A raft.'

'But what for?' demanded Lord Hood.

'Mr Christian said he wanted to quit the ship.'

The stir spread along the officers in the big cabin and several made notes. More evidence of a sort they hadn't expected, realised Hood. He determined to follow the same practice as the previous day and turn the questioning over early to the defence.

'The second-in-command *told* you he was going to desert?' pressed Sir Andrew Snape Hammond.

'Yes, sir.'

Hood leaned out, restraining the officer, nodding instead to Bunyan, urging him to his feet.

The lawyer rose, more sure of himself after the success of the previous day. Edward Christian would be interviewing Fryer now, he knew. The mutineer's brother had become increasingly excited the previous night as the decision to publish an account of the court martial had hardened. Now he wanted to meet all the witnesses, after their evidence had been given to avoid any suggestion of interference, to explore facts revealed but not pursued during the hearing. According to Edward Christian's clerk, there was a clamour in London for the daily reports.

'Why did he want to desert?' picked up Bunyan.

Purcell hesitated, trying to compose an answer that would cause him as little difficulty as possible.

'He was very distressed,' recalled the carpenter. 'He said he could no longer stand the treatment he was receiving from Captain Bligh and preferred to take his chance in the water ... we were sailing through islands at the time ... '

'And you helped him?'

'I gave him some planking ... he lashed it between two masts. And some nails, to trade, if he reached an island.'

'Do you think he would have succeeded?'

Purcell frowned, sensing a trap.

'We survived the open boat voyage,' he hedged.

'In an open boat,' rejected Bunyan. 'Do you think Mr Christian would have got to an island on the raft he had prepared?'

'I doubt it.'

'So he was, in effect, committing suicide?'

'Yes, sir.'

'Rather than continue on a ship of which Captain Bligh was commander?'

'Yes, sir.'

'So what did you do about it?'

'Do?' asked Purcell, uncertainly.

'Yes, sir,' enlarged Bunyan, aggressively. 'You were confronted with an officer who sought your help in a scheme that amounted to suicide. What did you do?'

'I told you. I helped him.'

'You helped him!' echoed Bunyan. 'Wasn't your responsibility to prevent it, rather than make it possible?'

Purcell nodded, head sunken forward. It was going to be worse than what had happened to Fryer, he thought.

'But you did nothing, apart from aid a distressed man in his ambition?'

'No.'

'Why didn't you alert Captain Bligh, as was your duty?'

'I didn't think of it.'

'You didn't think of it?'

The astonished question came from the President, pressing forward in his chair in his eagerness for the carpenter's reply.

' ... the *Bounty* wasn't like an ordinary ship,' tried Purcell, desperately. 'Most people felt sorry for Mr Christian. No one would have done anything to increase the man's hardship ... '

'Was there jealousy of Mr Christian, for his association with the captain?' asked Bunyan, suddenly.

Purcell stared at the lawyer, as if seeking hidden meaning in the question.

'Oh no, sir,' he said, definitely. 'No one envied Mr Christian that familiarity.'

'Explain further,' insisted Bunyan.

'Captain Bligh was not the sort of man with whom you attempted friendship,' asserted Purcell.

'What sort of man was he?' pounced Bunyan.

'A man impossible to please ... I've never known anyone for whom it was easier to find fault ... '

'And from whom you suffered?' scored Bunyan, again.

Damn the Timor enquiry, thought the carpenter. He'd been justified in what he'd done. Everyone in the boat knew that: it was going to haunt him for the rest of his career, he knew, becoming enlarged and distorted as every year passed.

'Sir?' he tried to avoid.

'Tell us about what happened in the open boat voyage,' demanded Bunyan. 'The incident that resulted in your appearing before a Dutch enquiry after your survival.'

'I think the captain suspected there had been some contact between Mr Christian and myself, before the mutiny ... ' started Purcell, disjointedly. 'That was my impression, anyway. He considered me differently from the rest ... singled me out ... said I wasn't doing enough. He commandeered my toolchest to store the food and kept the key to himself ... the bread supply began going quicker than we had estimated ... '

'And Bligh accused you of stealing it?' intruded Bunyan anxious to get some coherence into what Purcell was saying.

'Oh no,' rejected Purcell. 'Only one man had the key. Captain Bligh.'

'Was he taking more than his share, then?'

'No one was ever able to prove it.'

'But you suspected it?'

Purcell nodded.

'Did the captain know of the feeling aboard the launch?'

'He knew, right enough,' recalled Purcell, definitely. 'The

149

launch divided into two groups ... there was a great deal of distrust ... '

'The enquiry at Timor,' reminded Bunyan. 'Why were you summoned before it?'

'It happened about halfway through the voyage,' remembered Purcell. 'We'd reached an island ... we called it Sunday Island, after the day. We'd touched land before and managed to collect some shellfish and berries. Captain Bligh told us to forage again, the understanding being that each man provided for himself. I did rather well, collecting a lot of oysters and clams. But when I got back to the launch the captain, who had little, demanded I hand them over. He said the food was to be communal and everyone should benefit. I said that wasn't the agreement. He said it had been his order and we began to argue. I called him a confounded liar, as he'd proven himself to be in the past ... '

'You called your commander a liar?' interrupted the President, incredulously. Even allowing for the circumstances, for discipline to have collapsed to that depth was amazing, he thought.

'He was, sir,' defended Purcell, sensing the attitude of the court. 'Even castaways like we were, he was cheating us on our victuals, like he had aboard the *Bounty*.'

'Go on,' coaxed Bunyan.

'He started up at this ... said he was going to settle the dispute between us and with it all the disputes that existed in the boat. He grabbed a cutlass and slashed it over my head ... I could hear the blade whistling, it was so close ... he said I should take up another sword and we should fight, to see who was the better man ... '

'This happened *in* the launch?'

'No, sir,' clarified Purcell. 'We were on the beach. Almost everyone was watching. I refused. I said that no matter how badly I thought of him, I would not fight ... that he was still the captain ... '

'And there the matter ended?' encouraged Bunyan.

'No, sir. He kept cutting at me with the cutlass, so that I had to keep moving backwards. If it hadn't been for Mr Fryer, I think I would have been cut down.'

'What did Mr Fryer do?'

'He returned from his foraging at about this time ... he interposed himself between me and the captain and told the captain

it was not the way to settle any disagreement between us ...
it took a long time, but gradually Captain Bligh calmed
down ... '

Bunyan detected movement beside him and smiled, recognising his neighbour's agitation.

'Where did you get the cutlasses from ... those that were in the
launch?' he asked, helpfully.

'Mr Morrison threw them to us, just before we were set adrift,'
said Purcell, looking to the man on Bunyan's right.

'You saw him take no part in the uprising?'

'I saw him cleaning out the launch, prior to its being unshipped.
But I assumed he was doing that under the instructions from the
mutineers.'

'What about Mr Heywood?'

'I can't remember seeing him at all.'

Another excellent day, reflected Bunyan. From the evidence
they had so far heard, Heywood would have to be acquitted. He
nodded his thanks to the court and sat down. Morrison's cross-
examination, already largely covered by Bunyan's questioning,
was again very brief, and then Hood gestured along the table,
inviting questions from the officers around him.

Sir Andrew Snape Hammond responded, predictably, huddled
in his chair.

'Did you regard Captain Bligh as a good commander?' he
demanded, directly.

Purcell hesitated, more concerned at the interrogation from
naval officers than he was at that from a civilian lawyer.

'The ship was run efficiently,' he offered.

'Were the chance to present itself, would you sail again on a
ship under Captain Bligh's command?' pressed the officer.

'No, sir.'

'Why not?'

'He frightened me,' blurted Purcell.

The reply surprised everyone.

'Frightened you?' picked up Hood. 'What do you mean?'

'He was a man with whom it was impossible to feel anything
but unease,' replied Purcell, desperately. His earlier reply had
been instinctive and the truth. Bligh *had* frightened him. But he
knew it would be impossible for unsympathetic officers, in the
calm and safety of a ship at anchor off Portsmouth, to understand

what he meant. They sat waiting, staring at him, demanding more.

'... with most captains, you learn what sort of men they are,' groped Purcell. 'You come to recognise their ways, anticipate how they will react to certain situations. It's important, even. It's the sort of understanding that makes for the running of a good ship. But with Captain Bligh that was never possible. From the time the *Bounty* sailed from here, in December 1787, I was daily in the company of Captain Bligh for almost two years ... in the open boat voyage, I was but three feet from him all the time. Yet today I am no more able to say what sort of man Captain Bligh is than I was on the day I signed articles for that voyage.'

He'd failed, realised Purcell. Not one of the stern-faced men, examining him from the table eight feet away, had understood what he was trying to convey. Which was hardly surprising, he accepted. He'd never known himself why Bligh had created in him the apprehension he always felt.

'Only one person aboard the *Bounty* appeared able to understand the captain ... ' Purcell struggled on.

'Who?' demanded Hood, impatiently, anticipating the answer.

'Mr Christian,' responded the carpenter.

The President shook his head. The more he learned of the *Bounty* and its officers, the less he was able to understand why the mutiny had occurred.

'How can that be?' he demanded.

'Until we reached Tahiti,' said the witness, quite lost now and speaking as the words came to him. 'Mr Christian was the only person with whom I ever saw the captain conduct himself in a civil manner ... they would laugh and talk together ... '

'What caused the breach?' asked Hood.

'I do not know,' said Purcell.

'Are you sure?' demanded the President. 'It was you to whom Mr Christian came for help ... you knew he was setting out on a course that would cause his death ... he must have said *something* to you.'

Purcell shook his head.

'He was much out of sorts, rambling, incoherent almost ... all he kept repeating, again and again, was that he had to get away from Captain Bligh,' insisted Purcell.

'But without saying why?' asked Hood.

'It hardly made sense,' said Purcell. The words were colliding in his mind, like small boys released from school. He'd never be able to make them understand, he knew. Never. They'd think him an idiot.

'What didn't make sense?'

'He said the captain was trying to destroy him,' recounted Purcell, his voice jagged.

'He said the captain was trying to destroy him,' repeated Hood, spacing the words in disbelief.

'Yes, sir,' insisted Purcell. 'But I don't think he meant it as it sounded. I don't think he meant Captain Bligh intended him physical harm ... '

'Then what in God's name did he mean?' asked Hood, his temper barely controlled.

'I don't know,' apologised Purcell, hopelessly.

Hood sighed, his face reddening.

'I think, Mr Purcell,' he said shortly, 'that you had better stop before you succeed in completely confusing this enquiry ... '

The President looked beyond the witness.

' ... which will recommence promptly at nine tomorrow.'

It again took Edward Christian over an hour to read the transcript of evidence. Bunyan sat, contentedly sipping the wine that was now always waiting in the decanter for his arrival.

The lawyer smiled expectantly when the man finally looked up, but there was none of the euphoria that had greeted the previous evidence.

'Wasn't your meeting with Mr Fryer satisfactory?' queried Bunyan, trying to understand the change of attitude.

Edward Christian nodded, absently.

'Then surely what Purcell said today reinforces what you're doing?'

'Oh yes,' agreed the mutineer's brother. 'It's very good. You've done well again.'

'What is it then?' asked Bunyan.

'The *Bounty* was an unusual ship,' said the elder lawyer, reflectively.

'It was certainly that,' agreed Bunyan, missing the full meaning of the other man's remark.

'I wonder if Fletcher is still alive?' mused his brother. 'Alive and in hiding, somewhere in the world.'

Bunyan shrugged, confused by the man.

'And I wonder if he'd tell me,' continued Edward Christian.

'Tell you?' queried Bunyan. 'Tell you what?'

For the first time Edward Christian looked directly at Bunyan. 'Why it happened, of course,' he said. 'Why it really happened.'

16

His invitation to the council was almost an afterthought, Fletcher Christian decided, a reluctant concession the other mutineers had felt they should make and which they now regretted. Christian sat apart in the village square, the odd one out of their gathering, tormented by their attitude. His confrontation with Quintal should have imbued respect, at least from some of them. Young and Adams should have understood; they'd seen what had been happening. How would they have felt if Quintal had approached Susan or Paurai? He'd been friendly on Tahiti with the other botanist, William Brown. So why was he so hostile? And Jack Williams, the very reason for today's meeting, should have been more sympathetic than anyone. Since the Quintal episode, the division between him and the other seven white men had seemed to widen: there was, thought Christian, more intercourse between them and the natives whom they thought of as slaves than there was with him.

Slowly, Christian examined the men with whom he was sentenced to spend the rest of his life ... with them, but in virtual isolation from them, the cause of their unhappiness and therefore the person to be avoided, like an insane, embarrassing relative who has to be shut away in an unused part of the house and never spoken of unless for some cruel amusement. They blamed him for their predicament and hated him for it, Christian realised, just as he blamed Bligh and hated him.

'Jack wants a wife,' announced Adams, assuming the role of chairman.

Williams looked up, alert for any challenge.

'I've been alone for almost a year now,' he said, as if an explanation were required.

'The native men only have three,' pointed out Young. 'Which one do you intend taking?'

'I don't mind,' said Williams. 'I think Nancy is well disposed towards me.'

It was like an auction, thought Christian. They were sitting there calmly talking of taking a woman from her partner with the casualness with which he'd seen farmers debate the quality of cattle or pigs at Cockermouth market. They had become like animals themselves, decided Christian.

'It will cause trouble,' he said.

The other men looked at him, appearing surprised he had spoken.

'What?' said Quintal.

It was a curt, sneering question, the way he'd seen Bligh talk to the ship's cleaners. Quintal was anxious to recover, he recognised.

'It will cause trouble,' he repeated. 'There are only three women among six natives. We treat them like slaves and they resent it. So far, they've done nothing about it. But they will ... all they want is a cause and their rancour will explode. We've taught them how to use our muskets and now some of them are better than we are. If we insist that one of the women is taken from them, there'll be bloodshed.'

'We must remember that Mr Christian is an expert on sudden explosions of rage,' said Mickoy, trying to support his friend.

Christian sighed. It was pointless, he thought.

'What's the answer then?' demanded Isaac Martin. 'Are you prepared to share Isabella?'

Christian tensed and then smiled, glad the question had been put. He stared directly at Quintal, the expression still on his face but mocking now.

'No,' he said, definitely. 'I'm not prepared to share Isabella. I thought I'd made that quite clear.'

'Then stay out of the discussion,' rejected Williams, aggressively.

'Is anyone else?' came back Christian. 'You all know the truth of what I've said. To get Nancy from the natives, you will have to fight for her. Which one of you is prepared to share his wife, to prevent that happening?'

156

They were all unsettled by the question, even Quintal, who had less regard for his partner than anyone.

'Perhaps it could be resolved by negotiating with them,' suggested Adams, trying to defuse the tension that Christian had created.

No one bothered to reply, recognising the emptiness of the proposal.

'They're only natives,' said Quintal, defiantly. He paused, looking at Christian.

' ... despite what he says,' Quintal continued, with a contemptuous twist of his head. 'They know their position here. If we ask them, then they'll get ideas above their station and imagine they've a right to protest.'

'And haven't they?' pricked Christian.

'No,' retorted Mickoy, immediately. He reached behind him, groping for the bottle of taro liquor, and swigged from it before passing it to Quintal. The other man drank, deeply, then returned the bottle. Neither thought of offering it to anyone else in the group.

'I mind we should think hard on what Mr Christian says,' attempted John Mills, speaking for the first time. 'The natives might rebel against us.'

Christian looked at the seaman, surprised at the support.

'Share Vahineatua, then,' attacked Mickoy, identifying the man's wife.

'I didn't say we shouldn't do it,' immediately retreated Mills. 'I just said we should be careful.'

'Could we disarm them?' wondered Young.

'Probably,' said Christian. 'But before they had muskets they fought with stones. We can't put every rock and boulder on the island under guard. They could stone us to death as we slept.'

'Treat them rough,' insisted Quintal, the bottle in his hand again. Very soon he would be drunk, Christian knew. The man smiled, his mouth twisted. 'Kick them in the ass,' he said. 'Only thing they understand.'

'The teaching of Captain Bligh,' scored Christian. Nothing he said or did could reconcile them to him, he had decided, so he spoke carelessly, wanting only to expose their folly.

'I want a woman,' pleaded Williams, fearing the discussion was splintering into aimless, unresolved arguments.

'I don't see any alternative than of taking her, by force if necessary,' offered Adams. He was unhappy at the thought, everyone knew.

'And it must be a united decision,' added Young, looking directly at Christian.

So his invitation was not really an afterthought, corrected Christian. The mutineers recognised that the natives, at least, still regarded him as the leader of the community and that any decision they reached would have to appear to have his open support.

'It won't be, will it?' he said.

'Going to lead the destruction of what we've got here, just like you did last time?' demanded Mickoy.

'No one forced you to do what you did,' said Christian.

'You're the one worried about bloodshed,' reminded Adams, moving to block another argument. 'If you're not seen to enforce the decision, it'll be an encouragement for them to fight.'

The man was right, accepted Christian. For the doubtful peace of the island, he would have to appear in agreement with them. But why should he? he asked himself. What did he owe any of these men, except contempt?

'We need to move together,' enforced Young, carelessly.

'Do we, Mr Young?' snatched Christian, goading his former friend. 'This reminds me of a conversation of many years ago ... a conversation most of us here wish had never taken place ... '

Young flushed, annoyed at being caught.

Quintal was relapsing into the tipsy clown, turning the bottle upside down to examine the neck for any last drops.

' ... in the ass,' he advised, slurring. 'Kick them in the ass.'

'For the safety of the island ... ' began Adams, then stopped. 'For the safety of Isabella and the children,' he started again, the argument prepared. 'Will you come in with us?'

They'd won, accepted Christian. For any of the men with whom he was sitting he would do nothing, nothing at all. But to minimise a threat to Isabella, he would agree to anything.

'You know why I will,' he capitulated, staring around. 'But I want you all to know something else, as well. I think you are all scum, all of you. Worthless scum.'

They detested him, he decided again, looking back at their faces. Every one of them.

'Nancy,' said Williams, frightened once more the chance would be lost. 'Let's go to get Nancy.'

The mutineers shuffled into a group and moved off further down the village, towards the native settlement at the far end. Christian was manoeuvred into a leading position in the procession, but noticed that the other Englishmen managed to keep apart from him.

'She's in Talaloo's house,' advised Williams. He was smiling, eagerly, like a child being taken to a toyshop at Christmas. Animals, thought Christian, again.

Talaloo appeared in the doorway when they were about twenty feet away. The man had been expecting them, Christian realised. It was not surprising. The wives of the other mutineers would have known the reason for the counsel that afternoon and the Tahitian women gossiped constantly among themselves.

'You want my woman?' challenged the Tahitian, immediately.

'Mr Williams does not have one,' replied Christian, lapsing easily into the language.

'It is unfair,' protested the man. He was the leader of the natives, Christian remembered. For his partner to be taken would mean loss of face among the other Tahitians.

'It has been decided,' said Christian, awkwardly. Why did it have to be him? he thought. Why did he have to be the spokesman for a proposal to which he was the only objector? It was obscene.

The woman appeared behind Talaloo, looking out anxiously. She would want to join Williams, Christian knew. It was regarded by them as a greater honour to sleep with a white man than one of their own kind.

'I do not want it,' rejected Talaloo.

'What does Nancy want?' asked Christian. The others had withdrawn even further from him, he realised, standing at least five feet behind. He'd been trapped into taking the whole responsibility.

'It does not matter what she wants,' said the man. 'She is my woman.'

Christian detected movement behind and glanced sideways as Williams came level to him.

'I do not want us to become bad friends,' Williams said, moving further forward.

Williams had become the metal-worker on the island, setting up a forge on the outskirts of the village and utilising every piece of iron salvaged from the *Bounty*. The canvas bag he offered jingled with nails and trinkets he had prepared.

Christian winced, disgusted. *Just* like the cattle market, he thought again. Would they spit on their palms, then slap their hands together to seal the deal, as they did at Cockermouth?

Nancy moved past Talaloo, then stopped. Christian had not heard what the man had said. The conversation continued, very quietly, the woman frequently nodding, then shaking her head.

'You have guns,' accused Talaloo, coming back to the Englishmen.

'They mean nothing,' said Christian. 'We mean you no harm.'

'Yet you would shoot me, if I tried to prevent her leaving?'

'Damned right!'

The voice was Mickoy's and Christian half turned, furiously. Couldn't they keep quiet? he thought.

'So I have no choice,' accepted the native.

Christian could think of nothing to say.

Talaloo jerked his head at the woman who ran happily towards Williams. Would he feel her muscles and look into her eyes and examine the condition of her teeth? wondered Christian, bitterly. It was the level to which they had degenerated, after all.

Hopefully Williams extended the gifts he had brought, waiting for the man to accept them. Talaloo stared down, prolonging the rejection. Then he spat, carefully, not at Williams but at the group and went back into his hut.

'Wasn't too difficult,' judged Young, as they moved back into the village.

'Your part, at least,' stabbed Christian. 'Always the rearguard in times of action, aren't you, Mr Young?'

'We know your opinion of us,' sighed Young, patronisingly. He sniggered, anticipating his own joke. 'Why not catch the next ship out of here?'

'You'd have to fight your own battles then,' refused Christian. 'How would you do that, I wonder?'

He smiled up, expectantly, at the sight of Thursday at the far edge of the clearing. The child was moving slowly, looking around him, absorbed in some private game.

'Thursday!' called the mutineer. 'I'm here, son.'

The child looked towards the sound, but did not respond immediately.

'Come here, son,' said Christian, curiously. Normally the boy ran to him at the first shout. The men had stopped, grouped beneath the biggest banyan tree, all looking towards the boy.

Adams realised it first.

'He's bleeding,' he said.

Christian was already running, arms spread towards the child. Thursday stopped, eyes bulged and half turned to flee, but the man got to him, kneeling before him and holding the boy's shoulders.

There was a large bruise on the side of his face and the blow had driven his teeth into his lips, so that two tiny lines of blood felt their way over his chin. He was pulling back against his father, not recognising him, tears rolling soundlessly from those staring eyes and mingling with the blood.

'Isabella!'

The realisation wailed from the mutineer. He started up, turning behind him. All the mutineers stood there, gazing down, and nearly all their women were there, too. Unspeaking, Christian pushed the child towards the group and then ran to his house. His leg still hurt, slightly, so that it was an uneven, loping movement.

He realised the younger child was crying in its crib as he ran by, but didn't stop to look at it. The first room was wrecked, the furniture he had so carefully made and which the woman had delighted in arranging and rearranging, every day, splintered and smashed as if two people had not only fought among it, but tried to use pieces as weapons.

'Isabella!'

He ran into the second room, stumbling but continuing on, entering on his hands and knees. Here it was the same, the bed they had slept in and loved in and where he'd promised he would always protect her tipped on its side, so that the covering puddled in a heap. He threw the bed over, then groped into the blankets.

Outside the baby cried on, choking as tears ran back into its throat.

'Isabella!'

He pushed through the debris to the front of the house,

grabbing at the already broken furniture, throwing it wildly aside, chest heaving as he started to sob, unable to find her.

She was at the back of the house, in the small garden where they had cultivated the white frangipani with which she'd like to decorate the house and put into her hair. Isabella was spread on her back, legs splayed open as she had been left, her clothes ripped from neck to thigh and lying beneath her, like a mattress. She'd fought very hard, he realised. Her nails were cracked and some of her fingers were twisted and broken, where she had clawed at her attacker. Both eyes were puffed closed from the beating she had suffered and her teeth would be snapped, he knew, beneath those crushed lips.

The bruise across her throat was very evenly marked, where something had been pressed down, stifling her cries. And killing her. A musket barrel, he decided.

He began to cry at last, but like the boy his tears came without any sound.

'Isabella,' he moaned. 'Oh, my darling.'

He knelt beside her, like a man in prayer, angrily waving his hand to disturb the flies that had already begun to settle.

The clothing was bundled beneath her, so he had difficulty in freeing enough of it to cover her.

She had teeth marks on her breasts, he saw. Near each nipple. She had been gnawed.

He took off his jacket, covering her, then lifted her. She was very heavy and he staggered under the weight, heaving at the body to get his balance. Everyone was outside the house, at the edge of the garden. He stood in the doorway, arms weighed down, as if offering her for examination.

Isaac Martin's woman, Jenny, had Thursday's face held against her chest so that the child could not see, and he stayed there, numbed in his fear. Susan, who lived with Young, was cradling the baby in her arms and he'd stopped crying now, smiling up at her.

Isabella had loved to see the boy smile like that, remembered Christian.

He stumbled further into the garden, moving without thought, and as he did so the jacket slipped off, exposing her again.

He stopped, crouching down protectively, trying to huddle over her.

'Help me,' he pleaded, staring up at the onlookers. 'Please help me.'

Only the women moved into the garden. The white men remained where they were, all statued by shock. Not all, he corrected.

Matthew Quintal wasn't there.

17

William Bligh stop-started around the London chambers of Sir Joseph Banks in Soho Square, like a bird seeking breakfast crumbs. His face was flushed and there was a nervous tic vibrating near his left eye. He had to keep his temper, he knew. No matter what justification there was for his anger, it would be wrong to expend it upon Sir Joseph. He needed the man's help, not his animosity.

Sir Joseph had remained constantly loyal in his friendship, Bligh knew. So there must be a reasonable explanation for the lack of reception at Greenwich. And all the other things that were happening.

It was that damned court martial, he knew. God, the Admiralty were fools. Bumbling, incompetent fools. They'd sent him away, unpromoted, underpaid and without the protection of marines in the *Bounty*, then pushed ahead with the court martial without giving him the chance to appear in person.

Stupid, utterly stupid.

He'd raise it with Sir Joseph. The President of the Royal Society had wide influence in London. Frequently met the King at his levees at St James's Palace ... sounding-board for the politicians on colonial affairs, with his associations and knowledge of Australia now that America had seceded from the realm ... confidant of Pitt and Fox alike. So Sir Joseph would know about it. And be able to give him advice. It was so confounded unfair, Bligh thought, sitting down and clamping his hands on his knees, as if trying to push calmness into himself. Confounded unfair. Not more than three years before he had been one of the most sought-after people in London. King George himself had spent fifteen minutes with him, at the levee at

Windsor, showing a flattering knowledge of his career, discussing maps and charts in detail, even inviting him to peer at the heavens through the telescope he had had installed by William Herschel.

There had been suppers in his honour and society had clamoured for him to inscribe the book he had written about the voyage after he'd been set adrift from that damned *Bounty*.

He'd returned from the mutiny a hero, reflected Bligh. And come back now from the second expedition, upon which he'd succeeded in transplanting the breadfruit, to find himself shunned by those who had once ushered him into their houses and sought his favours and opinions.

The door behind him opened and Bligh rose, turning, to meet Sir Joseph. The President of the Royal Society was a burly, sharp-eyed man aware of his importance and influence but benevolent rather than conceited because of it.

Sir Joseph shook his hand warmly. The smile, decided Bligh, showed the genuine friendship that had arisen from their first meeting, when Sir Joseph had sailed the Pacific with him in the *Resolution*.

'Welcome to my house, sir,' said Sir Joseph, gesturing him back to his seat. 'Sorry I was not able to get to Greenwich, to greet you when you arrived.'

'Forced to say I was surprised, sir,' said Bligh, stiffly.

So he was offended, judged Sir Joseph. Natural enough. He sprawled back at his desk and examined the man sitting before him. One of the most famous figures in London, thought Sir Joseph. Or was the more correct word infamous? That was unjust, corrected the man. Bligh had earned his honours, every one of them. There wasn't a sailor in the kingdom who could match him for navigation. Good as Cook, by any standard. And he knew, having sailed with both. Doubted if even Cook could have managed that survival voyage.

'Your letter said you were much distressed,' prompted Sir Joseph.

'Distressed!' picked up Bligh, immediately halting, embarrassed. He'd shouted, he realised. And he'd determined to control his wrath.

'Indeed, sir,' he began again, speaking with difficulty. 'For more than a year I have sailed around the world ensuring the continued prosperity of the most important men of this country;

men already rich will make millions more from what I've done. Yet I arrive in Greenwich to be greeted by your clerk in the manner of a man returning from some ignominious defeat. I go to my home to find my wife in tears, the butt of jokes and humiliation and the Blighs the practical outcasts of London ... '

Sir Joseph sat shaking his head, sadly. He had been wrong in not going to Greenwich, he accepted. Already it had become yet another rumour against Bligh. The government had quite misjudged the effect an official welcome would have upon public opinion after the interest generated by the Portsmouth affair.

' ... and yesterday I requested a meeting with the First Lord of the Admiralty, Lord Chatham. He refused to see me ... '

'There could be a number of acceptable reasons,' Sir Joseph tried to placate. 'I know Lord Chatham is a much occupied man.'

'Too busy to see me,' said Bligh. 'Yet not too busy to receive my junior, Lieutenant Portlock.'

Banks grimaced at the rebuff.

'Why, sir?' demanded Bligh. 'Why am I being exposed to such ridicule? Why can't I go down to give evidence, at the court martial? It's ridiculous that I'm being denied permission.'

It *was* madness, accepted Sir Joseph. Even the younger Pitt had agreed the stupidity, yet appeared unwilling to impose his will.

'The enquiry was already well under way,' said Sir Joseph, the excuse prepared. 'The Admiralty had little hope you'd return during the hearing. For you to be called now would mean reconvening another court martial, with new officers ... It could take weeks, if not months. Your deposition is sufficient, surely?'

'No, sir,' rejected Bligh, adamantly. 'It's not sufficient and well we both know it. There's a campaign being built against me. A campaign of unjustified vilification and abuse, blatantly the work of the damned Christian family.'

'They appear implacable in their determination to retrieve the family name,' conceded Sir Joseph.

'The man was a villain,' insisted Bligh, his face purpling. 'Even the poxed enquiry at Portsmouth is proving that. Is it British justice to have a felon glorified and his victim castigated, without right of reply?'

It was an impossible argument to answer, thought Sir Joseph. Certainly the evidence being daily discussed by the government didn't have right and wrong balanced in such positive terms as they appeared to exist in Bligh's mind. But Fletcher Christian was appearing the undoubted ringleader of the insurrection.

Sir Joseph stood up, determined to mollify the man he admired.

'Come now, Captain Bligh,' he said, smoothly. 'Hardly castigating. And if any evidence were needed of your country's regard for you, then surely this will provide it?'

He offered the box to Bligh, who stared at it, his face twisting in renewed annoyance.

'The medal,' identified Sir Joseph, hopefully. 'The Royal Society gold medal, commemorating the success of your mission. Further, I'm proud to say the Society is electing you into its membership.'

'Here!' protested Bligh. 'To be given to me here, like a gratuity for a coachman for a successful journey!'

Another mistake, recriminated Sir Joseph. The man's outrage was justified.

'The King and the government are greatly occupied by the revolution in France,' apologised Sir Joseph, guessing the man's need.

Bligh held the box loosely in his hand, uninterested.

'The Christians,' he said, softly. 'The infernal Christian family.'

'It's a passing sensation,' assured Sir Joseph. 'London exists on gossip, the more scandalous the more acceptable. Is it likely that what's happening down there can have a lasting effect upon a man of your achievements?'

Bligh shook his head, refusing the flattery.

'William Bligh doesn't avoid conflict, sir,' he said, without conceit. 'I thought that, at least, would have been clear by now.'

'I don't understand,' frowned Sir Joseph.

'There isn't a coffee house or a salon in London that doesn't have one of the pamphlets ... they're everywhere.'

'But what can you do?' demanded his patron.

'Fight,' retorted Bligh, positively. 'If London society is minded to read, then so be it. Edward Christian is determined to publish his account of the affair, so now I shall publish mine. I shall answer the smears and innuendo, point for point, showing them to be what they are, lies and falsifications from a family unable to accept the existence of a cowardly blackguard bearing their name ... '

Sir Joseph shook his head.

'Think on it, sir,' he warned. 'What can possibly be achieved by a public quarrel of this nature?'

'The restitution of my honour,' replied Bligh, immediately. 'Do you expect me to sit idly by, becoming the joke of this city?'

'The public already knows your side of the affair,' avoided Sir Joseph.

'Then they need reminding of it again,' asserted Bligh. 'I'll not have my Betsy laughed at by women not good enough to be her laundry-maid. But for me, half the families in London would be facing bankruptcy and a debtor's cell in Newgate. What right have they got to laugh at me?'

'None,' agreed Sir Joseph, sincerely. 'And neither do they.'

'Oh yes, sir,' contradicted Bligh. 'They do and well you know it ... and the manner of my return serves only to heighten that ridicule.'

Amends had to be made, decided Sir Joseph. The man was being wrongly pilloried, no matter what his suspected faults. And that suspicion was only being created by clever innuendo, certainly not by facts.

'I believe,' blurted Sir Joseph, hurriedly, 'that the King is shortly to receive guests at the White House at Kew. The government is preparing a guest list. I believe your name features upon it, sir. Won't that allay the gossip?'

Bligh shrugged. Sincerity? he wondered. Or a belated attempt to recover from treatment the government now recognised was in error?

Pitt would be furious at the undertaking, Sir Joseph knew. But it was a problem that would have to be overcome. Bligh *deserved* the proper recognition, no matter how imprudent the invitation might be. To Pitt everything was politics, the pull and sway of advantage. That's why he'd remained in power for so long.

'I must assure you, sir, that the pressure of Royal Society work kept me away from Greenwich,' lied Sir Joseph. 'I now acknowledge that was a mistake, for which I am truly contrite. Rest assured that the *London Gazette* will carry the necessary information about your receiving the Society medal and of your appointment.'

169

'I'm minded to prepare a reply to the slanders being put against my name,' insisted Bligh, doggedly.

Sir Joseph sighed. It wouldn't help, he decided. In fact the man risked further humiliation attempting to out-argue an advocate as brilliant as Edward Christian. And Sir Joseph had no more doubt than Bligh that it was the mutineer's brother who was behind the present campaign. Some stories even had the man in residence in Portsmouth.

'I feel it is a mistake,' he cautioned.

'We'll see, we'll see,' said Bligh, briskly. Characteristically, once having decided upon a course of action, he was already convinced of its successful conclusion. Logic was on his side, determined Bligh. Who could fail to accept his side of the affair, once reminded of the true facts, not the distorted account that was being brought out at Portsmouth and published with such delight by his enemies?

'You'll not be dissuaded?' asked Sir Joseph.

'Not unless I can be permitted to attend personally at Portsmouth,' said Bligh, bringing his threat into the open.

'The government feels it would be a mistake.'

'Then the government must be prepared for me to defend myself.'

It was only when he was in the carriage returning home that Bligh realised he had forgotten to raise the problem of money with Sir Joseph. He sighed, dismissing the oversight. It had hardly been the proper occasion, anyway, he rationalised. Far better to wait until he had published his rebuttal of the lies being spread. The approach would be viewed far more sympathetically once he was in favour again. And he would be, he knew. Very soon. He frowned, reflecting upon the meeting. He had failed to get answers to nearly all his questions, he realised. Sir Joseph was an adept politician.

Bligh hoped his patron's ability would work to his ends.

18

The verdict of the court martial was very clear, determined Lord Hood, complacently. He'd conducted a good enquiry, he decided, only half listening as the gunner, William Peckover, moved towards the conclusion of his evidence. A very good enquiry indeed. And everyone recognised it. So there could be no criticism. And that was important. Rarely could he recall such interest in a naval matter.

They would have to acquit the sightless violinist, Byrn, together with Coleman and Norman, he knew. All the evidence showed them to be innocent. About four of the accused there could be no doubt whatsoever. From every witness had come support for Bligh's deposition that Ellison, Birkitt, Millward and Muspratt had been among the most active mutineers, armed, violent and behind Fletcher Christian in everything he did. For them it would be the yardarm. And quickly.

The intensity of public opinion, spurred on by what Bligh was doing, had surprised not only the President. The Admiralty were aware of it, too. And alarmed that it was almost unanimously critical of the authority represented by Bligh. Unquestionably, conceded Hood, that criticism was justified. But it was clouding the indisputable fact that a crime had been committed. A public hanging was needed to balance the affair, not a coffee-house squabble.

About Heywood and Morrison there was a lot of doubt, he thought, coming back to the court. Certainly there had been some conflicting evidence that Heywood had been seen with a pistol in his hand, but the explanation from the boy that he'd snatched it up unthinkingly, in the confusion of the moment, to put it down again within seconds was acceptable. From no one had come any indication that he was a supporter of Christian; he'd been a boy of little more than fifteen, after all, hardly responsible for his actions unless guided by a superior.

And Morrison, too, had made a convincing case. He'd actually indicated to Fryer that he would support any attempt to retake the vessel, recalled the President. And but for him, the launch would have sailed away without any weapons.

No, considered Hood, about Heywood and Morrison there was more than sufficient doubt. Not sufficient to acquit them, of course. But enough to recommend to the Admiralty that the strongest mercy should be shown towards them. And he'd personally reinforce it, to Lord Chatham, First Lord of the Admiralty. He smiled at the decision. It would enable the Admiralty to follow a course that might appeal to public taste. And they were anxious for that, he knew.

He became aware that Peckover had stopped talking and straightened in his chair. He had few questions of his own, he realised, but felt sure the Christian family spy would be well briefed. He nodded permission and Bunyan rose, with his customary eagerness.

'You knew Mr Christian well enough?' demanded Bunyan.

'Well enough.'

'Come now, Mr Peckover. Captain Bligh appointed you the man in Tahiti through whom the trading with the natives should be conducted. It meant you lived alongside Mr Christian for the six months he was shore commander there.'

'Yes,' agreed Peckover.

'Did you get on well with him?'

'Not particularly,' said Peckover.

'Why not?'

'He was not the sort of man I drew to.'

'Would you explain that to the court?'

' ... I thought of him as a lickspittle ... ' Peckover attempted to explain. 'He seemed altogether too keen for advancement.'

'Lickspittle to whom?' queried Bunyan.

'Captain Bligh,' replied Peckover, shortly.

'He was second-in-command,' reminded Bunyan. 'Wasn't it natural he should spend time in the captain's company?'

'I don't see how anyone could have happily spent as much time with him as Mr Christian did.'

Bunyan smiled at the admission.

'Your feelings towards Mr Christian,' qualified the lawyer, 'are tempered, are they not, by those you have towards the captain?'

Peckover shrugged, truculently. They wouldn't twist him, like they had Fryer and Purcell.

'Isn't your attitude towards Mr Christian one of not being able to understand how he could be able, for part of the voyage at least, to remain a friend of Captain Bligh?' pressed the lawyer.

'Yes,' conceded Peckover.

'You used the word "happily",' reminded Bunyan. 'Do you really think that Mr Christian was happy at the amount of time he had to spend in Captain Bligh's company ... or do you think he attended because he saw his future promotion dependent upon it, until the captain's behaviour became such that even he couldn't stand it any longer?'

'He appeared quite contented on the outward voyage,' refused Peckover.

'As we have already heard,' accepted Bunyan. 'But what happened at the end of that voyage ... in Tahiti? There was hardly anyone closer to him than you, at that time.'

'Life on Tahiti was very different from anything any of us had ever experienced,' recalled Peckover, smiling at the memory. 'Not one man aboard had known the like of landing at a more amazing place ... women would actually snatch out for you ... '

'And what was Mr Christian's reaction to that?' interrupted Bunyan, anxious to direct the man's thoughts.

Peckover shook his head.

'There never was such a man as Mr Christian for women,' he said. 'In every port it was always the same. In Tahiti it was two women a night, more often than not. It was like a farmyard ... '

'And the captain didn't like such behaviour from his immediate officer?'

Peckover hesitated at the question.

'There appeared no dispute at first ...' he recalled.

'Why not?'

'Captain Bligh was much occupied in getting the breadfruit. He had mind for little else, so the ship and men were left alone.'

'So the criticisms came later.'

'Things had changed by then.'

'Changed? How?'

'Mr Christian had met one particular woman,' said the gunner. 'Her name was Mauatua, but he called her Isabella, after a relation of his, here in England.'

'What was his relationship with this woman?'

'He settled down completely ... ' remembered Peckover. 'Told me he considered himself married. I recall I was surprised in the change in such a man ... '

'What was the captain's reaction to this?' pressed Bunyan.

'It was about this time that the arguments began,' said Peckover. 'Rarely a day passed without there being some dispute between them.'

'When the second-in-command was rutting ... to use your own expression, like an animal in a farmyard, Captain Bligh had no complaint. Yet when he reverted to a somewhat unusual but nevertheless settled relationship with one woman, the captain found fault. I don't understand,' prompted the lawyer.

'Captain Bligh was never a predictable man,' reminded the witness.

'Did Mr Christian talk to you about this?'

'No, sir,' said Peckover, shaking his head. 'I told you, there was no great friendship between Mr Christian and me.'

'Did he confide in anybody?'

'Not that I know,' said Peckover. 'He just withdrew more and more with the woman ... he did say one thing, though. He told me once that he'd never been so happy and that nothing Captain Bligh could do or say would upset him ... '

'Then how did he appear to you on that morning when he came to relieve you from watch?' pounced Bunyan.

'Very wild, sir,' accepted Peckover. 'I've heard people at this enquiry use the word demented and upon reflection that justly describes the state Mr Christian was in that morning ... he was badly out of sorts ... '

'So somehow Captain Bligh *had* upset him?'

'That remark was made to me in Tahiti, when he had the woman,' corrected Peckover. 'But she had been left behind.'

'Are you suggesting that Mr Christian seized a ship and cast eighteen men adrift because he could not bear to be parted from a woman to whom he was not legally married?' demanded Bunyan. 'Are you saying he did it for love?'

Peckover paused, considering the reply.

'I don't know, sir,' he said.

'What was it, Mr Peckover? What was it that drove Mr Christian first to think of desertion and then to mutiny?'

'I don't know, sir,' repeated the man. 'I don't think anyone does.'

Bligh might have known, reflected the President, at the top table. Arrangements should have been made to examine the man, now that he was back in England. The Admiralty and the government were being stupid.

Still, that was their decision, not his.

Edward Christian was grey with fatigue, Bunyan saw, so tired that he had difficulty in holding a thought longer than a few seconds and his conversation was rambling and forgetful.

It was hardly surprising, decided the younger lawyer. The man could not have had more than two hours' sleep a night since the commencement of the enquiry and sometimes had even abandoned that in his anxiety to publish an account of the court martial.

But he'd managed it.

Every day he had had printed the evidence produced before the court and as the examination had progressed had prefaced it with a summary of what had gone before, so that a complete narrative had been built up. To the evidence from aboard the *Duke* he had supplemented the accounts provided by each witness whom he had interviewed after they had appeared, contrasting their stories with those that Bligh had published upon his return from the mutiny and was reissuing now.

As careful as he had been in its preparation, Edward had been brilliant in its circulation, exceeding anything Bligh was achieving. Every High Court judge had received a hand-delivered copy, every morning. So had every Lord of the Admiralty, every M.P. and every member of the court of King George. Coaches had been hired to carry the pamphlets to church leaders throughout the country. Copies had been made available, free, in every London coffee house and according to the stories reaching Portsmouth, they had been read more eagerly than *The Times*.

The Archbishop of Canterbury had already preached a sermon criticising the enforced and unnecessary hardship of the British sailor, and the M.P. for Cumberland, a friend of the Christian family, had tabled his intention to force a debate when the naval estimates were considered.

'I don't think that even you guessed the success you would have, did you?' queried Bunyan.

Edward blinked up, focusing on the question.

'No,' he confessed, wearily. 'No, I didn't.'

'It's a pity, in many ways,' said Bunyan.

'Pity?'

'All this, for a dead man.'

Edward picked up his wine glass, then stared at it curiously as if wondering what it was doing in his hand. Shaking his head, he replaced it, then frowned up at the other man.

'Poor Fletcher,' he said. 'Poor, ill-used Fletcher.'

ᘓ 19 ᘔ

He was very close, Christian knew. He'd been searching for three days, setting out immediately after digging a grave in the garden of the house in which they'd known such happiness and stumbling, eyes fogged with tears, through a burial service.

Twice he'd actually seen Quintal, once in the south-west of the island, where the banyan roots were thickest and where obviously the man imagined he had the best chance of hiding, and again, after flushing him from there, to the north-west, scrambling in the foothills of the highest cliffs. So it wouldn't be long. The man was virtually trapped, herded towards the mountain. With every yard he climbed, his escape route narrowed.

It would have been easier had he accepted the offer of the other mutineers, he knew. Even Mickoy had volunteered help, but he'd spat at them, like the native whose woman they had taken. It was too late for them to salve their consciences now. Too late for anything, any more.

His unhealed leg throbbed and was swelling again, he knew. His clothes, stiff with yesterday's sweat, were glued to him by that of today and the insects, undisturbed, drank at his face and throat. Something larger than a fly had bitten him high on his left cheek and the inflammation was pushing his eye closed.

Christian stopped, hunched against a palm, gazing upwards. The volcanic rock climbed away, chipped by ravines and gulleys. A hundred hiding places, he thought. Or points of ambush.

He would have to be very careful, Christian decided. Quintal had run because it was the instinctive, panic-driven thing to do. But that hysteria would be subsiding now. He'd be thinking again, calculating. He'd know Isabella's murder would swing the mutineers behind Christian. There could be no other immediate reaction. But Quintal was cunning. He'd rationalise against that the contempt in which Christian was held. If it were he and not Christian who emerged from the jungle, then he'd know eventually that they would accept it. They'd despise him, at first, of course. But they'd come around, in time. Mickoy would be the first. Then Isaac Martin. Then John Mills. It would be inevitable that they would accept Quintal back, Christian realised, far more inevitable than that the sympathy with which they now regarded him would remain, after the initial shock had passed. He'd been right to reject them, Christian decided. Scum, all of them.

He felt his muscles setting and pushed away, grunting as the ground began to rise into the cliff. His cave was on the other side, he realised, suddenly, the viewpoint from which he'd looked down and first seen Quintal insult Isabella. She'd been very brave then, he remembered. And remained so, he thought, recalling the bruised, twisted hands. Quintal would have suffered already for the rape, he knew. But not as much as he was going to suffer. Christian carried a musket and shot. And a bayonet, too. But that wasn't how Quintal was going to die. It had to be slow, painfully slow. He wanted Quintal to scream and beg for forgiveness, and then hurt him even more, just as he had denied her any pity.

Which was why he had to be so careful. He'd lost Isabella and so he'd lost everything, the very reason for bothering any more about life. But he wasn't going to lose the final chance of revenge.

He had an advantage, he realised, despite his still bruised leg. Ever since they had arrived on Pitcairn he had climbed these cliffs and rocks, learning how to recognise footholds and vantage points and separate the safe ledges from those that crumbled under the slightest pressure. He'd kept fit and agile by climbing and felt more at home on the rockface than he did down below, in the sweating jungle.

But Quintal wouldn't. He'd done virtually nothing, except drink himself into obesity: even his garden and land had been tilled by either Sarah or by one of the bullied natives. So he'd already be greatly weakened, his muscles stretched and quivering by the unrelenting hunt.

Christian hoped he was in agony up there somewhere, crouched in a hollow or a cave, breath clogged in his throat, shoulders heaving like the animal he was, run to ground.

He was making too much noise, he realised, suddenly. Rocks

were skittering away underfoot, clattering down the cliffside and he had the musket looped in front of him, so that it scraped against the stone as he climbed. Christian slid the gun around behind him and began placing his feet with more care. He knew how to use the mountains, crabbing across in a series of traverses, so that he always approached a ravine or wide break in the rock from the side, never raising his head suddenly over the lip, where he would have presented a perfect target. And he was careful to find cover, moving nearly always under an overhang of rock or the shadow of a ledge, so that it would have been difficult to shoot at him from above.

The sun had baked the rocks, making them hot to touch. Twice a drowsing lizard scuttled away, jerkily, frightening him.

It was just after midday when he found Quintal.

It was an odd spot, where the rock had been hollowed out, the indentation like that of a hand being scooped into a flour tub. At the far end, the rocks had splintered and Quintal was pressed into the break, quite well concealed. He was crouched, knees held tightly under his chin and asleep with exhaustion, his head tilted back and his mouth half-open, like a man drinking beneath a water tap. He'd lost a shoe, Christian saw, and his foot was pulped and swollen into a bloody mass. His shirt was ripped, too. But that hadn't happened in the pursuit, guessed the mutineer. Isabella had done that, raking him with her nails. The man's face was scored, grooves furrowed down each cheek. Blood was congealed along the wounds, so that Quintal looked as if he were wearing war-paint. He'd obviously positioned the musket carefully, but he had dislodged it while he slept and it lay now almost out of reach, by his injured foot.

So easy, thought Christian, sighting along the barrel of his musket. His groin. That would be fitting. Or his stomach where it would take a long time to die. But not long enough. His knee-cap then. Cripple him, so that he couldn't run, then use him as a target, immobilising every limb before aiming at the body and even then taking care not to hit, not immediately anyway, any vital organ.

But he'd have to remain some distance away if he did that. And he wanted to be very close, to see the terror in the man's eyes. And hear him beg. It was important, to have him beg.

Soundlessly, without any hurry, Christian skirted where

179

Quintal lay, examining the route he would take when he fled. The crack in which he slept funnelled out, climbing gradually to a shelf of rock wide enough for several people to stand side by side. Like a rat up a drainpipe, thought Christian. The shelf projected on, almost forming a canopy over where he stood. He retraced his steps and stood at the spot where he had originally sighted Quintal, gazing directly up. Perfect. The cliff flattened here, so that it would be very easy to climb straight upwards, to the shelf. And when Quintal emerged, at the other end, he'd be waiting for him, musket primed again.

His first intention was to aim wide, merely to awaken Isabella's murderer. But once he had raised the gun, he knew that wouldn't be enough. The desire to hurt overwhelmed him, shaking through his body and oiling his face with sweat. The man's bleeding foot was alongside a rock, he saw, smiling as the intention settled in his mind. He steadied the musket carefully, wedging it along a wide piece of rock, and aimed at the boulder twenty feet away. Because of its trajectory, the ball would ricochet, flattened and razor-sharp, towards the man's out-stretched leg, carrying stone splinters with it.

It was a perfect shot, the ball striking just where he had intended and whining off to the left. Quintal's screams were inhuman, animal-like, as the pain jerked him awake. They would have heard, down in the village, realised Christian, already moving. They'd be huddled there, staring upwards and trying to determine what was happening. And how many would want him to win? he asked himself, clawing up to the ledge. None, he accepted.

He rammed the ball down the musket barrel, then primed the pin and crouched against the mountain, waiting. Quintal made a lot of noise scrambling up, his good leg pumping to push him through the funnel, sounds whimpering from him. He came straight out of the opening, not thinking that Christian could have got there before him. Christian had already positioned himself, musket trained upon the spot. A great sigh went through Quintal, at the belief he had reached not only safety but an excellent ambush position for the man he imagined would be pursuing along the same fissure he had just climbed.

Christian's shot was not as accurate this time. He aimed for the man's arm, the one supporting the gun, but missed. Instead the ball struck the rockface, spitting shards and dust up into the murderer's face. Again Quintal screamed, more desperately this time, confused by the attack. He lurched backwards, clawing at his face. The musket tipped from his hand, poised momentarily on its barrel against the ledge, then toppled away, bounding and leaping down the mountainside.

They could have seen that, down in the village, if they'd been looking carefully, he thought. Christian took care reloading, working unhurriedly. Quintal had no weapon now. And he had to be given time to clear his eyes, so he could see what was going to happen to him. Christian stopped, staring along the ledge. He hoped to God the man only had dust in his eyes and hadn't been permanently blinded. Quintal was shaking his head, as if he had been punched, but was slowly staring around, eyes squinted. Christian smiled, carefully tipping the powder from the horn.

'I'm going to kill you,' he shouted, along the ledge. The fear grunted out of the other man and he began groping backwards, shunting himself along on his behind and then twisting over, so he could crawl away.

'Just like you killed her,' added Christian. 'Very slowly.'

He spoke quite calmly, conversationally almost.

The ledge curved about twenty yards ahead, and the scurrying man was disappearing behind a rock outcrop. Christian walked forward, gun held easily in his hand. He was going to kill a man. And he felt very relaxed, he thought. Very relaxed indeed. He was looking forward to it, almost.

Quintal's attack was completely unexpected. He'd made the analogy of a rat, running up the tunnel. And he should have maintained the thought, knowing that a hopelessly cornered rat will eventually turn and fight. Christian had expected that Quintal would still be groping along the ledge, yards ahead, but instead he had stopped immediately around the bend in the shelf and pulled himself upwards. When Christian rounded the corner, Quintal was directly over him, the sort of boulder with which the Tahitians fought clutched in his hand.

Had Quintal not been wounded he would probably have succeeded in killing Christian. But he had only one foot upon which to support himself and as he moved, to leap upon his pursuer, he slipped, cascading stones ahead of him. Instead of hurtling down unexpectedly, he came down the cliffside on his back, but still with sufficient force to throw the other mutineer off balance.

Christian felt the musket knocked from his hand and skid over the edge. Quintal aimed the rock at his head, but off-balance he missed, crashing it down on Christian's shoulder, numbing it. Christian lashed out, grimacing as his knuckles smashed into the man's face and he kicked, too, remembering the other man's foot. The ball must have sliced into Quintal because the kick collapsed him, spinning him along the rockface. He landed hunched, snarling up. Blood was pumping from the foot, Christian saw. His face *was* ribboned, where Isabella had tried to protect herself.

'Frightened, Quintal?' he goaded. 'Frightened, like Isabella was?'

He lashed out again, kicking at the man's head. Quintal covered himself for the first attempt, but Christian lunged again, immediately, and Quintal's nose splintered under his toe.

The seaman fell back, unguarded, half supported against the cliff-face.

'No,' he said. 'Please no.'

Blood clogged his throat, making it difficult to understand what he was saying.

This wasn't right, thought Christian. He had wanted the man to fight, so he could have hit him, again and again. But he wasn't fighting. He was just lying there, beaten.

'Fight,' demanded Christian.

Quintal said nothing, hands cupped over his face.

'Fight, Quintal! Fight me!'

Quintal was looking at him, Christian saw, eyes alert, recognising the safety in inaction.

Christian snatched the bayonet from his belt and moved towards him. The man didn't cringe away, Christian saw. He was wedged against the rock and he thought he would survive. He imagined Christian would pull back, as he had so often in the past.

' *... you're not a brave man, are you ... you shout a bit and look good, but you rarely finish anything off, do you ...?*'

The taunt paraded itself in his mind. Quintal's words, he remembered: the defiance when he'd been confronted in the garden. Isabella had been there then. Brave. Unafraid. Unsullied.

He swept the blade forward, driving it into Quintal and the breath squeaked from the man, more in surprise than pain. Then Christian stabbed him again and then a third time, the anger pumping from him and Quintal screamed, again the dreadful, primeval sound.

The seaman slumped sideways and Christian stared down at the body. He should feel something, he thought. There should be the release of revenge, a pleasure almost. But there was nothing, not even disgust at what he had done.

What should he do now? he wondered. There was nothing, he thought. Nothing at all. The children, he supposed. But he didn't want them. Sarah could care for them better than he could. And she would, he knew. The Tahitians loved children. Even before he'd begun pursuing Quintal, the woman had chosen the role as mother to them. The baby was too young to realise what had happened, anyway. And Thursday was only four: he'd forget, soon enough. They'd be better, with Sarah.

His cave was the spot, he decided. It was to the cave he had come, within days of establishing the Pitcairn community. So it seemed right that it should be from the cave that he should kill himself. It would be very easy, he knew. Not even any pain. Unconscious by the time he struck the water, hundreds of feet below.

The ledge narrowed, but it was still quite easy to walk until he was only a hundred yards away. He picked up his normal route and spread across the rockface, finally reaching the little platform from which he could see the hidden village and the open sea beyond.

They *were* huddled down there, he saw, grouped together as if there were safety in numbers, some staring up at the mountain and others towards the jungle path from which the victor would emerge.

And then he saw something else. Along the path at the foot of the cliff, completely concealed from the waiting mutineers, crept Talaloo, musket in hand and with a cutlass in his belt. All the Tahitian men were with them, realised Christian, staring down ... Timoa and Mehow, both with rifles, too, and Menalee and Oho, clutching the stones with which they were so adept at fighting. Tataheite had a pistol, he picked out. And a cutlass, held ready in his right hand.

He looked back to the mutineers. Not one armed, he saw. He'd warned them and they'd laughed at him, like they'd always done.

He could alert them, he realised. If he went beyond the screen of trees, waving with his shirt, he could attract their attention. They wouldn't understand what he was attempting to indicate, but the natives below wouldn't realise that and almost certainly would abandon the assault.

Thursday would be safe, in any battle, he reflected. And the baby, too. It was only the white men who were being attacked … the white men who had discarded him. He squatted, unmoving, watching the hunched progress of the natives.

It would be very swift, he decided, with all the mutineers bunched together like that. And Talaloo was planning his revenge very cleverly, fanning the natives out so they attacked from two sides.

Suddenly Talaloo raised his hand, halting the assault, and Christian frowned, unable to see the reason. The natives appeared to be talking, arguing almost, and then Talaloo swept his hand out into the bay and Christian followed the gesture.

And saw the whaler that must have been tacking into anchor for some time, nearly all its sails reefed and the crew lining the decks, staring at the island.

20

Elizabeth Bligh sat hunched in her shawl, slightly apart from her husband, attempting to conceal her embarrassment.

'Please, Mr Bligh, don't,' she pleaded.

'The man's a fool,' insisted Bligh, speaking not to the woman but to the boatman whose ability to manoeuvre his craft he had criticised constantly since they had embarked at Westminster. 'A complete fool.'

The boatman rowed on, stolidly, glowering at Bligh.

'Ever thought of using the tide,' goaded Bligh, leaning forward to the man. 'We have been at Kew this hour past.'

Around them the river was crowded with boats and barges all heading towards the reception different from that which the King usually gave. Normally he held levees, for men only, or drawing-room gatherings at St James's, to which women were invited as well. Today's gathering was a political move, Bligh knew, the determination of the King and his court to prove they weren't frightened of being overthrown by the mob, like the French aristocracy.

A few of the surrounding craft, identifying Bligh, had come closer, Elizabeth realised. Hardly any had given any sign of recognition, she thought, although she knew nearly all of them.

His Betsy looked very beautiful, decided Bligh. She wore the dress of pink silk he had bought in the West Indies and although it had cost more money than he had been prepared to pay, he had had a jeweller make into a necklace the pink and red coral he had brought back from Tahiti.

'There won't be another woman with jewellery like that,' promised the man, looking away from the boatman. 'Unique, absolutely unique.'

'You're very kind, Mr Bligh,' thanked the woman.

Her husband looked tired, she thought. But that was to be expected, working as he did by candle-light into the early hours of every morning, answering the smears being manufactured at Portsmouth. But it wasn't just fatigue, she knew. It was costing a great deal of money to get the rebuttal printed; she suspected that the printer knew her husband's desperation and had even increased the cost, assured the acceptance was guaranteed. Thank God her father was so understanding. Mr Bligh would be very hurt if he knew the help she was receiving. Elizabeth didn't like keeping secrets from her husband, but felt it necessary in this instance.

They had to wait fifteen minutes for room to land and Bligh's exasperation with the boatman spilled over when the man missed two opportunities and was beaten to a mooring by other craft.

'Buffoon,' he shouted, ignoring the amused attention from the other boats milling about. 'Stupid fool.'

'Another mutiny, by God!'

Bligh snatched around, trying to identify the speaker. A lot of people were staring at him, he realised. And many were laughing at the anonymous remark. Why had Betsy wrapped the shawl so tightly around her? he wondered. It was really quite a warm day.

The boat moved away from the jetty the moment Bligh was stepping out, so that he stumbled forward and had to snatch out to a bollard for support to prevent himself falling completely. There was fresh laughter all around.

'Purposely,' accused Bligh, crouching on the quay so that he was almost level with the boatman. 'You let away purposely.'

The man stared back, saying nothing. Only his eyes moved, going to the people around, enjoying being the cause of their amusement.

'There's no point in arguing, Mr Bligh. Please,' said Elizabeth, still in the boat.

'Not a penny,' said Bligh, determinedly. William Bligh wouldn't be ridiculed by an illiterate man who couldn't control a dory in an inland waterway. 'For your insolence, you'll not get a penny for this trip.'

The man had taken the boat about a foot from the mooring. He shifted very slightly and Bligh followed the movement. The man had cupped the oar, he saw, in the separating water across which Betsy had to step. In the new, pale pink dress that she had never worn before. There was mud on the oar-blade.

'Hurry up,' shouted someone.

'Make room,' demanded another, enjoying being part of the theatre.

'We fixed a price,' reminded the boatman. He pressed very slightly on the threatening oar. If he completed the movement, Bligh realised, his wife would be soaked. And covered in filth.

'Hurry up, I say.'

Quickly, his face rigid with anger, Bligh threw the coins into the bottom of the boat, reaching out for Betsy's hand. The boatman carefully brought the boat in and steadied it as she disembarked.

'Four,' ordered Bligh. 'Be back here on the stroke of four.'

The boatman pushed away and when there was a boat's length between them shouted, over-loudly: 'Get yourself back, like you did from the *Bounty*.'

Bligh was shaking with fury, his mouth pumping for words. Elizabeth plucked at his arm, trying to pull him along the jetty.

'Please, Mr Bligh. *Please*,' she begged. 'They're all laughing at us.'

Bligh stumped angrily towards the park, holding his wife's hand in the crook of his arm. He was tense with rage, she could feel, the muscles strained beneath the cloth of his coat.

The palace grounds were crowded. Brightly coloured pavilions, like medieval jousting tents, had been erected in several places and two bands played at separate ends of the walkway. Two stages had been erected for theatrical entertainments and between the tents the servants moved in constant procession, burdened with trays of drinks.

The reception had been carefully planned. Every foreign ambassador was in attendance, in case another country imagined the King's weak health meant any more colonies could go the way of the Americas. To make the point as diplomatically clear as possible, the Prince of Wales had been sent to Brighton, to indicate his dispensability.

'It's so exciting,' Betsy glowed, hugging her husband's arm.

Bligh was staring around, looking for faces he recognised. He hadn't been at all satisfied with the acceptance within the houses of influence in the capital of his rejection of the court martial innuendo. Only four letters, he recalled. And two of them unsigned and abusive. Which was why this afternoon was so important. He had to meet the King, he decided. Only the briefest encounter would be necessary before such an audience. It would make him acceptable. And his narrative, too. Then they'd change their stance, these popinjays and fops with little ability beyond the bottle and the boudoir and even that open to question.

He felt his wife stiffen and followed her look. Lady Harpindene was parading slowly along the walkway towards them, a swarthily handsome, sharp-faced youth of little more than nineteen, dressed completely in white silk, even to his shoes, in fawning attention. Mrs Wittingdon was dutifully in place a few yards behind, her purple-faced merchant husband uninterestedly at her arm.

'Why, Mrs Bligh!' greeted the baronet's wife, in that familiar voice of constant surprise. 'And the worthy captain, too, I do declare.'

'Your servant, ma'am,' bowed Bligh. He could never understand why such people were so important to Betsy.

'I haven't made a mistake, have I?' giggled the woman. 'It is still captain? I haven't missed a promotion in the *Gazette*?'

Elizabeth felt her husband's arm go taut.

'No, ma'am,' she hurried. 'The only thing you might have missed was my husband's award from the Society.'

'Cleverly done,' praised Wittingdon, thickly, reaching the group. 'Country indebted to you.'

The man was drunk, Bligh realised. But the praise still warmed him.

'Thank you, sir,' he said.

'Such a brave man,' gushed Lady Harpindene. 'Despite all those nasty stories. I want you to know, captain, that everyone at my husband's club is laughing at them.'

'I mind they are, ma'am,' said Bligh, heavily. 'There seems to be much laughter these days.'

'Not at *your* expense, surely, captain,' intruded Mrs Wittingdon.

Both women were staring around them, Bligh realised, knowing themselves to be the point of attention and wanting to see who was observing them. Harpies, he decided. Both of them.

'What an unusual necklace,' said Lady Harpindene, turning to her youthful companion, so that he stared at Elizabeth's jewellery, eyes wide in mock amazement. Both women sniggered.

'It must be something very cute and unusual from the country,' patronised Mrs Wittingdon, whose décolletage was studded with rubies. 'Something native to the Isle of Man, perhaps.'

'I'm surprised at your mistake, ma'am,' returned Elizabeth. 'With the frequency with which you both go to the country, I'd have thought you would know that not to be the case.'

'It's called coral,' identified Bligh, sensing the importance to his wife of the exchange. 'Rarer than any gem. Only necklace of its kind in England. The King has some, of course. Personal present.'

Both women shifted, deflated.

'You must excuse us, ladies,' apologised Bligh, knowing they were ahead in the exchange. 'Someone I have to see.'

He hurried his wife around them, trying to keep Sir Joseph Banks in sight.

'I was very proud of you, then,' said Elizabeth, softly. 'And you didn't lose your temper.'

'Sluts,' dismissed Bligh, cursorily. 'Stupid to bother yourself with them.'

Sir Joseph saw them approach and turned gratefully towards them. He had been scouring the park ever since the man he had positioned especially to alert him of the Blighs' arrival had told him of the stupid scene with the boatman. Pitt had been furious at his promise to Bligh, Banks remembered, insisting he be personally responsible for the man during his attendance.

'Sir Joseph,' greeted Bligh.

'Your servant, ma'am,' said Banks, lifting Elizabeth's hand to his lips. 'You look quite lovely ... quite lovely ... '

'You're most kind, Sir Joseph,' blushed Elizabeth.

Slowly they began to move along the walkway towards the main building, from which the monarch would emerge.

'How is the King?' enquired Bligh, immediately. He felt very contented at having made contact with Sir Joseph before the sovereign came out to greet the guests. Now he was guaranteed an introduction.

'Occupied with affairs of state. But well,' reported Banks, discerning a point to Bligh's question.

Bligh frowned.

'Were it not for the problems it might have caused,' disclosed Banks, nodding towards where the foreign ambassadors were clustered, 'the event would have been cancelled. As it is, the King's appearance will be very brief.'

'How brief?'

'A walk along the main thoroughfare. Perhaps the briefest stop at the big pavilion, that's all.'

He'd rarely seen Pitt so agitated, reflected Banks. But for the man's concern with some unforeseen disaster that might befall the King, his annoyance over the Bligh invitation would have been far greater. Banks felt the ministers were far too nervous about the King's health: it had been several years since his last collapse.

'I had hoped ... ' trailed Bligh, still hopeful.

'Impossible, I fear,' refused Banks. 'We're anxious there should be no encounters whatsoever.'

'How much longer do you anticipate the enquiry will continue in Portsmouth?' asked Bligh. Banks would be receiving daily reports even more detailed than those being put into public circulation, Bligh guessed.

'Almost over now,' generalised Banks. 'Unpleasant business.'

'Have you read my replies?'

'Aye,' replied Banks. 'But there was little need for me to have done so. I've never doubted you.'

'For which I'm grateful,' said Bligh.

'Still wish you'd taken my advice and not involved yourself in a public argument,' said Banks, regretfully.

'It's been an expensive business,' embarked Bligh. It was an ideal opportunity to discuss his problem, he thought. But faced with admitting his penury to his patron, Bligh held back, embarrassed. It was not in his character to beg, for anything.

'Expensive?' helped Sir Joseph.

Bligh nodded. 'My only wish is to serve my King and my country,' he said, choosing an easy path. 'As well you must know. But I've made two trips to Tahiti now for less than a quarter of the salary I would be getting as a merchant captain.'

It had been careless of him not to have realised the difficulty, decided Banks. One of the favourite stories from the court martial was how Bligh had manipulated the *Bounty*'s victualling to make a profit. Here, perhaps, was the reason.

'The Admiralty still refuse to see me to discuss my next position. They plead embarrassment for the duration of the court martial,' said Bligh. 'So I'm considering accepting the offer from Mrs Bligh's family to return to the merchant service.'

Bligh's critics would see it as running away, decided Banks. Which perhaps it would be. He felt very responsible for the man. Whatever his personality defects, he was a brilliant seaman and a competent administrator. And undeniably brave. He needed help, not the treatment being presently accorded him.

Brave administrator. The phrase presented itself in the man's mind, as if for examination. Would Bligh be the man to solve one of the country's many problems? wondered Banks. At dinner only yesterday Pitt had been bemoaning the difficulty and the fact that there were more pressing problems nearer home which prevented him from giving it his full attention. The idea would arouse enormous opposition, he knew. Few would see Bligh as the ideal choice. But there was no argument that couldn't be overcome, if he were sufficiently determined. And he was determined, decided Banks. Bligh undoubtedly possessed the qualities necessary for what he was considering.

He stopped, so that Bligh halted alongside.

'Delay a while,' he advised. 'Keep your commission a few more weeks, at least.'

'Why, sir?' demanded Bligh, curiously.

'I've always been a good adviser to you,' avoided Banks. 'And I hope to remain so. Let's just get this damned court martial out of the way.'

'Another position?' anticipated Bligh, eagerly.

The King's arrival spared Banks from replying. The portly figure was surrounded by court intimates and there was an outer protection of politicians, both in and out of the government. Queen Charlotte was on the King's right arm. Bligh identified the Duke of Clarence and smiled in recognition. The King's son saw him and nodded. Lord Hawkesbury was in attendance, Bligh saw, with Henry Addington. And Lord Grenville, always the eager politician. The shy King was smiling, emptily, unhappy at so many people. His difficulty with a large crowd was legendary, remembered Bligh; he must be hating it. The promenade had been cleverly staged, with rehearsed people positioned at various spots where the King could appear to pause and engage in small talk. Even the bursts of polite amusement seemed spontaneous.

When the royal party drew level, the Duke of Clarence detached himself and moved towards Bligh. Elizabeth curtsied and Bligh bowed, slightly ahead of Sir Joseph.

'A pleasure to see you back among us, Captain Bligh,' greeted the Duke.

'It's been my pleasure, sir, to be of service to my country.'

'A service of which I know my father is well aware,' assured the Duke.

Bligh glanced aside, briefly, anxious to gauge how many people were witnessing the exchange. They were the complete focal point, he saw. Let them mock now, Bligh thought, confidently.

'I await only fresh orders,' said Bligh. He thought he detected the attention of the younger Pitt. Let that remark get back to him and the Admiralty, thought Bligh, hopefully. A feeling of great satisfaction suffused him.

'You must be very proud, ma'am,' praised the Duke, addressing Elizabeth. She was blushing, Bligh realised, glancing sideways. Darling Betsy. The harridans of society wouldn't ignore her after today. The royal group had passed Lady Harpindene without a glance.

'I am, sir,' replied the woman, shyly. 'Very proud.'

'You must call at my house,' invited the Duke. 'Certainly before you embark upon another enterprise. I share the interest of my father in navigation.'

'It would be the greatest honour,' accepted Bligh.

'Settled then. Excellent,' smiled the Duke, moving back to join the King.

Imperceptibly, Elizabeth squeezed her husband's arm. She felt very hot. Excitement, judged Bligh.

'Well, Captain Bligh,' said Sir Joseph. 'Do you need any further indication of how the establishment of this country feels about one of its most famous sailors?'

'Very comforting,' said Bligh, finding awkwardness with the words. Court etiquette and diplomacy was a damned nuisance, he thought, with impressions and attitudes decided upon with the exchange of a word. He felt far more at home on a quarter-deck, man to man, without this foppishness.

'They saw,' whispered Elizabeth, by his side. 'They all saw, Mr Bligh.'

She was very excited, he realised. He hoped she wasn't disappointed.

The royal promenade was almost over, Bligh saw, the King impatiently moving back towards the palace.

'Why not return to London in my carriage?' offered Sir Joseph, recalling his informant's account of the jetty argument. Nothing should be allowed to mar Bligh's triumph.

Bligh permitted his wife her exaggerated entry into Sir Joseph's ornate, crested carriage, as aware as she of the attention of a large group of people. Those who only an hour before had looked without recognition were now smiling and nodding, he saw. It was pleasant to ignore them.

Sir Joseph's importance was no secret, thought Bligh, happily. First conversation with the King's son. Now being escorted home by one of the most influential men in the land. That should halt a lot of tongues, he decided, seating himself comfortably on the rich-smelling leather.

He confided his hopes to Betsy that night, after all the children had been put to bed and they were alone, in the dining room.

'What sort of position?' she wondered.

'He wouldn't say,' admitted Bligh. 'But I'm sure that's what he meant.'

Elizabeth frowned, doubtfully.

'I pray he won't turn against you, Mr Bligh. Like all the rest.'

Despite what had happened that day at court, she was still suffering very badly, realised Bligh, sadly.

'They were laughing at us today, Mr Bligh,' said the woman, suddenly. 'I hated it.'

'Not in the end,' insisted Bligh. 'What happened today will halt the smears, you see.'

Elizabeth shook her head, unconvinced.

'There's rarely a day that passes, Mr Bligh,' she said, reflectively, 'without my lamenting the moment we first heard of the *Bounty*.'

'Hush, Betsy,' said Bligh, smiling across the table. 'Everything will be resolved, don't you fret.'

'That's the trouble,' agreed his wife. 'I do worry ... I worry nearly all the time ...'

Pitt laughed, uncertainly, imagining Banks was attempting a joke.

'I'm quite serious, sir,' asserted Sir Joseph. 'I say he'd be the ideal man.'

'But you can't be,' protested the politician. 'Why, it's madness!'

'Give the proposal proper consideration,' demanded Banks, undismayed by the opposition. 'He's got every qualification.'

'And I say he'd be a disaster, sir,' refused Pitt. Banks was too assured of his importance, decided the premier. Far too assured.

'But why?' asked Banks. 'Give me a reason, supported by fact, why William Bligh isn't the obvious choice. Fact, remember. Not a porridge of smear and rumour ... '

' ... it would be bad politics,' rejected Pitt, unable to give a direct reply. 'The man's surrounded by scandal.'

'So is Admiral Lord Nelson, because of his blatant association with the Hamilton woman,' scored Banks, not enjoying his descent to gutter argument. 'I don't see that deterring the Admiralty Lords from calling upon him.'

'The situation is altogether different,' replied Pitt, angrily. The man's face, coloured by his fondness for port wine, deepened and the redness was accentuated by the whiteness of his hair.

It was a wonder, thought Banks, that Pitt had been spared the severity of gout that had killed his father.

'I ask you only to consider it,' pleaded Banks. 'Consider it objectively, in the light of everything known of the man. I say he's the obvious choice.'

Pitt stared back at him, unmoved.

21

Lord Hood hated public hangings. They were necessary, for the maintenance of discipline, he accepted. But he still hated them. He stood uncomfortably in the main cabin of the *Brunswick*, feeling the vessel shift to anchor, his wine glass forgotten in his hand. The eleven other officers who had determined the verdict grouped around, all subdued at the thought of what was to happen. Hood stared through the port, at the other ships commanded to witness the executions, their crews lined up to order. Rarely, he thought, could so many ships be gathered at anchor with such little noise. It was always the same.

It had been a fair verdict, the President reassured himself. Heywood and Morrison had been rightly pardoned. Muspratt was the only man whose fate had not been decided cleanly. The man had been found guilty, like the remainder, but had won a stay of execution upon the technicality that he had been unable to call the proper witnesses for his defence. But that had not been his decision, recalled Hood. That had been the attitude of the Admiralty and any subsequent decision would have to be theirs, so any criticism would adhere to them, not him.

He heard the scuffle of feet on deck above. Any moment now, he knew, the yellow flag would be run up, calling the fleet to attention. He supposed he had to go aloft to watch it. The other officers were looking at him, expectantly. Slowly he put his glass on a table and led the way up the companion ladder, shivering as the wind swept round him.

Ellison, Millward and Birkitt were amidships, quite composed. Millward was even smiling. They'd been given rum, realised Hood, gratefully. It was a good idea to get accused men drunk. He'd once witnessed a hanging of a sober man and had been physically sick afterwards at the man's collapse.

There were other boats, Hood realised. Craft of every size had come out from Portsmouth and were circling around, to see the spectacle. Hardly surprising, he thought, after the publicity that had been generated by the trial. Ghouls, he criticised, silently.

The three men were slowly herded towards the ropes. Over their heads the flag burst open, climbing up the yard, and at a signal from the timekeeper the gun was fired, once. Not a sound, Hood realised, not even from the gawping public. They all died cleanly, just one quick snap. And then it was over. Hood was the first to turn away, hurrying back down the companion-way. He took the rest of his wine in one gulp and gestured almost irritably towards the steward for more.

'Always unpleasant,' offered Sir Andrew Snape Hammond, by his side.

'Yes.'

'And this a particularly nasty business.'

'And still unresolved, for my mind,' suggested Hood.

'Were the Admiralty insistent about young Heywood?' probed Hammond.

The rebuke to Bligh had astonished everyone, causing almost as big a sensation as the trial itself, and Hammond wanted to be the man with the accurate gossip.

'Absolutely,' insisted Hood. The Admiralty had been adamant that the action be interpreted correctly, so there was no indiscretion in talking about it, he decided.

'The First Lord himself said they wanted Heywood offered an immediate post,' he said.

'But for it to be upon your flagship, the very man before whom he appeared accused of the worst crime in the navy!' tempted Hammond.

'Lord Chatham was equally insistent about that,' provided Hood.

'So Bligh's out of favour?' mused Hammond.

'I'm not sure. He was well received at the King's reception, so I hear. There are some strange things afoot,' said Hood. He paused, playing with the stem of his glass. 'I knew the Christian family had powerful connections,' he said. 'But I never imagined they would be able to turn public opinion as successfully as they have. It's hard to imagine that Bligh was being received a hero into every salon in London such a short time ago.'

Hammond nodded.

'Were Fletcher Christian to reappear from the dead,' tried Hammond, 'I doubt that those same people wouldn't lionise him now.'

Hood nodded, becoming bored with the conversation.

'Let's hope it's the last we hear of the matter,' he dismissed. 'To my mind, the *Bounty* is just a confounded nuisance.'

Fletcher Christian had remained hidden for the three days the *Topaz* had lain at anchor in the bay off Pitcairn, witnessing every contact between the American crew and the mutineers. They'd been very frightened at first, he knew, remembering the panic of the six men who had milled around at the first sighting of the whaler, some making off towards the village, others abandoning flight almost immediately, resigned to whatever happened to them.

But now it was very different. He'd gazed down from his vantage point, prostrate against the rock so he would not be seen, and watched as the officers had come ashore and how the tensions had relaxed with present-giving and even a meal, in the village square, with them all sitting around the large table. They'd laughed a lot, Christian had seen: some of the native women had even sung traditional Tahitian songs.

There had never been such a relaxed feast on Pitcairn before, he realised. Certainly not with so much laughter.

And they'd found Quintal's body, as he had intended them to. Perhaps that was the reason for some of the laughter, he speculated. Because the body, mutilated as he had arranged for it to be by its fall down the cliffside and then immersed for two days among the scavenging fish of the bay, had been identified not as the murdering seaman's, but as his.

Never, thought Christian, had he imagined the intoxicated moment when he and Quintal had had their buttocks tattooed in Tahiti would become so important to him. He'd seen them crowd around on the beach and watched them draw the breeches away from the body for the definite identification. He'd carefully positioned other things, of course. He'd risked his life to retrieve his musket because it had his initials carved in the stock. And when he'd pulled the body from the water, early on the third day, he'd carefully placed the gun alongside. He'd looped his belt around Quintal's waist, too, knowing the buckle would be recognised by every mutineer on the island. He sighed, happily. Fletcher Christian was dead, he thought. As he should have been, years ago.

It was almost time to move, he decided. For over an hour now, there had been elaborate farewells enacted down there; and now the cutter was leaving the *Topaz* with what appeared to be supplies for the mutineers. It would return with the officers down there, he knew.

Christian started to descend to the west, away from the village and the risk of being seen, sure of his route. He went down almost vertically, careless of the noise, frightened he might have left his move too late.

He had to be aboard almost the moment the ship departed, he had estimated. And then conceal himself for at least a day, so they would be too far from the island for him to be put back.

Christian entered the water as the cutter beached. It was a good moment, he decided, striking out against the breakers. All the attention was on the jolly boat and what it contained. The exchanges would take more than an hour, he thought. He would need all of that.

Once in the water, he realised the whaler was anchored further from the shore than he had estimated. And the drift of the waves was against him. He swam slowly, as deep in the water as possible, recognising almost immediately how much the three-day pursuit and then the fight with Quintal had drained him. And it hadn't ended then, he thought. There had been the manhandling of the body and the descent and ascending of the cliffs again, to plant the evidence with it.

And he wouldn't be able to approach the *Topaz* directly, he knew. He would have to swim out and then circle back towards it from seawards. Any sailor looking out would be concentrating upon the island and its unusual inhabitants. He groped on, feeling his body numb not from the cold of the water but from fatigue.

He turned towards the ship before he had intended, knowing his strength was failing too quickly to enable him to make the approach he had wanted. Christian was almost unconscious when he grabbed out, seizing the bower cable. He hung there, arms locked around the mooring. The cable hole looked so far away, he thought, his mind as well as his body emptied by the exertion.

So very far away. And he had no strength to pull himself up. The current spun him, turning him towards the shore. The cutter had left, he saw. The men were bending at the oars and the officers were standing in the thwarts, waving back towards Pitcairn.

An hour, he thought. He had no more than an hour. He locked his legs as well as his arms around the cable and pulled upwards, lips clamped against any sound, not able to feel whether his limbs were moving as he wanted. It took him almost fifteen minutes to clear the water and then the climb was even more difficult. He hung suspended, the rope sliding between his hands and with nothing against which he could jam his feet, to push himself up. He could hear the creak of the oars and the shouts of the men as they came near, on the far side of the vessel. Less than an hour now. Far less.

But he was ascending. Slowly, perhaps too slowly. But getting near the deck. The knowledge spurred him. He paused, straining for sufficient strength, then jerked upwards in a rush, knowing that if he failed to reach the anchor entrance with this spurt there would be nothing left and he would fall back into the water. He felt, rather than saw, the cable door. He snatched out, missing it first time and almost pulling himself away from the rope, then grabbed again, finding hand-holds at last. He allowed the briefest hesitation, just sufficient to inhale, then hauled himself into the opening, jamming himself there.

He began shuddering, uncontrollably, at the very point of collapse. He'd succeeded, he told himself. He was aboard. Aboard and, for the moment, undetected.

The cable door was a good hiding place, he accepted. But a limited one. Once the anchor was lifted, he would be discovered. And that would happen the moment they got the cutter aboard. On the far side, he saw the pulleys go out to bring it in.

The layout of the whaler was new to him and he wedged there, studying it. Aboard a ship again, he thought, suddenly. For the first time, in so many years, he was on a deck, feeling a vessel move and shift beneath him. There was no excitement, not like there had been that day when he and Edward had travelled to Liverpool and he had seen his first ship and held his brother's hand with the thrill of it and promised, 'One day I'll be a famous mariner. You see, Edward. Famous.'

The rope locker. It was the obvious place, he thought, shaking

199

off the reminiscence and locating the tiny shed. And very near, too, little more than five feet away.

He tensed, awaiting the proper moment. It came as the cutter reached deck level and everyone's attention was upon it. He jerked away, bent double, body taut for any sudden challenge, scurrying across the intervening space.

He was very cramped. He had to pull himself down upon the coiled rope to prevent his body protruding the locker top off its rest. He lay there, tiredness pulling at him but resisting sleep, wanting to feel the ship move and know he was safe before he relaxed.

It seemed a very long time. He heard it first, the hiss of the cable up which he'd clambered being wound around the capstan and then there was the crack of sheets against the mast and the pitch of the ship under way.

It had been dusk when he got aboard and he waited for several hours, refusing to let his eyes close, before lifting the edge of the locker. They must all mess together on a whaler, he decided, sucking at the salt air. The deck was deserted, only the helm manned at all.

He crept out, accepting the foolishness of his action, but needing to do it.

He bunched in the cable door again, peering out through the tiny gap. He could just discern Pitcairn, jutting blackly against the horizon. Talaloo would attack almost immediately, Christian decided. The natives were probably on the cliff now, just waiting for the *Topaz* to get far enough away.

He'd warned them, Christian tried to assure himself. He'd warned them and they'd laughed at him, so there was no cause for remorse. He certainly didn't feel any. He paused at the thought. It would be difficult to know any emotion ever again, he knew.

'Goodbye, Isabella,' he said softly, in the darkness. 'Goodbye, my darling.'

22

William Bligh hurried impatiently across Soho Square, eager for his meeting with Sir Joseph. It had to be a position, he decided. Had to be. If it weren't, then he would have to tell the man who had befriended him that he had no choice but to quit the naval service. All right, so they'd laugh at him. But they were doing that anyway, despite what had happened at Kew. So it could hardly cause any more pain.

It was confounded unfair, Bligh told himself, gripping his hands in frustration. Even the court martial verdict, justification of his honour if ever justification had been needed, had not had the effect he had expected. 'Breadfruit Bligh', everyone was calling him. Or, worse, '*Bounty* Bligh'. There'd even been cartoons lampooning him, whip in hand. He deserved honours and got sneers. Confounded unfair. Didn't matter for himself, of course. He could have withstood it. Strong enough. And he'd been right, after all. Nothing to be ashamed of. Never had been. It was Betsy. She was suffering far more than he was. Several times he'd discovered her crying. She always made other excuses, of course. But he knew the real reason. Damn him, he thought. Damn Fletcher Christian in whatever hell he was in. And his family, too.

Sir Joseph Banks was waiting for him in the study, smiling his satisfaction. He was right in putting his confidence in the man, decided Banks. Bligh had the faults they all knew about. But he had the qualities, too. And they outweighed the disadvantages. Bligh wouldn't let him down, he knew.

'I trust you're well, sir,' he greeted the sailor.

'No, sir,' rejected Bligh, immediately. There was no point in avoiding the problem, he determined. That was not the way of

William Bligh. The propensity of politicians to wrap everything they said in a mess of pleasantries was damned stupid. Couldn't stand stupidity.

'I'm being sorely treated,' complained Bligh. 'Sorely treated, sir.'

Banks nodded, accepting the protest. It was impossible to prove, but he felt a great many powerful people had been influenced by the campaign against Bligh. He'd been so hopeful after Kew, he remembered. It was sad, very sad.

'The court martial was badly conducted, as far as your name was concerned,' apologised Sir Joseph. 'Much was said that could not be refuted ... '

' ... because I was denied attendance,' protested Bligh. 'It was a nonsense, as well you must know.'

The Admiralty *should* have delayed the hearing, Banks felt. Justice had unquestionably been done and the verdict had reinforced throughout the fleet the need for proper discipline. But Bligh *should* have been called, no matter if it would have entailed reconvening the court. Banks paused. What sort of witness would the man have made, he wondered, looking at Bligh. A clever lawyer would have inflated that temper within minutes, Banks decided, sighing. And done the man much harm. But not as much as had been done by relying solely upon his written deposition.

'It was unfortunate,' agreed Banks. He shrugged, discarding the past.

'I trust you've not taken any further your intention to leave the service,' he said, smiling at the news he had for the man. It would be compensation, Banks thought, happily.

So it *was* a position, guessed Bligh.

'I've spoken to my wife's relations,' Bligh warned. 'A place in the merchant fleet awaits me, should I so choose.'

If they wanted him, they'd have to pay, Bligh decided. There was no excuse for what had been allowed to happen.

Banks stood, pouring Madeira for them both. The man had a right to his attitude, he allowed. It had been very difficult to get the agreement about Bligh, reflected Banks. Even now the doubts remained among many in the government and he knew his critics were waiting for Bligh to create an incident that could be utilised as political capital. The appointment of one of the men who had been cleared by the court martial to an immediate post in the President's ship was worrying. Pitt was playing a dark game, determined Banks. Bligh would have to be closely advised. And warned.

'As you must know, there was a purpose to the advice I offered you,' commenced Sir Joseph, gently. He paused, sipping his wine.

'There was much made at the Portsmouth enquiry about your attitude to discipline,' reminded Banks, his speech prepared.

'I'm a direct man, sir,' interrupted Bligh. 'A man who believes in the value of discipline. Any who slack under me feel the rough edge of my tongue. I see no reason to change, sir!'

If only, thought Banks sadly, Bligh had been able to curb the quickness of that tongue.

'Captain Bligh,' he continued, gently. 'There is scarce need to defend yourself before me. Were I not convinced of your integrity, I would not have shown you my friendship for so long. If there is a crime to be proved against you ... '

He held up his hand, warningly, as Bligh looked sharply towards him.

' ... then I think it is too often acting towards people without mind for their feelings ... '

Were they Sir Joseph's views? Or those of people he undoubtedly represented? wondered Bligh. The remark deserved a reply. With difficulty, he held back.

'Your attitude towards discipline interests me far more,' continued Sir Joseph.

'How so, sir?' encouraged Bligh.

'I am, as you know, closely involved with the government. And with the King,' Sir Joseph said.

Bligh nodded.

'And I have been asked for my counsel on a matter causing the country a great deal of concern,' he continued. 'The settlements established around Botany Bay, in New South Wales, have become a disgrace to this country ... the lawlessness that exists there is almost unparalleled in our history ... '

Bligh was frowning. What had Botany Bay to do with him? He was a sailor. Damned good one, too.

'The current Governor-General, Philip King, is exhausted by his efforts to handle the matter. He seeks retirement ... ' Sir

Joseph paused. Bligh's refusal to shrink from his duty, no matter the personal consequences, made him ideal for the post. Bligh would not beg for relief if affairs went against him. If Bligh were successful in re-establishing order in the colony, it would erase a great deal of the current ill-feeling towards him in the capital. He could even become a hero again, as he had been after the voyage to Timor.

'... and I am empowered to offer you the appointment,' Banks completed.

'Me?' queried Bligh, incredulously. 'Governor-General of an Australian province?'

Banks nodded. It would be a difficult job, he thought. Even the King had been unreceptive, after Pitt's reluctant agreement, initially dismissing Bligh as 'that troublesome martinet' before being convinced it was precisely that attitude that was needed to defeat men who seemed to regard themselves as almost the same as the settlers in the American colonies. It was the argument that Australia might go the way of the Americas that had finally convinced the monarch, Banks remembered.

He'd exposed himself with his patronage of Bligh, Banks decided, worriedly.

Bligh was nodding, slowly, trying to assimilate what was being offered him. Betsy wouldn't accompany him, he guessed, immediately. She hated the sea, so such a long voyage would be impossible for her. Instead she could remain in London, the wife of a Governor-General. They'd come to her parties then, he thought, those snobs still convinced he was out of favour. And he *had* been shunned, he accepted. Until they realised they needed him. But he wouldn't agree so readily this time. He had almost bankrupted himself by the breadfruit expeditions. And suffered worse in other ways. Now it was time for them to make amends. It was a great honour, though. Betsy would be very proud.

'What will the salary be?' he asked, pointedly.

'£2,000 a year,' replied Sir Joseph, immediately. 'Which is £1,000 more than the present Governor is getting. The position is seen as one of much importance.'

Better than he had expected, thought Bligh. Betsy could become one of the most glittering hostesses in London on an income like that. He might even be able to buy some land as well. He wanted very much the security of property.

'And I could keep my naval pension? And seniority for promotion?' he pressed. By his demands he'd make them aware of his annoyance with their treatment of him.

'Agreed,' said Banks.

It would be good to get away from England, thought Bligh, where so many unseen forces seemed to be combining against him. People jealous of him. That's who were behind it, people who knew him, knew the drive and capability that were being recognised by the very offer he had received that day. The appointment would defeat those critics, he decided. It would be pleasant, laughing at them, when the announcement was made. It would mean being received by the King again. Properly this time. And with Betsy by his side. She'd enjoy that. It would wipe away the distress. And she'd no longer be ostracised.

'Would I have the King's understanding that it would be an appointment of a limited period, say four years?' asked Bligh.

Sir Joseph hesitated.

'Yes,' he conceded, after several minutes. 'I think such a condition can be allowed.'

Bligh was nodding, with growing acceptance. Strange, he thought idly, how every point he raised was so readily agreed by Sir Joseph. The government appeared very contrite. It was fitting that they should be, of course. Damned fools. Just like the Lords Commissioners of the Admiralty who had sent him away on the *Bounty* unpromoted.

'Understand the situation very clearly, though,' counselled the other man. 'What you're being asked to do here is a job far more difficult than controlling the most unruly ship. There is in Sydney a small group of men holding almost everyone to virtual ransom. They control all the importing, have created what amounts to a legal currency from the practice of paying for things in rum, the selling of which they keep in their power, and arbitrarily fix the price of anything else to their own whim. And they have a small army to support them. Unable to anticipate the problems it might create, the King allowed certain officers to raise a force; there are now almost 1,000 men, allegedly keeping order but in fact supporting a select dictatorship. The population consists largely of men sent there as convicts who have served their sentences. It is more natural in Botany Bay to break the law than to obey it.'

Bligh sipped his drink, smiling slightly. If he had not known the man better, decided Sir Joseph, he would have imagined Bligh were patronising him.

'Beware one man,' he enlarged. 'His name is John Macarthur.'

'What position does he hold?' asked Bligh, attentively.

Banks smiled.

'None. And all,' he replied. 'Macarthur is unquestionably the most powerful man in New South Wales ... during the sale of the King's sheep at Kew he was uncommon rude to myself and others, over the question of importing merino sheep into the province. He made it quite clear that he did not consider himself beholden to the home government in any way.'

Bligh frowned. Then why hadn't the man been brought to heel?

'And was allowed such disrespect?' he asked, the criticism obvious.

'Although they are the qualities you'll need, it's not the behaviour of the quarter-deck we're talking about, Captain Bligh,' lectured the other man.

'Yet Macarthur holds no official position?'

Banks shook his head.

'But he is without challenge the most influential man in the colony,' he repeated, trying to impress the fact upon Bligh. 'The richest, undoubtedly. And perhaps the most determined. He trades extensively with China and India through his shipping fleet, the traders look to him for guidance and almost everyone else for money. I'll wager there are few people upon whom he does not hold promissory notes and who are not, therefore, subservient to his wishes.'

Bligh covered another smile by raising the glass to his lips. Which made it all so easy, he thought. Pluck away the omnipotent figurehead and replace it with lawful authority and the problems would be no more. They really were quite stupid.

'These difficulties are well understood?' clarified Bligh.

'Completely,' assured Sir Joseph.

So the prestige of success would be correspondingly high, Bligh thought, happily. And he would succeed. He was sure Sir Joseph and the government and the King had over-estimated how entrenched the practices were, misled by a weak Governor. He'd be able to clean it up, Bligh knew. He'd stipulated four years because he did not want to be away from Betsy for any longer than that. But now he began regarding the time limit from another viewpoint. He'd let the condition be known, when the announcement was made, so that people would recognise his confidence. He'd show them, he determined, those people who'd laughed at 'Bounty Bligh' and labelled him a tyrannical despot. He'd succeed and damn them, just as he'd survived an open boat voyage that would have defeated anyone else to carry out his vow to damn Fletcher Christian.

'I shall have your full backing? You? And that of the government?'

'Yes,' responded Banks.

Bligh looked up at the doubt in the other man's voice.

'If things are as lawless as you say they are, then the situation will have to be met with determination and force,' anticipated Bligh.

'We accept that,' said Banks. 'As I said before, it's because you possess just those qualities that the position is being offered you. But be cautious, Captain Bligh. Sometimes problems are better handled by diplomacy and artifice than by direct confrontation.'

Bligh held his head curiously to one side. It had been a warning, he realised. This was to be his last chance. He had been selected because of his courage, he decided, but also because he was expendable, a man who might, just, defeat the racketeers but someone who could be sacrificed if he failed. The temper began to flare, but he controlled it. It was not Sir Joseph's fault, he repeated. The man had remained his friend, even remembering his financial difficulties. From every consideration, it was a damned good opportunity. He could have been pulled up on the beach and left to rot in some early retirement or ordered into a menial job commanding one of the Admiralty's coastal packets, like a street-hawker pushing a cart.

'You'll not find your confidence misplaced,' he told Banks.

'I'm sure I won't,' responded his patron. 'I'm just anxious that you should succeed and earn the proper recognition, not just for what you're going to do but for what you've done in the past.'

It was an admission of the government's guilt, Bligh saw. Or as much of one as the man could ever make. He'd clean up New South Wales, he determined: by God, he would. He'd scour it cleaner than a new pot and woe to anyone who tried to oppose him.

'It will give me great pleasure,' he said, formally, 'to accept the position.'

Banks hurried around the desk, hand outstretched.

'I'm delighted,' he said, sincerely. 'May luck and good fortune go with you.'

It would be the corrupt colonists of Australia who would need luck, mused Bligh, confidently. William Bligh made his own luck. And good fortune.

That night, in his Lambeth house, Bligh lay on his back in the darkness, his hand on Betsy's arm.

'Sure you don't mind me leaving you alone?' he persisted.

'You should know I don't, by now.'

'I wish you could come.'

'The voyage would kill me.'

'I'm going to succeed, Betsy.'

'I know you are, Mr Bligh.'

'We've had a lot of setbacks, but this time I'm determined nothing is going to go wrong. By the time I've finished in Australia, people will have forgotten about the confounded *Bounty* and Fletcher Christian. It will all be behind me, for ever.'

She'd be bruised in the morning, she knew, wincing at the grip he had upon her arm. If only he could control his temper, she mused, hopelessly.

'Be careful.'

'You know I will.'

'I'll think of you all the time.'

'And me of you.'

She felt him move in the darkness and shifted towards him, expectantly, and then remained there, feeling foolish and glad of the darkness.

He'd turned away from her, she realised, grunting up into a ball and already snuffling towards sleep.

She twisted away, sadly. Poor Mr Bligh, she thought.

BOOK THREE

'... he appeared to be very much agitated: indeed, I never saw a man so much frightened in my life, in appearance. When I went into the room, Governor Bligh reached out his hand to me and asked me if I would protect his life. I assured him his life was not in danger; and that I would pledge my own for the safety of his ...'

Lieutenant William Minchin, at
the enquiry into the overthrow
of Bligh as Governor-General
of New South Wales, 1811

23

The floods that had devastated the colony first in 1805 and then
again this year had scarred the settlers' minds, as well as their
land, decided Major George Johnston, gazing from the window
of John Macarthur's office out on to the Sydney streets. It was
very squalid, he thought. Squalid and disgusting.

Groups of ragged, broken men huddled exhausted on the
nearby corners, some of the braver actually waiting at the gate,
numbed either by rum or despair but drawn to Macarthur
because he was the richest man in the province and the only
person to whom they could come for help.

And Macarthur would help them, Major Johnston knew. For
a price. Macarthur owned these men out there in the dust, the
soldier realised, just as he owned the wives squatting in their
separate, complaining circles and the children, some of them
stark naked, playing their dispirited games.

Upon every one of them, against their property or their farm
implements or their stock or in some cases even the tattered
clothing they wore, he held promissory notes.

It was said, recalled Major Johnston, that there was nobody in
the whole of New South Wales who did not owe John Macarthur
something.

'So it's *Bounty* Bligh.'

Johnston turned back into the room as Macarthur spoke,
examining the haughty-faced, saturnine man.

'According to the reports,' he agreed.

The other men in the room shuffled, waiting for Macarthur's
lead. John and Gregory Blaxland were in several businesses with
Macarthur and looked constantly to him for guidance. Simeon
Lord actually admired the man, Johnston decided. And owed
him money, too.

'Appointed particularly because he can impose discipline,' enlarged Lord, knowing the remark would be regarded as a joke. Everyone laughed, dutifully.

'Well, the home government has failed with everyone else, so perhaps it's not surprising they should turn to a serving officer,' mocked Macarthur.

It was no secret, Johnston knew, that Governor King had been broken by Macarthur, like Governor Hunter before him. Macarthur was very proud of it, he guessed.

Johnston turned at a shout outside the window. One of those disgusting bucket parties was collapsing into the vicious fighting that usually broke out when the alcohol got to them. There had been five men hunched around the gallon bucket brim-full with rum, each initially taking orderly turns to drink from the ladle. Now one had keeled over, insensible, puddling the liquor all around him, and immediately an argument had arisen between the men on either side, each claiming they were due the unconscious man's share. What had been bartered for that bucket of rum? wondered Johnston. Whole acres were sometimes exchanged; in some cases, even entire farms. They were like animals, drink-besotted animals. Was it surprising, he wondered, when the majority had been criminals regarded so low they had been transported by a country anxious to get them as far away from society as possible?

'According to what I hear from the captains arriving from London, the government is concerned about events here,' said Gregory Blaxland, bringing the soldier back into the room again.

'Bah!' dismissed Macarthur, contemptuously. 'Wars with the French ... wars in Portugal ... a King whose sanity is in doubt ... what real interest can England have in us, 12,000 miles away?'

'According to Governor King, quite a lot,' suggested Johnston. He had dined with King the previous evening. It had been a carefully planned meal, Johnston recognised. The Governor who had conceded a little of his authority every month during his tenure of office now chose to make threats through intermediaries, rather than confront Macarthur directly. Obediently, Johnston had passed on the details that morning, interested to see how Macarthur would react to the impending challenge. The contempt had been predictable, the soldier decided.

'King is a weakling,' dismissed Macarthur. 'I'll wager he's no idea what the views of the government are.'

'London might regard us as being tainted by what happened in the Americas,' offered Lord, smiling hopefully. The man rarely expressed a view that wasn't guaranteed acceptance, thought Johnston.

Macarthur stood abruptly, pouring them drinks. The rum was much better than the filth that those poor unfortunates were soaking themselves in outside, decided Johnston, sipping appreciatively. But then it was natural Macarthur should have the best. Not a ship unloaded in Sydney harbour without his permission and not an article was sold without his being offered first choice.

'It's no more than a token gesture,' insisted Macarthur. 'Like it's always been. They've got too many troubles elsewhere in the world to worry about what's happening out here. We've no cause for concern.'

He hesitated at the doubt on the faces of the other men in the room with him.

'What's this!' he demanded, in mock belligerence. 'Lacking faith!'

He turned to Johnston.

'Is there a man in the regiment who won't be behind me, their old colleague?'

Macarthur had arrived in Sydney sixteen years before with the rank of captain in the New South Wales Corps, having bought the commission in England. Even though he had retired, he still affected fondness for the army life. It was a false attitude, Johnston knew.

'No,' guaranteed the soldier. 'The regiment are behind you.'

And with good reason, he added, mentally. Most were in debt to him. And looked to him as the supplier of rum for their grog-shops and convict-whored bawdy-houses to which they devoted more time than they did to their soldiering.

'And the traders?' demanded Macarthur, of Lord.

'Aye,' agreed the fine-featured sycophant. 'The merchants are all with you.'

For the same reason as the soldiers, thought Johnston. With this domain, Macarthur had more power than King George himself over all England.

Macarthur spread his hands expansively.

'So where's the danger?' he asked.

No one spoke and Macarthur stood there, smiling.

'I'm surprised at your weak hearts,' he said, going back to his desk.

They waited, expectantly, but Macarthur didn't speak immediately, allowing the silence to build up. The man enjoyed superiority very much, decided Johnston.

'I've determined not to be bested by *Bounty* Bligh,' assured Macarthur. 'And I've taken steps to see it doesn't happen.'

'What?' blurted Lord, who enjoyed gossip.

'Never you mind, Mr Lord, never you mind,' refused Macarthur. 'Just remain assured that things are afoot to thwart any quarterdeck tyranny in this colony.'

Three miles away James Hoare, three times convicted murderer, a sullen giant of a man, stood patiently while the guards broke away the bolts holding in place the metal punishment collar he had worn for the past three months. His neck and shoulders were calloused and there was an open sore on his collar-bone.

'There's no escape from here,' said the guard, emboldened because two others were standing with their guns at the ready. 'Three times you've tried and three times you've been caught and brought back to the collar. You're doomed, Jim lad. You'll see your days out and die here.'

Hoare walked back to the chain gang, without replying.

For almost two hours Edward Christian had been rigid at his desk, arms hard along the edge of his chair and his fingers white against the ends, as if he were physically holding on to reality.

Now, as the shock subsided, his tongue flicked out, wetting his lips, but he still did not speak, just nodding responses to what was being told him.

' ... and that's the whole account,' concluded Fletcher Christian. 'The whole of it.'

The mutineer looked apprehensively across the dimly lit desk at his brother. The lawyer was still very white, he could discern. But the shaking that had erupted at the realisation of who was facing him in the chambers of his London Inn of Court had gone.

When he spoke, Edward Christian's voice was as dry as the legal texts that lined the room from ceiling to floor and spilled over in places on to chairs and tables.

'... you committed murder ... murder as well as leading a mutiny?'

Fletcher nodded.

'Quintal killed my wife,' he defended. 'He took the last thing from me.'

The lawyer let out a deep sigh, the sound of a man who had been defeated after an arduous fight.

'So much,' he said, very softly. 'I'd achieved so much.'

The sailor frowned, wondering at the remark.

Edward stood at last, the smile forced but held on his face. He hurried around the desk and put his arms on Fletcher's shoulders, squeezing as if to reassure himself that the man really existed. Then he pulled him from the chair and hugged him, warmly. The man smelt, appallingly. And his face and neck were scabbed and dirty, the lawyer saw. Some of the sores were open and weeping.

'My God, Fletcher, it's good to see you ... to see you alive ... '

The mutineer tensed back from the affection, disconcerted by it, and stood away, relieved, when his brother released him.

'Some wine ... to celebrate at least ... and you look as if you could do with some refreshment. You look ... you look very tired ... '

Close to him for the first time, Edward stumbled to a clumsy halt at the complete awareness of how different Fletcher was from the man he had last seen ten years before. His hair had retained its blackness, but beneath the grime his face was burned to a teak colour and was patterned with suffering. The mouth, once so ready to laugh, was tight and unmoving and the eyes, which Edward remembered so calm and assured, flicked about, never focusing upon one spot for longer than a few seconds.

The man's demeanour was different, too. The Fletcher Christian whom he had known had been relaxed and confident. The person who stood before him now was never still. When he stood he went constantly from foot to foot, as if tensing himself for sudden flight, and when he sat, he did so with his legs stiff beneath the chair, ready to leap up at the first alarm. He recognised the sort of person who sat before him, the lawyer knew, suddenly. He saw them, every time he entered a court of law: the shifty, cunning habitual criminal.

The thought pricked the rising euphoria. He went quietly to the side table and poured the claret, needing the excuse to get away from the man.

His own brother horrified him, realised Edward.

'To your return,' he toasted.

Fletcher looked across the room, sad at the note in his brother's voice.

'That's little to celebrate, I feel,' he accepted.

'You're alive ... ' tried Edward.

' ... and as well might not be,' completed the other man.

The self-pity had been evident throughout the man's account of the mutiny and his subsequent existence on Pitcairn, recalled Edward. That was another trait in Fletcher's character of which he had been unaware. And there would be others, he guessed. He hardly knew the man at all, he thought.

Completely recovered, the lawyer went back around his desk and from habit drew paper and quill towards him, a counsel about to make notes of a case.

' ... so that's why you first thought of desertion, then led the mutiny ... ' he reflected, head down at his desk.

' ... I felt you, of all people, deserved the truth,' said Fletcher, conscious of the despairing criticism.

'It makes it possible to understand many things that were a mystery to me,' said the lawyer. Fletcher's reappearance presented him with an incredible dilemma, he recognised.

'There was no indication at the court martial?'

'None,' said Edward. 'There was evidence of everything but that.'

'What was it like, here ... the family, I mean?' stumbled the mutineer. Two hours and he had not enquired after his parents, he realised.

Edward sighed, suddenly aware that his brother had no way of knowing.

'Our parents are dead,' he said. 'There's little doubt the disgrace was the cause of mother's passing ... I'd managed to reverse the majority of public feeling by the time father died, but he still felt it deeply ... it killed him, too, I think.'

Fletcher nodded, showing no emotion. There was no feeling of any sort left, judged Edward, studying him: Fletcher was a hollowed-out man.

'So Bligh hasn't remained a hero?'

The fixation was absolute, thought Edward. His brother had dismissed instantly the death of parents he had adored, wanting only to know about Bligh. The damned man was an obsession with them all.

'Oh no,' said Edward. 'Bligh was exposed at the court martial and then again, in many different ways, by the efforts of myself and the Heywood family.'

'But he's still being accorded honours and high position,' said Fletcher.

For the first time his voice had changed from a level monotone, Edward realised, thinking of his earlier impression. His brother still possessed one feeling, he thought. He could still hate.

'But there's good point to that,' said Edward, urgently. 'We've both brought pressure, the Heywoods and myself, to get Bligh confirmed as Governor-General of New South Wales.'

'*Confirmed?*' echoed Fletcher, outraged. 'Into his most prestigious promotion yet! Why, for God's sake?'

'Because we know the man,' lectured Edward. 'He's bound to be defeated by events there. Neither he nor Sir Joseph Banks realise how the situation has been manoeuvred ... '

Fletcher moved around the room, fingering and then replacing ornaments and books.

'Are you sure?' he queried, at last.

'Sydney is a hell's kitchen,' said Edward, accepting again his brother would know little of the penal colony. 'It's defeated two Governor-Generals already who were better men than Bligh. There's no way he can succeed.'

'You appear to know a great deal about it,' prompted Fletcher.

'I've made a point of learning,' said Edward. 'One man, John Macarthur, virtually rules the colony. There's no one richer ... he's even got his own ships and companies, here, in England ... '

He paused.

' ... and I am the legal representative in London of these companies.'

Fletcher stopped his aimless wandering, staring fixedly at his brother.

'Why?' demanded the mutineer. 'Why have you done all this?

I'm consumed by the man, but for good reason. I cannot understand the degree of your feeling.'

The lawyer hesitated at the question, considering it for the first time. It was perhaps hard to understand, he accepted. But he'd been conducting the campaign for so many years now that the attitude seemed quite natural.

'He killed our parents,' Edward tried to explain. 'When he returned from that incredible voyage to Timor there wasn't a person of influence or position he didn't seek out, to sully the Christian name. Our family was ostracised and spat upon for years ... he even co-operated in the creation of a theatrical entertainment, in which you were represented a coward and a murderer and laughed at throughout London ... for years it was difficult for me to get any lucrative briefs.'

' ... *I'll damn your name and you with it in every part of the civilised world ...* '

Bligh's threat aboard the *Bounty* came back to him with the clarity of words spoken only minutes before. The man had kept his vow, Fletcher thought.

' ... I *am* a coward. And a murderer,' reminded Fletcher.

Edward shrugged, uncomfortably. Legally there was only one course open to him, he knew.

'Is that what you meant, about having achieved so much?'

The lawyer nodded.

'No matter what mitigation there can be ... and there is an overwhelming amount, I'll concede ... you're still a man who has broken the law,' said Edward. 'There can be no doubt that you led a mutiny. And by your own admission, you killed.'

'I've made a mistake,' apologised Fletcher, a cringing tone in his voice. ' ... I'm very good at making mistakes ... I've embarrassed you, by coming ... '

He had already spoken for almost two hours without pause, purging himself by confession, thought Edward. And still he wanted to talk.

' ... but I've wanted to come, for so long. I've been in London almost a year, labouring in the docks. I've watched you so often, from the alley opposite ... I know your carriage and your work habits ... especially your work habits. That's how I knew what time to call tonight, after your clerk had gone ... '

There was something else about his brother, decided Edward.

It wasn't just the attitude of the criminal. The man looked ill. He was very thin, the lawyer saw. And the clothes he wore were stiff with filth. It was little wonder he could detect the odour from where he sat, several feet away.

'Where do you live, Fletcher?' intruded the lawyer.

The mutineer looked up, amused by the question.

'Live?' he queried. He smiled, openly, his teeth green and discoloured. 'Address, you mean? People like me don't have addresses, Edward. We doss where there's shelter ... in a warehouse, if we are lucky. Among bales, on the wharf, more often than not, among the rats. Or in the hold of a ship we might be unloading ... '

The man's eyes narrowed and he waved a bony hand, cautiously. Cunning permeated his entire body, thought Edward.

' ... got to be careful of press gangs, though. People always disappearing, without a word ... '

Edward waited, knowing his brother had not finished.

' ... don't want to go to sea again, not for a while yet. Took me a long time to get home from South America, after I reached Montevideo on the *Topaz*. Always suspected that Captain Folger guessed who I was, but he never openly challenged me. I was a useful pair of hands ... '

'Whom *did* you say you were?'

'Quintal,' replied Fletcher, sniggering. 'Certain justice in that, escaping under the name of the man I'd killed!'

Edward managed to control the shiver of disgust. It genuinely amused his brother, he realised.

'Knew that the officers would have been told of the fight ... staged it so they'd find the body they imagined to be mine while they were there. But I knew the scum on Pitcairn better than they knew themselves. I calculated they wouldn't have given a true account of the reason and I was right. They hadn't said a thing to Folger about the rape and killing of Isabella ... just called it a dispute between the two of us for the leadership of the community. I told Folger that although I'd succeeded, I'd been frightened they wouldn't recognise me as the new leader ... never believed it, though. Sure he didn't. Useful hand, though. No point in bothering with too many questions, was there?'

Edward shuddered again, not bothering to hide the reaction this time. What sort of life was it, he asked himself, where a man would be prepared to condone and ignore mutiny and murder just for an extra pair of hands on a sea voyage? Where men just lay where they worked, expecting all the while to be snatched in their sleep and kidnapped to the other side of the world? Fletcher had become a sewer animal, realised the lawyer, just like the furry things that ran over him when he slept in his concealed holes and the parasites which no doubt infested his clothes and body as he sat across the room, physically ill and mentally uncertain.

Fletcher put aside his reminiscence, struggling back to the present, his lips working as he searched for the words.

' ... don't turn me in,' he whined, head cocked to one side. 'Know you should, after what I've told you. But give me a chance, eh? Just one chance, that's all I want.'

How many times would he have pleaded like that, wondered the lawyer, with someone's hand on his neck and whatever he was stealing still clutched in his hand.

' ... just need a chance, that's all. Couple of sovereigns wouldn't go amiss, either ... '

'Stop it!' shouted Edward, angrily. 'Stop it!'

Throughout the years, he realised, he had retained in his mind the recollection of an always-laughing Fletcher, debonair in his officer's uniform, wagering in pennies that he would never repay that he'd become the youngest admiral in the King's navy, struggling from his seabag bolts of silk and ivory carvings from places their excited mother had never heard of.

And that, stupidly and impractically, was how he had expected him to reappear, if reappear he ever did.

Instead he was confronted by a snivelling, smelling guttersnipe, begging for a few coins that would doubtless be swilled away in the gin houses and taverns of Fleet Street within an hour of being given to him.

'I'm not going to turn you in,' announced Edward.

It was a criminal commitment, he recognised. By this action he no longer had the right to wear the silk of the bar and argue right and wrong before the King's judges.

But he had no alternative, he rationalised. Shame had killed his parents and jeopardised his own career. It had taken years to rebuild the family name. And establish himself in the legal profession. Within two years, he knew, he would be Chief Justice of Ely. The Lord Chancellor had personally promised him the position. To produce that shambling apology of a man squinting at him from across the table and reopen the *Bounty* affair would create one of the biggest sensations in British jurisprudence. And destroy everything he had so painstakingly achieved. And more. His brother's mind would not withstand the strain, Edward thought. Fletcher would be incarcerated in Bedlam, hopelessly insane, before the end of any trial. And he'd never again appear before the English bar.

'Not going to turn me in?'

It was the question of a man so used to misfortune that any apparent kindness was immediately suspected as a trick that would be the cause of even greater problems.

'No,' said Edward, shortly, his resolution strengthening.

'What then?'

'I'm going to make you well,' promised Edward. 'I'm going to clean you and clothe you and try to restore you as the sort of man you were ... the sort of man I once knew.'

Fletcher eyed him warily, still suspicious. Reminded of his destitution, he groped beneath his left arm, scratching.

'Could do with a bath,' he remembered. 'Haven't had one for ... '

He grimaced, then shrugged, abandoning the recollection.

Edward began to stand, anxious now that he had made the decision to begin immediately the rehabilitation of his brother.

'Another thing,' stopped Fletcher.

'What?'

'Help me destroy Bligh. I know where he lives. I've been there even, watched him parade with his daughters, bewigged and dressed in silk, like a popinjay ... '

The mutineer groped inside his grime-stiffened jacket and pulled out a blade, twine lashed around one end to form a handle.

' ... was going to kill him, with this. That's why I really came here, tonight. Knew my identity would come out, if they caught me. Came here to say sorry, in advance, for any trouble I'd cause you ... '

The lawyer took the knife from the other man, holding it between the tip of his thumb and forefinger, as if it were contaminated. It was very sharp, he saw, honed for a special purpose.

He put it carefully in the drawer of his desk and locked it.

'We'll destroy Bligh,' he vowed. 'But not with a knife.'

And he would, decided Edward. What had happened to his brother had made him even more implacably determined to bring about the man's downfall than he had ever been. He already regarded his association with Macarthur as dangerous. Now he would have to become even more closely linked. But it was necessary for the purpose. Very necessary.

Edward snuffed out the candles and forced himself into contact with the vermin-ridden man, leading him down the narrow passageway and then out into Chancery Lane.

'A proper bed, Edward?' demanded Fletcher. 'Will it be a proper bed?'

The lawyer frowned in the darkness at the child-like question. 'Of course,' he said.

'I'm so tired,' muttered Fletcher, keeping very close, as if he feared being parted from his brother. 'So very tired.'

24

Bligh stood subdued at the rail of the *Porpoise*, gazing down at Sydney and the land beyond. He'd expected a shanty town. But despite the warnings from Sir Joseph at their first and then subsequent meetings, he'd not been prepared for what he saw.

There had been attempts to start a city, he recognised. But completion walls had sometimes not been added. Roofs had even been left off. Makeshift canvas fluttered and flapped everywhere from huddled lean-tos and tents. People and animals moved along dirt streets, scuffing dust clouds as they moved. In winter, Bligh knew, it would become a swamp. He smiled at the thought. Very apt, he decided. A human and natural swamp. And he had to drain it.

Although little more than ten in the morning, there was already ample evidence of the trade he had to eradicate. Shouts and yells echoed from a dozen drinking sheds along the wharf. He could see at least three men already lying senseless in their own vomit and excreta and fifteen minutes before he had watched without amusement the bizarre pantomime of two men, insanely drunk, lashing wildly and ineffectually at each other in a fight in which they had made little contact and from which they'd finally collapsed from exhaustion, not injuries.

And the whores were already out, plying for trade. One was even displaying herself, bare-breasted and skirts above her waist, in a window. Filth, disgusting degrading filth, he thought. Just like Tahiti, when the *Bounty* had arrived. He hadn't been able to do anything about it then. But he could here. He'd stamp out the sexuality, closing the brothels and driving the whores off the streets, into decent, God-fearing occupations. Clean it up, he'd promised the King and Sir Joseph. And he would. By God he would.

He turned at the movement at his side and nodded to Makins, the master. The man had approached for a reason, he guessed.

'Not a pleasant sight,' offered the officer.

'But one that will improve, sir,' assured Bligh, confidently. 'A year from now and you won't recognise Botany Bay.'

He was very sure of his ability, thought Makins. Where, he wondered, was the man's authority going to come from? It would be very different from a ship at sea.

'What about the captain, sir?' enquired Makins.

Bligh smiled. So it hadn't been a casual approach.

'Under arrest, as I ordered.'

'Sir,' tried Makins. 'His wife and family are very distressed. It'll mean disaster for them ... '

'Are you challenging me?' demanded Bligh, imperiously.

'No, sir,' collapsed Makins.

'Captain Short should have realised the consequences when he ignored my authority as superior officer on this convoy.'

And fired the shots across the *Porpoise*'s bows, when he'd made a necessary course correction, remembered Bligh. It was blatant, arrogant audacity. So Joseph Short would suffer for his insubordination. He didn't give a damn if the man had a land grant and had brought his entire family to Australia to settle. He'd go back in chains, with the returning Governor, to face the court martial he deserved.

From the rail he saw a larger dust cloud approaching and smiled at the approach of the carriages that were to take him from the ship to be received by the incumbent Governor. What a pity, he thought, that Elizabeth could not have been here. She so much liked pomp and ceremony.

Bligh stumped from the vessel, anxious to perform his first function as Governor-elect. Almost immediately his smile faded. They were rabble, just as Sir Joseph had warned, he decided, parading along the guard of honour formed by the New South Wales regiment. Twice he thought he detected men smirking at him in open contempt and nearly all stood just slightly away from the rigidness of attention. It was an attitude that could not have been questioned but which a sharp-eyed commander could recognise. And he was a sharp-eyed commander, Bligh told himself. And this bunch of impudent buggers would discover it, before long.

The reception in the streets surprised him, partly removing the irritation at the slovenly guard of honour. People were actually two deep in the centre of town and some had gone to the trouble of erecting bunting and giving their children flags to wave. That was important, decided Bligh. It showed the ordinary townsfolk were loyal and friendly. He'd need such support when he confronted the lawlessness he had come to put down.

A worry flickered through his mind. His authority was that rag-taggle regiment that had greeted him on the quayside. He might have misconstrued their demeanour, he accepted, but his initial impression had been that they regarded him as a figure of amusement, not a commander-in-chief whose orders they should unquestioningly obey.

He'd have to remain aware of that, he decided, as the landau swept in through the gates of the Governor's residence and began to circumvent the convict-tended lawns. Not as large as he had expected: quite small, in fact. But imposing, nevertheless. He was a Governor-General, he mused contentedly, an important, powerful man for whom people waved flags and stood at kerbsides, like they did at home for the King. And he would live in a house which in London would have befitted a lord. Well, a rich man, at least.

Governor King was on the steps to meet him, with his wife and the servants in the background. Where were the aides? wondered Bligh, the subsiding anger pricking up again. King's greeting was cordial, almost too effusive, gathering him into the study against any protest while his wife supervised the unloading of the luggage in the follow-up carriages.

'Welcome, sir,' said King, breathlessly. 'At last, welcome.'

Bligh stood in the centre of the room, frowning. It should have been a proper ceremony, he knew, a reception with all the civic heads in attendance and with a dinner to follow. He even had a speech prepared.

'Why the hurry, sir?' queried Bligh.

King held his head to one side, curiously.

'You snatch me off the steps like a man afraid of immediate attack,' enlarged Bligh.

'Glad to see you, sir,' replied King, badly. 'Native hospitality.'

'Then where is everybody else?' demanded Bligh.

He stood, studying the outgoing Governor. King was a pale,

faded man, like a garment washed too often and reduced from the colour it had once been. He had quick, nervous movements and the inability to meet directly the gaze of another man. Weakling, judged Bligh. Little wonder the lawlessness had proliferated.

'Everybody else?' echoed the Governor, inanely.

'I've remained on board that damned ship for three days in harbour,' reminded Bligh. 'I did so to enable the proper recognition of my arrival. God's teeth, sir! I even wrote you explicit letters of my intention, telling you I wanted every person of importance here today, to hear what I had to say.'

King shuffled, uncomfortably, gesturing towards the waiting liquor tray. Irritably Bligh shook his head, refusing the man his momentary escape.

'It was your letters that decided me against such a gathering,' said King, uneasily.

'But it was a specific request,' asserted Bligh.

'Made without proper awareness of the situation that existed,' said the worn-out man. 'You're not entering an affair to issue direct challenges.'

Bligh glared at the official, balefully. How the hell was he, a man who had failed so miserably in the duty entrusted to him, equipped to question the actions of a man ordered to clear up the mess? he wondered.

'You knowingly ignored my request?' demanded Bligh. It seemed pompous, he recognised. But commanding men were often pompous and that was what he intended to be, commanding. The sooner everybody in the colony realised that, the sooner order would be restored.

'Yes,' agreed King. 'I knowingly ignored your request because even though I think you are doomed to failure, I wish you success. And I know full well that if you disclosed your intentions to people who regard themselves as the civic leaders of this sewer, then you couldn't stand a chance in hell.'

Why was the other man regarding him so sadly? wondered Bligh. Immediately he corrected the impression. It wasn't sadness, he decided. It was the resignation of weakness. And if he had so abandoned pride, then the damned man should cast aside also the patronising attitude with which he had spoken for the past fifteen minutes.

King went to the drinks, pouring himself a full goblet while

Bligh watched, critically. Told to stop the rum trade and the man soaked himself in the liquor, thought Bligh.

'I wish you to succeed, Governor Bligh,' repeated the outgoing official, sincerely. 'I hope you have the success that has been denied me and the Governor-Generals of this confounded colony before me. But believe me, sir, you will fail more disastrously than any of us if you adopt the manner of a fairground pugilist, throwing the gauntlet to all comers.'

'I'm a sea captain,' rejected Bligh. 'My life is governed by carefully ordered regulations and those that transgress get punished. Soft hand a criminal, sir, and he'll spit in your face.'

'To control this colony, Governor Bligh, you need a militia. And you haven't got one. In the New South Wales Corps, you've got a collection of rum-runners, whore-keepers and price-fixers. What chance do you *really* think you have, when the men you have to use to enforce your orders are the very ones profiting most by the illegality of this place?' returned King.

Just like the *Bounty*. The thought came suddenly, surprising him. If he'd had marines aboard the vessel, then he could have maintained order. Once again the establishment had dispatched him on a mission and denied him the means properly to carry it out. Sir Joseph and the government had known the conditions, for God's sake. Why hadn't they provided him with what was necessary to put down this insurrection?

He altered his stance, controlling the belligerency. King had acted quite properly, he decided. Had he delivered the speech he could still detect in his breeches pocket, he could have made a fool of himself. And he couldn't do that, he recalled. There wouldn't be another chance after this. Sir Joseph had made that clear enough.

'I'll take that drink, sir,' he accepted, wanting to rebuild bridges.

He sipped the rum, grimacing at its harshness.

'And it seems, Governor King, that I owe you an apology. And thanks. I did not intend to be rude to you … unfortunately I am a naturally impatient man.'

The Governor nodded, looking at the rotund figure moving about the room before him. So this was the legendary *Bounty* Bligh, he thought. After so many setbacks, he would not have expected the man to have been so arrogant.

'To defeat them,' he advised, recognising the change in Bligh's attitude, 'you will have to bend with the wind until you discover their weaknesses. Men like John Macarthur have more power in this colony than King George himself.'

Bligh looked up sharply. That was treason, he thought. Governor King was either a very honest man, or very stupid.

'I have been warned,' said Bligh. 'Particularly of Macarthur. My very good friend Sir Joseph Banks, a man of great influence in England, has been deeply distressed by the rudeness shown to him by Macarthur over the matter of sheep importation into this colony.'

King refilled his glass, looking curiously as he did so at the newcomer. Bligh intended to settle his patron's grievance, as well as reforming practices carefully built up for a decade, he realised, uneasily.

There had for several months been rumours circulating in the colony about the new Governor, he recalled. They had appeared so informed yet at the same time so malicious that King had even considered them part of a campaign against the new man; some had even gone so far as to suggest they were the work of families damned by Bligh after the mutiny. He could find little exaggeration in what he'd heard, reflected the Governor.

'You're just one man against a well-ordered, well-organised society of corruption,' cautioned King. 'You'll only succeed by cunning.'

'Why haven't you adopted your own advice?' asked Bligh.

King smiled at the rudeness. A Governor's sash would sit uncomfortably about the shoulders of this irritable man of the quarter-deck, he thought.

'Because I arrived here with preconceived ideas,' rebutted King. 'And had no one to advise me against a course in which I faced unavoidable defeat.'

An honest man, thought Bligh. Weak and ineffectual. But honest.

'What *would* your guidance be?' he asked. He had meant the question to have the proper humility, but it had sounded condescending, he realised. So what? The man was an admitted failure and people who accepted defeat deserved contempt, thought Bligh. No matter what disaster had befallen him, he had never capitulated, recalled Bligh, warmly. Most men, ostracised

like he had been in London, would have been beaten; closed up
their London houses, even, and avoided the humiliation. Not
William Bligh. Elizabeth had been in tears, sometimes, almost
dragged from the house to appear at the theatre and the few
supper parties to which they were still admitted, more often as
objects of sniggering amusement than desired guests. But he'd
seen them all away. Now he was Governor-General of a British
colony and Elizabeth was on every guest list again, according to
the letters he'd received when they'd docked at Cape Town on
the outward voyage.

'Don't see them all at the same time,' guided King. 'They're a
close-knit, suspicious group of men. Receive them separately and
play a cautious game, hinting that the others have been indiscreet.'

Tea-party diplomacy, dismissed Bligh, like those scented
courtiers he'd seen around the Prince Regent, feigning insult and
flicking each other with their pastel-shaded gloves for imagined
revenge. The men he'd watched on the dockside that morning,
soaked in their own piss, were scum and he knew how to deal
with scum. And it wasn't done to the background music of the
harpsichord.

'I'm obliged for your suggestion,' he said, sharply, bored with
the conversation.

King looked at the man, caught by the tone in his voice. A
fool, he thought. A pig-headed fool. It was little wonder that
men found such difficulty in serving under him. But he'd tried,
the Governor contented himself. And it was time to move on to
other things.

'There is something else that would help you in your dealings
with these people,' he coaxed.

Bligh waited.

'You will be treated with more respect if you are a landowner
here. Accordingly I've prepared the conveyancing of some
property in your name. It's free, of course. As Governors we are
entrusted with such authority, when the occasion is deemed
necessary.'

Bligh frowned.

King went to his desk, smiling at the sea captain in the manner
of one man taking another into his confidence.

'Read your letters of appointment,' he advised. He offered his,
indicating the paragraph. Bligh scanned it, quickly. The authority

undoubtedly existed, he recognised. Australia was a developing country, he thought, immediately. To own land here would be to guarantee his family's future. He'd wanted for a long time to be a landowner, like Sir Joseph and all the other men of importance with whom he came into constant contact.

'Again, I'm obliged sir,' he said, accepting the papers that King offered him.

'There's provision for 240 acres of land for a private residence at Petersham Hill, on the Sydney to Parramatta road, adjoining Grose Farm,' listed the Governor. 'All that remains is for you to name it.'

It would have to be something fitting, decided Bligh, fingering the document. He'd served with undoubted distinction at Camperdown, he recalled.

'Camperdown,' he instructed, watching King complete the document with the name.

'And,' continued the outgoing official, 'I've allocated you 105 acres of land on the north side of the river at Parramatta ... '

He looked up, expectantly.

'Mount Betham,' decided Bligh, instantly. It would carry Elizabeth's maiden name and be bequeathed to her in his will, should he predecease her, he determined.

' ... and finally, 1,000 acres on the western side of the Hawkesbury road, near Rouse Hill.'

Another naval engagement would be proper, reflected Bligh. Nelson had personally praised him after Copenhagen. So that would be it.

He was a landowner, he thought happily, as King completed the third document. Just like his ancestors had been, in Cornwall. This was going to be a happy appointment, he decided.

King was proffering another book, which Bligh recognised as a record of previous Governors.

'It has become a custom,' continued King, gesturing as if it were one to which he was indifferent, 'for incoming Governors to initiate their land privilege by awarding a tract to the man they succeed.'

'Of course,' accepted Bligh, leafing through the book. Governors lived very well, he saw. Very well indeed. Sir Joseph had estimated he would be able to save at least £1,000 of his salary each year. There would now be a welcome addition to his income from the lands officially in his name. Never again, he thought, would he have to worry about money. It was a comfortable feeling. He would begin his letter to Betsy that night telling her of their unexpected good fortune.

'No doubt you've selected an area,' he anticipated. Perhaps King's hurry was that he was to sail for England so shortly, thought Bligh.

The Governor nodded. 'In the district of Evans,' he listed. 'I have other land already, of course. So I thought it would be a pleasant farewell present if it were in my wife's name.'

His first function as Governor, realised Bligh, affixing his signature to the document. He remained hunched over the paper, reading his own name. 'William Bligh – Governor.' It looked good, he thought, proudly. And the seal was heavy and impressive. An important man now, he realised. It was he, William Bligh, who ruled this colony, not a shambling collection of convict-soldiers and a few men who had been allowed to get ideas above their station because of the lack of previous authority. Sir Joseph was going to be proud of him. And perhaps the King, as well.

The reflection reminded him.

'When you return to England,' he said, firmly, 'I want you to take with you, under arrest, Captain Short.'

'Captain Short?' queried the Governor.

'The convoy captain,' enlarged Bligh. 'Damned man refused to accept my superior authority on the outward voyage ... actually fired warning shots across my bows and stern when I countermanded a ridiculous course he had set and changed direction. I've prepared the accusation against him. He's to be court-martialled.'

How easy, wondered King, would it have been for Bligh to have diplomatically handled the irritating difference in rank? He'd remembered the name as Bligh had been speaking.

'But doesn't he have his family with him ... an intention of settling here?'

'Don't give a damn about that,' rejected Bligh. 'I'll not have my authority flouted. It'll set an example to everyone here. I don't have time to waste on niceties. I want everyone to know the sort of man William Bligh is to be, from the outset ... '

It was a confounded pity about that speech which he would

never deliver, he decided, touching its bulk bulging his uniform. He'd seen it almost as an official proclamation, knowing how fully it would have been published in the *Sydney Gazette*. Couldn't be helped, he decided, briskly. The Short affair could be utilised, though. He'd use his newly discovered influence to ensure his decision was fully reported. It was good, to have such power. He carried more sway now than a captain at sea and he'd always regarded his authority there as absolute.

Why was King regarding him so dourly? he wondered.

The man hadn't understood a thing he'd attempted to convey, the outgoing Governor decided. Bligh still thought the situation in New South Wales could be stamped out with the ease of someone treading on a bothersome cockroach. Poor man.

Five miles from the Governor's residence, James Hoare, the habitual escapee, scraped his fingers around the food bowl, collecting the last scraps. Pigs on the meanest farms lived better than this, he decided, belching.

He squinted towards the fading sun. Almost time for another try, he decided. He reached up, feeling the hard skin on his shoulders and then moving to the almost healed sore.

But he'd plan it better this time, guaranteeing there was a ship lifting within the hour of his escaping.

He wouldn't be caught and strapped inside that collar again, he determined. This time he'd get away and they'd never catch him.

Fletcher was recovering remarkably well, decided the lawyer. The voyage had helped, of course. All those weeks at sea *en route* from London and Fletcher a passenger for the first time in his life. He'd laughed about it, which was important. The English physicians under whom he'd placed the sick, bewildered man had said several times that laughter would indicate a decisive step in his recovery, even though the precise causes of his breakdown, like his name, had been kept from them. But there was still a long way to go, Edward recognised. He'd missed two guineas from his purse that morning and knew Fletcher had taken it, like all the other money that had disappeared. He'd observe the doctors' advice, he determined, like he had on the other occasions, and make no reference to it. They were convinced it would cease when the man completely regained his confidence and stopped regarding the affluent environment in which he now lived as something that might be snatched away at any moment, sending him back to the gutters of London Wall or Greenwich.

Edward moved with distaste through the crowded, smelling streets. Sydney was a filthy place, he thought. And he had made a mistake in coming. It was a constant recrimination, growing with every day they spent in Australia.

The very lawlessness of Botany Bay gave them almost guaranteed protection, but his meetings with Macarthur were dangerous. Bligh's strength was still unknown. If the man managed to create any sort of intelligence system, then the association would be quickly learned. And that would destroy what they were trying to achieve. And wreck, too, his promised promotion at the English Bar, so long hindered by the *Bounty* affair.

Edward paused at the door of the lodging house in which he and Fletcher were living. Did he deserve the honour any more? Hardly, he thought. Harbouring a mutineer and a murderer: unjustified, either legally or morally, decided the lawyer. No matter how proper the campaign against Bligh.

He sighed, rejecting the doubt. It was too late, he knew. He had committed himself to a course and had to maintain it now. He stared back into the teeming streets. Nowhere else but here would he stand a chance of success, he thought.

'Well?' demanded Fletcher, immediately Edward entered the room. The lawyer had decided Fletcher should not accompany him aboard the *Porpoise* in case Bligh had been there, supervising the departure of his prisoner. The man was making so much of the affair that personal involvement had been possible.

'A good meeting,' reported Edward. He sat on the bed and began carefully wiping the dirt from his boots.

'In the event, Bligh wasn't on board,' he added. 'And it cost me only a guinea to get to Short ... people will do anything, for a price, here ... '

He looked up at his brother.

' ... Bligh's ruined him,' said Edward. 'The man had sold everything in England, to make a new life here. Because of the publicity that Bligh has generated over the matter, there's no one who doesn't know of his predicament. So he's been robbed at every turn, trying to sell his possessions to pay for the passage home of his wife and family.'

'How did he receive your suggestion?' probed the mutineer.

'Like a blind man offered his sight again,' recalled the lawyer. 'I've given him letters to my clerk, with full briefing instructions. There's another, containing my authority to draw, under my clerk's control, upon my account whatever sum is necessary for the defence and I've written to the best court martial barrister in London, with the personal request he takes the instructions. We were at Cambridge together and I know John Harrison well. He'll do it.'

'You said there was more,' reminded Fletcher. He'd return the money he'd taken from his brother, he decided. It had been an instinctive action, but now he felt ashamed. There wasn't any danger, he tried to reassure himself. Edward wouldn't abandon him.

'I went to the conveyancing office,' explained Edward. 'Harrison will need to introduce into the court martial documentary evidence of the land holding that Short has here ... '

Fletcher frowned, unable to understand his brother's enthusiasm.

' ... it is not a particularly big register,' continued the lawyer. 'But it contains some interesting information about the transactions of the last few weeks. Within four days of arriving to take up his position as Governor, Bligh became a substantial land-holder.'

Fletcher jerked up, the carefully repaired control going. He twitched in his excitement, the familiar perspiration bubbling on his face.

'I knew the man was a thief,' he snatched, eagerly. 'He always was, manipulating the *Bounty*'s victualling for his own profit ... '

He tailed away at the rejection on his brother's face.

'There's nothing illegal in what Bligh has done,' cautioned Edward. 'Not according to the strictest interpretation of the law.'

Fletcher slumped back into his chair, immediately crushed.

'Then why do you regard it as so important?'

The old Fletcher Christian would have recognised the significance, realised Edward, sadly. His brother was still far from well.

'We don't need criminality,' he lectured, softly. 'The innuendo will be sufficient. Imagine how it will look, when it reaches London at the same time as the court martial that the first action of the man appointed to do away with corruption and favouritism was to invoke his position to such advantage.'

Fletcher nodded, uncertainly.

'It's more than we could have hoped,' insisted Edward. 'Far more.'

'So you're happy?' queried Fletcher, like a child seeking reassurance from a parent.

No, thought Edward, in immediate reply. I'm a disgrace to the profession of a lawyer, attempting to extract an illegal revenge far out of proportion to the harm caused to me and my family. So I'll never be happy.

'So far,' he lied. If Fletcher ever learned of his misgivings, Edward thought, he would collapse back into the gutter and never get out again.

'What next?' asked Fletcher.

'The decisive meeting with Macarthur,' said the lawyer.

In the Governor's residence, four miles away, William Bligh shook sand upon the third letter he had written that morning and sat watching the ink congeal. He looked towards the harbour at the sound of the departure gun and strained to see the *Porpoise* edging out into the bay. The Short episode had gone remarkably well, he reflected. No one in Sydney could misinterpret the determination that indicated.

He came back to the letters he had just written, considering their tone. It was right to command their attendance, rather than invite, he decided. John Macarthur was unquestionably the man who had to be brought most sharply to heel. Defeat Macarthur and the whole colony would abide by the law again. Which was why it was important that George Johnston had to be present to be shown the sort of authority he would have to uphold from now on.

And Richard Atkins would be allowed no doubt about what was expected from him as Advocate-General, responsible for the administration of justice.

The outgoing Governor had warned him about Atkins, like so much else, remembered Bligh. Atkins was a weak man, the Governor had said. Almost certainly tainted with corruption.

And in debt to Macarthur, like so many were. It couldn't be helped, dismissed Bligh. The man held the appointment and would have to do as he was told, like they all would.

It was interesting, remembered Bligh, that there was said to be ill-feeling between Macarthur and Atkins. About a debt, Governor King had told him, unsure of the details. It was something to capitalise upon, decided Bligh. If there were bad feeling, then it would mean the Advocate-General was likely to become his first ally.

The three most important people in the colony, mused Bligh, summoning a convict-servant to deliver the letters.

It was time for them to realise that the old ways had come to an end.

William Bligh was commander now. As always.

25

They were resentful, judged Bligh, examining the men grouped
before him in the study. But they'd presented themselves, as
instructed. Which meant they were uncertain. It was an apprehension upon which he would have to exert pressure. Diplomacy,
Sir Joseph had advised. He smiled, waiting for them all to be
served not rum but the best claret he'd brought with him from
England.

What he intended to do was brilliant, he decided. It would be
impossible to criticise.

'To a successful governorship,' toasted Johnston, the military
leader, dutifully.

'I'll drink to that, sir,' agreed Bligh. 'Determined as I am that
it shall be one.'

He noticed the stir that went through them. Keep them
nervous, that was the way.

'And it's because of that determination that I have invited you
three gentlemen here today,' picked up Bligh. He moved from
man to man.

'You, Mr Macarthur, because you are undoubtedly the biggest
landowner and businessman in the colony ... '

And villain, Bligh concluded, mentally. Macarthur was smiling
back, happy at the description.

'You, Major Johnston, because you command the New South
Wales regiment ... '

The soldier began to smile, but the expression died as Bligh
went on: 'A body of men hardly fit to be described as the King's
soldiers, more interested as they are in running the grog-shops
and bawdy-houses of this place ... '

Bligh intercepted the looks that passed between Johnston and

Macarthur: it was an expression of men agreeing a mutual opinion, he decided. They'd guessed him a bastard and they were right in their assessment. He had every intention of being the biggest bastard they'd ever encountered.

'And you, Mr Atkins,' he completed, 'because as Advocate-General, it will be your job to impose the law that I intend enforcing in this province.'

Atkins nodded, like an obedient pupil being addressed by his headmaster. Even without the ex-Governor's guidance, he would still have judged Atkins the weakest of the three, he decided, a man always ready to give way to the strongest wind.

Johnston was the enigma, decided Bligh. Undoubtedly at the moment prepared to involve himself as deeply in corruption as anyone and to ignore the involvement of his men, but Bligh wondered how he would respond to strong leadership.

About Macarthur he had no doubt. The landowner would fight him, he knew, watching as the other man played with his glass, head sunk as if in contemplation of the wine. He was uncommonly like Fletcher Christian. The impression came to Bligh suddenly and he jerked back to the man, re-examining him. The same upturned, aristocratic nose and bearing. That same slightly patronising attitude of a man born into the ruling class who recognises subservience from other people as a matter of right. The same good looks of which he was boastfully aware, with his immaculate silk coat and burnished hat.

'You each must recognise the degeneration into which this colony has sunk,' continued Bligh. 'In some ways, there are good reasons, composed as it is largely of convicted felons who have earned their freedom ... '

Each man was watching him warily, Bligh saw, like animals unsure whether they were being welcomed into a new home or lured in to be put down.

'But I'm going to lift it out again. I am going to make it a fit place for these men who've earned their freedom and for the honest settlers who are being starved into a serf-like existence by the practices that have arisen here.'

'Brave words, sir,' said Macarthur. What would Bligh's reaction have been, he wondered, knowing that he was to sup that night with Edward Christian?

A well-modulated voice. That was like Fletcher, too, thought Bligh. The man seemed very sure of himself.

'And honest ones,' said the Governor, discerning the sarcasm with which the landowner had spoken.

'I am a sailor,' continued Bligh. 'I'm used to a rough way of life and well equipped to conduct myself in it.'

'So we've heard,' persisted Macarthur.

Bligh's head came up, but he bit at the words. The man was trying to goad him, he recognised. But he wouldn't let it happen. This encounter was going to conclude like every one in the future, with him the piper who called every tune.

'From this day,' announced Bligh, 'the settlers in this colony need not shop with the traders who have imposed a barter system, with rum the currency, and deflated the price of wheat and maize and mutton to starvation level. I am going to settle this season a price for next year's crops. It'll be a fair price and against that they can purchase every supply they're likely to need from the King's warehouses here ... '

' ... that's an order that won't be liked among the traders,' warned Macarthur.

And you the biggest, with a fleet of ships to bring in supplies and maintain your monopoly, thought Bligh. Macarthur's arrogance had slipped, he decided, at his announcement.

'I don't give a damn for the feelings of men who've shown themselves unfit to be traders,' snapped Bligh, pulling up from his chair and thrusting around in front of his desk. 'It is also my intention to close down these stinking brothels and sweep the whores from the streets. Botany Bay is to become a proper place to live in again.'

He wedged against the desk, the threat completed, looking down at the three men. About the traders he was not particularly worried, he decided. Civilians could register their protest. He was far more concerned with the rum dealers and whore-keepers in the New South Wales regiment.

Only Atkins was nodding doubtful approval but then his attitude was predictable, the constant obeisance to the man in command.

Macarthur stood, carefully placing his glass on a side table. Now he's going to show me he's not impressed or frightened, recognised Bligh.

239

'Excellency,' began the man, politely. 'You've been here for such a short time ... hardly long enough to learn the geography of the town, let alone its customs ... '

'Long enough,' interrupted Bligh.

Macarthur talked on as if nothing had been said.

' ... I can well understand your keenness, your resolve to make your governorship an outstanding one ... '

He paused here, smiling directly at Bligh.

The most cutting thrust yet, accepted Bligh, determinedly holding his temper. No one would ever be able to accuse Macarthur of making reference to the disasters that had befallen him in his earlier career, but that was unquestionably the direction of the remark. Johnston was even smiling, in appreciation.

' ... I've been here years. I know the people ... their feelings,' picked up Macarthur. 'I am the leading merchant in this city and my reaction will be that of them all. They'll resist you, at every turn.'

'Are you defying me, sir?' demanded Bligh. His temper slid, just slightly, so that the challenge was louder than he had intended. It didn't matter, Bligh decided. The impudence dictated such a reaction.

'Defying you! Of course not, Your Excellency,' responded Macarthur, hands lifted in apparent horror. 'I'm just trying to express the view that you're going to encounter.'

He was sure enough of himself to mock openly, even at their first meeting, thought Bligh. The man was placed to foment the protests. All the merchants and traders who would be outraged by the edict were concentrated within the town and easily able to organise themselves. The settlers whom he was lifting from serfdom by his decision and who would therefore be his supporters were dispersed over hundreds of miles in the hinterland. He was glad he had arranged the horseback tour to begin the following day. Everywhere he stopped he would guarantee the exploited, cowed people their freedom.

Macarthur had been very quick to realise his strength, thought Bligh, warily.

'And you, sir,' demanded Bligh, sidestepping the confrontation and addressing Johnston. 'What are your feelings on the matter?'

Bligh was purposely manoeuvring him into a corner, knowing his greatest danger lay in a rebellious militia, Johnston realised.

He held away from looking at his companion. Macarthur had been too confident, he thought. Like he always was. Now, realised Johnston, he had to commit himself. And there was only one commitment he could make. To talk of defiance, indicating his involvement in the illegality of the colony, would be treason. To say anything, in fact, indicating the participation of himself or his men in the corruption would be grounds for his immediate arrest and court martial. But the men wouldn't like it, decided Johnston. They wouldn't like it at all. He'd warned Macarthur Bligh might be different from the other Governors: why hadn't the confounded man listened?

Bligh was studying the man, impatient for his reply. He might have been better advised, decided Bligh in rare personal criticism, had he thought more deeply about today's confrontation. Perhaps Johnston should have been seen separately, as Governor King had recommended. Johnston and his militia held the key: he wondered if the man realised it.

'Well, sir?' he bullied.

'The business community of the town will not like it,' said Johnston, at last, choosing an easy path.

'But if it becomes a law, as I can make it, then it will be the duty of yourself and your regiment to enforce it,' pressed the Governor.

The look that passed between Johnston and Macarthur was almost imperceptible. But there had been an exchange between them, Bligh knew.

'Of course, Your Excellency,' capitulated the soldier.

'And it will be your job to adjudicate, within the defined limits of the law, upon anyone who defies or attempts to avoid the new regulations,' said Bligh, moving to Atkins.

'Oh yes,' agreed the Advocate-General, hurriedly. 'Of course, sir. Of course.'

Macarthur and Johnston were looking at the third man in open contempt, thought Bligh.

'I shall promulgate the order in tomorrow's *Gazette*,' said Bligh, satisfied with his conduct of the meeting. 'Already hand-bills have been printed and are being circulated to all the settlers, informing them of the new system. And tomorrow I begin a tour, to meet and explain to them personally ... '

'You mean you've already made the Order ... that today's

meeting wasn't for advice and consultation?' blurted Macarthur.

In his surprise, Macarthur was unable to keep the incredulity from his voice. It was the first time for many years, Bligh realised, gratified, that anyone had had the courage to disregard the man so openly.

'Of course,' said Bligh, emphasising his arrogance, aware of the annoyance it would cause the other man. 'I need no counsel or permission to act as I have done. I asked you to attend here today as a matter of courtesy, to inform you ahead of the official announcement, nothing more. There is no way my decision will be reversed. By now half the settlers will have been told. The rest I shall acquaint personally.'

Macarthur was shaking his head, in refusal.

'I am afraid, sir,' he said, 'that you have created for yourself a turbulent situation.'

'My life has been a turbulent one,' responded Bligh. 'It's a condition I'm well used to.'

'I'm afraid this one, sir, might well be beyond your expectation.'

'What, sir!' challenged Bligh, immediately affronted. 'You dare question my wisdom!'

'No, Governor, I do not question you. I merely give you due warning that other Governors have tried to do as you are doing. And been unfortunate in their endeavour,' said Macarthur.

Bligh positioned himself purposely only feet from Macarthur. What transpired in his study today would be gossiped around Sydney within the hour, he knew. So every word was important.

'Let us understand the way of things, Mr Macarthur,' he said, his voice very even. 'For too long, affairs of this colony have been overlooked by the government of King George. But that is now over. The King wants a dutiful, obedient colony and by God, sir, I'm minded that he shall have one. The person who opposes me in my ambition will be the person who suffers.'

Macarthur stared back at him, unafraid.

'I fear, Your Excellency, that you are in for a stormy passage.'

'That concerns me little,' returned Bligh, suppressing his temper at another defiant reference to the *Bounty*. To show the other man his rejection of the sneer, he added: 'It's always others who are undone in battles with William Bligh, sir. For some it's a lesson hard learned.'

Johnston and Atkins were sitting stilled with embarrassment,

Bligh realised. It was right the colours had been broken out so early. The quicker the confrontation, the sooner his success. Bligh prolonged the silence, knowing they could not quit his presence without permission and determined to show them, by every action, his awareness of his power.

At last he conceded. 'I feel that we have said today all that need pass between us.'

'Aye, sir. That's true,' admitted Macarthur.

'I trust, sir, that I shall have your support, as the leading man of commerce in this colony?' Bligh pressured.

'Doubtless we shall see much of each other,' avoided Macarthur. 'I foresee our futures much intertwined.'

'Much intertwined,' agreed Bligh, happy at the feeling he was able to impart by echoing Macarthur's words.

Still he refused them permission to leave his presence.

'No doubt,' he said, 'there will be discussion among the towns-folk and the traders about the orders to be issued. I shall not take it amiss, gentlemen, if upon being questioned about it, you let them know from our meeting here today my determination about the matter.'

'We will let your attitude be known, rest assured,' guaranteed Macarthur, pointedly.

'Let us meet again, gentlemen,' said Bligh, finally releasing them. 'I look to you for support in my endeavours.'

Within minutes of their departure, William Gore, whom Bligh had appointed Provost Marshal upon his arrival, entered the room.

Bligh smiled at the man. He was, decided Bligh, the nearest he had to a confidant.

'Squally,' announced Bligh, cheerfully. 'They didn't like the pronouncement at all.'

'I knew they wouldn't,' said Gore.

'I have decided,' said Bligh, hands contentedly across his stomach, 'that I am going to like being a Governor. Like it very much indeed.'

'Do nothing?'

Macarthur halted, wine glass half to his mouth, staring across the dinner table at Edward Christian.

'Yes,' advised the lawyer. 'Do nothing, sir.'

243

The landowner looked from Edward to the other Englishman. They were uncommonly alike, thought Macarthur. Yet the lawyer had introduced the other man as his legal assistant. A man didn't obtain a complexion like that as a legal assistant locked inside an office, decided the merchant. It didn't matter: the lawyer seemed determined to help him defeat Bligh and that was the only consideration. He could surround himself with whatever men he wanted, providing they did not interfere with that object.

'But I can't ignore it,' Macarthur protested. 'I lead the merchants and the traders here. How can they exist, without custom?'

Edward looked down at his plate, toying with his food.

'It *is* a fact, Mr Macarthur,' he said, 'that there has been introduced into the colony a harsh system of monopoly.'

'Sound business protection,' defended Macarthur, defiantly. 'This is an unpredictable climate. Twice, in successive years, floods have washed away crops. If the men I represent didn't protect themselves during the good times, they'd go out of business during the bad.'

'A monopoly,' refused Edward. 'If this meeting is to be of use to either of us, let's not play with semantics, Mr Macarthur.'

'Why should I do nothing, in face of what Bligh has proposed?' hurried on Macarthur. The other man had a fine brain, he judged.

'Because Bligh has right on his side. And the law,' said the lawyer. 'Fight Bligh with his weaknesses, not his strengths.'

'And the man is his own weakness,' added Fletcher.

Macarthur looked at the second man. An educated voice, certainly. But he was no lawyer, Macarthur decided.

'I know Bligh well,' continued Fletcher. 'He's a man who will always overstep himself. To play the waiting game is good advice.'

Macarthur frowned at Fletcher Christian, curiously. No, he dismissed, after consideration. It couldn't be. Every official account had the man dead.

'But create a traders' association,' suggested Edward, concerned at the attention that the other man was paying his brother. 'Dissent will disappear like mist unless there is some forum where it can be expressed. But don't allow yourself to be chairman or president. Nothing you do must be construed as a direct challenge to the Governor.'

'Never directly challenge him,' counselled Fletcher Christian, distantly. 'Openly defied, the man becomes insane.'

Perfect, decided Hoare, from the protection of the deep shadows of the wharf. Three people, each unknown to the other in the grog-shop, had insisted the *Parramatta* was lifting on the morning tide. A Macarthur boat, to boot. Which would mean the legally prescribed search for escapees, if made at all, would be so brief as to be a joke. He waited patiently until well after midnight, when the dockside was deadened by either alcohol or sleep. He shinned nimbly up the after mooring rope and within minutes was safely concealed in the wood locker.

26

The King was furious, Sir Joseph Banks saw. His face was purple with emotion and he kept gasping to a halt, his exasperation robbing him of the words necessary to express himself. Everyone in the court was frightened of another mental collapse, Sir Joseph knew. And if it happened now, he would be blamed for it. He and Bligh.

'Outrageous,' the King managed at last. 'Disgraceful. What? What?'

'I will accept it was very unfortunate, sir,' apologised Sir Joseph. Had it not been for the King's anger, the habitual demand for a reply would have sounded amusing, thought Banks. No wonder the pamphleteers had seized upon the mannerism.

'You told me you'd instructed the damned man as unequivocably as possible that he was to be a diplomat.'

'I did so instruct him, sir,' insisted Bligh's patron. Both Lord Grenville and the Duke of Portland were moving apprehensively towards them, alarmed at the King's outburst.

'Then what, sir, is this?' demanded the King, hurling the papers screwed up in his hand across the chamber at the other man.

' ... a trivial quarrel over who's the superior officer,' persisted the monarch. 'And your protégé sees fit to incarcerate someone who dared question him upon a 12,000-mile voyage, with a destitute wife and six children, during the worst season of the year. It's little wonder the poor woman and one of the children died. Now the court martial not only finds no case to answer, but honourably acquits the wretched man. Is that your idea of the diplomat needed to solve the problems in New South Wales? Is it? What? What?'

'I agree, sir, it was a gross error of judgment,' conceded Sir Joseph, miserably.

'An error of judgment!' echoed the King. 'And what sort of judgment was shown, pray tell me, sir, when the man sat in the comfort of the Governor's mansion while Short was on his way to ruin and apportioned himself something approaching 1,500 acres of land. I thought Mr Bligh had been sent to Australia to suppress corruption, not actively participate in it!'

'It was not a corrupt action, sir,' defended Sir Joseph, emptily. There was no other subject of discussion in London, Sir Joseph knew. Even the cabinet and the Privy Council had officially debated it, after the pamphlets had begun to circulate and then the details of the land deals had been confirmed, quite openly, in a dispatch from Bligh himself.

'I know it's not criminal!' accepted the King, irritably. 'But is it *really* the action you expected from a man specifically sent, by me upon your recommendation, to curtail the sharp practices in others?'

'No, sir,' accepted Sir Joseph.

The King gestured, calling the Admiralty Lords nearer.

'I want the man Short well treated,' he ordered. 'I want lucrative employment found for him. And as the land grant was denied him by someone holding my warrant of appointment, then I'll have him compensated. See to it ... '

He waved them away, impatiently, coming back to Sir Joseph.

'And you, sir,' he threatened, 'see to it, as well. Write to the man in whom you place such trust. Write to him and advise him that he's coming dangerously close to incurring not only your wrath, but the displeasure of his sovereign. I'll not tolerate any more stupidity, d'you understand?'

'I'll tell him, sir,' undertook Sir Joseph, sincerely. 'I'll leave him in no doubt of our feelings.'

Damn Bligh, thought Sir Joseph, as his carriage moved away from St James's Palace. Couldn't the confounded man ever learn? He looked up, halted by a sudden thought. Had he been wrong about Bligh, for all these years? Had he misplaced his trust, when all the time he should have been listening to the critics, not dismissing the rumours as malicious gossip?

Edward Christian finished reading aloud the letters he had received that morning from the barrister who had defended Captain Short and then the longer, more detailed account of that and other developments from his clerk. The lawyer was hoarse from speaking and gratefully drank the tea that Fletcher poured for him.

The house into which they had moved was far more comfortable than their initial lodgings, decided the barrister, gazing upon the imposing view of the harbour. He sighed at a thought. Thank God his practice was so profitable now. And that he had been able to take such a leave of absence. His impetuous, emotional agreement to Fletcher's wish to see Bligh's downfall was proving damned expensive. Edward was still uncertain of Macarthur's discretion. Just one word, thought Edward in familiar fear, and he would be ruined.

He smiled across the room at his brother. What did the money count, or his career, for that matter, compared to the almost complete recovery he could now see in the other man?

Every trace of the hardship Fletcher had suffered had gone, he saw. Fletcher's face had filled again and he no longer held himself in the cramped, protective way of a man expecting to be kicked at any moment. And the other indications had vanished, too. Fletcher had actually returned the last amount of money he'd stolen, Edward recalled. For weeks now he'd left his purse lying carelessly around the rooms, testing the man. Always the carefully counted coins had remained intact.

'That was wise advice of yours,' praised Fletcher, reading again the message from Edward's clerk.

The lawyer nodded agreement.

'Every one of Macarthur's captains has spread discredit on Bligh's name in London,' he said.

'It was hardly necessary, was it?' demanded Fletcher.

'Necessary?'

'Our coming here,' expanded Fletcher. 'We've exacerbated and utilised every error that Bligh has made. But it's the man himself who's making the mistakes.'

'We've properly brought them to public attention,' reminded Edward. 'That wouldn't have happened if we had stayed in England.'

'I couldn't have killed him, you know,' confessed Fletcher, disjointedly.

'What?' queried Edward, confused.

'In your chambers, that first night,' recalled Fletcher. 'When I produced the knife and said I was going to kill Bligh. I had intended to ... wanted to, desperately. I'd actually gone to his house, before coming to you. It would have been so easy. At one point he was no more than ten feet away, quite alone and unguarded. But I couldn't do it.'

Yet the man *had* murdered, balanced Edward. He stood unmoving by the window, waiting.

When Fletcher looked up at him, his eyes were wet, the barrister saw.

'I'm frightened of him, Edward,' moaned the younger man, despairingly. 'After all these years and all the misery for which he's been responsible, I'm still terrified of him.'

An atmosphere crowded into the room, embarrassing both of them.

'I would have so much liked you to meet Isabella,' said Fletcher, suddenly. He was staring at the ground between his feet, lost in memories, Edward saw.

'She was so very beautiful,' he said, softly. 'So very good and so very lovely ... '

His shoulders began to shake. He would cry soon, Edward knew. Usually he managed to prevent the tears until the privacy of his own bedroom.

27

Bligh had listened with mounting excitement to the Provost Marshal and sat waiting now for the arrival of Atkins. It would provide an example, decided the Governor. He'd bring Macarthur down and show those doubters in London, who found it so easy to criticise from a safe distance of 12,000 miles. The King might be displeased, thought Bligh, recalling Sir Joseph's letter. But he wouldn't remain so once the corruption in the colony was smashed.

And it would be destroyed, by the move he could now make against Macarthur. It was exactly what he needed, an incident in which he would triumph. And he would triumph, he determined.

He picked up Sir Joseph's letter from his desk, idly rubbing his finger along the edge. Even Sir Joseph was turning against him, he decided, worriedly. That was very obvious from the tone of the letter. And the whispers had started against him again in London, he knew, turning to Betsy's correspondence that had arrived in the same vessel from England. But he'd show them. William Bligh wasn't beaten yet. Far from beaten.

Atkins flurried in, nervously jerking his head between the two men. The strength of the traders' opposition was worrying the Advocate-General, Bligh knew. Now the man regretted the endorsement he had so readily shown to Bligh's reforms, placing him on what he now thought to be the weaker side.

'We've got him,' declared Bligh, eagerly. 'We've got Macarthur.'

Atkins frowned, suspiciously. Bligh was too keen on an open clash, he felt.

'Remember the disappearance from the penal colony of Hoare, the murderer?' demanded Bligh.

Atkins nodded.

'He escaped on the *Parramatta*, a Macarthur boat,' revealed Bligh, triumphantly.

'You sure?' said Atkins, apprehensively.

'The master and the crew openly depose it,' said Gore, offering the documents. 'He's free, in Tahiti.'

'And Macarthur himself provided the declaration under the terms of the penal code, asserting his ship had been searched before sailing. So he's responsible for aiding the escape of a wanted man.'

'Technically,' admitted Atkins, uncomfortably. 'Nothing more than a technicality.'

'He's refused to provision the impounded vessel, forcing the crew to break the law by disembarking,' added Bligh. 'That's an offence that carries a jail sentence. Legally we can remove the man from any position of influence in the colony. We've won!'

Atkins nodded, uneasily. Bligh was definitely manoeuvring the confrontation, decided the Advocate-General. Manoeuvring it, without properly considering the implications. Bligh needed something to demonstrate his authority, Atkins agreed. But this wasn't it. The merchants hated him. And the regiment were as near rebellion as he had ever known because their rum and women trade had been taken from them. Bligh couldn't possibly win, even if Macarthur were removed.

'It's not sufficient,' he cautioned.

'Of course it is,' rejected Bligh. 'The law has been broken, by Macarthur. So he'll be brought to trial.'

'But he won't accept my jurisdiction,' warned Atkins. 'There's a civil dispute between us, over a trifling debt. It would give him grounds for refusing to accept me as his judge.'

'Rubbish,' swept aside Bligh, swollen with the conviction of his success.

Atkins was a coward, decided Bligh. A miserable coward, trying to evade his responsibilities. Governor King had mentioned some money transaction between the two men, he remembered, but his recollection was that it had been settled. Atkins was trying to resurrect an old score as an excuse to avoid involvement and ingratiate himself with the other faction. But it wouldn't work. He wasn't going to be denied the opportunity of deposing Macarthur and gaining unchallenged control of the colony.

'Arrest Macarthur,' Bligh ordered, addressing Gore. 'In the next few days, we'll see who's in command of this damned colony.'

We will, thought Atkins, worriedly. Why the hell was Bligh so pigheaded?

'It's a small amount,' offered Edward Christian, guardedly.

'But it's a debt,' insisted Macarthur. 'And I've got a letter against Richard Atkins's name, attesting that he owes the money.'

The lawyer stood up in the wealthy man's second-floor office, gazing out of the window overlooking the brawling dockside. Fletcher had been right, he thought. Bligh would have destroyed himself without any prompting from them. At best, they'd precipitated what was to happen. But it would have certainly occurred. For the remainder of his life, Edward knew, he would be ashamed of what he had done. And deserved to be.

'It's grounds for refusing to accept him as a judge,' agreed the lawyer.

'Will you defend me?' demanded Macarthur, unexpectedly. The Englishman would be a good advocate, he knew.

Edward shook his head, definitely.

'The brother of the man who mutinied against Bligh!' said Edward, needlessly. 'We want to defeat the man, not provide ammunition for him.'

'I know every other member of the court who will sit in judgment upon me,' said Macarthur, pointedly.

The lawyer turned, recognising the reason for the remark.

'That would be stupid,' he warned. 'Why bother, when you can't possibly face trial before Atkins anyway.'

'Because I always like to be sure,' smiled the merchant.

'You *can* be sure,' insisted Edward. 'At the moment, you can't be tried, not before Atkins. Continue the way you're thinking and you'll give Bligh the proper excuse to arraign you, not one he's had to go out of his way to manufacture out of technicalities.'

Macarthur shook his head, refusing the advice.

'You can counsel me about the law, Mr Christian,' he said. 'But you can't tell me about the ways of Botany Bay.'

'But it's so stupid!' repeated the lawyer, trying to retain something of his integrity.

'That's for me to decide,' rejected the merchant leader.

28

He needed Johnston's support, decided Bligh, pacing his study. His *declared* support. If the reports he was receiving were to be believed, the town was in a dangerous state following the arrest of Macarthur. And he had to believe them, he knew. The details agreed from too many different sources for it to be idle gossip. Macarthur would have inflamed it, of course. No doubt about that. The merchants would not have formed such a cohesive force without the man's leadership. And the regiment, aware the penalty for rebellion was death, wouldn't have been so openly defiant if there had not been someone co-ordinating and feeding their anger. He wouldn't have thought Macarthur clever enough to have orchestrated the opposition so well. It was almost as successful as that in London.

Bligh stopped at the window, staring out towards the town. They'd come along the main highway, he thought. Wide enough for ten men moving abreast. They'd be difficult to stop, a crowd that big. One or two men, perhaps. It was always easy to dissuade one man. But a crowd was more difficult. He paused at the thought. Fletcher Christian had been one man, he recalled. And they'd talked alone, in his cabin. He hadn't dissuaded Mr Christian. He shrugged aside the memory. Didn't apply, he rejected. The circumstances were completely different. How many supporters did he have? Gore was with him, he knew. And perhaps twenty soldiers, immediately assigned to the Governor's residence. But they wouldn't fight, he guessed. If they saw the regiment or even the townspeople approaching in force, they'd abandon their posts.

So Johnston was the key. As he'd always been. The man had supported him once, when he'd announced his reforms, remembered Bligh. But unwillingly, tempered the Governor. Now he saw the tilt of opinion, Johnston might be more difficult to persuade.

Atkins was still with him, he thought, suddenly. With increasing doubts, perhaps. But still loyal for the moment. If the man performed his function as Advocate-General properly today, then any crisis could be averted. If they could get Macarthur to jail, then the defiance would crumble. Just as the opposition to his reforms would collapse. He looked at his watch: too late to see Atkins now. He was due in court within the hour.

Bligh shivered, frightened for the first time. It was bad, he accepted. Very bad. Not his fault, though. Just like the *Bounty*, all over again. Sent away without any soldiers to enforce his orders. And they were proper orders, quite legal and justifiable. That's not how it would be seen in London, though. It was clear from what Sir Joseph had written that his enemies were working hard, turning opinion against him again. He looked at his watch for the second time. No way he could speak privately to Atkins before the hearing, he decided, definitely. Damn.

He rang the bell, urgently, and when the servant came summoned Gore. The Provost Marshal arrived in minutes, flushed and slightly dishevelled. Scared, judged Bligh, regarding the man. Everyone was scared except William Bligh. Not him. Never scared. Beat them yet.

'What do you hear?' demanded the Governor.

'It's not good, sir,' warned the soldier. 'The people are gathering at all the main places, holding protest meetings. The court building is almost surrounded.'

'And the regiment?'

'In their barracks.'

'Quiet?'

'For the moment,' reported Gore. 'But the townsfolk are there, too. There's much discussion among them.'

'I need Johnston,' announced Bligh. 'Send a trooper for him. Tell him I want him here immediately.'

Gore remained standing in the room.

'Sir?' he said, apprehensively.

'What is it?' queried Bligh, irritably. Why the hell was the man wasting time? Didn't he realise the urgency?

'There's no way we could oppose an uprising,' warned Gore.

'I've no more than a handful of men and their loyalty is in the gravest doubt.'

'I know that,' snapped Bligh, impatiently.

'Isn't there another way this matter could be resolved?' asked the Provost Marshal, knowing he was exceeding his position.

Bligh's face burst red and his eyes flared. Would no one accept his authority any more? Cowards. Why was he always surrounded by cowards and blackguards?

'Are you saying I should retreat, sir! Are you saying that William Bligh should turn away from a rightful, legal course, just because the weight of opinion is against him?'

'I was suggesting ... ' tried Gore, but Bligh talked him down.

'About your business, sir,' he hissed, twitching in fury. 'I'll hear no more of this turn-the-other-cheek nonsense. Macarthur has broken the law and shall be punished for it. I've instructed so and my word is law, as soon everyone here shall learn.'

Bligh stalked about the room after Gore had gone, forced into movement by his irritation.

Careful, he told himself. Lost control there. Stupid to have done that, to the only man remaining loyal. Apologise later. Mustn't lose control. Needed calm, wise thinking to resolve this. His last chance, he remembered. Sir Joseph had let him know that, during his appointment meeting in London. Mustn't fail them. Keep his temper and play a clever game. That was the way. Where the hell was Johnston?

It was a rigged court, thought the Advocate-General. The realisation came immediately Atkins entered the chamber, flustered and annoyed at having to force his way through the mêlée of people outside. It was jammed inside as well, the public seats abandoned, with people standing on and around them to witness the proceedings.

A soldier recognised him at last and made a desultory attempt to clear a way and it was then that the impression settled in his mind. He was to sit with six other officers. They were already there, he saw, grouped in a circle on the raised area at the far end of the room, laughing and gesturing among themselves, all the time slightly facing the dock in which Macarthur had already been arraigned.

Atkins bustled up, nervousness pulling at him.

'Who put the prisoner up before I arrived?' demanded the Advocate-General, pompously.

There was a snigger. Atkins was sure somebody had laughed. He looked around the officers, trying to detect it. Every face looked back at him, set and rigid.

'I did,' said the deputy chairman, Captain Anthony Fenn Kemp. 'It was far too hot below. And besides, he's not convicted yet. So why should he be treated as a felon?'

It was an open challenge to his authority, Atkins recognised immediately. And should be put down.

'You don't object, do you?' said Captain Kemp, looking to the other soldiers for approval.

'No,' said Atkins, wearily. 'No point in reversing it now. But don't take such decisions in the future. Always wait upon me.'

'I'll remember that,' promised the captain, smiling.

There *had* been a laugh, that time. Atkins was sure of it. He jerked along the bench, brow furrowed in distress. Blank-faced, all of them.

He turned back into the room. There were a lot of officers and soldiers from the regiment as well as civilians, he saw. He identified almost every merchant and trader in Sydney and there were others whom he didn't know.

In the line of people nearest the dock, Edward Christian leaned across to his brother.

'It's a farce,' anticipated the lawyer. 'Bligh's lost.'

'Sure?' demanded the mutineer.

'Watch. And listen,' advised the lawyer.

So Macarthur had ignored his advice and tampered with the court, thought Edward, staring up at the man positioned above him. And he'd known it was to happen. Nowadays shame was an almost constant feeling, thought the lawyer.

It was several moments before Atkins could bring order into the room and even when he began the proceedings it was over a groundswell of noise. It was a regularised procedure, the oath being administered to the officers by the Advocate-General who then, finally, took it himself.

Atkins had the Bible in his right hand when Macarthur shouted.

'I object to the Presidency of Richard Atkins,' he announced, standing. 'There is personal animosity between us and we are engaged in civil proceedings. Therefore a fair hearing is impossible.'

It was as if everyone had known in advance of the outburst. From the back of the room, where it was impossible to detect the culprits, cheering broke out.

'Continue with the oath,' Atkins instructed Kemp.

'I will not accept the jurisdiction of this court,' insisted Macarthur, loudly. 'I have a deposition to make before the commencement of this hearing with Richard Atkins as my judge.'

'You will sit down, sir!' ruled Atkins, turning back to the man.

'I will not,' rejected Macarthur, to fresh laughter from the well of the court. 'I will not be tried on what amounts to a technicality by a man who could benefit from my conviction.'

'This court will not begin until I am sworn,' announced Atkins, from the bench. 'Anything you have to say in your defence will be considered at the proper time, according to law.'

'No, sir.'

The challenge came from his right and Atkins turned to Captain Kemp, apprehensively.

'We are sworn,' said the soldier, indicating the other officers. 'We will hear the accused's protests to your Presidency to decide whether they are valid.'

'That is illegal,' protested Atkins.

'We will decide the legality or otherwise.'

Atkins remained where he was, standing awkwardly like a child that has wet itself at a birthday party and knows movement will disclose the secret.

Kemp gazed at him for a moment, considering the impasse, then signalled the other members of the court and they all sat down, leaving Atkins upright and foolish. Hesitantly, looking back as if he expected them to change their minds and recall him, he moved to the end of the dais and perched on a chair. Everyone was laughing openly now, he saw. He'd supported Bligh and been humiliated because of it.

Macarthur was an excellent performer, thought Edward Christian, looking up again as the man spoke. He could have acquitted himself well in an English court of law. The man gestured with a sheaf of papers, like a flag-carrier showing a banner to be followed. He outlined the debt dispute between himself and Atkins, repeated a fair hearing was impossible and listed in detail the arguments and rancour that existed between them. A justified legal objection, thought Edward Christian, gazing around the court. Why, he wondered despairingly, had the man had to interfere with the other officers? It had been so unnecessary. Atkins had recovered his composure, the lawyer saw. The man had prepared an answer and was moving impatiently to deliver it.

Captain Kemp moved to speak when Macarthur had finished, but Atkins anticipated him, scurrying back to the centre of the dais.

'Contempt,' he spluttered, to Macarthur. 'I am the duly appointed Advocate-General of this colony and what you have just done is contempt. Therefore, with the power invested in me by King George III of England, I commit you, John Macarthur, to jail for contempt of court.'

Fool, decided Edward Christian, watching the poor man's attempt to regain control. To the lawyer's left, Macarthur lounged against the dock-rail, grinning broadly.

'Jail, sir!' said Captain Kemp to Atkins. 'It is I who will decide the outcome of this matter.'

'This is not a proper court,' shouted Atkins, his command slipping away as he turned to the room for support. 'I order the court to be cleared.'

'Stay,' countermanded Kemp.

It *was* becoming a farce, thought Edward Christian. As a lawyer, it offended him. But the real sufferer was William Bligh, he tried to convince himself.

Edward shook his head, rejecting his attempted reassurance. It wasn't sufficient any more, he knew. There was no justification for what he had done.

'I will withdraw,' threatened Atkins, desperately, his face flushed and his voice edged with hysteria. 'I shall withdraw, taking with me any legal authority for this hearing.'

'Yes, sir,' agreed the captain, bullyingly defiant now. 'Why don't you leave?'

Atkins hurried head down from the room, through a line of laughing, jeering people, lips quivering with emotion.

'Were you right?' questioned Fletcher Christian, to his brother.

Edward stared after the Advocate-General.

'There,' he said, his voice soft, 'go the hopes of William Bligh.'

And the last of my self-respect, he added.

'I can't believe that Bligh has been bested,' refused Fletcher, shaking his head.

29

'Won't come!' echoed Bligh, outraged.

'I'm sorry, sir,' apologised Gore, uncomfortably. 'He says he had an accident disembarking from his carriage last night and is too unwell to leave his bed.'

Another coward, thought Bligh. Johnston was so scared he was prepared to hide in a nightshirt rather than obey his sworn duty to uphold the law. He'd have him court-martialled. He'd have the man shipped back to England and dismissed his commission. Enemies everywhere. All against him. A conspiracy, nothing less. Obeying the law, that's all. Why didn't he get any support in enforcing the law?

'He *is* bruised, sir,' offered Gore, hopefully. 'All down the right side of his face. And his right leg appears very stiff.'

'What's the truth of the matter?' demanded Bligh.

Gore shifted, disconcerted at informing upon another officer.

'I gather he was drunk last night and fell upon arriving home.'

Bligh jerked his head, exasperated. He had no military backing, he accepted. Or civil support, either. His only following was among the settlers, straggled away in the outback. All alone, he thought. As always.

'It's very worrying, sir,' offered Gore, guessing the other man's thoughts.

At that moment the study door thrust open and Atkins bustled in, wet-faced and breathless.

'They ejected me from my own court,' he complained, like a spoiled boy who'd lost his cricket bat because he'd insisted on first innings. 'They laughed at me and let Macarthur read out a long prepared statement ... '

'Is Macarthur free?' snatched Bligh, realising the significance.

'Not yet,' said Atkins, slumping uninvited into a chair. 'But he will be, within the hour.'

'Oh, my God,' said Bligh, quietly.

'You've already manipulated a court when you didn't have to,' criticised Edward Christian. 'You don't have to do anything more. Let the authorities in London decide the matter.'

Macarthur shook his head, defiantly. It was very hot in the cell below the court-room and both men were sweating.

'For God's sake, man,' Macarthur yelled to the jailer. 'Hurry with that release order.'

The man was as implacable as Bligh, determined the lawyer, looking at the merchant. Or as Edward himself had once been. But not any more. Please God, he thought, let not what was building up here end in bloodshed. He'd condoned every other illegality and he didn't want that.

'Bligh's thrown out a challenge,' repeated Macarthur. 'One of us must be faced down.'

'He is the Governor-General,' reminded Edward Christian. 'No matter how clumsily he's carried out his instructions. You can't openly oppose him.'

Macarthur jerked his head to the hubbub outside.

'There'll be an insurrection before day-break,' he said, confidently. 'Everyone who has had his livelihood taken away by that damned man is just waiting for the signal to storm the Governor's mansion.'

'Don't give it, then,' instructed the lawyer, refusing to pander to the man's charade. 'You control what's happening out there in the streets. We both know that. If you tell them to disperse and go, then they'll do so.'

Macarthur shook his head, smiling.

'It would give Bligh time to recover,' he said. 'I can't afford that.'

'I was prepared to guide you on matters of law,' began Edward, slowly. 'But what you're considering now is, in my opinion, openly criminal.'

What right had he to make a judgment like that? thought Edward.

'So our association ends?' guessed Macarthur.

'Yes,' said Edward. He wondered if he were concealing his apprehension from the other man.

'You've no need to be concerned,' said Macarthur, smiling up at him from the table.

'Concerned?'

'Our contact has been a secret one. And will remain so.'

He paused, as if expecting the lawyer to respond. When Edward said nothing, Macarthur continued: ' ... remain secret ... and so will the fact that it was not only with Edward Christian, lawyer, but with Fletcher Christian, mutineer.'

Edward started, as if he had been slapped.

'I'm surprised you took the risk, even here in Botany Bay,' criticised the merchant.

'I regret it, now,' confessed Edward. 'It was very stupid ... like so many things ... '

'You can be sure I'll keep my word,' guaranteed Macarthur. 'And don't think there's anything altruistic about it. If I thought it would bring me some advantage, then I might use it. But to have openly consorted with a mutineer makes me an accessary. I've got more to lose than to gain by disclosing it.'

Edward nodded, accepting the man's honesty.

'Thank you,' he said.

'What will become of your brother?' asked Macarthur, unexpectedly sympathetic.

'I don't know,' confessed Edward. 'I wish I did.'

Fletcher's inability to comprehend the meaning of the court hearing that afternoon had worried him, Edward realised. His brother had obviously not recovered as fully as he had believed.

'Take him away from this place, quickly,' advised Macarthur. 'Botany Bay corrupts people, turns them into animals. Take him away, somewhere safer.'

Edward rose to leave.

'I intend to,' he said. 'As quickly as possible.'

'And try not to be too self-critical for whatever you've done.'

Edward turned at the door.

'Is it obvious?' he asked.

'Just go home,' said Macarthur, avoiding the question. 'Go home and try to make William Bligh a less important part of your life ... yours and Fletcher Christian's.'

30

Major Johnston positioned himself at the centre of the table in the officers' mess, nervously irritating the edge of his tunic with his fingers. He was doing the correct thing, he told himself. He'd be upheld when London learned what had happened: he knew he would.

His face still hurt, where he had fallen the previous evening. He reached up, gently feeling the bruise.

The officers who had formed the court that had decided the unsuitability of Atkins to sit in judgment upon Macarthur were grouped immediately to his right and left, and facing him on the far side was every leading businessman in Sydney. Macarthur was seated directly opposite, unable to control the triumphant smile that constantly hovered in the corners of his mouth.

'It's clear what's got to be done,' he prompted.

Johnston scuffed his chair, uneasily. This was different from making Governors' lives so uncomfortable that they sought voluntary retirement.

'I don't like it, sir,' protested the soldier.

'Listen,' commanded Macarthur.

There was noise from every direction outside the barracks, occasionally bursting out into bouts of jeering. Macarthur's men were serving rum, free, guessed Johnston.

Macarthur swept his hand around the table.

'There's every civic leader in the colony here behind you,' he said.

'I'm not convinced we're faced with open insurrection,' rejected Johnston. It would be his career and reputation on the line if this went wrong, thought Johnston, not Macarthur's.

'We *are*,' insisted Macarthur. 'That's plain for everyone to see.

If the settlers start moving in to support Bligh, it'll be open battles in the streets. It's known he's dispatched Gore to muster help.'

'There's no sign of it arriving,' protested Johnston.

'Not quite true, sir,' disputed Captain Kemp. He'd grown very sure of himself since the court hearing that morning. 'From the soldiers I have on the outskirts of the town there are indications that some *are* coming into the city. It could be bad, by morning.'

There was a fresh burst of shouting from outside and Macarthur moved his head towards it.

'Order's broken down,' he insisted. 'None of your soldiers would support Bligh. You wouldn't yourself. And none of the traders will. And if Bligh is still free when the settlers gather, you'll have two opposing armies. There's only one course open to you.'

'Martial law?' queried Johnston, hopefully.

'That,' agreed Macarthur, the smile registering quickly. 'And more. You'll have to appoint yourself Governor-General. And arrest Bligh.'

'I've already signed the warrant for your release,' complained Johnston. 'I'm not sure I've the power to do even that.'

'It's too late for those doubts,' said Macarthur, briskly. He stared around the table, enlisting support. 'Anybody who feels differently from the way I do?'

The civic leaders shuffled among themselves. There were several mumbles of 'we're with you' and a lot of head nodding. Johnston looked around him, apprehensively. Everyone of importance in the colony *was* there, he tried to reassure himself. John Blaxland, Macarthur's partner ... James Mileham ... Gregory Blaxland ... Nicholas Bayly ... Thomas Jamison ... it was all powerful support. But what they wanted him to do was frightening.

'What if Bligh resists?' he asked, worriedly.

'Resists what?' mocked Macarthur. 'A troop, nearly 1,000 strong, against a Government House guard of about twenty men and they doubtful. Don't be silly.'

'I don't want killing,' said Johnston.

Again there was the flicker of excitement from Macarthur as he realised Johnston was accepting the demands.

'Our overthrow of Bligh must be lawful,' demanded the

soldier, suddenly. They all stared at him, bewildered by the contradiction.

'I must have a written petition to usurp his office,' announced Johnston, trying to clarify himself. He should have used the same excuse with Macarthur as he had with Bligh and insisted he was too ill to come into town, he decided. Only disaster could come from this.

The others in the room stirred at the thought of probable involvement.

'I won't do it, without such a document,' continued Johnston, seeing the reaction and hoping fervently it gave him an escape. They'd abandon him if things went wrong, he thought. A letter would prove at the enquiry that would inevitably follow that he'd acted to preserve order, according to his warrant, and upon the wishes of the colony leaders.

Macarthur sensed the uncertainty of the men around him at the same time as Johnston. 'A paper and quill,' he called, quickly. It was Kemp who provided it, enjoying his new status.

Macarthur scribbled hurriedly, careless of style or punctuation. Without this doubtful authority, he knew Johnston would back away. And given time to consider what they were doing, the merchants and the businessmen would avoid participation, too.

Macarthur held up the paper, reciting the petition. ' ... the present alarming state of this colony, in which every man's property, liberty and life is endangered, induces us most earnestly to implore you instantly to place Governor Bligh under arrest and to assume the command of the colony. We pledge ourselves, at a moment of less agitation, to come forward to support the measures with our fortunes and our lives.'

Johnston nodded. 'Upon that, I'll move,' he promised.

Macarthur stared around the room again, seeking corrections. No one spoke. And very few looked directly at him, he realised.

'And I'll be the first to sign,' he encouraged, adding his name with a flourish. He shoved the paper across the table, towards Blaxland. Another few minutes, he thought, and they'd start finding excuses not to endorse the petition.

There was, thought Johnston, miserably, no way he could avoid it now. Damn Macarthur.

It took Edward Christian nearly an hour to reach their rented house, buffeted and hindered by crowds making for the barracks. Macarthur would be there by now, the lawyer knew, surrounded by frightened, malleable men planning yet another mutiny in the life of William Bligh.

So many insurrections against a man who used authority like a hammer, to batter, rather than a guide, to be followed, reflected the lawyer.

Macarthur's prescience had surprised him. And the man was right, he accepted. He had allowed Bligh to obsess him, turning him into a criminal like the men in the jails on the outskirts of town, breaking stones in retribution for their crimes. He deserved no better, thought Edward. For Fletcher, there was an excuse at least. But for him there was nothing.

He had to get away, taking Fletcher with him. He'd been wrong about his brother's recovery, he realised, thinking again about the oddness following the court hearing. The man was better, certainly. But there was still the tendency to withdraw inside himself and build disasters from the shadows in his own mind. That was certainly what had happened after the Macarthur court appearance. Fletcher had left the chamber where Bligh, by open inference, had been humiliated quite convinced that the Governor had, after all, succeeded. Edward had delayed by thirty minutes his appointment with Macarthur trying to persuade his brother how irrational the conviction was and although the man had professed to understand, the lawyer had left their house knowing he was still uncertain.

'Fletcher,' he called, from the doorway.

There was no reply, but that was hardly surprising, decided Edward. The street noises overlaid everything. He walked expectantly into the sitting room. It overlooked the streets and Fletcher had been watching, fascinated by the build-up of the crowd, before Edward had left to meet Macarthur. The room was empty.

He checked the dining room in seconds, his panic rising, then took the stairs two at a time, knowing even as he began his search of the bedrooms that they would be empty.

He stood, panting, back in the drawing room, staring out. It had been an inviolable rule since their arrival in Sydney that Fletcher never left the house unless they were together. And it had been an easy edict to enforce, recalled Edward, because of Fletcher's nervousness.

It would have been a powerful emotion to have overcome that perpetual apprehension of arrest. And Fletcher only possessed one feeling any more. Hatred. Of William Bligh. He hadn't succeeded in convincing his confused brother that Bligh had lost the day, realised Edward. Which meant there was only one place where Fletcher would have gone.

It was almost impossible to move in O'Connell Street. Edward entered the mass of people like a man wading into a fast-flowing stream, trying to move against them towards Government House. Men and women were grouped around braziers and lantern poles wigwammed together to form patches of brighter light. At several places a few men attempted to make speeches against the Governor, but rarely finished because of the lack of interest of the people milling around. In the backwater of street corners, children played and giggled and ignored their mother's restraints, believing it was the biggest party they'd ever attended.

The majority of the crowd had been swilling up and down the street for two hours, stoking through rumour and imagined anger the tension of mob hysteria. The rum that Bligh had impounded hadn't been wasted, realised Edward, as men he casually passed stumbled at his touch, two even falling.

There were shouts, but Edward ignored them, not believing they were directed at him. The inaction and the rum had fed, rather than reduced, the hysteria and an irritable man, actually hitting out at them, was a welcome excuse to release some of the pent-up feeling.

Two men began jostling the lawyer between them and immediately a circle formed.

'Let me through. For God's sake, let me through,' pleaded Edward. It was exactly the reaction they wanted and they began howling at his impotent frustration. Another man entered the circle, so that the lawyer was pushed between them in a triangular pattern.

Fletcher would be almost there, at the gates, Edward thought, desperately. He strained up, as if expecting to catch sight of him. His only vision was a circle of sweat-smeared, mob-blanked faces, grotesque and distorted in the guttering torches that blazed from the poles above their heads.

'I must get through. Please. Please let me through.'

The crowd picked up the chant, hurling it back at him.

Edward dropped to his knees, destroying their roundabout, panting his exasperation. Please God, he prayed, let the guards still be at their places, preventing anyone entering. Let them turn Fletcher away, believing him to be part of the mob.

'I'm sorry,' said Edward, still kneeling. He looked up at his tormentors. 'I'm sorry I pushed you. I meant no harm. Please. Just let me through.'

Robbed of movement, the crowd appeared embarrassed at their game. A child bustled in, jealous of the attention. The circle straggled open and one of the men who had done the pushing backed away into the darkness. Slowly, still apprehensive of moving too quickly and irritating them again, Edward stood.

'Me,' demanded the child. 'Now me.'

'So sorry,' Edward kept repeating, protectively. 'So very sorry.'

They actually parted, eager to rid themselves of him. Shown a pathway, he jerked forward, breaking into a run when he cleared them. The lawyer kept running, realising from the pain as he moved that he had been bruised by the crowd. He turned the corner into Bridge Street, staring expectantly up towards Government House, hopeful for the lonely, upright figure.

The road ahead, right up to Bligh's mansion, was deserted.

And the guards had fled, he saw.

All alone, realised Bligh, staring down from his bedroom window towards the town. He'd strained for several minutes, trying to detect the guards at the gates, before reluctantly admitting that they'd deserted. Discipline the cowards, he decided. Provost Marshal would have a guard list. Look to it the moment he returned from organising the settlers. Damned man would have to hurry.

He'd flog those who'd run away, he decided. That was the answer to desertion. Put them against the mast and strip their backs. No, careful. Not on a ship now. On land. They're soldiers, not sailors. Have to be a court martial, first. Silly mistake, thinking of a ship. Wasn't scared. Take more than a few arrogant men to scare William Bligh. Only one with rightful authority.

They'd recognise it, in the end: once Gore got back. Need his uniform, to enforce it.

Bligh turned away from the window, scrabbling hurriedly through his wardrobe and selecting every item of his Governor's apparel. He dressed carefully, stopping to admire himself in the full-length mirror of the dressing room. The last article was his Governor's sash. He ran it through his fingers and then looked down, as if seeing it for the first time, before slipping it over his shoulder.

Governor William Bligh. Good sound. Important man, at last. Well off, too. Landowner. Betsy was very proud. Told him so in every letter ... letters, that was important. Have to destroy the official letters. Couldn't let those fall into the mutineers' hands. Mr Christian would like to read the letters. Always was a nosy man, prying into everything, wanting to know every secret. He'd beat him yet. Mr Christian wasn't going to succeed with this mutiny. He'd address the men, from the mizzen. Give them the chance of being forgiven. That was it, tell them there'd be no punishment. Not Mr Christian, though. He'd have to be punished. By God, how he'd have to be punished, for what he'd done. Bligh jerked back from the fireplace, as if one of the burning documents had flared in his face. Why was he thinking about the *Bounty*? Wasn't the *Bounty*. That had happened years ago. He'd become famous, because of it. And Mr Christian was dead. Long ago. Had to be.

He watched the flames brown the edges of the papers, spluttering at the official wax seals. King George's own seal. Being burned now because of a bunch of crooked buggers who wouldn't accept his word as law. Always a mistake when people ignored William Bligh. They'd learn, like everyone else. Court-martial them, that's what he'd do. Macarthur ... Johnston ... the whole lot. Ship them to England in chains and have them arraigned before a court martial and see to it they were punished. So many court martials. More than he could remember, almost. Tyrant. Bigot. Foul-mouthed. Bully. Always the same slanders. Rubbish. Wasn't a tyrant. Regulations, that's what was important. Follow regulations, through to the end. Other people couldn't do that. Too busy being diplomats and interpreting the rules to fit the circumstances, like the soft wax melting there before him. So he'd run a tight ship and flogged a few. Not many, though. And he'd brought them to Tahiti without the scurvy, no matter what that drunken sot of a surgeon had said. Tahiti was the trouble. Too much sex. Big-breasted women, flaunting themselves. Men, too, painted like birds and gaudy in their dyed clothes. Filth. That's what it was, filth. No one spared. Mr Christian worst of all. Bewildered by it. So easily led. Always had been. Poor Mr Christian. Didn't have to do this, though. Not just captain and second-in-command. Friends, after all. Too late now, though. Deserted. No, not deserted, mutinied. That was it, mutiny. Have to punish him, for leading the mutiny. No allowances possible. Regulations. That's what mattered. Regulations.

The fire was dead, he realised. He stood, shaking his head. Not the *Bounty*. Got to stop thinking about the *Bounty*. Australia. That's where he was. Australia. Governor-General of New South Wales. King's appointment. Specially selected, a rigid disciplinarian for a difficult job. Should have given him troops. He could have done it, with troops to back him. Company of marines would have kept him in command. Needed marines on the *Bounty*.

He gripped his hands against his thighs, forcing his nails into the palms of his hands. Not the *Bounty*. Definitely not the *Bounty*. Had to stop thinking of that damned ship.

There appeared to be some cohesion forming far away, where he could just detect the lights of the lanterns and flares. The barracks were lighted as bright as day, he thought, braziers everywhere. The soldiers were still inside, he could just discern. But they appeared to be gathering for something.

A movement brought him back to the mansion perimeter. A man was hurrying through the open, unprotected gates. Sent ahead to establish the resistance and report back, guessed Bligh. He stood quite still, staring down into the courtyard. He knew him, decided Bligh, watching the shadowy figure cross the lawn. He recognised the gait and the way the man held himself. Irritably the Governor shook himself again. Damned stupid. Of course he didn't know him. How could he? He turned back to the bedroom. He'd hide, he determined. If the spy reported that he'd fled, perhaps they wouldn't search the house for him. The Provost Marshal would return with the outlying settlers to support him. Sure of it. And if he still occupied Government House, then he was still Governor.

Bligh hesitated on the landing, listening. The intruder's footsteps sounded very loud down below, he thought. The man was walking with measured, almost leisurely steps, apparently unafraid of being suddenly confronted by a defender's musket.

Arrogant bugger, thought Bligh, creeping further along the corridor.

\mathscr{CCG}\ 3\ \mathbf{I}\ \mathscr{DC} 31

Fletcher Christian had actually turned to leave the abandoned house, convinced Bligh had fled to the settlers for protection, when he heard the door close above.

He stopped, motionless in the hallway, head held to one side, unsure whether he had imagined the sound.

There were no footsteps. And there would have been footsteps, surely, if there were somebody up there? So it could have been imagination. Or the wind, blowing the door shut. There were a lot of windows open, the curtains billowing in. And the front door gaped wide where the occupants had run away.

Far better to get back to their house, before Edward returned. Shouldn't worry Edward. Been a good friend. Loyal brother.

He had to be sure, Christian knew, turning towards the stairs. He couldn't leave the house, without knowing for certain. Wouldn't take long. Quite a small house, really, for a Governor's mansion.

He was creeping now, he realised, as he began to mount the circular stairway. He was moving on the balls of his feet, testing each step. That's how he'd walked on the *Bounty*, all those years ago, edging towards Bligh's cabin with Quintal and Churchill jostling behind. Was he still frightened of Bligh? Would it be there, that apprehension that bunched in his stomach, like a physical pain? Christian stopped again, hand gripping the balustrade. He could still go back: wasn't too late. Nobody would ever know. He *wouldn't* be frightened, he decided, his lips moving with the determination, hands white against the rail. He *wouldn't* let Bligh win, not this time, if he were up there. He'd face him as an equal. And destroy him. He knew how to do it, Christian convinced himself. And he could do it now, not like on the

Bounty. Destroyed Quintal, after all. And against Bligh he possessed a more effective weapon than he had had in his fight with the other mutineer.

Just had to control the emotion, that's all. And he could do it, with just the two of them.

He prodded open the dressing-room door, immediately impatient with his hesitation. Like the cabin door on the *Bounty*. He shoved it again, hard, so that it bounced against its hinges and upset the small wine table behind. That was the way. Defiant. Nothing to be afraid of.

Disordered, Christian saw, clothes dropped where Bligh had stepped from them, the wardrobe door wide open. And a heap of ash in the grate. Christian turned away, then came back to the room, halted by a thought. Quickly he went to the fireplace and ran his hand through the blackened paper. Hot: not more than fifteen minutes ago, he guessed.

So Bligh *was* here, somewhere.

He shuddered at the acceptance, like a man exposed to a cold wind. He faltered at the door. He could still walk away, he told himself again. He could go unhindered down the stairs and back to the house and watch from the protection of his darkened room as the mob overran the building and flushed Bligh out.

But that would be running away, he countered. And he wasn't going to run away. Not any more. That was the point of confronting the man, to prove he wasn't a coward. Bligh had to know that: be shown it, in fact.

Christian put his back to the stairway, moving positively, going further along the corridor.

A bedroom, he realised, coming to the second door. But not used, obviously. All the furniture was covered in dust sheets and the mattress was the only bed covering. Mrs Bligh's, he decided, had she accompanied her husband.

The mutineer walked through the connecting door and smiled at Bligh's bedroom. Not as disordered as the dressing room, but still showing evidence of a man leaving in haste. The dressing-table drawers were jerked out, he saw. And coins littered the floor, where Bligh had fumbled to fill his purse and dropped them in his anxiety.

Always thought of money, remembered Christian. He went slowly around the room, fingering objects. Bligh's belongings, he thought, the possessions of the man he hated. He put them down, hurriedly, like a man fearing infection. There was a miniature of Bligh's wife, mounted before a mirror, and two others, of children. The daughters, Christian knew. Had they been the ones he had nursed, in Lambeth? Or were these the children who had come later? Bedding was pulled almost on to the floor, as if Bligh had started up suddenly, catching the covering against his clothes, and a quill lay across the writing desk, staining the top with its ink.

Bligh would have hated the room disarranged, Christian knew. A fastidiously neat man, recalled the mutineer, everything folded and stowed into its appointed place and locker. So the man must be distressed, very distressed indeed. That was good.

Christian had begun walking towards the door leading back on to the corridor when he saw the entrance to the second room, to his right. It was a narrow, small-framed opening. Not a room, decided Christian. A cupboard, perhaps. He moved on, then stopped again. Wouldn't it be more likely that the man had concealed himself in a cupboard than an open room?

Christian heard the sound as he reached out for the latch. It was the scuffing of someone pulling away, trying to hide.

Christian didn't pause this time. He pushed forward almost angrily, thrusting his shoulder against the door. It wasn't locked and so he stumbled on, stopping with his hand still against the edge, for support.

It was a room after all, a tiny storage cell. At one end, neatly stacked, were Bligh's trunks. A narrow bed fitted against the far wall. And by its head, immaculate in his official uniform and with his hand on his sword hilt, as if posing for an official portrait, stood William Bligh.

He stared unblinkingly at Fletcher Christian, his face without any expression.

'No,' he said, very softly. 'Please, no.'

Edward Christian ran into the house and stopped before the stairs, uncertain.

'Fletcher!' he shouted.

His own voice echoed back.

'Fletcher! For God's sake, where are you?'

The lawyer stared back to the entrance, listening. Were the

sounds of the crowd getting nearer? It sounded like it. Perhaps fifteen minutes, he thought. No more. If he didn't get his brother away by then, they'd be trapped by the mob. Or the soldiers. It hardly mattered which.

'Fletcher!'

Instinctively Edward hurried up the stairs, following the same route as his brother, but more impatiently, flurrying from room to room.

But he didn't enter Bligh's bedchamber through the connecting door, but through the main opening, from the landing, and almost missed the small room. He was pulling back when he heard the sound, difficult at first to establish as a human voice.

'Dead,' it wailed. 'You're dead.'

It was all right, decided the mutineer. He *wasn't* frightened. The hatred was there, all right. And the loathing, too. Particularly the loathing. But there was no fear. So he would be able to do it.

'No, Willie,' he said. 'Not dead.'

It was perfect, decided Christian. Exactly the right tone. Bligh had always been very insistent about the softness of the voice.

'Know you're dead,' mouthed Bligh, doggedly.

'I survived. Just like you, I survived.'

'Go away.'

'You don't mean that, Willie. You don't want me to go away ... you never did ... '

' ... laughed at me ... sneered ... '

'You wouldn't accept it though, would you? Thought it was going to be the same on the homeward voyage ... '

' ... shouldn't have laughed ... won't be laughed at ... important ... in command ... shouldn't laugh ... '

'But you looked so stupid, in just your shirt, pleading ... important people shouldn't plead ... '

'Tahitian whore ... all she was ... Tahitian whore ... '

'Told you not to call her that, Willie. I loved her ... really loved her ... '

' ... not ... not possible ... '

'Yes, it was. I loved her properly. Not like you.'

'Don't say that.'

'It's true. Just her. Not you. Never wanted you ... always laughed at you ... '

'Not true.'

'But it is true. Does it hurt, to know that someone you loved was laughing at you, all the time?'

'Did love me.'

'No, I didn't, Willie. I did it because I was terrified of you ... because I believed you would make public what I had become ... '

Christian moved into the room, reaching out to the other man.

' ... but that was our private joke,' said Christian. 'Now you'll become a public laughing stock, a man unable to control his own colony. Think what that'll mean, back in London, Willie.'

'Not true ... restore order ... in command soon ... '

'No, Willie. You're disgraced.'

The mutineer moved abruptly, as if afraid the other man would jerk away. He seized him first by the shoulders, holding him hard.

'Feel it, Willie? I'm not a ghost. It's really me. It's Fletcher.'

Bligh was straining back, twitching at the contact.

'Don't pull away, Willie. You never pulled away before.'

He made another sharp movement, cupping his hand behind Bligh's head. And then he pulled the man towards him and kissed him, open-mouthed, holding their faces together, driving his lips open.

Bligh was resisting so hard that when Christian released him he toppled backwards, across the bed. For a moment he stared up, eyes protruding from his face. Then they clouded, like a curtain being pulled down. And he screamed, a desperate, empty sound. There were no words, just the moan of a man retreating into a private, safe world, where no one could reach him.

Fletcher Christian felt a movement against his shoulder and turned to his brother. Edward wanted to touch him, he realised, his hand outstretched. But the man had stopped, inches away, revolted by the idea of contact.

'For God's sake,' said the lawyer, face twisting in disgust as he dropped his hand. 'Let's get away from here ... and from him ... '

32

The Prince Regent was very controlled, realised Sir Joseph Banks, gratefully. He had expected a tirade, but so far the conversation had gone remarkably well.

'We're glad the whole matter has ended,' said the Regent, formally.

It was important to get lodged in his mind that Bligh had acted according to regulations, decided the man's patron.

'The court was unanimous in its verdict that Johnston was guilty of mutiny,' he reminded. 'That he's been cashiered will show the public that Governor Bligh was at all times acting properly.'

The Regent shrugged, impatiently. He was bored with the Bligh business, realised Sir Joseph.

'Not important,' he said.

'And from the evidence called, the man Macarthur was shown to be a blackguard, as well,' persisted Banks. 'Bligh's been completely vindicated.'

'Could still have been handled differently. And to more credit to the Crown,' insisted the Regent, as if his sick father needed defending. 'Don't forget he was held for nearly a year in that damned mansion. Imagine it, the Governor of a British colony, almost a common prisoner. Too bad, altogether too bad.'

The man would not be half the King his father had been, when he finally acceded to the throne, decided Banks.

'How is Bligh, by the by?' asked the Regent.

'Much improved,' reported Sir Joseph. 'The promotion to admiral did much to restore his health. Now that his wife is dead, he's moved to a country house quite near mine, in Kent.'

The Regent nodded. The boredom was increasing, Banks realised.

'No question of him ever being appointed to any responsible position again, of course,' said the Regent. 'For appearances' sake, there'll be no rebuke. But we're much displeased.'

It was almost as if he were seeking reassurance, thought Banks. And that was hardly necessary. He'd made his wishes very clearly known.

'No, sir,' agreed Banks. 'Admiral Bligh has been very definitely retired.'

'Damned glad,' said the Regent, closing the subject. 'Never want to hear the man's name, ever again.'

The Cumberland sunset was spectacular, the whole hillside bathed in red and colouring the milky clouds that would bring rain during the night. Edward stood at the window, staring down over the well-tended small-holding. So very peaceful, he thought. Hardly the house of a man so much involved in violence and conflict.

The lamp flared behind him and he turned, to look at his brother.

'I'm sorry I'm not able to visit you more often,' he said. The emptiness of the apology was obvious.

Fletcher shrugged.

'I'm happy enough, by myself. I live a lot in my mind, back on Pitcairn.'

Edward came further into the room. He *could* have made more frequent visits, he knew. But he found it increasingly difficult to speak to his brother. With Fletcher he was reminded of his own mistakes. And embarrassed by them.

'The land looks very good,' he said, trying to find a subject between them.

'I was well taught,' reminded the mutineer. 'Don't forget I lived alongside the botanist Nelson for six months in Tahiti. And his assistant Brown came to Pitcairn.'

There was little way of avoiding the past, thought the lawyer, miserably.

'Have you had any difficulties?' pressed Edward.

'No,' reassured Fletcher, immediately. 'No one knows me. Or wants to. I occasionally go into the village, but the world has forgotten the mutiny on the *Bounty* and a man named Fletcher Christian. There's no danger. And I know Cumberland too well to make any mistakes. I've been four times to our parents' grave and know nobody suspects me.'

Edward hesitated, wondering whether to make the announcement. Finally he said: 'Bligh has been retired.'

The other man seemed completely uninterested, thought the lawyer. Even hatred was erased now.

'He's utterly despised,' added Edward.

Fletcher began laying the meal for them. Suddenly he stopped, looking down at the older man.

'It seemed so important, didn't it?' he said. 'All that money and all that effort, to prove him the villain and me the victim.'

Edward waited, curious at the outburst.

'And there was no satisfaction, you know? I'd planned that moment for so long. I'd rehearsed the words and the way I would stand ... I was obsessed with his destruction and to make it as obscene as possible. And when it happened, I felt nothing.'

'He was a disgusting man,' offered Edward, hopefully.

Fletcher smiled down at him, shaking his head sadly.

'You don't understand, do you, Edward?' he said. 'You still don't understand.'

'Understand?'

'It wasn't Bligh for whom I felt disgust ... it was for me ... I was disgusted with myself.'

'But why, for God's sake? He corrupted you, when you were little more than a boy ... tyrannised you by his authority and by threats into doing what you did ... '

'But that's the whole point,' contradicted Fletcher. 'That was my protection ... it always has been, all these years, the way I convinced myself that I was blameless and Bligh was responsible for everything. But it isn't true.'

Edward looked away, embarrassed by the other man. He wouldn't come again, he decided. He'd say his new position as Chief Justice of Ely made it impossible for him to travel so easily. Fletcher's admission had erected completely the barrier between them.

'That's the burden, Edward,' confessed the mutineer. 'Bligh didn't corrupt me ... I did it willingly ... I wanted to ... '

Edward could find nothing to say.

'Only with Isabella was I complete ... only Isabella ... that's why she meant so much ... '

Fletcher looked pleadingly at his brother.

'Can you forgive me?' he asked.

So much destruction. And so much wasted, reflected the lawyer.

'No,' he refused. 'No, I'll not forgive you, Fletcher. You made your hell. I'll not make it easier for you to live in it ... '

He paused.

' ... like I've got to live in the hell you made for me ... '

Bibliography

Ball, Ian, *Pitcairn, the Children of the 'Bounty'*, London, 1973

Beechey, Captain F. W., *Narrative of a Voyage to the Pacific*, two vols, London, 1831

Belcher, Lady D., *The Mutineers of the 'Bounty'*, London, 1870

Bligh, William, *A Narrative of the Mutiny aboard H.M.S. 'Bounty'*, London, 1790

Brooke, John, *King George III*, London, 1972

Danielsonn, Bengt, *What happened on the 'Bounty'*, London, 1963

Fryer, Mary Ann, *John Fryer of the 'Bounty'*, ed. Owen Rutter, London, 1939

Hughes, Richard, *Captain Bligh and Mr Christian, the Men and the Mutiny*, London, 1972

Mackaness, G., *The Life of Vice-Admiral William Bligh*, two vols, Sydney, 1932

Nicholson, R. B., *The Pitcairners*, Sydney, 1965

Ross, A. S. C., *The Pitcairnese Language*, London, 1964

Rutter, Owen, *The Turbulent Journey*, London, 1936

—— (ed.), *Court Martial and the 'Bounty' Mutineers*, London, 1931

—— (ed.), *The Log of the 'Bounty' Mutineers*, London, 1931